DESCENDING SON

DESCENDING SON

Scott Shepherd

47NORTH

Text copyright © 2014 by Scott Shepherd
All rights reserved.

Printed in the United States of America.

Published by 47North, Seattle

www.apub.com

ISBN-13: 9781477808733
ISBN-10: 1477808736

Cover illustration by Larry Rostant

Library of Congress Control Number: 2013936772

To Holly

She's the One

PROLOGUE
JESS BELOW

When Jess regained consciousness the first thing he heard was a whooshing sound.

Something rhythmic in the night air. It was in the distance, but steadily getting closer. The noise hurt his aching head.

What the hell did he get hit with?

He was having a hell of a time wiping away the cobwebs.

Two men? A car trunk?

The thoughts jumbled together. . . .

One thing he knew for sure. He was being dragged across the desert floor, his body assaulted by every possible pebble and rock. He couldn't see what or where the sound was coming from—the only thing in sight was the evening sky.

Damn, there were a lot of stars. The Milky Way washed across heavens that glittered like God's jewelry box. It brought back childhood memories of being on the roof with the telescope his father had given him. (And the report he demanded on precisely which constellations Jess had seen and berating him for the ones that he had missed. That memory wouldn't go away no matter how many times he got hit on the head.)

He worked harder on trying to clear his brain. Realizing one might only have a few minutes left on Planet Earth will do that to you.

Suddenly, the blades appeared—swooping down out of the moonlight. Jess thought the windmill was going to scoop him up and hurl him further into the desert. The actual blades weren't even close. It was the overwhelming size of the structure and magnificence of the twirling works that made him imagine it was going to swallow him up whole.

More windmills appeared, pumping energy through the Coachella Valley. In their immediate proximity the roar was earsplitting, whereas if you were just traveling along Highway 111 they looked more like mirages on a hill waiting for mythical conquistadors to ride by and tilt.

Someone continued to drag him along the ground, past the windmill field and deeper into the desert. Even the moonlight wasn't enough to illuminate the dark sands. A flicker of light caused Jess to twist his head.

He saw a ski-masked man about twenty yards away aiming a flashlight into the desert. Clearly, there was a destination in mind.

As the whooshing blades lowered to a hypnotic hum, Jess suddenly realized they weren't moving. He was yanked to his feet and brought face-to-face with the dragger: another ski-masked man. His natural instinct was to try and resist.

For his efforts he got a gun embedded into the small of his back.

He figured this was the blunt object that had knocked him cold. He fell into a ski-masked sandwich—one step behind the man with the flashlight and the gun-toting thug at his rear.

"What do you guys want from me?" Jess asked.

The answer was another gun thrust into an already way-too-sore kidney.

A few more steps; then Jess saw something reflect off the flashlight.

A glint of metal.

As the beam located the object, it became abruptly clear to him that this was a one-way trip.

A shovel was sticking out of the ground. Next to it was a freshly dug hole.

A grave. In the middle of nowhere.

Panic raced through every blood vessel in Jess's body. He whirled around on the gunman—and got pistol-whipped. Jess tumbled to the ground and was immediately kicked in the ribs by the flashlight wielder.

More kicks followed from the gunman—each one propelling him closer to the open grave.

"Noooo . . . ! Please . . ."

But no amount of begging, cajoling, or praying stopped the assault. Jess rolled over the edge of the hole and fell into the open pit. He landed in a heap—on something hard, made out of wood.

Jess rolled onto his back and his arms bumped against the walled sides of the casket into which he'd dropped.

The gunman stepped away from the grave's edge to make room for his partner, who was carrying a large wooden object.

The casket cover.

The two men quickly worked together, holding either side of the coffin lid while standing on opposite sides of the grave. Then, lining it up like a champ about to sink that last eight ball in the corner pocket, they let it drop into place.

Jess screamed.

All that remained were a few precious seconds until the inevitable sound. The sound no man is ever supposed to hear.

The clank of a shovel as it scoops up the first mound of dirt to pour on his grave.

PART ONE
SUN CITY

1

"Some asshole dumped his rig on the 405 just north of Bellflower. Better tell Safeco I'm gonna be an hour late."

Jess Stark leaned forward and tapped the dispatch mic. "And you're where exactly?"

"Not even crawling by the Los Alamitos exit," came the frustrated voice over the radio speaker that sat right next to Jess's computer.

Jess clicked the mouse a few times, scanned a couple of Los Angeles virtual traffic pattern maps, and then spoke into the mic again. "Swing onto the 605 North."

The squawk over the radio was equally mechanical and human. "Oh, man. That's completely the wrong direction."

Jess kept his voice at an even keel as he offered up auto guidance advice to the miffed messenger. "You head up to the 91, then go west. If that blocks up, which it probably will, get on the 710 North and take it up to the 105. Go west until you hit the 110 and you'll cruise north into downtown from there."

"That's like a dozen freeways, Jess . . ."

"Five. Six counting the one you're stuck on."

"How am I supposed to keep track of all that?" whined the driver.

"You don't. That's why I'm here. You just drive." Jess patiently began repeating the numbers in sequence—605, 91, 710, 105, 110—till it became the messenger's mantra. By the time the driver got onto the 605

North, the anxiety had fled from his voice and Jess clicked off, knowing the package would reach its destination on time.

"I could've just called the client and told him we were running late," said Rose, Modern Messenger's Jill-of-All-Trades. Twenty-something, she was getting some kind of degree over at Cal State LA in the evenings, while during the day she answered phones, billed clients, and tried to keep the books in line.

"And because we missed our one-hour guarantee, the run goes to AAA Delivery next time, or whoever is listed first in the Yellow Pages." Jess tapped the radio. "Plus this way, Clayton learns more shortcuts and I hold his hand less."

Rose harrumphed. "Long as he doesn't miss an off-ramp. Then he'll never get there."

Jess chose not to respond. Rose was one of those girls who needed to get the last word in, which meant this conversation could continue until next Tuesday. But she was a whiz with a calculator and balance sheet, and those were two things he was happy to keep on her portion of the double-sided partners' desk that sat in the center of the tiny El Monte dispatch office.

Jess had driven for the company before taking the desk job. Blowing out an engine on his old Nissan by piling up close to a hundred thousand miles in less than three years and a multitude of speeding tickets had made the decision simple. (And he couldn't stand one more day at the so-called Comedy Traffic Schools to wipe out a violation—Jess's own private tour of hell.) When Old Man Martinez decided to retire, it left an opening behind the dispatch mic; Jess was happy to fill it. Running two dozen drivers all over town wasn't quite working the LAX control tower, but he liked the fact that most people he dealt with were just faceless voices pouring over the radio speaker or out of a phone headset.

Jess took pride in the fact that he had upped the on-time delivery percentage from under eighty percent to ninety-eight percent in the year he'd been behind the desk. Occasionally, circumstances beyond his control would cause a run to slip through the cracks—a package that wasn't ready, a wrong address, the two percent. But recently he had found drudgery creeping into the job; Jess could tell because he was doing more Sudoku puzzles and reading two detective novels at once while dispatching his fleet.

The challenge had been laid down and met. Jess knew he was ready for greener pastures, but didn't have the slightest idea where to go look for them.

It was one of the reasons he had taken to doing the Santa Anita run himself (even though it meant tempting the Engine Trouble Fates or the El Monte cops chasing a citation quota). Sure, he could have worked it into one of the drivers' schedules, but it got him out of the office four days a week and let Rose feel like she was steering the ship for a bit, though upon his return Jess invariably had to reroute messengers she had spread all over the City of Angels.

At two thirty, Jess walked out to the parking lot, jumped into his year-old SUV, and headed up Peck Road toward Arcadia. Shortly before three, he pulled into the racetrack parking lot, which was so vast it had doubled for Wally World, the amusement park in *National Lampoon's Vacation*. He paid his admission and once inside sat on a bench in the paddock to study the entries for the nightcap, the last race of the day. He scribbled all over the Daily Racing Form with two pens—one a red-felt Flair, the other a Pilot blue very fine ballpoint—and picked the four horses he figured had the best chance to win. This day, in no particular order of preference, Jess chose numbers 3, 5, 6, and 9.

Then, he walked up to a teller and placed a twenty-four-dollar wager boxing the 3, 5, 6, and 9 in the trifecta, which meant buying every possible combination using his four selected horses to finish one-two-three in exact order. After that, he purchased two dozen Racing Forms and programs for the following day to deliver to Fleishman, and returned to the parking lot.

Five minutes later, Jess walked into Arcadia Liquor and handed over the forms, programs, and purchased trifecta ticket to Fleishman, the gray-haired proprietor whose wardrobe alternated between four different way-way-too-bright-colored sweat suits. Fleishman handed Jess twenty-four dollars for the wager and they shot the shit until the last race went off on the TV hanging from the ceiling above the fine-aged Scotches.

The nine horse won by three lengths at 17-1 odds and the favorite (the five horse) finished second. But what got Fleishman whooping and hollering was when the six horse got up for third—completing a winning trifecta that paid $435—a nifty profit of just over four hundred bucks.

Fleishman patted Jess on the back. "Boy, can you pick 'em or what?"

"Sometimes it works out like you figure it," said Jess.

"More often than not with you, kid. Tell me you bet it for yourself this time."

Jess shook his head. "Nah. You know me. I just like the puzzle."

"Puzzle, schmuzzle. We're talking four hundred smackers. What's with you and money anyway? You allergic or something?"

Jess shrugged and told Fleishman he had to get going.

No point in telling him the truth. When it came to money and all the things it did and didn't do, Jess could sum up his feelings in four words the liquor store owner would never understand.

Been there. Done that.

※　　※　　※

Jess thought about the trifecta on the drive back to his apartment. Surprisingly, it wasn't the "Woulda, Shoulda, Coulda Had It" that obsessed most gamblers after they missed out on a score. It wasn't that his wallet had four hundred fewer George Washingtons in it; Jess had helped Fleishman cash tickets for three times that amount without regret. What he wondered about was why the handicapping and waiting for the result appealed to him so much. As he dropped out of Pasadena onto the 110 freeway, he could only come up with one answer.

It kept him occupied.

He was always looking for something to fill the waking hours. It kept his brain whirring, problem solving, just plain dealing.

Dr. Clifford had tried to tell him he wasn't dealing at all. But Jess didn't want to hear that.

A few months after he ended up in Los Angeles, he landed on a shrink's couch (didn't everyone?) because he was unable to sleep, his mind was on overdrive, and he knew every infomercial by heart. He was only halfway through his first session when Dr. Clifford said Jess was suffering from anxiety.

On his second visit, Dr. Clifford suggested they try biofeedback. Jess had never heard of it and asked Clifford to explain. The shrink said he would hook him up to a small machine that measured one's anxiety level.

(Some kind of pulse reader, Jess figured.) There was an arrow on the main display. The further it swung left, the more relaxed the patient was. If it went to the right—well, that wasn't ideal. It meant all your synapses were on high alert.

"The idea is to do exercises that urge the arrow left, getting you to relax," explained Dr. Clifford. "Making that happen in this office will help you apply those techniques in the outside world to calm down when you feel anxious."

Jess figured it was worth a shot. Clifford pummeled him with all kinds of questions—name everyone from your first grade class, recite the presidents, say your Social Security number backward. He threw enough at Jess to make an ordinary person sweat and rocket the arrow toward the danger zone.

But a strange thing happened.

The more tasks Clifford gave him, the further the arrow drifted left. His head filled with dozens of assignments, Jess was actually relaxed.

"Let's start over," suggested the shrink, scratching his head. "Imagine you're on a beach, it's a sunny day, and you're thinking of absolutely nothing."

Zing. The arrow swung to the right.

Jess practically had an anxiety attack right there in his shrink's office.

Dr. Clifford decided Jess wasn't a candidate for biofeedback.

Jess figured he wasn't cut out for any more therapy.

He knew what the problem was—what was driving him crazy.

When Clifford asked him to clear his mind, Jess tried really hard to do just that. But the arrow picked up on the truth and made a hard right toward Anxietyville.

The truth was that whenever Jess tried to think about nothing—all he could do was think about her.

The Dodgers blew another lead in the ninth. They went down in order right around the time Jess finished writing his last check. That was synchronicity for you—both hit rock bottom at the same time. At least the

Dodgers would get another chance the next night. Payday wasn't for another week at Modern Messenger.

He put the checkbook in a desk drawer and then glanced at the one framed photograph on the desktop. The Coachella Valley shot from up high on a hill. Sun City, as the Rat Pack once called it, spread out in all its desert splendor.

He drifted across his one-bedroom Echo Park apartment to the front windows. Bright light from the stadium in the ravine filtered into the living room, washing the blank walls in sheer whiteness. In an hour or so, the light would disappear along with thousands of disappointed fans.

On home stands he would sit in this room with Vin Scully's voice coming from the television in the bedroom. The TV director might select what he wanted viewers to see, but Scully's mellifluous tone allowed pictures to form in Jess's head. That way he could hang on to images as long as he wanted—sometimes for hours after the stadium lights flicked off and the taillights faded down the hill.

❄ ❄ ❄

Rose smiled as he came through the front door. "Hi Jess."

She never smiled. Something was up. "Rose. Nothing as usual?"

She dug a message slip out of a rack. "Actually, you got three calls. All from the same woman."

"Really."

"Kate Stark." Rose handed over the slip. "I didn't know you had family."

He stared at the message, tight-lipped. "I don't."

"She said she was your mother."

Jess stuffed the piece of paper in his pants pocket.

"I'm sure she did."

❄ ❄ ❄

Thirty minutes later Jess was still staring at the message. He had already un-crumpled and re-crumpled it a half-dozen times. He had even folded it in half, then into quarters. He was lucky a window wasn't nearby—otherwise he would have thrown the paper outside, which would have meant hauling his ass outside to go retrieve it.

Finally, he asked Rose to make a Starbucks run. Jess wasn't really thirsty, but he didn't want her listening in on the phone call he finally decided to make.

A woman picked up on the first ring. "Hello." She sounded precise and sophisticated. Even saying just the one word.

"It's Jess."

"I didn't think you'd call."

"Me either," he admitted.

Kate Stark waited a moment, choosing each syllable carefully. "He wants to see you."

"Bullshit."

"Jessie, don't . . ."

"Seven years I don't hear a word from the bastard. And suddenly he has you call me out of the blue?"

Kate took a deep breath. "You're right. I'm the one who wants you to see him. It's his birthday and—"

"You've got to be shitting me! You're actually inviting me to *his* birthday party?"

"Your father's dying, Jessie. I really think it would be a good idea if you got down here and saw him."

2

Most people didn't realize Los Angeles was two big grids bisected by a mountain range. On one side you had the San Fernando Valley, which was once nothing but orange groves. Now it was a bunch of strips—malls, clubs, and land boasting Spanish names like Reseda and Tujunga. On the other side of the Santa Monica Mountains was the LA Basin, some parts glitzy, other sections you might not get caught dead in. A half-dozen arteries split the mountain range, allowing drivers to get from one grid to the other. Whether it was a couple of large ones that could double as parking lots (the 405 and 101) or narrower roads (Beverly Glen, Coldwater, Laurel), from thirty thousand feet above it looked like ants crawling back and forth over one humongous hill.

Not exactly a description of paradise. But put a gun to any Angelino's head and they'd tell you they wouldn't live anywhere else. Name another place you could find such beaches and weather. And the "Rich and Famous" to boot.

Jess Stark would list any number of cities along the French and Italian Rivieras. People would respond by saying no one spoke English there. He'd be tempted to say more than half of Los Angeles didn't speak it either, but he knew that wasn't very PC.

For Jess, Los Angeles was just a place to bide time. If he only knew what for, he would have headed there long ago. No sense moving on if there wasn't a good reason or place to move on to. As a result, he'd been biding for almost seven years now. It wasn't lost on Jess that he was still only two hours from the desert where he'd been born and raised. He didn't need Dr. Clifford's couch to understand why he let himself be tethered by this one-hundred-mile umbilical cord. He just didn't want to own up to the reasons.

Jess always knew the day would come when he would get pulled back into the Coachella Valley for some reason. His father being on his deathbed fit the bill. As Jess got into his SUV, he wondered if he was going because he felt an obligation, or to make sure the old fucker really was going to end up six feet under when he got back home.

Either way, Jess had a feeling that his "biding" time was about over.

"If I could just get off that LA Freeway without getting killed or caught . . ."

Jess had survived seven years in the Big Bad City without either happening, provided he made safe passage across the county line.

It wasn't a coincidence that Jerry Jeff Walker was singing about packing up dishes and throwing out LA papers. Jess had popped "LA Freeway" on the iPod as he drove up the on-ramp.

Interstate 10 started at the Santa Monica Pier and came to an end somewhere on the Florida coast. Jess had only made it as far as Phoenix on a couple of family vacations, back when he agreed to go on them. Jess got on the 10 just west of downtown.

For a good hour, it seemed impossible to outrun Los Angeles—the malls got bigger, the car dealerships larger, and neon signs brighter as they beckoned the weary driver to come in and spend a load of money they didn't have.

A few miles outside of Riverside it all changed.

The air got clearer. In the mornings it would be a good deal cooler and the afternoons were a whole lot hotter. Large rock formations cropped up on the side of the road and suddenly there were literally fields of grain and purple majestic mountains. White sands stretched for mile upon mile.

As Jess dipped into the Coachella Valley, he noticed a few citified touches had sprung up in his seven-year absence. Where once stood a small building housing the Morongo Indian Casino, there now was a hotel the size of the Washington Monument. It looked bizarre; it was the only structure over two stories for a dozen miles. The outlet malls in Cabazon that were just going up when Jess left were now doing booming business even in the pre-noon hours.

But some things forever stayed the same. Big billboards tempted tourists with sunny skies, golf courses, and resorts. Hadley's Orchards, where you never could imagine that so many different kinds of fruit could be dried, pitted, and placed in a plastic baggie. The rest stop with the life-sized brontosaurus slide had children racing up and down it, no different from when Jess was a child and insisted his parents take him there each week.

And the desert had lost none of its beauty. Sure, housing developments had sprung up all over the white sand floor, but zoning restrictions made sure there was enough room between communities to still boastfully refer to Palm Springs as "the Desert" (as opposed to Vegas, where all one ever heard of was "the Strip").

Jess swung onto 111, the main thoroughfare into downtown Palm Springs that split off Interstate 10. High up on the northern hills, windmills reigned over the valley, pumping energy for all they were worth. Jess passed by the Aerial Tramway, where one could take a funicular to the mountaintop and have a snowball fight, then half an hour later enjoy a tennis game in the ninety-degree sunshine down below.

Jess checked the dashboard clock. Not even noon. Pretty darn good. The empty road promised he'd reach his destination in less than two hours—an excellent time even in the good old days when Indian Wells was reservation land instead of a place where they held professional tennis tournaments.

Up ahead, a dust storm suddenly appeared. For a moment Jess wondered if he was about to fly into the teeth of a freaky bout of weather or if he should be on the lookout for Dorothy Gale's house being blown into the sky by a twister. But it quickly turned out to be a pickup truck that had carelessly swung off the road and kicked up a ton of dirt into the morning breeze. The pickup began weaving back and forth. At first it seemed like the driver was on a twenty-hour bender and the bartender had forgotten to take his keys.

Then, Jess saw the motorcyclist.

The rider was trying to run up on the heel of the pickup. Each time the truck driver tried to let the cyclist by, the biker would chase the pickup's tail.

Jess wrenched the SUV into a hard right and a quick brake as he had no interest in playing a game of chicken with a crazy man. The moment Jess swung onto the right shoulder, the pickup barreled by on the wrong side of the road with the motorcycle in hot pursuit.

Jess got a quick glimpse of the cyclist as he sped by. He was well built, dressed in black from head to toe except for a scarlet red helmet and silver gloves that clamped down on the accelerator. The tinted face mask betrayed not a single feature of the rider. He could have been the Pale Horseman on a modern metal steed.

As Jess tried to maintain control of his own car bumping along the shoulder, he heard a gigantic crunch. He glanced in the rearview mirror to see the pickup fly off the road and roll end over end at least four times.

The motorcycle and its rider remained unscathed. It buzzed around the bend and out of sight without missing a beat.

Jess screeched to a complete stop and jumped out of the SUV. He raced across the highway, onto the hot sand and past a snapped-in-half cactus, which had taken the brunt of the pickup that lay twenty yards farther on. The driver was pinned beneath the scrunched door. Jess's heart skipped a beat when he spotted gasoline leaking from the tank.

He dropped to his knees to check on the man and fought the instinct to turn away—the pickup driver was in such bad shape. His face had numerous deep gashes and blood seeped through his mangled clothes. He was in his late twenties, but even with all the facial wounds, Jess could see he was handsome and athletic. Jess got his arms under his shoulders.

"We need to get you away from this thing," he said.

The pickup driver lay limp in his arms. Jess didn't know if this was because the man was unconscious or agreeing with him. Surprisingly, he was able to yank the guy halfway out of the pickup on the first try.

The driver's eyes popped open. He gripped Jess's throat and shook him wildly.

"D . . . don't . . . don't make me go back!"

Jess was confused. "Huh? What . . .?"

"I can't go back there!"

Jess forcefully removed the man's hands from his throat. "I don't know what you're talking about! C'mon, let's move!" Another yank allowed Jess to pull the man clear of the pickup and drag him forty yards further into the desert.

Seconds later, the truck exploded in flames.

Jess threw himself over the injured driver for both of their protection as pickup parts scattered all over the sand.

Once the sky stopped raining auto parts, Jess straightened up to find that the man had lost consciousness. His breathing was labored. Jess rooted around for his cell phone and suddenly realized it was in the SUV that was parked at least two hundred yards away.

He started to get to his feet to run for the phone. Then, thinking better of it, he dug into the driver's pockets. He came up with a cell and a handful of blood from the gaping wound in the man's abdominal area.

"Damn." Jess clamped down on the rising nausea in his own stomach and the feeling of doom beginning to take residence.

He punched in 911 and quickly walked an operator through the situation. He tried to approximate his location, but was told it wouldn't be necessary.

"We can trace your cell, Mr. Cox."

"Cox? My name's Jess Stark."

"This isn't Tom Cox?" asked the operator.

He suddenly understood. "No, that must be the injured party. I'm using his phone."

The operator said they would have the paramedics out there as quickly as possible. He should just hang tight. Jess said he would. He remained kneeling in the middle of the desert—sunbaked and in mild shock himself.

Waiting. Drenched in a young man's blood.

Tom Cox died in Jess's lap three minutes before the first paramedic arrived.

3

Jess immediately noticed three things about Thaddeus Burke. First off, the man was absolutely no-nonsense. If he was born with a sense of humor, it was long gone by the time he reached adolescence. Second, he loved being sheriff. If the man was literate, which Jess would wager the jury was out on, he would consider Jim Thompson a god, and any of that writer's lawmen a role model. Finally, his middle initial was probably an "S," standing for Suspicious. Burke seemed like a man who never took anything at face value—which was validated by the sheriff's shaking head as he handed Jess back his driver's license.

"Good Samaritan fresh out of Los Angeles, that's what I'm supposed to believe here," Burke said.

"Label me whatever you want, Sheriff. I saw the guy go flying off the road and ran over to see if there was anything I could do to help."

Burke was in his early fifties; his standard crew cut gleamed blond from too much time in the sun. Jess didn't know what was more remarkable about the man: the apparent absence of body fat (indicated by his form-fitting uniform) or the impeccably seamless tan. Burke glanced over at Jess's SUV. "Most people wouldn't have stopped."

"I didn't have much choice. I almost got run off the road. If I hadn't pulled over, you'd be making room for both me and Cox."

Jess indicated the coroner wagon parked behind Burke. The paramedics had left twenty minutes earlier. A few cop cars still remained.

"You know Tom Cox, then?" asked the sheriff.

"The 911 operator told me his name when I used his cell phone to call in the accident. I'm an innocent bystander, Sheriff. No reason to turn this into something it isn't."

Jess looked past Burke again. The medical examiner, an attractive woman in her mid-forties, her scarlet hair in a tight bun, was wrapping things up.

"What about the motorcycle rider? Any luck finding him?"

Burke offered up a slight grin. "Innocent bystander, huh?"

"Just making sure you know that the biker definitely drove Cox off the highway."

"Appreciate the help. I'm sure we would've figured it out from the skid marks." Burke looked back up Highway 111. "Didn't get a look at the guy's face?"

"Seemed like he was deliberately trying to keep it covered. The face shield was completely black. I'm surprised he could see anything."

"Probably custom-made—one way tint." Burke checked the pad he'd been taking notes on. "Red helmet, silver gloves. Don't think that'll narrow it down much. We've got a lot of bike shops in the Valley—and it doesn't necessarily mean he bought the stuff local. All the same, we've put an APB out on the guy, for all the good it'll do. Probably halfway to Hemet by now."

He shoved the pad in a back pocket, his first move indicating he was done with Jess. "Thanks, Mr. Stark. If you think of anything else contact me at the station." The sheriff dug a card out of his vest and handed it to him.

Jess stuck it in his wallet. "There was one other thing about Cox. He was scared to death when I pulled him from the pickup."

"Kind of natural, wouldn't you say? Nasty crash like that?"

Jess shook his head. "I don't think it was about the accident. He begged me not to make him 'go back.' What do you think that meant?"

Burke chewed on it, and then shrugged his shoulders. "Beats me. Maybe the place he worked. The Oasis."

"The bar off Ironwood?"

"Tom was the short order cook there the last few months." The sheriff took another hard look at Jess. "Oasis is a local place. Thought you were from Los Angeles."

"I grew up here."

The sheriff's eyes lit up like the proverbial light bulb. "Jess Stark. You're Walter Stark's kid."

Jess stomped down the reflex to frown and eked out a nod. "That's right."

"You've been gone a while, haven't you, son?"

"Seven years or so since I moved to Los Angeles."

"What brings you back down here?"

"My father's birthday. My mother's got a party planned."

"Wish the old man a good one for me."

"I'll make sure and do that."

Burke placed a hand on Jess's shoulder. Discovering Jess's parentage had suddenly brought a degree of familiarity to the proceedings.

"Hell of a homecoming, kid."

Burke traipsed through the sand to check in with the medical examiner. The redheaded woman was just getting to her feet. She motioned to a couple of her men that they could transfer Cox to the coroner's wagon. She started to confer with Burke—then, her eyes strayed past the sheriff to look over at Jess. But the eye-line was cut off a few seconds later when Burke shifted a bit to his right.

Jess couldn't tell if the sheriff had done it on purpose, but he wouldn't put it past him.

One of the coroner's men draped a sheet over Cox's body and then pulled it up over the dead man's head.

It occurred to Jess that the desert sun would never shine down on Cox's face again.

Hell of a homecoming indeed.

4

The iron gates were large enough to protect Troy. Jess wasn't planning a surprise attack, but he hadn't committed to coming when he talked to his mother. Like the ancient Greeks, he figured he would gain entrance to the compound because he was Kate's birthday gift to his father. Of course, all hell broke loose once the Trojan horse was safely ensconced in the city, and Jess expected nothing less from the father-and-child reunion.

The family surname was etched in wrought iron over the entrance gates to the mountainous estate. The patriarch had spent years climbing to the top of this hill and wanted to make sure everyone knew he wasn't planning on leaving it anytime soon.

It hadn't always been that way. Walter Stark came to the Coachella Valley as an ambitious young man in the early sixties. This was right about the time Sinatra had taken residence in the heart of Palm Springs. The Rat Pack played golf and drank at Tamarisk Country Club during the day, then went back to Frank's to eat and drink a whole lot more. Walter, who was failing at one entrepreneurial scheme after another, got his big break parking cars at one of Sinatra's all-night shindigs.

A platinum blonde overdosed in one of the cabanas. Unfortunately, she had been with a man she wasn't married to. At a time when the only focus of *Variety* and *The Hollywood Reporter* in the desert was who came and went at the Sinatra house, ambulances and cop cars pulling up the main driveway was the sort of publicity nobody wanted. The Sinatra majordomo begged Walter to escort the fallen woman to a clinic that happened to be owned by her cuckolded physician husband. The ashamed doctor was so appreciative of Walter's discretion that he immediately hired him to work at the clinic.

Three years later the platinum blonde had run away with a TV Western star, the doctor had taken early retirement, and Walter Stark was sole owner of the newly branded Stark Medical Clinic. Flash forward four decades and Walter owned six more medical facilities, twice as many desert properties, and every year was among the richest and most influential people in the Desert.

Walter liked to tell everyone that he made his fortune from the ground up. Jess knew this had to be bullshit; if Walter Stark wanted something, nothing stood in his way of getting it. Jess had no proof but was certain that Walter got his hands on that first clinic by blackmailing the old physician.

Jess stopped at the foot of the driveway and rolled down the window. He looked at the gate bell and hesitated. It wasn't too late—he could still turn around and make it back to LA before rush hour hit. Then, he glanced up at the security camera. His arrival was on tape. Beating a retreat would only result in another call from Kate Stark and him looking like a chickenshit.

His brand-new Oxford shirt crinkled as he reached for the bell. (He'd tossed the one with Tom Cox's blood on it after purchasing new threads at Target.) The intercom over the speaker crackled and a woman's voice laced with Spanish methodically spoke.

"Stark residence."

For the first time since he had returned his mother's call, Jess smiled. "Lena? It's Jessie."

He could hear the intake of breath, almost a "whoopee" if people still talked like that. A happy, thankful murmur in Spanish followed, and then the gates were buzzed open.

Jess navigated the SUV up the steep driveway. Enormous cacti of every exotic variety surrounded desert flowers on both sides of the asphalt. The driveway bent to the right where jagged shadows from the mountain ridge cast a shadow over the car. He rounded the last bend and sunshine poured over the mountaintop, revealing the Stark manse in all its pueblo glory.

It took four architects (and countless arguments between his folks that kept Jess and his siblings up many a night) more than three years to build the showpiece that got a six-page spread in *Architectural Digest*. It was his mother Kate's pride and joy—but Jess always considered it a soulless mausoleum his parents chose to occupy on this side of the grave.

The concrete driveway gave way to thousands of pebbles collected from a La Quinta quarry, and the SUV kicked up more than its fair share as Jess parked. The manse's front door—which could exist at the Prado without shame—swung open and a tiny Latina woman in her late fifties and wearing maid's uniform came bustling through. She raced across the pebbled car port and threw her arms around Jess.

"*Ay, Dios mío;* I told your mother—no way he comes!"

Jess returned the hug—awkward since her head rose only halfway up his chest, but genuine because there was obviously a good deal of history and affection between them. "I can't believe you're still putting up with her, Lena."

The woman smiled. "She won't let me leave." They both laughed and finally broke apart. Lena gave him the once-over. "You look tired."

"I'm not used to the long drive."

She poked him in the stomach with a quick finger. "You're not eating either."

"I'm twenty-nine years old . . ."

"I'm the one who wears her age, *muchacho*." Lena ran a hand through her reddish hair that had its modestly placed share of gray.

"You look terrific, Lena."

She smiled, gratefully accepting the compliment she was fishing for. Lena Flores was the one servant Jess's parents could never bring themselves to dismiss. That was because Jess knew she had more pride and resilience than any other person to reside under the Stark roof all these years—including the Stark children.

"How's Maria?"

"She graduated in May."

"From high school? Wow . . ."

"Not high school. College."

"Little Maria who used to run out of the room whenever I came in it? That Maria?"

"First in our family to go and finish." Lena reveled a bit in the incredulous look on Jess's face. "You've been gone a long time, Jessie."

He thought back to the conversation with the sheriff out on the highway. "Not the first time I've been reminded of that today."

Lena started to walk toward the back of the SUV, her indentured instincts taking hold. "You have luggage . . ."

Jess gently pulled her away from the car and steered her in the direction of the house. "One step at a time. When walking into the lion's den, it's good to have both hands free and an escape hatch." He dangled the SUV key.

That gave Lena reason to chuckle. But as they got closer to the house, a cloud slipped over her demeanor. She gripped Jess tightly at the elbow, pulling him close. "It's good to have you home, Jessie."

"I'm glad to see you too, Lena."

Her tiny dark eyes searched his face, finding satisfaction and solace in that truth. But Jess could tell she saw something else there as well—his intention.

"You're not staying, are you?"

"Just as long as necessary." He held the front door open, motioning for Lena to enter first.

"Your mother is in the garden."

"Does she know I'm here?" asked Jess.

Lena shook her head. "She pays little attention to the phone or door. *Señora* Kate keeps to herself a lot these days." She stepped inside the house.

But Jess hesitated, lingering at the threshold with trepidation. He had never expected to enter this house again. The day he had left, Jess had made a solemn vow never to return. But he had never imagined his father on his deathbed. He figured the bastard was going to live forever.

Lena was already walking down the hall when Jess called out to her.

"Lena?"

She turned around. "Yes, *muchacho*?"

27

Jess swallowed before asking, "Just how bad is he?"

"Not good," she replied glumly. "Not good at all."

❉   ❉   ❉

Growing up, if Jess ever needed to find his mother, the first place he checked was the Cactus Garden. There, Kate would sit on the gypsum bench and he would lie on her lap and listen to fairy tales and Aesop fables. Eventually, Jess was able to read to himself and spent many an afternoon curled up on the same bench buried in the latest Hardy Boys case while Kate tended to some desert rarity or trimmed her orchids in the greenhouse at the rear of the garden. By the time he was a teenager, the visits to the Cactus Garden were more infrequent—usually to ask for the car keys or tell his mother that he wouldn't be home for dinner.

Upon entering the enclosure this time, it occurred to Jess that the two of them had been passing through the garden in different directions all those years. He was growing up and questioning everything. She was getting older and retreating into a world where she didn't want to provide any answers.

He stood under the canopy of cacti that formed the garden's entrance and watched his mother clip and trim a bulbous cactus. Kate Stark was an impressive woman in her early fifties. She possessed movie-actress good looks and an exquisite bone structure that made one think New England crusty when in fact she was a tomboy who had surfed the Wedge in Newport Beach every weekend in high school. This accounted for Jess's athletic prowess on the football field. He certainly didn't inherit any physical talent from his father's side of the family.

Finally, Kate took a step back to admire her handiwork and became aware that Jess was watching her. She dropped the pruning shears to the ground and started to bring a hand to her mouth. Then, she became aware of this grandiose gesture and was remarkably able to effortlessly lower her hand without reaching its original destination.

"You actually came."

Jess was pretty sure she wasn't going to race across the garden and throw her arms around him, but he figured he ought to at least give her the chance. Kate didn't disappoint—she stood her ground.

"You didn't leave me much choice," Jess said.

Kate motioned toward the house. "You should have told me. Lena could have had lunch prepared, made up your room . . ."

"I'm not going to stay here." Jess really hadn't decided until that very moment, but two minutes in the Cactus Garden had made the choice clear.

"But . . ."

"I just came to see Dad." His tone made Kate back off. She looked back over her shoulder, then at her watch. "We'll have to see if he's up. He sleeps a lot—especially during the day. Nights seem to be better."

She walked forward until she reached the son she hadn't seen in seven years, and laid a gentle hand on his arm. "Thank you, Jessie."

He let her hand remain for a moment, and then nodded. The fables and fairy tales seemed as distant as the time in which they were written. His mother prattled on like an anxious child. "I didn't tell Walter that you were coming. Just in case . . ."

"I didn't show?" Jess said, finishing the thought. "It'd be a shame to disappoint him."

He turned around to leave the garden.

"You really hate us that much?"

Jess didn't miss a step as he passed beneath the canopy. "Let's just go see Dad and get it over with, huh?"

The living room could easily host a state dinner or a decent touch football game. As Jess followed his mother through it, he couldn't recall spending more than five minutes at a time in it as a child. He was commanded to come and say hello to dinner guests or good night to his parents. The one time he had ventured in to read a book, he sat on the sofa with his feet up on the antique coffee table. His father found him there, and after that Jess found it painful to sit down on anything else for a good week.

In seven years the house had changed about as much as Jess's feelings— very little. Every wall, each nook and cranny, reminded him of what had transpired here. The familiar trappings made him want to get out the door, down the hill, and back onto Interstate 10 that much quicker.

The only real difference he could see was that there were more photographs, mostly of famous people. There was not one single picture of the Stark brood. No surprise there. Jess couldn't remember ever posing for a family portrait. The fact that his father was in every single picture was candid proof of whose realm Jess was walking through.

The only photograph of Walter and Kate was in a frame on the piano. Both were dressed in formal wear. Kate sported a lot of jewelry and whatever else it took to look picture perfect. Jess thought Walter Stark had the same expression as the rest of the photos in the living room—a no-nonsense attitude that said he was doing you a favor allowing himself to be captured on film.

Kate pointed at the picture frame. "That was taken three months ago on our anniversary. It's hard to believe."

As if to demonstrate her point, Kate opened the lanai door. She stepped outside and motioned for Jess to follow.

The first thing Jess saw was the wheelchair.

For a moment he thought there was just a blanket piled on the seat, but then realized it was covering somebody.

"Walter. There's someone here to see you."

A heavy sigh, then a groan emerged from beneath the blanket. Kate motioned for her son to step around the chair and join her.

Jess looked down into a pair of cold piercing eyes. It was the man from the photograph on the piano. But he looked at least fifty years older.

Walter Stark could have been a living ghost.

5

Walter Stark looked at Jess like he was a mirage. The old man's mouth opened to speak but then quickly shut. For the first time in Jess's life, his father was at a loss for words. Someone had to break the ice.

"Hi, Dad."

This time Walter mustered a nod and soft response. "Jessie."

The blanket shifted. He thought the old man was trying to find a comfortable position. He was shocked when he saw his father's withered pale fingers emerge from the blanket. Jess couldn't remember a handshake between himself and Walter. That would signify a warm greeting, or, heaven forbid, an acknowledgment of a job well done.

Jess reluctantly offered Walter his hand in return. The man who ruled boardrooms with an iron fist could barely grip his son's palm. They only shook hands briefly but Jess was shocked by how cold Walter's fingers felt.

The doorbell rang deep from inside the house. Kate checked her watch. "It's three o'clock. That must be Edward. You'll excuse me a moment?" She bent down and dutifully kissed her ancient husband's forehead.

She slid open the screen door and entered the house. With great effort, Walter turned to watch her disappear. Jess noticed his father trembling. Whether this had something to do with Kate or his illness, he couldn't tell.

As Walter turned back to face Jess, he gripped the armrest for support. This quieted the shakes and allowed him to focus on his son.

"What are you doing here?"

"I heard you weren't feeling well."

"That's an understatement."

An awkward silence followed. This was nothing new to Jess. On the rare occasion he had dinner with his parents growing up, barely a word was spoken between him and Walter. Maybe one of them asking to pass the butter. Usually it was Jess asking to be excused.

"This was your mother's idea, no doubt."

"She reminded me it was your birthday."

"Whoop-de-doo."

Walter began trembling again. The blanket slipped halfway down his torso. Jess leaned over him to help pull it back up but Walter waved him off.

"I can do it, damn it!"

As Walter managed to yank the blanket away from Jess, their hands brushed again.

"You're freezing . . ."

"That's me. Cold-blooded as always."

Jess moved around to the back of the wheelchair. He grabbed the handles and started to push Walter toward the patio edge where the desert rays beat down.

"Maybe we ought to get you some sun."

"No!"

Walter kicked out with his dangling feet. The commandment of his voice and the tone that had filled his son with dread his entire life caused Jess to let go of the wheelchair. His father immediately calmed down.

"Here is fine," he murmured.

Footsteps approached from the living room. Jess started to turn to see who was coming when his arm was clutched by his father's icy hand.

"Jessie."

Jess swiveled back toward him. For the first time since Jess had come out onto the patio, Walter's bloodshot eyes looked alert.

"Come closer."

Jess leaned forward. Walter pulled him further until they were face to face. For seven years Jess had put a hundred miles between the two of them—now they were inches apart.

"They're killing me," Walter whispered.

Jess looked stunned. "They? Who?"

Walter started to respond, but a booming voice cut him off.

"And how are we feeling today, Walter?"

Jess turned to face the thirty-five-year-old man who had come through the screen door with Kate. Walter glared at the man without loosening his grip on Jess's arm. "Like crap."

Then Walter lowered his voice and whispered quickly in his son's ear. "We'll talk more tonight."

Jess stared incredulously at him. Who was this man in the wheelchair masquerading as his father? Walter Stark never wanted to talk to his son. He was never frightened or delusional. But not this new sickly version—he was all of the above.

Jess had dozens of questions, but was unable to ask them because the new arrival was already approaching with an extended hand.

"You must be Jessie."

Jess nodded and instinctively took the proffered palm.

"Dr. Edward Rice. I've been looking after your father. Give me a few minutes with him and we'll chat. I'm sure you have plenty to ask me."

"That's an understatement," replied Jess, echoing his father's earlier response. He glanced at Walter. Was Jess imagining things, or did the old man actually crack the most infinitesimal of smiles?

Kate motioned for Jess to follow her back inside the house. "Let's get you something to eat and drink. Then you and Edward can talk."

Jess couldn't believe it but he was actually reluctant to leave his father. For years, all he had thought about were ways to get away from him. But it wasn't every day that the man cried out for help.

In fact, Jess could never remember it happening.

He looked one final time at Walter. Father and son locked eyes. The meaning on Walter's face was crystal clear—they were by no means finished.

And strangely enough, Jess could feel himself in violent agreement. "I'll see you later, Dad. Promise."

Half an hour later, Jess took the last bite of a childhood memory—Lena's triple-decker BLT. To this day she wouldn't reveal the secret spread she placed on each piece of toast, but Jess was sure she could open a franchise of restaurants with the concoction.

"Chili pepper and Thousand Island?" he guessed.

"I'll never tell," said Lena.

"Am I even close?"

Lena laughed and took the plate toward the sink. She almost bumped into Rice as he walked into the kitchen. "Excuse me, Doctor," Lena mumbled. She quickly rinsed the plate and placed it in the dishwasher. "Let me know if you need anything." Lena made herself scarce before either Jess or Rice could take her up on the offer.

"Mind if I join you?" asked Rice.

Jess motioned for him to sit in the chair across the breakfast table. He studied the physician as he seated himself. Jess had no idea where Rice had gotten his medical degree, but had no doubt that the man had aced the interview process. Rice was extraordinarily handsome, but it was more than just the perfect tan he got on the Ironwood fairways every Wednesday afternoon. Rice possessed that certain charm women succumbed to and men envied—unless you were someone like Jess who wondered why Rice walked around the Stark mansion like he owned the place.

Rice's eye drifted back toward the doorway. "How many years has Lena been with the family?"

"Ever since I remember. So at least thirty." But Jess was never one for small talk. "How long has my father been like this?"

"A few months," Rice said. "Damnedest thing. Severe anemia, abnormal platelet count. Absolutely no response to drugs. If I didn't know better, I'd swear someone was poisoning the man right under my nose. It's been difficult to make an exact diagnosis."

"After all this time?"

"I've had patients for over a year and not been able to tell you what's wrong with them."

"I wouldn't go advertising that."

Rice flashed that smile which Jess was certain opened more than its fair share of doors. "I'm sure you're aware of the trials and tribulations of modern medicine, Jessie. We've taken giant steps forward in diagnostic techniques and research to identify obscure diseases and germ cells. Consequently, we've developed some remarkable vaccines and medicines to combat these maladies. But the body is an amazing instrument—it constantly tries to improve on itself. It throws up a wall to fight off one particular bacterial strain and does a damn good job of it. But it gets caught looking when the next disease comes along and bores through that wall, whereas the previous one lay down at its feet."

"So my father is just a casualty."

"Not if we can build that wall strong enough."

"Why isn't he in one of his hospitals? God knows he owns enough of them around here."

"Don't think I haven't tried to persuade him. Walter is convinced if he checks in, he'll never check out."

"That sounds like my father."

"Nothing would please me more than to have him at Meadowland. I could keep an eye on him better."

"You work at the hospital?"

"Actually, I'm Chief of Staff." Rice immediately caught his expression. "I had my lucky share of breaks. Starting with your mother. She came in for a minor procedure a few years ago and I assisted. Kate was impressed by whatever she thought I did and obviously said good things to Walter."

"I did more than that. I raved about you."

Both men turned to see that Kate had entered the kitchen.

"What minor procedure?" asked Jess.

"Female thing. Run-of-the-mill. And don't give me that look. None of us had heard from you in two years by that time."

Jess didn't respond. He knew he had no right.

"The hospital was being mismanaged," she explained. "Walter was constantly complaining about it. I convinced him to give Edward more responsibility."

"I wouldn't blame him for doubting that decision right about now," Rice said with what Jess would classify as false humility.

But Kate refused to hear anything along those lines. "You're doing everything you can for Walter. We all appreciate it, Edward. So much."

Jess was done with the plaudits. "How long does he have, Dr. Rice?"

Rice hesitated before answering. "I wouldn't be leaving town so quick."

From the resigned look on Kate's face, Jess surmised that this pronouncement wasn't newsworthy.

Rice got to his feet. "I'll check in before the party."

"Thank you, Edward. For everything."

Rice gave her a reassuring hug and said goodbye to Jess and that he would show himself out. The moment the doctor left the room, Jess whirled on his mother.

"Party? What party?"

"The one Clark James is throwing for your father's birthday tonight."

"Jesus."

"I knew you wouldn't have come if I told you."

"Damned straight."

Kate took Jess's hand. "You're here, Jessie. At least go to your father's party. You heard the doctor—it's more than likely his last one." She squeezed his hand tight. "I really think your father would like to have you there."

Normally Jess would have chalked that up as the Bullshit Statement of the Decade. But he couldn't stop thinking of Walter's whisper in his ear and the fear in those bloodshot eyes.

His father had been scared to death.

So when Kate repeated her plea for him to attend the party, Jess gave the only possible response. And it was an honest one.

"I wouldn't miss it."

6

The developed community started on the Florida coast and was refined in the Arizona desert. It was in full force by the time it hit the Coachella Valley as real estate barons decided to expand Palm Springs into smaller townships with names like Rancho Mirage, Indian Wells, Palm Desert, and La Quinta. Each had a number of planned developments, sporting cookie-cutter but pay-through-the-nose-for-them houses with adobe roofs and white sandblasted walls surrounding a signature golf course designed by a retired PGA player or A-list links architect. Retirees spent their golden years trolling fairways by day and living in clubhouses at night, mixing it up with timeshare holders who got one week a year under the desert sun, along with Angelinos and frozen Canadians rich enough to afford a second home.

That was the Palm Springs Jess was happy to leave behind. Still, he had to admit that despite whatever problems his family posed, and there were plenty, he did like the neighborhood he grew up in. It was more than just being affluent—it had a sense of character and integrity. Each house was distinct and blended into the gigantic mountains, surrounding sands, and desert flora as if it had been there since the beginning of time.

In Palm Springs proper, the town took on a post-Dustbowl feeling. The houses were distinctively smaller, their occupants way down the tax basis chart. The homes and businesses had not changed one iota since the fifties, when they were built.

Jess navigated the SUV past homes where children ran through sprinklers to keep cool. Other houses had inflatable pools set up in their front yards. More than a few had pickup trucks advertising businesses—this was where the hotel and country club workers returned at night, the heart and soul of the Valley whose denizens tended to the rich man's needs and the tourist's every want.

Eventually, the homes disappeared and the road split into just plain desert. If Jess drove four more miles, he'd pick up Interstate 10, where he would have to decide whether to head back to Los Angeles or turn right and mosey on toward Arizona. He slowed down a mile before the junction and pulled into a dirt driveway. He drove under a neon sign that would have read "The Sands" if it had been night, lit up, and the capital "S" weren't gone.

The motel had a couple of dozen rooms and four cars in the parking lot. A placard above the office read, "Free TV, Internet Available." Jess parked next to a yellow sixties Mustang—someone's pride and joy as it was the only thing without five coats of dust on it. He got out of the SUV and walked inside the office.

The only thing missing was Norman Bates. A nudie calendar hung on one wall. Appropriately, it was from 1992. The owner must have had a crush on the half-clad Miss October or was extremely lazy. On another wall, *Star Wars* posters hung on either side of a Marvel Comics dartboard. Above the desk was an old-fashioned peg bar full of iron keys with wooden room numbers.

Jess approached a man who didn't believe in treadmills but had a lot of faith in Corona and Budweiser. He was bent over fiddling with a television. His wide jeans had unfortunately slipped way too far below his waist, which made Jess grin.

"I thought it looked bad *outside*."

Benji Lutz, all 240 pounds of him, turned and hitched up his pants. He returned the smile. "Jess. You should've said you were coming."

"Why? You would've demoed the place?"

Benji laughed. "Just because of that, you don't get the Friends and Family discount."

❈   ❈   ❈

Jess drained his beer and tossed the empty can over his shoulder. It clanked off the rim of a metal trash can and dropped to the ground beside its twin.

"Now I remember why you didn't make the basketball team," said Benji. He tried to punctuate his statement with a seated sky-hook and his can landed beside the two dead soldiers.

"Least I hit one out of two," Jess countered.

Benji popped open a third beer and offered it to Jess, seated in the rocker beside him. Jess waved it off.

"Probably should keep my head clear for my dad's party."

"That sucks." Benji took a big gulp. "The news about your dad, I mean. Not the party."

"No. The party is going to suck too."

"Sounds like he's pretty sick."

"Doesn't look good." Jess glanced up from the motel porch at the night sky. The Sands might not be an establishment with four stars but there were a million visible ones above. A perk when you're out in the Middle of Fucking Nowhere.

"What happened, man?" asked Benji. "You just blew out of town right after that summer. No one heard word one from you."

"That was kind of the plan."

"You like LA better than the desert?"

"I don't like it at all."

"So why live there?"

"You're going to have to start charging me by the session if you want me to answer that."

Benji chugged and chucked the beer. Total air ball. "I stink."

"But you were a hell of an offensive tackle."

"Certainly took enough hits for you. Enough to deserve a phone call before you split."

Jess walked right into that one. "Sorry."

Benji began to reach for another beer, but then curiosity got the better of him. "You really run a messenger service?"

"For the time being. You still subscribing to *The Amazing Hulk*?"

"It's *The Incredible Hulk* and *The Amazing Spider-Man*."

"That just answered my question," Jess said with a chuckle.

"Don't knock my stories, man. They're doing awesome shit at Marvel these days."

"Maybe you oughta get a job working for them."

Benji made a grandiose gesture taking in the entire Sands Motel. "And give up all of this?"

Both men busted up.

Benji was the first to recover. "So how long you in town for?"

"Not sure. I'll swing by James's house and take things from there."

Benji blanched. "Clark James?"

"Uh-huh."

"You didn't say the party was at his house."

Jess avoided his old friend's gaze. "I might have neglected to mention that."

"Yeah, you did." Benji popped the top off another Bud. "That ought to be really interesting."

Until Jess dashed up the interstate for La-La-Land, Benji Lutz knew him better than anyone. Certainly than any member of the Stark clan. Not only had he covered his ass on the football field for three years, he'd also blocked a lot of interference for him with both the Stark and James families. Benji was probably the only person besides Lena Flores that he trusted or felt he could ask anything.

Even the question he'd been dreading.

"How's she doing?"

"Tracy?"

Jess finally looked back at Benji and nodded.

"Let me put it this way."

He took a big swig of Bud, then waved the can pointedly at Jess.

"You're going to be real sorry that you left."

7

Clark James's house was an eyesore. At least that was Jess's opinion. It appeared overnight above Palm Springs, paying no heed to neighborhood association or architectural restrictions. As far as Jess was concerned, a Tudor mansion had as much business in the desert as a polar bear. But James's most famous role was playing a patriarch in a gothic horror film that had made gazillions. He actually bought the New England monstrosity featured in the movie, had it carted across the country, and plopped atop the hill. The print media ate it up and it had been featured in numerous photo spreads over the past decade and a half.

The actor threw infamous all-night parties that somehow the paparazzi always seemed to know about. Jess suspected it was James himself who clued them in. The actor may have been a relative newcomer to the Coachella Valley (fifteen years were dwarfed by the Starks' half-century residency) but he made damn sure everyone knew he was around. With Sinatra, the Rat Pack, and even Bob Hope dead and buried, Clark James had ascended to the throne of Palm Springs royalty.

Walter Stark's birthday celebration was just one more big bash. A couple of photographers were perched within two feet of the valet parkers. Flashbulbs popped, digital cameras clicked, and hundreds of shots were snapped with the hope that one picture could sell for a few grand. If the shooter was lucky enough to get a wardrobe malfunction or a flight of fisticuffs on film, the price could command five figures from the right tabloid. Jess was tempted to tell the paparazzi to keep their Nikons trained on him—the odds of him getting into a fight were fifty-fifty. He thought better of it when he realized the press didn't give a shit. They had no idea who Jess was.

The valet parker opened the driver's door, took Jess's car key, and gave the dusty SUV a quick once-over. The valet's look of disdain spread to Jess's five-year-old sports jacket and khakis.

"Put it by the servants' entrance for all I care," Jess told him. He made his way inside before the valet tried to park him over there as well.

The entryway was tall enough to launch the space shuttle. Jess passed on the flute of champagne offered by a tuxedoed waiter and squeezed past a dozen partygoers clamoring for glasses off the tray. He knew most of these dolled-up women and men in slick suits were James's hangers-on and probably couldn't identify his father in a lineup. (The truth be told, Jess had hardly recognized the old man himself that afternoon.) Jess would bet that very few of the guests were close friends of his parents.

Jess moved down a hallway that had gigantic framed one-sheets of Clark James's films on both walls. It actually made him appreciate the photographs in his parents' living room. The ambience of the house he grew up in usually felt like an icebox, but at least there was a modicum of class about the place.

The living room was jam-packed. Most men were wearing dinner jackets. The women were trying to out-dress each other—most of them by seeing who could be the most tastefully underclad.

"Wow. Mom said you'd be here but I was absolutely sure you wouldn't show."

Jess turned around. A stunning redhead in her early twenties and a designer gown that left little of her flawless body to the imagination had come up behind him.

"Nice to see you too, Sarah."

"You just in town for the party or you sticking around for the reading of the will?"

"The body's not cold yet. In fact, I've got a news flash for you—it's still breathing."

Sarah took a healthy sip from her champagne flute. "Semantics."

"A little heartless?"

"Coming from my brother who ran out on us seven years ago and dropped off the face of the earth, your opinion means shit."

It had only taken two minutes with his sister for Jess to see how long seven years could actually be. When he had left Palm Springs, Sarah had been a sophomore in high school who had kissed maybe two boys and had only started to develop the curves she now flaunted. The only person she talked back to was her mother (like any red-white-and-blue-blooded All-American girl).

Now, the beauty in front of him exuded sexuality, defiance, and a whole lot of dislike for her wayward brother. Jess couldn't help but wonder how much of this was due to his absence or Sarah having to live under the Stark roof as the eldest child by default.

"I guess I missed the my-baby-sister-started-drinking stage."

"Only by half a dozen years. I've also had *sex*." She uttered the last word in a conspiratorial whisper and finished off the champagne with a flourish.

"Looks like someone needs a refill," a baritone voice said.

"Absolutely," said Sarah, waving the champagne flute.

The man whose face graced the movie posters in the hallway had joined Sarah and Jess. Clark James was silver-haired with eternally youthful skin at what had to be sixty-plus years old. Even if you'd never seen one of his films, you knew he had to be a movie star—he had that commanding presence of a matinee idol from days gone by. Jess knew he had retired a few years ago after a big film had gone bust, but James was still as much in demand as when he made his debut four decades earlier.

James flagged down a server and exchanged the empty for a fresh, full glass.

"It was really kind of you to arrange all this for my father," Sarah said in a buttery-up tone.

"I've known Walter forever. I'm just sorry he's been so ill." James's voice boomed through the living room; he couldn't help his theatricality. "But I do think the old man is rallying for the occasion."

The actor glanced across the room where Walter and Kate were greeting guests. Jess was surprised to see his father out of the wheelchair. Walter was actually up on his feet and his color was better. He still wasn't wearing his age well but Jess had to admit that it was a definite improvement over his condition earlier that afternoon. "Seems like it," Jess agreed.

Clark James took notice of Jess for the first time.

"You remember my brother, Jess?" asked Sarah.

James overacted, which many critics would tell you was his natural tendency. "Ah, the prodigal son returns."

Sarah made a big production out of a sudden realization. "Silly me. Of course you two know each other. Your daughter and Jess . . ."

Jess cut off his sister. "I'm sure Mr. James isn't interested in reminiscing. Besides, it's Dad's night." He extended a hand toward James. "Thank you for hosting this, sir."

"My pleasure. You're just in time. I was about to toast your father." James gave Jess a healthy pat on the back and then crossed the room to join the Parents Stark.

Jess glared at his sister. "You've become quite the bitch."

"Just not yours. I'm sure she's around here somewhere." Sarah flashed an eat-shit-and-die grin and moved off to get a ringside seat for the actor's toast.

Jess didn't have time to consider following her as he felt a tug at his sports coat. Standing right beside him was the definition of a lanky brooding teenage boy in a form-fitting dinner jacket. The kid looked as uncomfortable as Jess.

"Hey Jessie."

Jess looked more dumbfounded than when he first saw Sarah.

"Harry?"

"Sarah's still a pain in the ass, right?"

"Wait a minute. Did my not-so-baby brother just say 'ass'?"

"I've learned a whole lot of new words since you left," said Harry Stark.

"I'm sure you have."

Whereas the changes in Sarah were certainly considerable, at least his sister was recognizable after Jess's seven-year absence. Harry was a completely different being. The adolescent beside him bore no resemblance to the eight-year-old whose sole ambition had been to build the perfect Lego castle. Jess couldn't have been less interested in helping out his baby brother growing up—he had games to win and girls to chase—but now he was genuinely pleased to see Harry and didn't hesitate to hug him.

"I didn't even know you were home."

"Mom brought me back for the school year when Dad got sick. I'm not really sure why. It's not like we've spent quality time together."

"I'm sure she's had her hands full." Jess shocked himself by suddenly defending his mother. He chalked it up as a rote response.

"Nah. She just knew it'd look bad if she didn't."

Jess didn't disagree with his brother, who had grown both older and wiser. "You going to Desert Chapel?"

"Yeah. Sophomore year."

"Playing sports?"

"They tried to get me to go out for football. Figured maybe it ran in the blood." He gave Jess a self-effacing shoulder shrug. "Like I could ever play quarterback."

"Wouldn't know unless you gave it a shot."

"No way. They'd expect me to be you. By the way, you still hold half a dozen records."

"Teams must have really sucked since then."

"Yeah. Kind of." Harry chuckled. "I might try golf in the spring. Depends on how long Mom wants me to stick around."

"You don't have a say in the matter?"

"Hell no. You did the right thing leaving, Jess. This place is fucking weird and depressing."

He didn't know what was more surprising: his younger brother possessing such a colorful vocabulary or feeling the exact same vibes that Jess had sensed since he rolled into town that morning.

"This ought to be a crock of horseshit," said Harry.

Harry was staring at Clark James. The actor had one hand on Walter Stark's shoulder, the other holding up a champagne flute. "Can I have your attention, please?"

The hubbub died down as all eyes turned toward their host. James took the pregnant pause he'd used in dozens of films to feign sincerity and then launched into his toast. The first part was all about himself instead of the honoree, which didn't surprise Jess in the least.

"You make a bunch of movies and you start believing your own press. You get used to getting lots of free stuff, moving to the head of any line, and people looking at you all googly-eyed wherever you go. But when I got to Palm Springs fifteen years ago, I became aware of another man getting that same treatment. I couldn't help wondering who was stealing my thunder."

A healthy dose of laughter filled the room. Some forced, most genuine. Jess thought that these people were easily entertained.

"Walter Stark. Who was Walter Stark? I'd never heard of him. I hadn't seen a picture he'd made, a ball game he'd played in, or an elected office he held. I wanted to know—I needed to find out—who the hell was Walter Stark?"

James gripped Walter's shoulder tighter. "Walter Stark turned out to be a humanitarian—a foreign breed in Hollywood. He built hospitals to take care of the sick and elderly, made countless donations to numerous charities, and could always be counted on to lend a helping hand."

"Like I said, horseshit," murmured Harry.

James built toward his ending. "I got to know Walter and it has cost me a shitload of money in donations." There were more hearty laughs. "But I am extremely honored to call him my friend. And happy to share the press with him any time he sees fit."

James raised his glass up high. "So, here's wishing Walter a happy birthday, a speedy recovery, and that one year from tonight we'll be throwing him a bigger and even better party!"

Everyone took sips of bubbly and responded with plenty of "Hear, hear" and applause. James leaned closer to Jess's father. "Anything you'd like to add, Walter?"

"Just one thing," said Walter.

Jess thought it remarkable that his father's voice was so much stronger than it had been on the lanai only a few hours earlier. "I'd like to know if you've got a picture in some closet getting older every day. Because if you do, I'd love to meet the artist. You look like you did in a movie you made ten years ago."

James laughed. "I might have quit but that doesn't mean my makeup artists aren't still on salary."

Harry nudged Jess. "Glad you came home for this crap?"

But Jess's eyes had drifted to the French doors leading outside, where a drop-dead gorgeous girl was watching the proceedings. Raven haired, with alabaster luminous skin and just the slightest trace of rouge and ruby lipstick, she was a vision in a white cocktail dress. Her eyes landed briefly on Jess and then she walked outside.

Clark James and his father continued to chat away to the delight of the crowd, but it was just so much white noise for Jess. He stood transfixed on the carpet, eyeing the empty French doors. He'd often wondered what he would do when it came to this moment. Would he beat a hasty retreat, or go and confront the past?

The latter won out.

Jess looked apologetically at his brother. "I'll catch up with you in a bit, Harry."

Then Jess headed for the French doors—following the girl who broke his heart.

She stood on the grass-lined rim of the infinity pool staring out at the twinkling lights of Palm Springs below. Her exquisite skin took on a porcelain sheen in the moon glow, and as Jess crossed the lawn his heart skipped a beat. He hadn't seen Tracy James in seven years and she still took his breath away.

"Not a word all this time. Now, suddenly you show up in my living room," she said.

"It wasn't my idea, believe me." Jess stopped when he was two feet away. Part of him wanted to hurl her into the pool or off the cliff. The other part wanted desperately to pull her into his arms.

"You could've called. Told me you were in town," she said.

"I didn't think you'd want to see me."

"Always, Jessie." Tracy offered up a sad smile. "Maybe you're the one who didn't want to see me."

"That was true for a long time."

"And now?"

Jess wrestled with what to say. Did he dare tell her how he'd thought about her every day for the first two years? And how that basically hadn't changed over the next five? Or did he come clean about all the pain she had left him with? Maybe he ought to tell her how she'd caused him to flunk Dr. Clifford's biofeedback test.

Jess went with a convenient truth instead.

"I came here to see my father."

Tracy lowered her eyes. "I'm so sorry about all that."

Jess couldn't help himself. "Are you really?"

She looked genuinely hurt. "Of course I am. About everything." Her eyes drifted back to the party inside. People were continuing to hobnob and drink, oblivious to the fragile reunion happening poolside.

"I think about you all the time, Jessie." She moved almost imperceptibly. But definitely closer. "Do you ever think of me?"

There it was. A second chance to fork over the truth. But he had waited too long to speak up.

"Isn't this nice? The happy couple together again."

Jess felt a chill as he turned to face his father. Could this really be the same man who hours earlier had been shivering to death under a blanket? Tracy looked out at the city lights, avoiding Walter Stark's penetrating gaze. Jess instinctively stepped in front of her. "Your party's inside, Dad."

"Not as interesting as what's happening out here," said Walter.

The nasty grin was what made Jess finally snap. "You really want to get into all that? Right now?"

"You wouldn't do that to your mother." Walter looked back toward the house.

"You don't think so?"

Tracy tried to step between father and son. "Jessie . . ."

But Walter wouldn't let it go. He glared menacingly at Jess. "You don't have the nerve or the guts."

Maybe it was a lifetime of built-up anger toward Walter and having to toe the line. It might just have been Tracy standing by his side. But Jess found himself doing what his father thought him incapable of—issuing a threat.

"What you said earlier? About what *they're* doing?"

Walter backed off a bit. Once again, Jess saw fear in his father's eyes. "Watch what you say, boy."

"Maybe they ought to finish it."

Walter waved a pale finger in his son's face. "You'll regret saying that."

Tracy finally couldn't take it. "Stop it! Both of you!"

The two men were taken aback by her sudden outburst.

"I must have been out of my mind coming back here," said Jess. He turned away from both of them and made a beeline for the side exit.

Walter yelled after him. "That's right. Run off. Just like you did before!"

Jess didn't let that faze him and kept on walking. He was in the yard just long enough to hear Tracy call his father a bastard before he disappeared into the desert night.

JESS BELOW

Jess stopped screaming after the sixth or seventh shovelful. Not only did his assailants have no intention of pulling him out of the grave, he knew there was a limited amount of oxygen in the enclosed space. He had no idea how long it would take to use up the available air and no interest in rushing the process.

Eventually, the thudding clods of dirt ceased. Jess heard a car door opening. When an engine revved, and tires screeched, his heart sank. Suddenly his plight hit him full force—buried alive in the middle of the desert and no one knew where he was.

"OhGodohGodohGodohGod . . ."

He kept up the frantic mantra until he remembered the price of overexerted breaths. It took every ounce of willpower to try and calm himself down.

Once his breathing became less labored, Jess faced the next obstacle—escaping before he ran out of oxygen. He tried pushing up against the coffin lid, which, of course, didn't budge an inch. There was a ton of caked dirt piled on top of it.

Horrific thoughts raced through his head. What sort of creepy crawly things were living down here with him? What if he managed to poke a hole in the coffin lid, dirt poured into his mouth, and he choked to death on his own burial ground long before he would have asphyxiated? These fears were fueled by not being able to see a damn thing.

That was when Jess remembered his cell phone.

He'd always made fun of people who went to rock concerts and held their iPhones up to replicate the classic lit match from days gone by. Now he wished he had a dozen of them.

There was very little room in the coffin. Jess thought it might take him a good hour to turn himself around. It took ten minutes just to extract the cell from his pants pocket. He said a silent prayer his phone was holding a full charge—it was half-answered when he saw the battery bar was at fifty percent.

It illuminated his surroundings: simple carved wood. Wherever his ski-masked captors had obtained the coffin, they had bypassed the showroom models. He was just relieved to see he wasn't sharing the space with a rodent, reptile, or nest of worms.

Suddenly, something obvious occurred to him. He was holding a cell phone. It was probably a long shot but what harm was there in trying to dial 911?

He punched in the three digits and hit "Send."

The display screen immediately flashed "No Signal."

Jess groaned. He was tempted to hurl the cell but knew it would bounce off the lid and hit him square in the face. With his luck, it would probably land directly in his open head wound and he'd end up passing out again.

Jess regained his composure and as he stared at the phone, he became aware of a few things.

He could see the walls of the coffin.

The time was 2:42 a.m.

And he was completely fucked.

8

Jess was in the passenger seat of the family station wagon punching radio presets. A newscast, a ball game, and a couple of rock stations blasted out of the speaker he'd cranked up to drown out his parents, who were arguing in the driveway. Sarah was behind the wheel with her hands over her ears and eyes shut, trying to wish it all away. Jess was nine and Sarah was seven. She punched the horn in frustration and accidentally hit the gear shift. The station wagon lurched down the steep driveway.

Sarah screamed. Jess yelled at her to stomp on the brake. Her feet couldn't reach it. A hysterical Kate shoved Walter toward the car, which was picking up momentum. Walter stumbled and fell to the ground, helpless to come to his children's aid.

As an AC-DC tune blared on the radio, Jess tried to grab hold of the steering wheel from the passenger seat and got Sarah's hands clawing in his face instead. Jess grabbed his door handle and screamed for Sarah to do the same. But the doors wouldn't budge—they'd automatically locked when the car started to move.

Kate keened at the top of the driveway. Sarah's face was drenched in tears. Jess noticed something in the rearview mirror.

The adult Tracy James stood at the bottom of the driveway.

She was wearing the white cocktail dress from Walter's birthday party and it was drenched in blood.

The nine-year-old Jess screamed as the car hurtled on a collision course with the impassive Tracy.

Bang!

Jess bolted up in bed.

There was another sharp bang. He whipped around and realized something was slamming against the motel room wall. Blue neon washed above the bed; it came through the thin opaque curtain of the room's only window. The wind howled outside—an endless echo.

Jess hopped out of bed. He wore a white T-shirt and pair of sweatpants. He crossed to the window and peered outside. The neon sign was on (the "S" still wasn't fixed) and spread a turquoise glow across the parking lot. Jess's SUV and the vintage Mustang were the only two cars. The Santa Anas blew sand all over both of them.

There wasn't a living soul in sight.

Jess closed the flimsy curtain and headed back to bed. He chalked the nightmare up to desert winds, an old love, and general familial unpleasantness. He looked at the clock radio on the nightstand—just past four in the morning. Too early for a cup of coffee and way too late to analyze a bad dream. He lay back and tried to drift back to sleep.

This time, a scratching sound got his attention.

He sat up slowly, trying to ascertain where the noise was coming from. The wind continued to blow but there seemed to be something else. It sounded like a moan, as if someone was calling his name.

Jess was tempted to pinch himself. Maybe he was in one of those horror movie sequences where you're dreaming and wake up in a cold sweat, only to throw open a door and wake up again because it was just one big fucking nightmare. But he was pretty sure he was wide awake and someone was at the door.

He climbed out of bed again. "Who is it?"

The answer was a more pronounced scratch and a heavy blast of wind. He placed his hand on the doorknob and hesitated before throwing it open.

The scratching stopped.

So did the wind.

Jess opened the door and his father fell onto him.

Walter was a mess, with blood trickling from his mouth. He was ghostlier than he'd been in the wheelchair. His father started to slip, so Jess tried to pull the old man up but was dragged out the door for his troubles. They tumbled to the ground in the parking lot.

Walter gasped for breath but barely found any. "Son . . ."

Jess clung to his father. "Who did this?"

Walter didn't have strength left to answer. His bloodshot eyes drifted to the wall beside Jess's motel door.

A bloody "T" had been scrawled there. The horizontal slash was thick; as if it were being emphasized.

Jess couldn't help raising his voice. "Did you do that? What does it mean?"

But Walter didn't respond.

He died in his oldest son's arms.

9

By the time the cops arrived, the wind had died down to a slight breeze. The morning sun crested over the eastern mountains, throwing sparkles off the purple quartz. It was cold. Unless it was the dead of summer, the days started out frigid even if the mercury climbed into the high eighties by noon. For Jess, that chill was going to linger a while. There was a litany of unresolved issues between him and Walter, and now Jess was forced to carry a one-sided burden for the rest of his days.

For the second time in less than twenty-four hours, Jess found himself with Thaddeus Burke while the sheriff's men tended to a dead body. This wasn't lost on the lawman, who sucked coffee from a 7-11 Big Gulp while waving at the coroner van with his free hand.

"This is becoming a nasty habit, son."

"Tell me about it," Jess replied.

"I'm sorry for your loss. Walter Stark was a great man."

Jess just nodded. The sheriff was entitled to his own opinion.

Burke finished off the coffee, crumpled the cup, and tossed it in a trash can. "I know you've been gone a long time. But I'm sure you're aware of all the good things that your father did around here."

"I wasn't close to my father, Sheriff." Jess's eyes drifted toward the coroner van. The scarlet-headed medical examiner was examining his father's bloodied body. She was bundled up in a parka and sweats; the 911 call had

55

obviously pulled her out of bed. "We didn't see eye to eye on most things. If we did, maybe I would have never left. It's even possible I would've been working for the man. The truth is, I hardly knew him. Yesterday was the first time I had talked to him in over seven years."

"At least you got to spend some time together."

Jess thought back on seeing his father the previous day. The weakened man on the lanai. The nasty patriarch by Clark James's pool. Neither version of Walter Stark was going to rank up there as a fond memory to hold onto.

But what did stick in his mind was his father asking him for help. And how Jess had done absolutely nothing.

"Not enough," he honestly replied.

"You know what he was doing all the way out here in the middle of the night?"

"I've no idea. He died before he could say anything."

"We've been looking for his car but it's not here. The only two in the parking lot belong to you and your buddy."

"Maybe someone dropped him off," suggested Jess.

"We'll check up at the house. He could have called for a taxi. I'm sure we'll figure it out."

Burke asked Jess to tell him exactly what had happened. Jess recounted the banging noise that woke him up. The sheriff suggested it might have been a car door dropping Walter off. Jess said it sounded much more violent, like something being slammed against the wall in the desert wind. He mentioned the scratching sound, which led him to the door where he found his father with the life oozing out of him.

"I wonder what he wanted to tell you," said the sheriff.

"Maybe the name of the person who killed him?"

Burke's eyes narrowed. "Jumping to conclusions, aren't we?"

"His body was covered in blood."

"He could've been in some kind of accident. Wandered off the road."

Jess couldn't believe the ludicrous theory the man was offering up.

"And he ended up right outside his son's motel room? Right after seeing him for the first time in years? A little convenient, don't you think?"

"I'm supposed to believe that someone murdered Walter Stark and dumped him on your doorstep."

"Sounds just as likely a scenario to me."

Burke looked dubious. "And who do you think killed him?"

"Who knows? My father might have done all the great things for this town that you say, but I'm sure he pissed off bunches of people and stepped on lots of toes along the way. Maybe you oughta start with whatever he was trying to write in blood on that wall." Jess pointed at the bloody "T" next to his room.

"You said you opened the door and found your father?" asked Burke.

"That's right."

"Ever occur to you he held onto the wall for support and his bloody hand left that imprint?"

"Looks drawn to me."

"Sounds more like an overactive imagination." Burke shook his head. "Look, Mr. Stark, you've had quite a couple of days. I wouldn't be surprised if you were in shock. You ought to let the paramedics take a look at you when they're done . . ."

"I'm fine, Sheriff."

"Okay. Say that you are." He stuck his notepad in his back pocket. "I'll tell you what I know. Your father had a disease that completely stumped Doc Rice. No telling what kind of toll it was taking on him. I've got to believe a midnight stroll didn't help matters any."

Jess was trying to keep track of everything. "You know Edward Rice?"

"This town is a lot smaller than you think, son."

"You're going to stand here and really tell me that my father died from natural causes?"

"I'm saying he was a very sick man with an undiagnosed disease. Burke pointed toward the medical examiner. "Lilah will file her report and then we'll get a better idea of what's what. In the meantime, maybe you should let me do my job while you go on about your grieving."

Burke patted Jess on the back, signifying that the interview was over. The sheriff crossed the parking lot to confer with Lilah, the medical examiner. Jess stood in the doorway and watched the proceedings. Half an hour later when the coroner van pulled off with his dead father and the cops trailing right behind, he was still standing there.

It was starting to warm up.

But Jess still felt that deep chill.

"How long are you going to stick around for?"

Benji and Jess were back in the rockers. Benji was working on another six-pack; Jess was nursing a water bottle. "Can't say for sure. I'm still working up the nerve to head up to the house."

"Your dad just died. I'm sure your family wants you around."

"I wouldn't count on that."

"What are you talking about?"

Jess told Benji about the party and ensuing fight between him and his father.

"What was Tracy doing the whole time?"

"Trying to decide whether to break it up or run for the hills. I tried to keep her out of it."

"What finally happened?"

"I actually threatened him. Then I stormed off in a huff. Can't say I was quiet about it." Jess lowered his eyes. "Or proud."

"That's not good, man."

"No kidding."

"I didn't mean you, Jess. I was thinking about Burke."

"The sheriff?"

"Let's say you're right and they find out your dad was actually murdered. They're going to be looking for someone with a motive."

"I'm sure there's a laundry list. He screwed over tons of people in business."

"And they just happened to pick last night to kill him? The same day you come back to town after not seeing your father in seven years? A man you've made no bones about hating. Now you tell me you got into a big fight with him?" Benji pointed his beer at Jess's room. "Six hours later he's dead outside your door."

Jess saw where Benji was headed. "I called 911 right away."

"Burke would just say you were trying to be clever, bro. It's not going to stop him from looking at you as Suspect Numero Uno."

10

Jess was in the kitchen with Lena when Kate got home from the mortuary. Jess's mother looked like she'd put on ten years since the previous evening. She wore a simple black dress and shoes; he couldn't help but notice that she had the perfect bag to match. Kate immediately opened her arms and he dutifully went to her.

"I'm sorry, Mom," he said while they were still entwined.

Kate eventually let go. She wiped her tear-welled eyes and nodded. "I can't imagine what it must have been like for you, finding him that way."

"What was he doing out there? Did he tell you why he was coming to see me?"

"I didn't even know he was gone."

"I don't understand."

Lena brought over a freshly brewed cup of tea. Kate thanked her and then turned back toward Jess. "Ever since your father got sick, we thought it better to be in separate bedrooms. He had such trouble sleeping, I didn't want to risk waking him when he finally drifted off. You know how it is when you aren't well. You don't want to be bothered with anything or anybody. Imagine feeling that way day after day. Week after week . . ."

Emotion flooded over her. She broke off and gripped the teacup with trembling hands. Lena leaned in to steady the cup but Kate indicated she had a grip on it. She held onto Lena's hand for a moment. Despite everything Lena had witnessed in the Stark house over the decades, Jess could see a deep-rooted affection and devotion between these two women that nothing would tear asunder.

"He never mentioned me?" asked Jess.

Kate offered up a sad smile. "Oh, he mentioned you. I came outside looking for him at the party and he said the two of you had fought. When I pressed him about it, he refused to say anything else." The ensuing silence made it clear she wanted Jess to fill in the blanks.

"It was just the same old stuff, Mom. You know Dad and me. One says black. The other mentions every color in the rainbow before agreeing on anything."

"I'd concocted some fantasy in my head that the two of you would forget about the past and start over again. But your father was so damn stubborn."

The cup started to shake again. This time he reached over and took Kate's hand. "At least we know what side of the family I got that from." As easy as it had been for him to get a rise out of his father, Jess could always offer a soothing balm to Kate.

"No question about that," mumbled Lena, who was preparing sandwiches by the sink. Kate and Jess shared a laugh of relief.

"Now that you know he left the house, think back. Do you remember hearing a car? Anything like that?"

Kate shook her head. "I was pretty wiped out after the party. I made sure your father was in bed and then went to my room. I think I was asleep before my head hit the pillow."

"So, Dad got undressed, put on pajamas?"

"I actually helped him," Kate said.

"And there weren't any wounds or blood at that point."

She shook her head. "That's when we got to talking—well, tried to talk—about you. He was all worked up. I was happy to see it. He'd been so weak these past few weeks. I actually went to bed thinking maybe we'd gotten over the hump with his illness. I was crazy enough to finally feel a little hope."

Jess felt plenty of sympathy for his mother, but his curiosity won out. "He obviously wanted to see me for some reason. It wasn't an afterthought.

He got himself fully dressed—different clothes than he wore to the party. Casual slacks. A white shirt that . . ."

Jess stopped mid-sentence. The least he could do was spare his mother the gruesome details.

"He tended to wander around at night."

Those words came from Edward Rice as he walked through the garage door. He placed a car key in a bowl on the kitchen table. Once again, Jess was disturbed by the sense of familiarity the physician had in the Stark house. It was a whole lot more than Jess had ever felt in his two decades under the same roof. Kate could sense her son's discomfort.

"Edward was kind enough to take me to the mortuary."

Jess chose to ignore that for the moment. "What do you mean he 'wandered around'?"

"Walter had taken to sleepwalking over the past couple of weeks." Rice looked over at Lena. "When did you find him out by the pool at four in the morning? A week ago?"

Lena rinsed her hands and nodded. "It was very strange. A noise outside woke me up. I thought it was the wind. Then I noticed the alarm was off. So I got a flashlight and went outside. That's when I found *Señor* Stark standing by the pool. He was only wearing the pajama pants and no shoes—and it was ice cold. I told him to come inside before he froze to death. But he didn't answer. He was asleep!"

"In the night air?" asked Jess.

Lena nodded. "I tried to shake him awake. He kept saying 'Noooo, noooo' when I pushed him toward the house. He was still moaning like that when I called the doctor."

Rice took up the tale. "Walter didn't wake up till the next morning. Couldn't remember a thing. He thought he'd been in bed the whole night."

Jess attempted to reconcile this with what he had experienced early that morning. "You're saying that my father sleepwalked himself six miles to my motel in the middle of the desert?"

"Not at all," said Rice. "But he could have wandered out of the house that way. If he got as far as the pool the other night, maybe this time he made it down the driveway. Some motorist could have picked him up, took him where he wanted to go. You were obviously on his mind from your fight earlier in the evening."

Jess was surprised the physician knew about the altercation with his father. But then he realized word of it must have spread through the party like the plague after Jess stomped out the side gate.

"Supposing that was remotely feasible, don't you think that person would have noticed he was drenched in blood?"

"I don't think your mother needs to be saddled with details, Jess."

"No secrets, Edward. We agreed," Kate said. Jess wasn't happy to see her hanging on Rice's every word.

"Walter was probably fine till he got to the motel. He must have gotten confused and wandered into the desert. He could have stumbled through cacti and sustained his wounds that way, which would account for all the scratches the M.E. found."

"You talked to the medical examiner?" asked Jess.

"I just got off the phone with Lilah Webster. I know her quite well. You run a geriatric hospital, you're going to cross paths with the M.E. more than a few times."

"What else did she say?"

Rice hesitated. But Kate wasn't going to let the doctor off the hook. "Edward. What else?"

"There were bite marks. A lot of them. Lilah thought he must have fallen and some wild animals probably went after him." Rice turned back and addressed Jess. "He somehow managed to get back on his feet and make it to your motel room."

"I didn't see or hear any animals."

"They wouldn't follow him out of their natural habitat. Especially with cars, people, and the highway nearby. From her preliminary examination, Lilah seemed to think it was cardiac arrest."

"I would have known if my father had a heart attack."

"Ever witnessed one before?"

Jess couldn't admit that he had.

"What exactly transpired when he passed away?" asked Rice.

"He was weak. Having trouble breathing. He said my name, closed his eyes and . . . faded away." It had been much worse than that, but Jess found he was carefully choosing his words for the benefit of his mother.

"That sounds like a heart attack, Jessie." Rice's tone became much more somber. "These past few months were extremely traumatic for your father. His disease took quite a toll. Last night was probably the final straw. By the time he went through those last exertions to reach you—it was too much. His body finally gave out."

Rice turned to Kate. "Lilah should be through with the autopsy by tomorrow. You can proceed with the funeral arrangements and cremation after that."

"Cremation?" asked Jess. "What about the police investigation?"

"According to Lilah, there isn't going to be one. Her report is going to say Walter died from natural causes. Case closed."

"You've got to be shitting me!" Jess whirled on his mother. "You can't agree to this."

Kate didn't respond. Instead, she stood up and handed her teacup to Lena. "Could you show Dr. Rice into the living room and let me have a moment with Jessie?"

"Absolutely, *Señora*." Lena motioned for Rice to follow her out of the kitchen.

"You shouldn't overdo it, Kate," the physician said.

"I'll be with you in a few minutes, Edward."

Lena led the doctor out the kitchen door but not before tossing a sympathetic I-wish-I-could-help-you look Jess's way. The moment the door closed, Kate's mood did a one-hundred-eighty-degree swing.

"Why are you doing this?"

"Doing what?"

"Looking for things that aren't there? Why can't you just accept the facts you're being told?"

Jess was completely caught off guard by his mother going on the offensive. "I just want the truth, Mom."

"Your father is dead, Jessie. No truth is going to change that." Anger bubbled to the surface as Kate spoke. Jess could only imagine how long it had been submerged. "Maybe if you hadn't left the party last night things would have been different. Have you considered if you'd stuck around and talked to your father in a civil tone, maybe he wouldn't have had to go chasing after you in the middle of the night . . .?"

Kate trickled off. She choked back a sob.

"So now you're blaming me for this?" Jess asked quietly.

Kate looked startled, realizing that was exactly what she had been doing. She tried to correct course. "I never blamed anything on you, Jessie. I just missed you."

"I got the impression from Sarah that everyone couldn't stand me."

"That's Sarah being Sarah. You're my son. The only thing I hated was that you felt you had to run away from all of us."

Jess knew he should have left things at that. But now that he was face to face with his mother, he desperately wanted to know more.

"Did Dad ever tell you why I left?"

Kate shook her head. "I didn't care. I still don't. I'm just glad you're back."

"I'm glad I could be here."

For a moment Jess thought he might have been throwing his mother an emotional bone. But then he realized it was the honest-to-God truth.

"It would be good for you to stay and grieve with your family," Kate said. She leaned over and kissed her son gently on the cheek. "Don't run away so quickly this time."

Jess followed the sound of the bouncing ball into the Stark backyard. An Olympic-sized pool, a guest house, and tennis court were strategically situated for optimum sunlight. A basketball hoop hung atop one fence on the tennis court. Harry was shooting free-throws from the baseline that doubled as the makeshift court's charity stripe.

He watched his younger brother's methodical approach. Harry was so wrapped up in shooting and rebounding the ball that he was unaware of having an audience. Jess felt regret begin to sink in for all the years he'd missed with Harry, when the boy became a young man who could have used his older sibling's shoulder to lean on and look up to. It was time they would never get back and Jess wondered if it would have an enduring distancing effect on their relationship going forward. In that moment, Jess knew the onus was on him; he couldn't let that happen.

Jess waited till Harry made five in a row (which didn't take long) before entering the tennis court.

"You'll break your golf coach's heart when you make junior varsity."

"You haven't seen me when there's a hand in my face. I can't shoot for shit." Harry tossed the ball to Jess.

"You talk like that around Mom and Dad?"

Harry cracked a smile. "What do you think?"

"That you wouldn't be able to sit down if you did." Jess tried a twenty-footer. It clanged off the rim and Harry caught the rebound.

"I let down my guard around Mom once and she washed my mouth out with soap." Harry tried the same shot that Jess missed. It swished through the net. He grabbed the rebound and threw the ball back to Jess.

"H."

"I get a chance to make it first," said Jess.

"You won't."

Harry was proved right when Jess's attempt banked off the rim again. He tapped the ball back to his little brother, more than happy to get involved in a spontaneous game of H-O-R-S-E.

"Talbot still coaching the team?" asked Jess.

"He died three years ago. I went to the funeral with Mom and Dad." Harry threw in a reverse no-look layup. Swish again. "Now we have to go to his."

Jess replicated the shot perfectly. "Yeah," he grunted.

Harry looked for a place to attempt his next shot. "You sticking around for it?"

"Of course."

Harry didn't betray a reaction to this. But Jess surmised from the confident way his brother made his next shot that he was happy about it. Jess's try from the same spot was an air ball.

"O," Harry said gleefully.

Jess was happy to see his brother smile. He imagined it was a rare thing these days. Jess remembered being Harry's age in the Stark mansion and the paucity of happy times that came with being under Walter Stark's thumb.

"So how's it been being back home?" asked Jess.

"The same. Sarah's a pain in the ass. Always arguing with Mom—mostly about money. Mom's overly protective but could be a whole lot worse. She could be like Dad." This time Harry missed an easy shot, a ten-footer that didn't draw iron. "I can't believe he's gone."

"Me either," said Jess. He tried a free-throw and was surprised when it went right through the center of the net. Harry rebounded the ball, tried a free-throw and made it. Jess grabbed the ball and moved to the corner.

"What happened between you and Dad before you left?" Harry asked. Jess missed the shot by a mile.

"Play fair," Jess said.

"You're not going to tell me?"

"Someday maybe. Not now."

Harry realized he could jinx shots all night for Jess and wouldn't get an answer. "Maybe if I come and crash on your couch up in LA?"

"Yeah. Maybe then." Jess retrieved the ball, dribbled it a couple of times, and handed it back to Harry. "I'd like that. I'd like that a lot. So. What is it?"

"H-O. You're a Ho."

"Funny kid."

Jess lost, with Harry only getting an "H" for himself. Then they played P-I-G. Jess found a rhythm and shut Harry out. Another game of H-O-R-S-E followed. Harry won that. They played different words—like "S-U-C-K-S" and "B-I-T-E M-E." Each won his fair share.

They played until the sun went down and couldn't see anymore.

Then, they played a little longer, knowing that nothing good waited for them inside.

11

Over the years, Jess had watched his fair share of funerals for heads of state on television. Inevitably, in the days before the actual service, news anchors would plant themselves outside the deceased's home or church where the funeral was going to take place and watch the mourner's parade come and go. Walter Stark might not have ruled a country, but the turnout at the mansion was indicative of the influence Jess's father had on the city of Palm Springs.

The stream of visitors started out slowly. Couples his parents occasionally dined with; old family friends whose kids Jess romped with after grade school. Some of those playmates were now working men and women. Jess had lost touch with most of them way before he headed to Los Angeles. They were nothing more than perfect strangers offering condolences.

Kate stayed on the living room couch, receiving guests one by one. They sat or knelt beside her for maybe five minutes before Edward Rice gently urged them aside and brought the next one forward. Jess grew increasingly irritated at how easily Rice stepped into the host role. He wasn't sure what bothered him more, Rice walking around the house like he owned it or his mother letting him do so.

Jess helped Lena pass out hors d'oeuvres while the guests depleted his parents' liquor supply. He asked her how many of the mourners she'd met before. Lena said she barely knew a third. She guessed a good number were employees from Walter's various businesses. Jess thought there were probably a bunch of curiosity seekers as well, and Lena didn't disagree.

By eight o'clock, it was standing room only. Lena had to call the local deli for reinforcements. Jess was having difficulty trying to find a corner where he wouldn't have to put on a funereal face.

Kate insisted on introducing him to a few distant relatives. He couldn't sort out a third cousin from somebody's aunt, so he accepted their sympathies and feigned interest. Jess was trying to escape a close-talking uncle-by-marriage when he bumped into a handsome Latino man. The drink Jess was carrying spilled onto the man's three-thousand-dollar suit.

"Damn it. I'm sorry," said Jess.

"No trouble at all. It was overdue for a cleaning anyway." The man's English was flawless and his Spanish accent exuded sophistication. Jess was surprised when Kate actually rose off the couch to introduce the man.

"Jess, this is Jaime Solis. He was a close friend and business associate of your father's."

Solis's eyes lit up. "Ah, Walter's son. I've heard a lot about you."

"If it was from my father, I doubt much is worth repeating."

Solis just laughed and dabbed at the wet spot on his jacket with a cocktail napkin. He was in his mid-forties. He looked born into his designer suit. His bronze skin glowed off his gold and blue tie and he held out a perfectly manicured hand to Jess. "I'm terribly sorry about Walter. These past few months had been so difficult for him."

"Thank you. How did you meet my father?"

"A mutual friend introduced us," Solis said. "Walter and I shared a lot of the same interests and I ended up offering him a few business opportunities. He reciprocated by inviting me to invest in a couple of medical clinics with him."

Solis said he had been spending more time in the desert the past few years and recently bought a house down the road.

"Along with the country club," Kate pointed out.

"You must have really wanted to get a good tee time," Jess said.

"I don't even play. But the chef is exquisite and the view from the dining room is to die for. You'll have to be my guest."

Jess told Solis if he stayed in town long enough he'd take him up on the offer and would try to keep his drink in his glass. He apologized again. Solis waved it off and sat down between Kate and Rice. Jess turned toward the front door just in time to see Sheriff Thaddeus Burke arrive.

He crossed the room to intercept the lawman. Burke was out of uniform. He wore a suit that hadn't been pressed in ages—it probably only got trotted out on rare occasions. "What's this crap about saying my dad died from natural causes?"

"This isn't a business call, Mr. Stark."

"Doesn't mean I can't ask the question, Sheriff. You saw his body. Did that look like a man who suffered a heart attack?"

"I can only go by what the M.E. tells me. She's got the medical degree and fancy equipment. I'm just here to pay a condolence call."

Burke's smug face got Jess's skin crawling. "Maybe you ought to consider it paid and go back to doing your job."

"I saw your father a lot more than you did the last few years. I'd say that gives me as much right to be here as you." This truth caught Jess off guard and he reluctantly allowed Burke to slip past.

The evening continued to go downhill from there. Jess was particularly disappointed by Sarah's actions. Her voice got louder and her laughter more frequent with each drink. He couldn't even hang with Harry. His brother got corralled by their mother and was stationed on the couch like one of the von Trapp children. But instead of obediently singing "So Long, Farewell" and sent to bed after one performance, Harry had to endure encore after encore of condolences and variations of, "It'll-get-better-I-promise."

The final straw was the arrival of Clark James. Jess suspected it was commonplace for the actor to take over a room upon arrival. But he found it particularly nauseating that his father's "best friend" wouldn't even try tempering the attention-getting. James took a seat beside Kate and within minutes it was the thespian holding court, not the grieving widow. Jess decided it was time to leave the living room.

He walked down the long corridor toward the back of the house. The hallway walls were lined with more Stark memorabilia. There were pictures of Walter playing golf with dignitaries, shaking hands with governors and senators, dedicating desert museums, hospitals, and retirement homes.

Again, the most glaring omission was family pictures. Like the living room, the trek down the carpet toward Walter's office was intended for the visitor to know whose turf they were traversing.

Jess hesitated outside heavy oak wood doors. He thought he heard whispers coming from inside. Jess knocked on the door. The whispering stopped. He turned the knob and entered his father's inner sanctum. Of course, it was empty. The acoustics in the house must have been playing tricks on his ears or he was imagining things from yesteryear.

The office was from the era preceding the man cave. It wasn't tricked out with every electrical device known to humankind. The computer was puny and at least five years old. Walter didn't even have a wireless router. But the room still oozed power and success. Two deep leather chairs sat by the fireplace where late night brandies had been imbibed while business was discussed. The desk was an antique from which Walter ruled the desert. Jess settled into the chair where deals were brokered and broken.

He had just opened the top drawer when Tracy stepped into the room.

"It's strange to see you sitting there instead of him."

He automatically eased the drawer shut, feeling like he'd been caught with his hand in the cookie jar. And by her, of all people.

"I didn't know you were here."

"I came with Dad. He sort of sucks up the air in a room."

"I hadn't noticed."

Tracy grinned. "I saw you duck out of the living room. I thought I'd follow. I didn't need to stick around and watch him entertain the troops."

"His specialty," Jess said.

Tracy walked across the office. She took in the surroundings. Jess could see being in Walter Stark's private office was having a similar effect on her. "This is sorta strange."

"On so many levels," agreed Jess.

He watched as Tracy started to settle down in the chair across the desk, but then changed her mind. It felt way too formal for the two of them. Whatever their present was, Jess and Tracy's history begged for something more intimate. She moved to the edge of the desk and leaned against it. Being that close made him think of Dr. Clifford's biofeedback machine— the arrow would have been rapidly approaching the Danger Zone.

"I'm sorry about last night. I didn't mean to get in the middle of an argument," she said.

"It wasn't your fault. My dad started it. As usual."

Tracy looked around the room and repressed a chill. Jess could tell they were feeling the same thing. It was as if they were walking over the dead man's grave. "I can't believe he's gone," Tracy said. "I knew he'd been sick but last night he seemed like his old self, willful and belligerent as always. I would've bet he was going to outlast us all."

Jess didn't disagree. "What happened after I left your house last night?"

"You mean after I called your father a bastard?"

He chuckled. "I managed to catch that."

"I still feel awful. It's the last thing I ever said to him."

"What did you do after that?"

"I went inside. Kept my distance." She thought back. "I think I saw him talking to your mom for a little while. Maybe with my father too. I ended going upstairs to bed shortly after. The whole thing was just too upsetting."

Tracy was near enough for Jess to feel her breath. Once upon a time Jess had lived for that, but the ensuing years of pain and trying to forget her had changed things. So, even though she was now only inches away, those feelings were just something from days gone by.

Or so he hoped.

"It's pretty bad that it took your father dying to let us see each other again."

"It certainly wasn't the way I imagined it."

"And how was that?" she asked softly.

Jess decided that was a slippery slope and flipped through the papers on the desk instead. He wasn't really looking at anything in particular, just as long as it wasn't Tracy's eyes. He knew he could get lost in them. No way was he letting that happen again.

"I know you hated him, Jess. There wasn't a whole lot to love, that's for sure. But he was still your father. I can't tell you how bad I feel about everything that has happened."

He continued to shuffle his father's papers. Tracy took hold of his fingers and made him stop. Jess hoped his palm wouldn't begin to sweat.

"I had no way of getting in touch with you. No one knew where you went."

"I made sure of that."

Tracy's eyes welled with tears. She let go of Jess's hand to wipe them clear. His palm was still dry. Thank God for small favors.

"Are you going to hate me forever, Jess?"

"I could never hate you, Tracy. I just don't think things can go back to the way they were."

Tracy forced a smile. "You left an opening there."

But Jess didn't answer. He had come across a notepad under some manila files and noticed the letterhead on it.

The Oasis Bar and Lounge.

"Jess?"

"One sec." For a moment he couldn't remember where he'd seen that name—so much had happened in the past twenty-four hours. He knew the Oasis was the bar off Ironwood.

Suddenly, he remembered.

The dead man on Highway 111 had worked there.

Jess ripped the sheet off the notepad and stood up. "Sorry. I gotta go."

"What?" Tracy looked confused.

"Do me a favor."

"Sure."

"Tell my mother I'll call her in a bit. I don't think I can face that crowd of hangers-on in there."

He went out the office French doors before Tracy could respond.

The office doors led directly to the cactus garden out back. Jess figured he could swing around to the gate leading to the side yard. That way he could bypass the multitude of mourners inside, extract his SUV from the driveway, and head off without making excuses.

He passed the greenhouse on his way to the gate. Jess heard some giggling. The greenhouse door cracked open and Sarah stepped out. The first thing she spotted was Jess.

"Oh. Jess. What are you doing out here?"

Jess was about to ask the same thing but his sister was already trying to beat a hasty retreat back inside the greenhouse. But someone was behind her and she almost crashed into him.

Edward Rice.

Jess's first reaction was distaste, then disappointment. He finally landed on the idea that they deserved each other.

Sarah looked embarrassed and angry. "It's not what you think."

"Since when did you care what I think?"

Rice stepped forward to try and offer an explanation. "Jessie . . ."

Jess cut him dead with a look. "You two enjoy yourselves."

He left them standing there, wondering what he was going to do with this newfound discovery. They probably would've been thrilled to know he was less interested in them than the notepad he found on his father's desk.

Two minutes later he was back on the road.

12

Palm Springs was definitely not a nightlife Mecca. It had its share of clubs and even a teensy red-light district, but it wasn't South Beach by a mile, or even a block of the Sunset Strip. They didn't exactly fold up the sidewalks on Palm Canyon at night but foot traffic was minimal, window-shopping nonexistent, and most restaurants could barely fill one seating, and never two. Tourists came to the desert to bask in the sunshine, have an early dinner with a few cocktails, go to bed early, wake up the next day, and start the process all over again.

So, when Jess came down the hill from the mansion, it was smooth sailing through the heart of town. He made it to the Ironwood turnoff in less than ten minutes and hung a left. A hundred yards down the road he swung into the Oasis's parking lot. The neon sign was a palm tree with alternating blinking red words on the fronds: "Cocktails," "Food," "Sports TV."

There were a half dozen cars spread through a lot that could handle twenty times the amount. Jess took a spot near the entrance of a ramshackle building that last got a facelift during the Eisenhower administration.

As he approached the front door, Jess thought about what he hoped to accomplish inside. He was well aware that he had walked out on the Stark family's version of a wake in a desert palace to question strangers in a gone-to-shit bar. Some might find that a peculiar choice, but Jess was looking for any excuse to get out of there. Plus, he had always been intrigued by things that didn't add up—and his father's death certainly fit the bill.

But Jess knew it was more than that. He couldn't stop thinking of the terror in Walter's eyes when he told Jess someone was trying to kill him. Finding a message pad on his father's desk from the same bar where another frightened dead man had worked further activated Jess's shit detector. The irony that he was doing this on behalf of a man he'd spent most of his life hating wasn't lost on him.

He swung open the screen door and entered the bar. "Hotel California" tinkled through stereo speakers as old as the song. As Jess approached the bar, a Steely Dan tune came on next. He would have bet the same mix tape had been playing in the Oasis for three decades. A couple of regulars hugged barstools and their beers. Two old-timers pushed balls around a pool table in back. A Latina waitress in her early twenties sat in a booth, sorting through a paucity of tips. She looked up when Jess entered and started to get on her feet, but Jess waved her off, indicating he was going straight to the bar.

As he crossed the room, he wondered what his father was doing at a dive like the Oasis. Walter Stark threw five-course dinners at home and entertained guests by the dozens at the country club. Jess couldn't remember his father ever stepping inside a coffee shop or fast food joint, let alone a roadside bar.

The bartender was watching a muted college basketball game on a TV that still used an antenna. He swung his gargantuan frame around as Jess took a seat on a barstool. The man couldn't have been less interested if Jess had been peddling Tupperware.

"What can I get you?" he asked, not bothering to stifle a yawn.

Jess nodded at the beer spigots. "Whatever's on draft."

The bartender pulled an iced glass out of a lower drawer and drew down on the Stroh's lever. He handed the beer to Jess, who dug a ten out of his wallet and motioned that the bartender could keep the change. It raised the man's eyebrow and his suspicion—no one left five-dollar tips at the Oasis unless they were drunk off their asses.

"Is Tom around?" asked Jess.

The barkeep's eyes flickered. "He doesn't work here anymore." He started to move away.

"Funny," Jess said. "My dad said he did. Maybe you've seen my father in here? Walter Stark?"

"Sorry. Doesn't ring a bell." The bartender turned away, clearly shutting him off.

Jess took a swig of the Stroh's. He was considering using the direct approach and asking the man about Tom Cox's death when a voice whispered behind him.

"Finish your beer and go out back."

It was the waitress. Jess was surprised he didn't notice it the first time— but he actually knew her. Of course, when he last saw her she'd been fifteen and running around the servants' quarters in the Stark manse. Now she was a woman who would take any man's breath away.

"Maria?"

"Hi, Jessie. I would've said something when you walked in but I couldn't believe it was you."

"My God. Lena . . . your mom . . . said you'd graduated college but I never imagined . . ."

Jess broke off, continuing to stare. Her brunette hair had hints of blond from the desert sun, her eyes were dark pools that beckoned without a hint of makeup, and her uniform did nothing to hide the fact that she was long past being the awkward teenager that Jess used to tease.

Maria's eyes took on an insistent, desperate quality. "You don't want to ask questions here."

"Why not?"

"Your father came in here a few times and met with Tom Cox."

She didn't have to connect any more dots.

"And now they're both dead," Jess stated.

"I wouldn't want that to happen to you."

JESS BELOW

His wireless provider would have been upset—they weren't going to be able to charge Jess for extra minutes. He doled out his cell phone usage sparingly. It was a good light source and Jess was kicking himself for not getting the souped-up battery package when it had been offered.

He was already tired from thumping his foot against the coffin walls. He checked the cell's time display: 4:05 a.m. He'd been at it for over an hour and a half. He continued kicking the wood panel in front of him, but all he had gotten for his trouble so far was a sore arch, which he knew would hurt like a son of a bitch when he put some weight on it.

He managed an insane chuckle. Who gave a shit if his arch hurt right now? To put weight on his foot he had to be standing up, which meant getting the hell out of this damn grave. A whole bunch of good saving a little pain would do him when he suffocated to death.

Something obviously was making his brain circuits go a bit haywire. Maybe he was running out of air.

Jess started slamming his foot against the wall again.

The monotony set his mind adrift. He remembered being twelve and his mother forcing him to take ten-year-old Sarah to the park for the afternoon. Jess wanted to play catch but his sister insisted on flying a kite she'd gotten for Christmas. Jess showed her how to get it airborne. Sarah demanded taking over, promptly got the kite stuck up in a tree, and let go of the string.

She began whining for Jess to climb up fifty feet and get it. He picked up a baseball he'd brought and tried to knock the kite off the uppermost limb. His first ten throws didn't come close. Sarah wanted to try and suddenly it turned into a game. Pretty soon they were both laughing and providing pitch-by-pitch commentary as they tried to dislodge it with the baseball. When they finally freed the kite three hours later, the sun hugged the horizon and they caught hell from Kate when they got home. But that was one of the few times Jess could remember having a good time with his baby sister.

Something cracked.

The sound snapped his daydream in half. Jess fumbled for the cell phone and aimed it at the coffin wall by his feet. The fluorescent glow illuminated a distinct split in the wood.

He wasn't sure what that would gain him, but was happy to have made some kind of progress.

Then, he heard the *dripping* sound.

Jess swung the light just below the crack he'd made and saw another one had formed. This curbed any enthusiasm the first breakthrough had provided.

Water was starting to drip out of the new crack.

13

The fluorescent lights in the Denny's were a sharp contrast to the dim glow of the Oasis. Same number of customers, but a distinctly different midnight clientele. The Oasis patrons were regulars who didn't have anywhere else to go, while the Denny's denizens were people headed somewhere. Travelers making a pit stop on an all-night trek to Los Angeles or Phoenix. Nightshift workers stopping for dinner before heading to bed. Others were getting sustenance before heading in to work graveyard. Maria and Jess were the only ones who couldn't be categorized.

He couldn't get over that this was the girl who had been so shy she hid behind Lena's skirts when she was growing up. Age and gender had been the obvious reasons separating Jess from Maria. The *Upstairs, Downstairs* dynamic insisted on by his parents (especially Walter) widened those gaps. Jess remembered the time his father discovered him putting a dollhouse together for Maria. Walter berated him for playing with "the help" and Jess was dragged out of the room, embarrassed and feeling bad that the seven-year-old girl was too proud to cry.

Maria had quickly changed out of her uniform while Jess waited in the Oasis parking lot. When she opened the SUV door and climbed in, Jess couldn't help but notice the way her silk blouse clung to her body, the slight V-neck just suggestive enough. As Maria strapped herself in, the seat belt secured tightly across her chest and her flowing skirt hiked just above the knee—giving further evidence that this wasn't Lena Flores's little girl anymore.

On the short ride to the Denny's, they'd exchanged pleasantries and did a little catching up. Jess told her his dispatch job kept a much smaller roof than the one at the mansion over his head, but he was fine with that. Maria gave him an understanding nod. She'd grown up in the back rooms of that house. She might have been an awkward teenager when Jess left Palm Springs but there was nothing wrong with her eyes and ears. She was well aware of the tension between father and son.

Maria had done well in high school and gotten a scholarship to Pomona. Tons of competitive science classes had worn her out and she was taking a gap year before applying to medical school. Working at the Oasis gave her enough money to live in a small apartment just outside of downtown. She actually didn't mind waiting tables at the bar; it gave her time to think really hard if she wanted to become a doctor. At the same time, she didn't want to disappoint her mother.

"The medical profession would be lucky to have you," he said as they settled into a genuine Naugahyde booth. "But Lena would support whatever you chose to do. One hundred ten percent. She beams whenever she mentions you."

"That's because she can't wait to introduce me as 'my daughter, the doctor.'"

"I've known your mother longer than you. If you're happy, she's happy."

A bored waiter brought coffee. Jess realized he hadn't eaten since that morning, so he ordered an omelet. Maria nursed the coffee cup. Once the waiter shuffled away, Jess brought the conversation back to where he had started with the Oasis bartender.

"What was my father doing with Tom Cox?"

"I'm not sure. But he was there on more than one occasion."

"Any idea what they were talking about?"

"Not really." Maria lowered her eyes and studied the coffee cup.

"But . . .?"

"I did overhear them once."

"And?"

"Your father kept saying he wanted Palm Springs back like it was before this all happened."

Jess lowered his cup. "Before all what happened?"

Maria shook her head. "I didn't hear that part. Like I said, I was eavesdropping."

Jess continued asking questions about Walter Stark having clandestine meetings with a short-order cook in a bar like the Oasis. Maria really wanted to help and constantly apologized. He told her that was ridiculous; she was doing the right thing by not listening in.

"I was there when Tom died," said Jess.

"You were?"

He told her about the motorcyclist and ensuing accident. "When I pulled him out of the car, he was absolutely scared to death. He grabbed me by the neck and begged me not to make him 'go back.' You think he meant the Oasis?"

Maria pondered the question. "I doubt it. The owner, Gus? The guy behind the bar you talked to? He's not exactly your dream boss. But I wouldn't waste my dying breath on him."

"So what do you think Tom meant?"

"He was probably talking about Meadowland," Maria answered.

"My father's retirement complex?"

Maria nodded. "Tom worked as a chef there. He got fired about three months ago. That's when he started at the Oasis."

"That doesn't make sense. My father cans Tom Cox and then shows up weeks later to talk to him?"

"Your dad wasn't the one who fired Tom. He told me it was the doctor who runs the place."

"Edward Rice?"

Maria caught the distaste with which Jess mentioned the name. "I see you've met him."

"He seems to be running the house when he's not fooling around with my sister."

Maria's eyes widened. "Ah. That's what Mom was hinting about."

"What's that?"

"You know my mother," Maria said. "She won't come right out and gossip so she has a way of mentioning people's names in the same breath without linking them up. I haven't been around much, so I guess I missed it. But Sarah and Doctor Rice sort of fit."

"How long has he been running Meadowland?"

"Quite a while."

The waiter came over with the omelet. Jess waited for him to move off before he took a bite and continued. "You have any idea why Tom was fired?"

She shook her head. "We didn't talk much even though I got him the Oasis job."

"You did?"

"I was at the house when he came looking for your father a few months ago. He was really upset about getting let go—and our cook had just been deported. So I told him there might be an opening."

"Nice of you."

"He was a good guy. But he pretty much kept to himself the months he worked at the bar. When I asked him what it was like at Meadowland, he got nervous talking about it."

"What did he say exactly?"

"That a lot of creepy stuff was happening out there."

"Such as?"

Maria hesitated, and then leaned forward in the booth. At first glance someone would think she was striking a provocative pose for her boyfriend.

She was actually making sure no one could overhear.

"He said that way too many people were dying."

14

Jess had been dreaming of his father when the noise woke him up.

He couldn't remember the last time he'd dreamt of Walter Stark—maybe the first few weeks after he'd taken off for Los Angeles. Jess chalked those up to rage during the day that gave way to repressed anger in the supposed calm of night.

This dream had been strange because it wasn't a nightmare. Nor was it combative. The two of them were sitting in the stands at the Palm Springs Little League Field after a game, Walter trying to console his son after he'd struck out three times. Jess knew he was dreaming as it was happening. His father had never come to one of his games. But there was Walter Stark talking about nasty curve balls and strike zones, words he couldn't imagine coming out of his father's mouth. In the wacky way dreams and reality fold onto each other, Jess said his father shouldn't be sitting in the stands with him.

"Game's over, Dad. You're dead," said Jess the Dream Boy.

"Doesn't mean we can't sit here and enjoy ourselves," replied Dream Man Walter. He reached over and rubbed Jess's back. It actually hurt and Jess told his father to stop. Walter ignored the complaint and dug in with his nails, starting to scratch Jess's back so hard you could hear the fingernails on the uniform shirt.

That became the scratching sound that brought Jess out of Dreamland.

He quickly rolled over and checked the luminescent clock radio. 3:15 a.m. The scratching continued and grew louder. Jess sat up, reached for the nightstand, and flicked on the lamp.

The room looked no different. It was totally devoid of décor, style, or inhabitants. Jess's clothes were strewn on the desk chair; his shoes sat by the bed. He had been so exhausted that he'd fallen asleep before his head had hit the crummy foam pillow.

Jess noticed that the bathroom door was cracked open; no light came from within. He got out of bed and started to cross the room—then stopped in his tracks. He glanced around, looking for some weapon to fend off anything that might pop out of the bathroom, but Benji ran a no-frills operation, and that meant most things in the room, like the television set, clock radio, and lamps, were nailed down so no one could steal them.

Jess approached the bathroom door and banged his fist on it, hoping to scare someone hiding inside. He threw open the door and a startled gecko raced through a crack by the window. Otherwise, the bathroom was unoccupied.

Jess sighed, pissed at his imagination working overtime.

The scratching started up again.

Jess beat a path to the front door. He flung it open and was greeted by a blast of desert night air. At least a dead body didn't collapse in his arms. The parking lot was empty except for the SUV and Benji's Mustang. Walter's death and ensuing police commotion had scared away the last of the Sands's clientele for the time being.

He turned to go back inside, but stopped when he heard the chug-chug of a motorcycle on the road. It wasn't very loud and got softer as it moved deeper into the desert night. Jess couldn't be sure it had been in the Sands parking lot, but it gave him a reason to check things out.

He looked for tire tracks and found far too many to sort out, the culprit being the excessive police activity the previous morning.

Jess stopped looking in the dirt the moment he stepped in front of the SUV.

Moonlight cast a scarlet glow on the SUV's windshield.

When he got closer he saw the color came from something spread across the glass.

Blood.

A simple one-word message had been drawn in it.

LEAVE.

15

"Think someone might be trying to tell you something?" Benji asked.

The sun was barely up when Jess showed him the message on the windshield. The blood had begun to dry. As morning progressed, it would get darker and crustier.

"Don't suppose you saw or heard anything in the middle of the night?"

"I was out cold, man." Benji's sheepish grin would have done a Cheshire proud. "Sort of had a one-man wake after you took off yesterday. The coroner showing up doesn't do wonders for business."

"Right. Because it was booming before that."

"Economic slump, Jess. Give things time to turn around."

Benji's lack of conviction told Jess his old friend thought this was a long time coming. "How are you making a living anyway?"

"I actually rented a few rooms out as office space. Don't have any tenants right now, but I had an insurance guy for a year or so. Then there was this startup Internet company." Benji coughed, and corrected himself. "Well, I thought that's what they were till I realized they were shooting a porn movie."

"You kicked them out?"

"I should have. But I let them finish the flick and then they skipped out without paying me."

Jess tried to withhold the smile. "Imagine that."

"I need a better class of citizen in here." Benji suddenly looked at Jess like he was manna delivered from above. "Maybe we oughta start a business together!"

Jess was frightened to ask—but took the plunge anyway. "Like what?"

"How 'bout one of those sci-fi horror collectible stores? We could carry comics, graphic novels, movie posters . . ."

"Isn't there one on the main drag downtown?"

Benji waved it off. "Real shit business. No one's ever in the place. We could do so much better."

"'Cause you get so much foot traffic out here."

Benji frowned. He tried to make one more half-hearted attempt. "We could advertise."

"I'm not the best business partner, Benji." He glanced at the SUV again. "Especially seeing as how someone wants me out of town."

"I'm really sorry 'bout that."

"Not your fault," said Jess. "It was right outside my door and I slept through it."

"You gonna call the cops?" asked Benji.

It had been more than two hours since he'd discovered the bloodied glass. He didn't relish another faceoff with Thaddeus Burke. The sheriff was sick of dealing with Jess—and the feeling was mutual. The man had been so unwelcoming in his three previous encounters, it wouldn't surprise Jess if Burke or one of his minions had left the message.

"I don't think so," Jess said.

"You figure Burke would sweep it under the rug like everything else?"

"Pretty safe bet."

Jess opened the SUV trunk and rooted around inside. He found an old towel and used it to start wiping the blood off the windshield.

"So you're not going to do anything?" Benji asked.

"I didn't say that."

"You have an idea who might have done this?"

"Possibly."

Benji got that excited look in his eyes, which scared the shit out of Jess. "I know! Maybe we ought to open a private eye agency . . ."

"Now you're pushing it."

❋　❋　❋

One thing that Jess could say about his late father was he didn't skimp. When he had acquired Meadowland, it had been a broken down series of ranch houses sitting on farmland. He tore down the structures and built a much larger one that looked like an ultra-fancy Indian pueblo. Sheep had actually grazed in the pastures and Walter sold them for a nice profit to a stockyard up in Fresno and transformed the land into beautiful gardens. He called it Meadowland to give historical reference to the previous four-legged residents and moved the geriatric set in to replace them. State-of-the-art medical equipment and a first-class staff of trained medical professionals (nurses, doctors, orderlies, and therapists) provided long-term care for the aged and infirmed.

Jess had been forced to volunteer there by his father one teenaged summer. All he could remember was the smell of human life wasting away and Walter insisting it built character. Jess remained convinced the only thing his father wanted was to torture him and not have to pay Jess a salary for it.

He parked the SUV in a circular driveway lined with citrus trees and multicolored perennials. A gardener who looked as if he had been planted in the flowerbed dutifully waved at Jess. He nodded back and moved inside. The main lobby had a pastel motif that washed across the furniture, area rugs, and wallpaper. Jess approached the reception desk, where a ma-tronly woman with too much bottled blond in her hair wore a pleasant lime-green uniform and a practiced smile.

"Can I help you?" she asked in a sing-songy tone.

Jess identified himself and the woman's smile dipped into sincere sym-pathy. She must have had a lot of practice with numerous family members over the years being the bearer of bad news.

"I was so sorry to hear about Mr. Stark's passing."

Jess accepted the condolences and said he was just going to drop by the kitchen. The matron found this rather odd.

"Is there something I can help you with?"

Jess knew there were situations when evasion, not honesty, was the best policy. "No, thanks. Just checking on something for my mother." She offered to help him again, but Jess begged off and headed down the hallway.

Breakfast was finished by the time he walked into an industrial-sized kitchen. There was a small cleanup crew and a man wearing a chef's apron eating oatmeal at a tiny table.

"Guest rooms are the other end of the hall," the chef said between spoonfuls.

"Presuming you're the chef, I was looking for you."

"Chef? That word doesn't get tossed around here too much. Usually it's 'cook.' And other things depending on what the main course is." The man was reed-thin and florid-faced. Jess remembered an old adage—never trust an underweight chef. Or at least his cooking.

"I'm Jess Stark."

"You related to the old man?"

"If you mean Walter, yes. I'm his son."

"Sorry to hear 'bout your dad. I'm Meany." The two of them shook hands. "Haven't seen you around here before."

"I just got back into town. I worked here one summer as a kid, but that's about it."

"Way before my time," said Meany. "I've only been here for three years."

"Did you work with Tom Cox?"

"Rarely. I covered his days off. Rest of the time they had me doing odd chores around the joint. When Tom left, they offered me the job full time." Meany hesitated, starting to feel a little uneasy. "Why are you asking questions about Tom? You know he's dead, right?"

Jess saw no reason to lie, so he came out with the truth. "I was at the scene of the accident yesterday."

"Wow. I saw it on the news. Looked gnarly."

"It wasn't pretty. Do you know why Tom left?"

Meany shook his head. "I just know he was fired. Everyone was pretty mum about it. One day he was here, the next he was gone, and they had me coming up with new menus."

"I take it you weren't close with Cox?"

"Like I said, we worked different shifts."

"So, if he was worried about something or poking his nose into a situation he shouldn't have, you wouldn't know anything about that?"

"He didn't talk to me about it."

"But maybe someone else?"

Before Meany could answer, the matronly bottled blonde entered the kitchen.

"Mr. Stark, a moment please?"

An officious man in a suit bought off the Macy's rack appeared beside her. He addressed Meany. "I'm sure you have things elsewhere to catch up on, don't you, Mr. Meany?"

The cook nodded and started for the door. As he passed Jess, he mumbled "Human Resources" in his ear. This was only a momentary heads-up because the man introduced himself the second Meany left the room.

"I'm Gordon Chalmers, head of HR for Meadowland. Can I ask you what you're doing back here?"

"Just talking to your chef for a couple of minutes."

"I'm sorry, but we just can't have anyone wandering wherever they want about the premises. We have very strict rules here at Meadowland."

Jess couldn't stand the bureaucracy dripping off Chalmers's every pore. "Well, I'm not exactly sure which rule I'm violating. And it's not like I'm some stranger—my father owns the place."

"But he doesn't anymore, Mr. Stark," Chalmers said.

"Okay, I get the fact that he's dead so I guess technically he doesn't. But it reverts to his family and I am his son."

"And I'm terribly sorry for your loss," Chalmers said. "That doesn't change the fact that your father sold Meadowland a couple of months ago."

"He did? To who?"

The moment Jess asked the question, he felt the answer in the pit of his stomach.

"Edward Rice," Chalmers said.

Jess got no satisfaction out of being right.

"If you've got any questions about Meadowland, I strongly suggest you address them to him," Chalmers added.

Jess swallowed some pride. Then he asked Chalmers if he knew where he could find Edward Rice.

16

Palm Springs Country Club was one of the desert's grand old dames. In a time when a golf course sprang up in the Coachella Valley as often as a blemish on a teenage girl, PSCC was a throwback to a different era. PSCC didn't allow cell phones or BlackBerrys in the dining room. If you wanted to make a note during a meeting, a pad and pencil, with the club's logo neatly embossed on both, were hand-delivered by a tuxedoed waiter. You might not recognize the designer of PSCC's course (built in the late thirties) but if you Googled him you would see he had five tracks listed among *Golf Digest's* "Top Fifty Courses in America."

Jess gave the SUV to a valet. Self-parking was not allowed at PSCC and neither was the tip he offered. He entered a lobby that had museum-quality paintings on either side of a Mexican tiled floor that had been hand-laid more than a half century ago. The bright colors were still vibrant after all those years. He was certain someone was polishing them weekly, if not daily.

He hadn't even gotten to the reception desk when a maître d' stepped through the doors leading to the dining room with a sports jacket in hand. "Dr. Rice is waiting for you on the veranda," the man said as he helped Jess slip on the coat.

"I see they haven't loosened the dress code," Jess remarked.

"Never, sir. If you'd follow me."

Jess walked through the dining room that would do any four-star restaurant proud. There were maybe a dozen members in a space that sat one hundred and fifty, their average ages somewhere between seventy-five and recently deceased. The tables were appropriate for a state dinner—complete with designer linen tablecloths and napkins, fine china, and Baccarat stemware. The walls had murals of golf landscapes that looked so real, one would want to tee up and play them. The real deal—eighteen holes that had hosted PGA events for five decades—lay directly outside the windows that ran the length of the dining room's north wall.

The maître d' led Jess through plate glass doors onto a balcony, where Edward Rice was finishing a Cobb salad by the rail above the eighteenth green. "Mr. Stark, sir," the maître d' introduced with an over-the-top gesture.

"Thank you, Max," Rice said.

"Yeah. Thanks, Max." Jess wiggled around in the sports jacket. "A perfect fit, by the way."

"But of course, sir." If Max meant that with a bit of smug satisfaction, he wasn't letting on. He disappeared inside the club.

Rice waved his fork in the air. "I would've invited you for lunch but I figured you would have grabbed something in my kitchen."

"The receptionist obviously called you," said Jess.

"Veronica is nothing but thorough. You could have phoned ahead."

"You could have told me you'd bought the place," countered Jess.

"I never met you before yesterday, Jessie. Besides which, I think that should have been handled by your father." Rice put the fork on the salad plate. "Oh, that's right. The two of you didn't talk for seven years."

Jess refused to get into a pissing contest with the man. "When did he sell Meadowland to you?"

"Not too long ago. When he got sick, I refused to charge him for my services. He was able to do less and less at Meadowland, and was grateful for everything I had accomplished as chief of staff. He wanted to ensure the place was in good hands should the inevitable come to pass, and he gave me a wonderful opportunity at more than a fair price."

"And I'm sure my mother and sister just went along with it."

"I can't speak directly to their finances," said Rice. "But given your father's substantial holdings, I don't think the turnover of one convalescent facility was going to put your family in the poor house." He sipped some water. "But I feel uncomfortable talking about these matters. It seems more suitable for you to bring them up with your family."

"If that's true, it's the only thing you're not comfortable with regarding them."

Rice lowered the water glass. "Why were you asking about Tom Cox?"

"He worked there. You fired him."

"That's right."

"And now he's dead."

Rice nodded, nonchalant. "A sad turn of events."

"Why did you let him go?"

"He stole some files."

"What sort?"

"The confidential sort." Rice straightened up. At first he had seemed bemused by Jess confronting him. But with each ensuing question, the physician got more irritated, though he was trying not to show it. "What's going on with you, Jessie? Doing a little amateur sleuthing?"

"I've had two men die on me in less than two days. One happened to be my father. It's only natural that I'm interested."

"Actually, I'd say that's unnatural, given your involvement the past decade."

"I'm a late bloomer," Jess retorted.

Rice smiled. "You're more like your old man than you'd ever admit." Jess didn't bite, so the doctor pushed on. "Let's say I understand you're upset about Walter's death. It was sudden and peculiar, certainly traumatizing. What I don't get is your interest in Tom Cox."

"He was meeting with my father recently in a bar, more than once. Now they're both dead."

"I never would have taken you for one of these conspiracy nuts."

Jess ignored the dig. "Those files were on residents who died recently, weren't they?"

"If you already had your answer, why are you asking me the question?"

"How many deaths have there been at Meadowland?"

"People die all the time, Jessie, in Palm Springs more than other places." Rice looked out at the sparsely populated golf course. "After all, it is a retirement community."

Rice's iPhone dinged, he checked it, then excused himself to drop off some paperwork for Jaime Solis, the owner of the country club who Jess had met at the house. Moments later they reconvened under the porte-cochere. The valet nodded at Rice, then took back the sports jacket and ticket for the SUV from Jess.

The two men stood in silence as the wind decided to pick up at that very moment. Rice wiped some passing dust from his eyes. "What's really on your mind, Jessie?"

He decided to pull no punches. "Everywhere I look, you're involved. My father's health. You bought his business. You've been consoling his widow and now you're seeing his daughter. Speaking of which—how long has that been going on?"

"That's really none of your business."

The valet pulled up in a nifty sports car. Rice said goodbye to Jess and started toward it.

"I thought you rode a motorcycle," Jess called out, trying to catch the physician off guard.

"I gave up dirt biking in my teens." Rice laughed loudly. "Your fishing technique needs some work, Jessie. Maybe you should stop playing P.I. and look after that family you ran out on."

Rice fired up the sports car and took off. Jess's eye followed it down the driveway and then glanced over at the golf course. He was focused on a blood-red bridge in the distance when the valet arrived with the SUV.

"Hold it a few minutes, okay?" Jess asked. Again, his rote response was to dig in his pocket to tip the man, but the valet motioned to put his money away and take his time.

Jess walked down the cart path toward the bridge. He passed the driving range. It was deserted—perfect pyramids of golf balls waited for someone to come and hit them. The sprinklers arced over targets on the grass, the sputtering rhythm of the water providing the only sound. The scarlet bridge connected the driving range to the first tee and spanned a creek, which was wedged in between dramatic rock formations one hundred feet below.

Harry stood in the middle of the bridge. He had his Sunday bag casually slung over his shoulder. The wind continued to whip up the desert sand but he seemed oblivious to it as Jess approached the bridge. Harry was staring down at the creek, lost in thought.

"Harry . . .?"

The younger Stark brother didn't budge. Thinking that the howling wind might have swallowed up his voice, Jess called out again. Harry continued to be transfixed by the creek and rocks below. Jess didn't like that Harry was precariously close to the bridge's edge, despite the guardrail.

"Harry. You're too close."

This time Harry responded, but his voice seemed distant—even from only five feet away.

"I thought I heard him."

"Heard who?"

Harry kept his eyes on the creek. "Dad. Last night. Outside my window."

Jess placed a gentle hand on his brother's shoulder. It seemed to bring him out of his trancelike state. "Bad dreams, Harry. I've had a few myself the past couple of nights."

Harry managed a not-quite-sane-sounding chuckle. "You know what's funny? I thought I heard him just now. Down there. In the creek."

Jess looked where Harry was pointing. The sand was blowing off the rock formations. "It's just the wind, Harry."

Harry leaned forward to look: Jess reached over and pulled him back. The boy's eyes cleared and it was as if he was seeing Jess for the first time.

"I didn't mean to scare you."

"Too late for that." Jess, certain that Harry was back on firm footing, released his grip on him. "I didn't come back home to go to two funerals."

Harry's face brightened. "Does this mean you're staying?"

"At least till I get a few things settled," Jess said. "But I'm around whenever you need me."

"Really?"

"You can get me anytime you want." Jess urged Harry to walk off the bridge back toward the clubhouse. "I'm sorry I've been gone all this time. I should've been here for you. But I just had to go."

"Because of Dad?" Harry asked.

96

Jess nodded.

"What did he do?"

"Nothing you have to worry about."

The two brothers fell into step and walked past the driving range. The wind died down as they approached the parking lot. Jess took the car keys from the valet.

"Give you a ride home?"

"I rode my bike. I'll be okay."

Jess gave Harry a quick hug, and then opened the car door. As he was climbing in, Harry tapped him on the shoulder.

"Have you forgiven Dad?"

Jess considered how he wanted to answer this.

"Not yet." He was saddened by Harry's look of disappointment. "But I'm starting to work on it," he added.

Relief appeared on his brother's face.

A few minutes later when Jess was back on the road, he realized maybe he'd been telling his brother the truth.

He was working on it.

17

Jess had Googled three Tom Coxes and half a dozen Coxes with just the initial "T" in the Greater Palm Springs area. Phone calls established that the former were all alive and kicking, while the latter weren't named Tom and also on the right side of the grave. Luckily, Maria Flores had given Jess her cell phone number and she picked up when he dialed it. She was concerned when he asked for Tom's address and wanted to know what Jess was planning. He told her he wanted to swing by Tom's place and check it out. The truth was Jess wasn't sure what he was going to do once he got there, but it seemed like the logical place to start digging. Maria told him to be careful and let her know if he found anything. He didn't make any promises but thanked her and headed for the suburban heart of Palm Springs.

Tom's neighborhood had tiny houses with lawns the owners were in a constant struggle to keep from turning brown. When Jess pulled up in front of 1536 Tamarisk, he saw that Cox had thrown in the towel on that battle and had planted a small cactus garden in the front yard. Sand was never in short supply in a desert community—just wait for the wind to pick up and a whole new batch got dumped outside your door for absolutely free.

Jess parked a couple of doors down and checked out the neighborhood as he approached the house. It was early afternoon, so most people were still working and kids hadn't gotten home from school. It was a good time to be the only person in sight on the block and easy to slip through a side gate and come around the back of the stucco house.

The kitchen door hadn't been updated since the house was built in the fifties and Jess put his credit card to use for something other than running up debt. He had seen doors jimmied open that way on TV cop shows, and figured it was worth the shot. At first he got nothing but resistance—along with the increasing feeling a neighbor would report him and a squad car would pull up, spilling out cops with pointed guns. Just when he expected the card to break in half, leaving his name and number wedged in the door, the lock actually clicked open. Shocked but pleased at his neophyte skill, he would have suggested Cox get a better security system, but a whole lot of good that would do a dead man.

Jess was prepared to run for his car if an alarm sounded, but his presumption that a cook at a dive like the Oasis didn't have anything worth stealing proved to be correct as he entered the house in silence. Jess eased the door shut and started to explore.

The kitchen wasn't going to win any *Good Housekeeping* awards. Dishes were piled in the sink. *Architectural Digest* wasn't going to be popping by any time soon either: the décor was early Ward and June Cleaver.

The unimpressive tour continued as he moved down a narrow hallway and entered the living room. The furniture appeared to be the kind of stuff that came in a box and needed to be assembled. He'd lived in similar apartments in Los Angeles. You make one call, a truck pulls up, drops a few boxes on your doorstep, you get a screwdriver, unfold some instructions and voila—you have the drabbest living room imaginable.

Tom Cox's bedroom was just as fashionable. The bed was hastily made. Clothes were stacked haphazardly in dresser drawers and a few pairs of shoes were tucked into a corner. The television wasn't even digital—Cox had either owned it forever or had picked it up at a swap meet. There was one book on the nightstand: *Mexico—Off the Beaten Track*. Jess flipped through it. A few pages were dog-eared in a section detailing towns in Central Mexico. He wondered if Tom had been planning on leaving Palm Springs for a different life, one he wouldn't be scared to go back to.

There was one more room across the hall. Jess was surprised to find that the door was locked. So far everything he'd found in Cox's house had a net worth of a used set of golf clubs. He dug out his trusty credit card and actually had more trouble with this lock. It took a good couple of minutes to get it open.

The room was pitch black. Not a single stream of light came from the window. When Jess flipped on the light switch, he understood why.

The window was boarded up. A heavy piece of plywood had been nailed over it.

The rest of the room was just as bizarre. The walls were completely covered with papers and photographs. Most were pictures of elderly people. Jess had never seen any of them before. Next to most of them was a corresponding personnel file emblazoned with the Meadowland stamp.

Jess was disheartened that Edward Rice's accusation of Tom Cox stealing files from the convalescent home seemed to be true. Someone, presumably Cox, had used a red Sharpie to scrawl a date on both the pictures and files, along with the notation D-O-D.

Date of Death.

Tom Cox had obviously swiped files that didn't belong to him. But they substantiated his claim to Maria that an extraordinary number of elderly people had died within the past year at Meadowland. Jess lost count by the time he got past a dozen. This certainly didn't do wonders for Edward Rice's recent acquisition advertising itself as a "long-term" care facility.

Above the desk was a different set of photographs, pictures of a small town. Some were snapshots. Others were either ripped out of books or magazines. A few featured a run-down Spanish church with bougainvillea draped over an ornate jeweled cross.

The town was too small to be Palm Springs. At first Jess thought it might be one of the outlying cities, Indio or Blythe. But he didn't recall a church like that in any of those places.

Jess examined one of the photographs more carefully. A couple of cars lined the streets. Jess was able to make out a couple of license plates on beat-to-shit vehicles. Both were from Mexico. He suddenly understood why he'd never seen the town before. He had not ventured farther south than Tijuana in years.

He considered taking some of the files, but he had already broken and entered. He didn't think Thaddeus Burke would know he'd been in Tom

Cox's house, but he could only imagine the sheriff's reaction if he caught Jess with stolen files from Meadowland.

Jess decided to grab one of the Spanish church pictures instead. He stuffed it in his pocket and looked around for a pen and paper. He figured he could write down half a dozen names from the stolen files.

That's when he spotted the picture of Clark James on the desk.

Tom Cox had used his red Sharpie again. He had drawn a big "T" across the actor's smiling face.

It was the exact same "T" (the one with the thick horizontal slash) that Jess's father had scrawled in blood on the wall outside his motel room.

Jess started to pick up the photograph when he heard a noise behind him. He whirled around just in time to see something swinging through the air toward his head.

Too late to avoid getting smacked in the temple, he dropped to the ground, writhing in considerable pain.

Jess looked up and saw the Motorcycle Man looming above. He wore the same black suit from head to toe. The scarlet helmet covered his head and one of his silver-gloved hands held the object that had clubbed Jess in the head.

A gasoline can.

The Motorcycle Man uncapped it and began pouring fuel all over the floor. Some of it splashed onto Jess, who tried to roll away.

"Noooo!" he yelled.

But the man paid no heed and emptied the can. He kicked Jess in the side of the head with his pointed black boot.

The room went fuzzy. The last thing Jess saw was the flick of a match as everything went mercifully black.

JESS BELOW

The dripping was getting softer, but that didn't give Jess any solace. He flipped open the cell phone and trained the light toward his feet. The water level had risen halfway toward the top of the casket wall. This confirmed his suspicions about the diminishing drip sound: As the water rose, the drops had less distance to travel from where they leaked in.

He'd given up trying to staunch the flow about an hour ago. He had tried jamming his foot into the coffin corner where the water was coming through. The pressure against the sole of his foot had intensified immediately and water dribbled over the edge of his shoe. His instinct had been to push harder. The coffin wood started to creak. Jess instantly lowered his foot, realizing if it remained there, the coffin would split open and a tidal wave would pour in.

The dank cold from the water caused Jess to shiver. He lifted the cell phone off his chest, and checked the charge bar on the display—maybe fifteen percent left. He lashed out with his foot in frustration and got a mouthful of water for his trouble. And then dropped the phone. It splashed, gave the water a luminous glow for a few seconds, and then the display went black.

"Damn it!" Jess frantically rooted around in the darkness and rising water. "Where are you? C'mon!"

Finally, he felt it roll under one of his soaked thighs. He picked it out of the water and flicked the power switch. Nothing happened.

"No!"

Jess tapped it against the coffin lid. The first couple of times didn't change anything. He was about to smash it hard when the display flickered. He shook the phone back and forth—and miraculously the light clicked back on.

"Thank you, thank you." Jess laughed, realizing the insanity of the situation. It wasn't like anyone would hear him. Certainly not God. If a higher deity was listening, the first thing Jess wanted to ask was why did he end up down here in the first place?

The phone charge was visibly decreasing; it was twelve percent and Jess sighed as it dropped to 11. He shut off the phone before it hit single digits. Not that it made much difference—permanent darkness was on the way.

The water continued to drip as Jess weighed his choices. He could wait for it to fill up the coffin and gasp for air till the last possible moment, or he could plunge down into the cold liquid and see if he could pass out and let nature take its course.

He thought back to the swimming lessons he took at the Stark mansion when he was eight years old. The swim teacher his parents had hired was having trouble getting Jess to hold his breath underwater for the entire length of the pool. He had nothing against the woman. She was actually quite attractive and sweet, a college student making money between semesters. He just wasn't ready to try the entire distance underwater. Jess liked the fact that the girl didn't push him. She was encouraging as long as he swam a little farther below the surface each week.

But this didn't sit well with Walter Stark when he checked in on one of the lessons. The swim teacher tried to stick up for Jess, but his father wouldn't hear of it. He made his son swim the entire length of the pool underwater by using the pool scooper to shove his head under each time he tried to come up early. The first time Walter tried this, Jess dodged out of his reach. Walter told him if he did that again, he'd fire the swim teacher. Jess made it all the way across the second time and broke the surface huffing and puffing. He hugged the wall and was still gasping for air when his father dismissed the college student anyway.

The terror of that trip across the pool had stuck with Jess ever since. The thought of willingly forcing himself under the surface till he couldn't breathe filled him with dread. He realized he was determined to cling to every last breath of air possible, even though he knew it was only a matter of time until the water swallowed him up whole.

At least when that happened, Jess figured he wouldn't have to listen to the monotonous dripping sound.

He laid back and gratefully took in another breath.

The drops got softer and softer as the water continued to rise.

18

Tracy was giggling as she led Jess down the hallway toward her bedroom. She was wearing a string bikini that could double as a postage stamp, her hair still damp from the pool. Jess was also wet and concerned he was leaving footprints on the plush carpet. Tracy shut him up with a long kiss and then fiddled with the door. Jess yanked her back. Smoke billowed from under the doorframe. As they fell to the ground there was a gigantic smash of glass.

Jess snapped back to reality.

Tom Cox's house was in flames and Jess was lying in the middle of it. He began coughing and rolled away from the approaching flames. He bumped into a scalding hot table as he heard more crashing glass. It came from the living room windows, not that Jess could see them. Giant flames and black smoke obstructed his vision. He got on all fours and crawled toward the tinkling glass.

Tom Cox's furniture was already burned beyond repair. The television exploded as Jess crawled by. Glass shards sliced his face and hands. The flaming drapes were fit for a Hieronymus Bosch canvas, flickering, daring Jess to run their gauntlet. He collapsed on the floor in another coughing fit, about to lose consciousness once again.

There was another burst of glass. A silhouette loomed amongst the drapes, towering over him like the Devil himself ready to escort a doomed man Down Below. An arm reached for him. He didn't care whom it belonged to. Jess grunted and grabbed it with a superhuman effort.

The fact the arm was smooth and feminine was worth bonus points.

Maria Flores screamed at Jess through the roaring flames. "C'mon, Jessie! C'mon!"

The draperies started to fold into themselves as she tried yanking him over the window threshold. He was halfway out when the curtains collapsed over the lower part of his body. Flames licked at his jeans as the two of them tumbled outside in drapes of fire.

They landed in a heap on a grassy patch below the window. Maria was thrown free and scrambled to her feet. She carefully grabbed the portions of the curtains that weren't lit and quickly used them to smother the flames on Jess. Then she grabbed him by the arm and pulled him up.

"We've got to get away from here."

Jess kept coughing but was able to move under his own power. A few minutes later they were leaning against Maria's car across the street.

She asked him half a dozen times if he was okay. Jess said yes and thanked her repeatedly. Finally, when his coughing subsided and his eyes cleared from the smoke, he was able to ask what she was doing there.

"When you called me for Tom's address, I got worried you might get into some kind of trouble."

"Good thinking."

He asked about the motorcyclist. She told him the street was deserted when she arrived. No motorbike, no rider. Jess quickly brought Maria up to speed, telling her about Tom Cox's eerie rogue's gallery of pictures and files.

"You think that's why the guy set fire to the place?" she asked.

"Most likely. If he just wanted to get rid of me, he didn't have to burn down the entire house."

"Too bad none of that stuff will see the light of day."

Jess wholeheartedly agreed. But something jogged at his smoked-out memory. He looked back at the burning house and suddenly reached in his back pocket to pull out a crumpled photograph.

It was the picture of the Mexican town he'd grabbed off the desk.

"That church looks familiar," said Maria. She was peering over his shoulder at the photo.

"I'm pretty sure it's not around here."

Maria was fairly certain it wasn't either.

Minutes later the entire house was engulfed in flames. Neighbors congregated on the sidewalk. At least one thought to call 911. The fire department showed up within five minutes.

By then, the house was long gone.

"Trespassing. Then there's breaking and entering."

"That's going to be really hard to prove, Sheriff, considering there isn't a house anymore," Jess said.

This gave Thaddeus Burke pause. It was the first time Jess had been in his office—the other encounters had been at crime scenes and a bereavement call. Since this was Burke's home turf, Jess was willing to try almost anything to gain an upper hand. Maria, who sat in the chair beside Jess, took up the protest.

"What about the man who attacked Jessie?"

"We'll do a proper investigation, ma'am."

Jess let out a derisive snort; Burke turned a shade of red.

"Got something on your mind, son?"

"I want to know who killed my father."

"And I want you to stop looking for a zebra in a pack full of horses," Burke retorted.

"What about the papers in Tom's study?" asked Maria.

For the first time the sheriff looked surprised. "What papers?" he asked Jess.

"Files. Photos. Stuff Cox was collecting."

"Could you be a little more specific?" asked Burke.

"I didn't get a good look. But it doesn't matter anymore. Everything was destroyed in the fire." From the corner of his eye, he caught Maria staring at him, obviously remembering the photograph in his pocket. "Not that you give a shit about anything I have to say."

Burke got up from his desk and began pacing. Photographs of dignitaries lined the walls. Like Jess's father, the sheriff wanted anyone who walked in his office to be aware he knew powerful people. Jess wondered if that was just the man's ego—or did Burke actually have an inferiority complex that needed bolstering by the pictures? He suspected a little of both.

"Let me set things straight for you, son."

Burke sat on the front edge of his desk directly between the two of them.

"Tom Cox had a car accident. Your father died of a heart attack. That's it, pure and simple. I need you to quit trying to turn this into something it's not."

"Are you ordering me to stop questioning my father's death?"

"Ordering? I wouldn't say that. More like . . . strongly suggesting it . . ."

"Does that sentence end with 'for your own good'?"

Burke stared him down. The man was clearly trying to hold onto what was left of his temper. He responded with enough ice to service a frat party.

"I don't make idle threats, young man."

Jess nodded. "I think that's the first thing you've ever said that I actually believe, Sheriff."

※　　※　　※

It went back and forth like that for another fifteen minutes until Burke finally kicked them out of his office. They were halfway down the corridor when Maria asked Jess about the photograph.

"Why didn't you show it to the sheriff?"

Jess didn't break stride, keeping his voice down. "You just spent an hour with the man. You trust him?"

Maria didn't even have to respond. Her smile was enough.

"Exactly my point," said Jess. "No way I'm giving it to that lard ass. Then I'd have nothing to go on."

"So you're going to ignore him and keep digging into this?" asked Maria.

Then it was Jess's turn to smile.

19

Jess found Lilah Webster in the cafeteria loading up a tray with "healthy food" items. Watching her pay for lunch, he once again thought she was a woman who went to great lengths to hide her attractiveness. She wore the white lab coat as a shroud; her body language indicated an intention to cover her femininity and advertise to one and all she was a proud member of the medical profession.

He waited until she sat down at a table in the corner. Once it was clear she was eating alone, he crossed the room and slipped into the chair across from her. She didn't favor him with a big reaction, but his scrapes and singed clothes didn't go unnoticed.

"You look like someone who belongs on one of my lab gurneys, Mr. Stark."

"Too much desert sun." Jess pointed at her food tray. "Can I ask you a couple of questions while you eat?"

Lilah took a bite of fruit salad and shook her head. "Long as I get back to my office in fifteen minutes. I've got an autopsy scheduled."

"That's exactly what I wanted to talk to you about. Not the one that you've got coming up. My father's."

She stopped mid-bite. "We didn't do one."

"Excuse me? Did you see my father's body?"

Lilah lowered the fork. The friendly façade was immediately dropped the moment Jess started to question her work. "You know I did. You saw me at the motel."

"Then you saw the condition my father's body was in."

The medical examiner went into full-bodied defense mode. "And it was ruled a cardiac arrest at the scene—death by natural causes."

Jess could tell that Lilah Webster believed every single word she uttered. But it didn't alleviate his suspicions. "Still, I would've thought you'd do one, just to make sure."

"If I double-checked every case that came through this building, I'd have bodies piling up around here for months, Mr. Stark." Lilah actually smiled; validating Jess's surmise—the medical examiner would have been a stunner if she had let down her scarlet mane and guard. "Besides which, the family didn't want one."

"My mother told you that?"

"She wasn't the one who contacted me."

Jess didn't even have to ask the obvious question. He knew the answer. "You talked to Edward Rice."

She confirmed it with a slight nod. Jess rubbed a finger across his temple, the throbbing no longer just coming from the burn mark.

"Your mother had given him written permission to speak for the family," Lilah explained. "He said everyone was in enough pain and saw no reason to put them through more than necessary."

"I'm sure he did."

Lilah Webster continued to express her regrets and condolences to Jess. But he had already tuned her out. He was too busy wondering if he could turn a corner in Palm Springs without Dr. Edward Rice waiting there.

Lena opened the front door. Concern immediately spread across her face upon seeing Jess. She had tended to his scrapes and bruises since he was a toddler and her first instinct was always to try and make things better. She indicated his singed clothes. "*Mi Dios*, what happened?"

"I see you haven't talked to Maria yet."

He slipped inside and closed the door. Lena looked at him, confused. "Maria?"

"Don't worry, Lena. She's perfectly fine." He gently dissuaded her from tending to his wounds, insisting he was going to be okay. Lena kept pressing him about her daughter, so Jess offered up a G-rated version of Maria coming to his rescue. Lena was still horrified but Jess assured her that Maria had never been in any danger. She finally took his word for it and Jess asked where he could find his mother.

"In the Cactus Garden. She's been spending more and more time there."

Jess declined Lena's offer of food and drink. He started down the hallway, then, turned back around.

"By the way . . . Maria?" He paused, wanting to express how bowled over he'd been by the girl who had blossomed so much in his absence. He could only come up with one word. "Wow."

Finally, Lena had something to smile about. "I know."

Jess continued down the hall and almost crashed into Sarah coming through the French doors.

"Jess . . .!"

"Not staying long, Sarah. I'll try and not mess up the rug."

He fingered his tattered wardrobe but Sarah had other things on her mind. "What the hell were you doing giving Edward the third degree at the country club?"

"You really don't want to get into this."

"Damn right I do," she seethed.

"Okay. Sure." No sense in beating around the bush with his sister. "Who the hell is this guy, anyway? He shows up out of thin air. Next thing you know Dad gets sick and he turns over Meadowland to him. And as if that wasn't bad enough, he's now got his hooks into you . . ."

"You've got no right putting down the man who has been here for this family when they needed someone."

That stung more than a bit. But it didn't stop Jess from continuing. "I just talked to the M.E. Did you know your boyfriend stopped her from performing an autopsy on Dad?"

"He said we'd been through enough sadness."

"Or maybe he wanted him cremated before they could look into it further."

Sarah started laughing. "Edward's right. You've completely lost it."

"He's got you believing everything he tells you? Come on, Sarah—how much do you really know about him?"

Sarah answered with a touch of sadness. "A lot more than the guy who walked out on us seven years ago."

Jess didn't have a comeback for that one. Sarah brushed past him and headed for the stairs. For a moment he thought about chasing her, wondering if they could start the conversation over. It had been at least a decade since the two of them had a civil one. There was probably too much water under the bridge to try now, yet she was still his sister and had grown up with him in this house. Maybe not as much under Walter's severe eye and hand as Jess, but after he left, Sarah had to endure seven more years of their father. It was no wonder she had hardened so. God knows how Jess would have turned out if he had stayed. He also knew Sarah well enough that reconciliation would have to come on her terms, so he gave up the fantasy and headed outside through the French doors.

He found his mother clipping cacti in a corner of the garden. She'd done away with the funereal black. She wore capris and a flowered blouse. A wide-brimmed hat shielded her from the beams of the setting sun. Kate continued clipping away methodically and Jess noticed that despite the mourner's togs being put aside, his mother moved like a woman in a drug-induced state.

"Hi, Mom."

Kate didn't turn around. She continued to clip thorns. "Your father loved the desert. When we first moved here, he said 'Katie, this place is an oasis people will flock to. And I'm going to lead them to it.'"

Jess continued to approach, but his mother still didn't face him. "He had vision. I'll give him that."

"It didn't help him see what was happening to him. Not until it was too late."

"Most people don't."

He sat down on a bench close by. Kate turned around and saw his bloodied bruises and tattered clothes. "My God, Jess . . ."

111

She brought up a hand in concern. Jess eased it away and motioned for her to sit down instead.

"I'm all right, Mom."

Kate let the clippers drop to the ground. She sank down onto the bench beside him with even more invisible weight on her shoulders.

"I'm so sorry this is what you came home to, Jessie."

"I wish I had gotten here sooner."

Kate took her son's hand and gripped it tightly. She didn't have to tell him she wished the same thing.

"I need to ask you about Edward Rice," he softly said.

The mention of the physician broke the tender moment. Kate let go of Jess's hand. "He's been so helpful the past few weeks."

"Did you tell him not to do an autopsy on Dad?"

"I didn't see the point. What good would cutting him up do?"

"It might tell you if someone killed him. Wouldn't you want to know who and why?"

"Would it bring him back? That's the only thing I want—your father back. But I can't have that, can I?"

She stared off into the garden, lost in memories Jess had no way of sharing. His relationship with Walter had only been worth forgetting. He gently turned the subject back to Rice. "Don't you think it's odd that Rice has become so involved with this family?"

"Not at all. He's been a godsend."

"How'd you meet him anyway? He wasn't even in the picture when I left."

"He was introduced by a mutual friend."

"Mutual friend," repeated Jess.

"Clark James."

Thoughts raced through Jess's head. He remembered the toast James had given Walter at the birthday party. And the picture of James he'd found in Cox's apartment—the one with the mysterious "T" scrawled on it. Too bad that had gone up in flames with everything else.

"Clark James was no friend of Dad's."

"I know that," Kate said softly. She turned to face her son. Jess was surprised to see the hurt in her eyes.

"You do?"

"For social purposes, they kept it civil. But I know Clark hated your father because of what happened seven years ago."

Jess was shocked. "When did you find out?"

"Not right away. The longer we didn't hear from you, the more I put things together."

"Did you ever talk to Dad about it?"

Kate shook her head. "He was the father of my children. The man I'll always love." She took Jess's hand again. "Your father changed after you left."

"I find that hard to believe."

"Take my word, Jess. He did. He never was the same afterwards." There was an inherent plea in her eyes and voice when she asked the next question. "Now that he's gone, can't you finally forgive him?"

This time it was Jess who let go of her hand. "Obviously Clark James never did. Otherwise he wouldn't have sicced Edward Rice onto him."

Jess stood up. Kate's eyes were filled with tears. "Jess, you should leave this alone."

"I wish I could, Mom."

He left Kate alone amongst the cacti where she could regret all that had passed. Jess headed for the side gate, feeling increasingly woeful about what was yet to come.

JESS BELOW

The cell phone was dying.

Jess tried not to flip it on, but it was becoming increasingly difficult to lie in the darkness. His body was completely submerged in water and he could feel it climbing up toward the base of his neck. The more Jess willed himself not to use the cell phone, it got overruled by wondering how much charge he had left.

He tried to distract himself with the circumstances leading to his predicament. Who were the two men that had knocked him out, tossed him in the car trunk, dragged him across the desert, and thrown him in an unmarked grave? He was fairly certain one had to be Edward Rice. Jess had been pretty vocal about his suspicions regarding the physician—it didn't seem farfetched that his questions had led to the man taking desperate action. It gave Jess some solace he'd gotten under Rice's skin. But in the end, who cared? Look where he wound up.

He figured the other man had to be the mystery motorcyclist. If so, this had been the third time in forty-eight hours they had crossed paths. Violence had ensued each time: a deadly car crash, a house burnt to the ground, and now outright—unless some miracle occurred—murder.

He wondered how his disappearance would be explained. Jess had been pretty intent on looking into his father's death. Wouldn't his family question his dropping off the face of the earth? Then, he imagined the trusted Dr. Rice counseling his mother and love-struck sister. Why should they be surprised? Jess ran out on them seven years earlier and they never heard once from him. How was this any different? Sarah would immediately subscribe to this theory, and sadly, rather sooner than later, Jess suspected his mother would too.

Despite trying to breathe steadily and distract himself, he couldn't stop thinking about the cell phone. His heart raced like something out of a Poe story and he knew only one way to slow it down. He raised the phone up and flicked it on.

His heart began beating even faster.

The water was no longer dripping into the coffin. It was at the level of the crack in the casket wall and was pouring through an even larger hole. He was horrified to see the water level actually rise as he watched it.

The digital phone charge was maybe two percent. The luminous glow in the water turned the color of blood as the ice-blue phone readout flashed "Low Battery" in bright red. The display light flickered. Jess frantically fumbled for the button to save power for one last look—but the battery died before he could punch it.

He was thrown into complete darkness.

Jess felt the water move up his neck and his heart pummel faster. He instinctively tried to fend it off, pushing his feet against the casket wall to thrust himself backwards, but ended up smashing his head against the back wall. He opened his mouth to yell in pain—and got a big dose of riled-up water for his trouble.

Jess spit it out and choked. He tried to remain still as the water continued to rise, tickling the base of his chin. He was able to slowly back up a few precious inches and raise his head until it hit the casket lid. The effort put a ton of strain on his arms, holding his upper torso aloft in the water. He didn't know how long he could keep himself up. The sad fact was even if he succeeded, the water would eventually have its way.

He could only hope that Tracy had phoned someone. She had to call somebody, didn't she? Tracy wasn't going to just sit there and do nothing. If he had ever meant anything to her at all—and he knew he had once meant everything—she would send someone to find him.

Right?

But how would they know where to look? He was in the middle of nowhere. The only way he would get discovered was when the State Highway Commission decided to put in a feeder road to Interstate 10 and started digging things up.

Jess willed himself not to think about that. He focused on one thing and one thing only.

The only person who knew he was missing.

Tracy.

Tracy . . .

20

The Jameses' house looked deserted when Jess pulled into the driveway. No parked cars, only a couple of lights on in a palace that had more than five hundred. He had thought about calling ahead but nixed the idea. A phone call would give Clark James time to either bug out or concoct a story.

Jess rang the bell and got no response. He tried again and was about to head back for the SUV when a light flicked on in the hallway. Footsteps approached. Then the curtain in the side window slipped aside.

Tracy appeared on the other side of the pane. Her smile cut right through his heart. The drape slid back into place, the front porch light came on, and she quickly unlatched the door.

"Jess. Wow. This is a surprise."

"Actually, I was looking for your dad."

"He's not here."

She couldn't hide her disappointment, but it was quickly replaced by concern. Jess had changed out of the singed clothes, but he still wore the telltale signs of going three rounds with a fiery blaze. "What happened to you?"

"It's one of the things I want to talk to him about."

"I don't understand."

"You weren't supposed to."

She didn't rise to the bait and instead opened the door further. "Come on in. You can wait for him. He went to the country club for a dinner meeting. He shouldn't be that long."

Jess hesitated on the threshold. Tracy's smile was coy, scolding, and alluring all at once. "I'm not going to bite."

He gave in and entered the house. Tracy wore a halter top, shorts, and sandals. Simple threads, plain colors, a beautiful girl. Jess followed her into the living room. His mind went back to a time when they would have made an immediate detour upstairs and not emerged from her room till the next morning.

But seven years was seven years. And though there might still be torrents of water under all those broken bridges, Jess knew in his heart they were beyond repair.

Tracy turned on a couple of lights and had him sit down on the couch. He passed on anything to eat or drink—even though he couldn't remember when he'd last done either.

"Some Band-Aids? Soap for the wounds?"

"I'm okay, Trace."

"You don't look it." She settled down beside him on the sofa.

"Been a long couple of days."

"Did you find what you were looking for the other night when you ran out of the office?"

Jess thought about how much he wanted to tell her. He wasn't really sure what he knew or surmised. It jumbled all together and most of it didn't make sense. He chose the safest path. "I'm still trying to figure it all out."

"What did you want to talk to Dad about?"

Jess figured there was no harm getting her objective view on the subject. "How long has your father known Edward Rice?"

Tracy frowned. Whatever she was expecting Jess to say, this wasn't it. "For a while. Five years, I'd say. Why?"

"He's gotten pretty tight with my family, in case you haven't noticed."

"I've heard people talk. Can't say I've witnessed much with my own eyes. I haven't spent a lot of time with the Starks since you left. As you can well imagine."

"I heard your father introduced Rice to my dad."

"I think that's right. I can't say for sure. He took care of my dad when he was in the hospital. It makes sense he would have met Walter during that time since he owned the place."

"When was your father in the hospital?"

"Right after *The Seventh Day* shut down. He was really sick. We did a good job keeping it out of the tabloids."

"I make a habit out of ignoring them, so I had no way of knowing."

"There was so much bad publicity about the movie that Dad's publicists were able to shift the focus from his illness to the film shutting down. When he finally got better, he did one press conference announcing his retirement and that was that."

"What was wrong with him?"

"Dr. Rice never pinned it down. Dad got so weak during filming he couldn't leave the tents they were camped out in. He finally collapsed and by the time Rice brought him back home, Dad's blood counts were either off the chart or nonexistent . . ."

"What do you mean 'brought him back'?"

"Edward Rice was the physician on the film. He finally stood up to the director and said if they didn't get Dad into a proper hospital, *The Seventh Day* would be the great, late Clark James's swan song. In the end, they shut the movie down, paid off the locals, and the rest of the crew came back from Mexico."

"Mexico?"

Tracy smiled. "You sure you've been working in LA all these years? It was a really big deal."

"My clientele isn't exactly the Hollywood jet set. Mostly escrow companies and banks."

"Well, Dad was hell-bent on making this apocalyptic Western that no studio wanted to finance. He put up half the money himself. He would tell you they went to Mexico because the look was perfect, but it's no big secret you can get a crew to work for thirty cents on the dollar down there. Luckily, it saved him a ton of dough when he had to pay everyone off."

Jess was rapidly processing all this information. He dug in his pocket and pulled out the picture of the church he'd taken from Tom Cox's locked room. He showed it to Tracy.

"This look familiar?"

She looked at the photograph with great scrutiny. "Where'd you get this?"

"Doesn't matter. You've seen it before?"

Instead of answering, Tracy got to her feet. "Gimme a second, okay?"

"Sure. I think I need some fresh air anyway."

Tracy disappeared into the bowels of the house while he headed outside. Even though Jess was hit by a blast of hot air the moment he opened the glass door, he had to repress a shiver. Things were folding on top of one another and he was feeling more uneasy than ever.

Jess sat at the edge of the Jameses' pool and stared out at the desert night. So many things still bothered him. Clark James's illness was front and center. It sounded eerily similar to what had befallen his own father—anemia, loss of strength, and a diagnosis that befuddled his physician, the same physician in fact. Jess was beginning to lose perspective. Was Edward Rice behind everything that seemed wrong in Palm Springs? Or was his dislike for the man so intense that Jess wanted to lay everything at the doctor's feet?

The Mexico angle was equally troubling. Instead of tying things closer together, the strange events seemed to be spreading. What started as a man dying of old age in the desert was suddenly moving across the border and back five years in time. No wonder Jess's head hurt so much.

He dipped his hand in the pool and dabbed the water across his singed forehead. The coolness stung a little, but still soothed. A hint of jasmine swept through the night breeze, then grew stronger. He turned around and realized that the scent was coming from Tracy, who had slipped up from behind and settled beside him while barely making a sound.

She put a tender hand on his shoulder, apologetically. "Sorry. Didn't mean to sneak up on you like that."

"That's okay," said Jess. "Daydreaming."

He didn't remember smelling the jasmine scent in the living room. She must have put the fragrance on since he came outdoors. Tracy placed her hand over his wet brow. Jess didn't rush to remove it.

119

"You going to tell me why you decided to jump into a barbecue?"

"Let's just say it wasn't my choice and leave it at that?"

Jess smiled and could tell Tracy was happy for the olive branch. She offered up an eight-by-ten photograph in return. "It took a little while to find this, but I thought I'd seen it among Dad's things."

Jess studied the photo. Clark James had his arms around a curly haired guy wearing glasses, a loud tropical shirt, and a crooked smile. Jess had never seen the other man, but the church behind them was the same one from Tom Cox's photograph.

"It's a publicity still from the movie. Since the film was never finished, none of these ever got released. I guess Dad kept a few for posterity."

"The church is in Mexico," Jess realized.

"It's a small town called Santa Alvarado, about fifty miles inland from Puerto Vallarta. Dad's character was a former preacher who became this mythic gunman."

Jess pointed at the man in the Hawaiian shirt. "Who's this guy?"

"The writer of the film. Had a strange first name. Tag, I think. I could easily find out. Is it important?"

"I don't know what's important right now."

Tracy continued to gently stroke his brow. Jess was so exhausted that he didn't stop her. He never imagined it would be his father's death that would lead to a moment like this. It was so ironic that Jess had to wonder if he and Tracy were an inescapable force.

"What are you hoping to find out, Jessie?"

"I keep asking myself that. I guess I just want to know what happened to my father. Which is so damn strange that I'd even care. After everything? Doesn't that strike you as being totally fucked up?"

"He was still your father." Her finger continued to gently massage his brow. "I just think he was really sick and his heart finally gave out."

"After crawling halfway across the desert to find me?" Jess stared at the valley below. "I'm having a hard time getting past what he whispered to me the day I got back here."

"Which was what?"

"He said 'they' were killing him." Jess turned to look Tracy in the eye. "I'm now wondering by 'they' if he meant Edward Rice and your father."

"That's crazy sounding," Tracy said.

"I know. I know." He shifted around, uncomfortable in his own skin. "I never should have returned my mother's phone call. Then maybe none of this would have happened."

Her hand traced the side of his face. "You don't know that." Tracy's fingers dropped further and moved down his neck. "Besides, if you hadn't called her back, I wouldn't have gotten to see you again."

Jess raised his own hand to meet her groping fingers. And just held them.

"I've missed you, Jess. I really have." She let out a gentle sigh as if just saying it out loud had lifted a huge burden off her shoulders. "Have you missed me?"

Jess let go of her hand. He didn't avoid her eyes and answered with the truth. "I miss what we once were."

"Doesn't mean we can't try again." Her hand moved back to his face.

"I'm not sure. The only thing I know is that I can't stay here."

"Maybe I could come with you." Jess flinched as her finger hit a singed sore spot. "You're really hurt, Jess."

"I don't feel much of anything."

"I haven't either. For a real long time."

Tracy brought her lips close to his cheek and barely grazed the burn mark. Then, she broke away and cried out.

"Noooo!"

Jess turned to see two men emerge from the darkness.

Both wore jeans and dark long-sleeved shirts. They had ski masks over their faces. One carried a baseball bat.

Jess tried to get to his feet, but the man with the bat swung first. The Louisville Slugger bounced off the side of his head and Jess tumbled to the ground. He could hear Tracy screaming for them to stop—right before a second swing knocked him out cold.

❉   ❉   ❉

It was either a big-assed bump or his head smashing off a wall that made Jess come to.

He tried to straighten up and got another head clobbering for his trouble. Moaning softly, Jess turned to see a sliver of moonlight pouring in through a tiny hole. He reached out and traced its shape, then shuddered when he realized what the hole was.

The opening in the lock of a car trunk.

Jess tried to throttle down the ensuing wave of panic that came with extreme claustrophobia. Not bad enough that he was crammed into a space for someone half his size; his plight was worsened by the driver navigating a road with a billion potholes.

Fiddling with the lock proved worthless; it was jammed on the outside and didn't have a mechanism inside to pop the trunk. Jess tried to swivel onto his back, which proved anything but a cinch. There was no wiggle room. Plus, his right shoulder was killing him. It took a good five minutes to flip over, all while his body continued to be pounded by the bumpy road.

Once on his back, Jess found his nose was less than three inches from the trunk lid, which made an MRI seem like a spacious condo and ratcheted his freaked level up a few notches.

The car wrenched to the right and slowed down.

The bumps got even nastier, rattling the scrambled eggs that filled his brain.

Then the vehicle braked to a thankful stop, giving Jess one more good head jolt.

Jess suddenly realized whoever was driving might open the trunk. He needed to figure out what to do if that happened.

What if it didn't open? Maybe they were going to dump the car in a river. He immediately dismissed that notion. What river? They had to be in the middle of the desert. And, wouldn't they be moving still, rolling down an embankment so that the car could sink? Jess shook off that horrible thought and tried to come up with a game plan.

After being jammed into the tight space for God knows how long, he didn't think he could move fast enough to attack whoever put him in the trunk. His best bet was to act like he was still unconscious. Let Whoever-It-Was drag him out of the car. Once he was in open space, he could make his move.

He heard a car door open. He waited for what seemed like forever, and then it slammed shut. Good. Only one guy. And Jess had the element of surprise on his side.

A second door opened.

Shit. The odds just got a whole lot worse. Jess shut his eyes and did his best possum impression as footsteps approached from both sides. Words were murmured that he had no chance of making out. A key scraped, fiddled in the lock, and then clicked. The trunk lid started to open.

Jess allowed his eyes to flicker open a microscopic inch—just enough to make out two shapes. Framed against the moonlight and stars, two ski-masked men loomed over the open trunk.

One guy reached in and grabbed him. The hand brushed against Jess's burnt shoulder, resulting in the greatest acting performance of his life—pretending to be unconscious when he wanted to scream at the top of his lungs.

The man hauled him out of the car and onto his feet. Jess purposely let himself slump like dead weight onto the man's body. Not a big reach—he felt like shit.

He heard the other man slam the trunk shut and figured this was it—catch them by surprise, jump in the car, and take off.

Now or never.

"I think he's awake," one of the masked men mumbled.

Jess's eyes snapped open.

Just in time to see a blunt object coming straight for his head.

The next thing Jess knew, he was being dragged across the desert to his own private hell.

JESS BELOW

Tracy.

What happened to her after he'd been knocked unconscious? Had she been able to evade his attackers? What if there were others lying in wait for her after he was dragged away? He tried to think positively. Maybe she had been able to race off and call the police.

Then, the negatives took over. What would she tell them? Two unknown men had attacked her old boyfriend, thrown him into a car, and driven off into the darkened desert? Even if she had taken down a license plate, hours had passed since Jess was thrown in the grave. For Jess to be saved, someone had to have spotted the car on the highway, tailed it to the middle of the desert, and known exactly where to dig.

None of that had happened.

Jess began to accept his fate. He could only hope Tracy had been able to avoid a similar one.

As the water reached the bottom of his chin, Jess knew he had precious minutes left before it would cover his face. The fight had gone out of him. All that remained were questions. What would the end be like? Would he feel anything? Would anyone ever find him—and if they finally did, would there be anything left to identify who he was?

And then there was the most gnawing question of all. As the old Pet Shop Boys song went, "What Have I Done to Deserve This?"

For someone to go to such drastic lengths to get rid of him, Jess must have been on to something. Ironically, his premature burial meant that he was probably right that Walter had been murdered. You don't get rid of the Boy Who Cried Wolf unless he had something to back it up. But Jess had nothing concrete, only suspicions.

Then he thought about Tom Cox's house.

The mystery motorcyclist had set the place up in flames. If he had wanted to just kill Jess, he could have done it in a less destructive way. The cyclist must have wanted everything in Cox's locked room burned to a crisp. That included Jess. That way anything he'd found would die with him when the house went up in smoke. But then Jess escaped, so the cyclist came to the Jameses' house to finish the job.

Was it because Jess had seen something on those walls? If so, what? The missing patient files from Meadowland? Was it the pictures of Santa Alvarado and the church? Or Clark James's photograph with the mysterious "T"? Some, none, or all of the above?

This train of thought was interrupted by water lapping into his mouth. Jess spit it out and tried to back away again. But there was nowhere to go. He could barely lift his head above the rising surface.

"Oh God . . ."

This was met with another blast of water in his face. He choked this time and the ensuing coughing fit made him lose the boost he was getting from his hands on the coffin floor. Jess sunk under the water, started gagging, and tried to kick his way back up.

But water was sloshing everywhere. A giant thud rocked the coffin. The water pressure got stronger and Jess felt his head begin to cloud over.

Disjointed images bopped around his brain as he started to flit in and out of consciousness.

"*. . . Your father's dying, Jess,*" Kate said on the phone.

. . . Tom Cox lying on the bloody desert sand begging Jess, ". . . don't make me go back . . ."

. . . Walter Stark grabbing hold of Jess's arm on the lanai. "They're killing me."

The coffin thudded again. Jess's head bobbed above the surface for a second but another thud caused the wood to splint. The increase in pressure sucked him below the surface again.

More images assaulted his head.

. . . The bloody "T" on the wall of the Sands Motel.

. . . ". . . too many people were dying," Maria said.

. . . The windshield with the bloody message: "LEAVE."

. . . Harry on the bridge. ". . . I heard him . . ."

Jess felt the world slipping away. He thrust himself up from the bottom using his hands, and his head smashed against the coffin lid.

The wood cracked in half.

Jess sputtered as water poured off his face. The thudding gave way to banging. Another crack appeared in the coffin lid.

And then the cover began to slip aside.

Jess was able to raise his head above the water and enough cobwebs cleared for him to realize someone was trying to open the coffin.

"Help! Help! Please help!" His screams were compromised by coughs, so they sounded garbled.

The coffin lid cracked in half. Dirt fell on top of Jess and sent him sinking under the water again. It was so unexpected he gulped down a huge amount of water and started to lose consciousness.

Something slapped him across the torso, enough to snap him awake. He reached out and his hand grabbed the business end of a shovel. Whoever was above pulled on the other end—enough so Jess cracked the water surface. He sputtered, gagged, and coughed.

A familiar voice called from above. "You've got to help."

Jess could see dirt covering the remaining half of the casket cover. It needed to be cleared away for him to squeeze out. Jess was able to shove some dirt away.

His silhouetted rescuer scooped up a bunch more with the shovel. Finally, enough was removed so Jess could break part of the coffin lid away. His savior lowered the shovel for Jess to grab onto once again. The man yanked and was able to pull Jess up enough so he could grip onto the grave's edge.

Jess hung there for a moment and then pushed with all of his might. He went up over the edge and rolled onto his back. He lay there, panting on the desert sand.

The sky was lavender. Early morning stars were beginning to lose their twinkling luster as the first glimmers of an orange dawn winked above the far horizon. Jess had never seen anything so lovely. He turned the other way to thank his rescuer.

And almost fell back in the grave.

Standing over him was his father.

"Whha—?"

"Sssh . . ." Walter inched toward him.

"Dad? I don't understand . . ."

Walter didn't look like the man Jess could have sworn died outside his motel room. He had regained most of his color. His father looked as strong as Jess remembered him when he hit the road for Los Angeles seven years before.

Which was impossible.

"I tried to warn you. I left a message for you."

Jess shook his head incredulously. "On my car? Telling me to leave?"

Walter nodded.

Jess's mind raced. "And the 'T' on the wall?"

"It's a cross."

His father edged closer. Jess couldn't go anywhere. The open grave was still behind him.

"But you're dead. I saw you. They put you in the coroner wagon and took you away." Jess's voice was quickening; sheer panic and hysteria settling in.

Walter leaned down to put his arms around his oldest child. Jess tried to wriggle away but was shocked to find his seventy-year-old father was overpowering him.

"You must leave. While you still can."

"Why? I don't understand what's happening!"

And then Jess did.

His father opened his mouth—revealing sharp, pointed fangs.

PART TWO
DARK SANDS

TRACY BEFORE

The first time she saw Jessie Stark since high school, he almost ran her over with his car.

It was her own damn fault; she had been walking in the middle of the street when he came barreling around the corner. Tracy was so busy digging in her purse for Kleenex to wipe her teary eyes she didn't notice she had drifted off the sidewalk. By the time she became cognizant of the blasting horn, it was too late to dive out of the way. It was only the quick reflexes of the driver—spinning the vehicle into a hard left, expertly tapping the brakes, and plowing into a bunch of roadside trash cans—which prevented both of them from becoming fatal highway statistics on the eleven o'clock news.

Perfect, thought Tracy. A fitting end to what ranked right up there as maybe the Crappiest Night Ever. She ran across the street to check on the black BMW and its owner. By the time she got there, the driver side door had swung open and her life had changed.

"I'm so so sorry," Tracy said. "I'm such a stupid fucking idiot. I didn't even know I'd wandered out into the street."

"Are you okay?" Jess asked, stepping out of the car.

"Am I okay? Me? You're the one who pulled off that sweet NASCAR move."

Jess didn't answer right away. It was that awkward moment when two people reconnect in the most bizarre way imaginable.

"Tracy? Tracy James?"

"Oh my God. Jess Stark." She practically blushed. "This is getting more embarrassing by the moment."

When she had last seen Jess, he was being carried off a football field on the shoulders of his teammates after leading them to a comeback win for the Southern Section Championship. Tracy had avoided the cheerleading experience at Desert Chapel, depriving the squad of the prettiest girl in school. She spent most of her time curled up with a book in a corner of the library; Jess and his crowd's all-night beer-pong-a-thons weren't her idea of "good times." They had exchanged maybe half a dozen sentences during her junior year, mostly at functions they'd been dragged to by their fathers.

"What are you doing out here all by yourself?" Jess asked.

"It's a long and not very pretty story," admitted Tracy.

"It could have had a real downer of an ending."

"Tell me about it."

"Can I give you a ride somewhere?"

"Interesting question."

Tracy pointed at the wrecked trash cans with a BMW sticking out of them.

"You tell me."

❋　❋　❋

It turned out they needed AAA. Jess said they could hike up the hill to his folks' house, where he could call the tow service and get a taxi for Tracy. She told him she was happy to wait for the tow truck and offered to pay for the damage. Jess said it was his fault—he shouldn't have been going so fast. By the time AAA arrived, they were busily catching up on the years since high school.

About an hour (and two tire changes) later, they were in a twenty-four-hour Denny's, still talking.

Jess had just graduated from Cal Poly San Luis Obispo with a degree in history and a minor in English. He had purposefully forsaken the scholarships offered by a few Football Is King universities in the South and Midwest. Nor did he pursue the business school Ivy League track his father had so wanted him to get on.

"Sounds like you did everything in your power to piss off your parents," Tracy observed.

"Well, if you know anything about my father, it doesn't take much."

Tracy said you'd have to be an ostrich with his head buried in the Coachella Valley sand not to know Walter Stark's ways. "He's definitely a guy used to getting what he wants."

"Which makes our upcoming family reunion really pleasant," he said.

Jess told her that his mother was the only family member who attended his college graduation the previous month. His sister, Sarah, was too busy spending his parents' money touring the great palaces of Europe. For Harry to be interested in something, it needed to have a Transformer involved. Walter had flat out refused to go because it would mean he supported his older son's decision to throw his life away.

"I'm surprised they got you back here at all."

"It's their twenty-fifth wedding anniversary. I considered not coming but then decided I could pick up a bunch of my stuff before I hit the road."

"And where would that road lead?"

"Anywhere my father doesn't own something."

Tracy couldn't suppress a smile of admiration. She certainly had her own daddy issues, which she readily admitted as she brought Jess up to speed.

Sometimes she wished she had the nerve to stand up to Clark James like Jess had with his father. She wasn't going to cry "Poor Poor Pitiful Me" as Warren Zevon had once so deftly written—there were definite perks that came with being the daughter of a Mega Movie Star. More often than not, she found it easy to be Daddy's Little Girl to get what she wanted, and Clark was happy to serve her every whim as long as she asked nicely.

But the truth was that Tracy yearned for privacy. Her mother had died when she was just seven and she had grown up accompanying her father—a perennial "*People*'s Hottest Bachelor"—to every press junket or red carpet that came down the pike. By the time she hit puberty, she felt like one more flashbulb in her face would make her melt like the Wicked Witch of the West. Which led her to transfer into Desert Chapel her junior year. She had to beg Clark to let her enroll in high school down in the desert (where they had a vacation mansion) instead of the ritzy actor's–kid school she'd been at since she was a toddler. She liked the anonymity she got being away from the Hollywood paparazzi, and the fact that she missed most of the high school cliques by getting to DC late was just fine.

She'd graduated from Desert Chapel with honors while existing below the radar, and chose Dartmouth as a collegiate destination—as far across the continent as one could get from sunny Southern California. She took every liberal arts course available and ended up drifting into a string of relationships with older men, mostly teachers and alumni donors. Most of them fizzled out for her by the time they had barely begun.

Tracy drained the rest of the black-and-white malt they were sharing. "Famous Dad that no woman can nail down. Motherless Daughter looking for love in all the wrong places. Dr. Phil could dedicate an entire week to us."

Jess laughed. "You've got one more year left?"

"I start back right after Labor Day. Going to be one long hot summer."

Jess was surprised she was going to remain in the desert. "You do know that the average temperature is one hundred five in the shade?"

"Dad is shooting a movie in LA. No way am I spending three months in that circus show. The house here is empty. I can catch up on my reading, camp out in the pool, and turn into a prune."

"I don't think we have to worry about that happening," said Jess.

Instead of taking the compliment, Tracy lowered her eyes and stirred the last drops of malt with the straw. She could feel Jess watching her as a muzak version of "A Horse With No Name" mercilessly assaulted anyone who dared pay attention.

"You still haven't talked about it," he said.

Tracy stopped stirring. "*It* being what had me crying in the middle of a Palm Springs street at midnight?"

"Yeah."

The gentleness of that one word got her to look up from the malt glass. Hedonistic hero, hell. Where had this man been all her life? Or even an hour ago.

Her eyes had started to well up again. "One of those wrong places."

"You still in it?" Jess asked.

"I hope not."

Six weeks later, Jess was still in Palm Springs and Tracy had seen him every single day since the night he almost ran her down.

1

Benji Lutz was actually the night manager at the Sands Motel. It was true that he owned the place, but since occupancy was rarely above a single digit and he lived in the best room, perfectly situated right behind the office so he'd hear anyone ring the bell, Benji figured he could save money by filling the position himself.

Once Ella, the ditzy college dropout who worked the day shift, bounced in around seven a.m., Benji followed a daily routine. He spun the Mustang into Palm Springs proper and ordered a well-done sesame bagel and Coffee of the Day at the local deli, and then turned around and drove the five miles back to the motel. He punched on *Sports Radio* and listened to Dan Patrick; once back and firmly ensconced in his office chair, he continued to watch the rest of the show on Direct TV. When Ella asked why he didn't just buy the bagels and java in bulk and invest in a toaster and coffeemaker, Benji told her the morning drive cleared his head. She wanted to ask him what could warrant wiping out his brain since he did absolutely nothing. But she also knew Benji *was* her boss and she needed the job, as bored as she was out of *her* totally blank mind.

Benji would check the receipts, and five minutes later when that was done, he'd settle down with the latest *X-Men* issue or read a classic graphic novel for the umpteenth time. Once a week he ventured back into town for Comic Day when the new issues hit the stands, and spent at least an hour flipping through the mags, though he always ended up buying the same four series. While perhaps not a man of vision or one to roll with change, Benji was loyal to a fault. After that, he picked up a greasy meatball hero from his favorite food truck and headed back to the office to enjoy an afternoon filled with superhero feats of derring-do, topped off by some Pepto-Bismol.

On this particular day, he'd scooped up the latest *Hulk*, *Thor*, *Iron Man*, and *Avengers* issues, and spent the journey back debating which one to dive into first. He had settled on David Banner and his green raging alter ego and was chomping down on the sandwich when he entered his back office. He almost choked on the last meatball.

Jess Stark—or more specifically some gone-to-shit version of him—was in Benji's office chair.

Jess looked like he hadn't taken a bath in a lunar cycle. His shirt was ripped to shreds: mud and dirt caked every visible inch of skin. The exception was his neck, where he held a bloodied bandage he'd extracted from the emergency medical kit that Benji kept on the shelf above his desk.

Benji dropped the Marvel quartet and meatball special on the floor. "Whoa, man. You look like something out of a Sam Raimi movie."

Jess replied with great effort. "Funny you should put it that way."

Half an hour later, the comic books were still lying on the floor. Benji had made a pot of strong coffee, but Jess's hands continued to shake as he replayed the events that led to him occupying a desert grave.

"Who do you think attacked you at Tracy's house?" Benji asked.

"I'm pretty sure one was Rice. I turn over a rock; the man crawls out from underneath it. Wouldn't surprise me if Burke was the other guy."

"Burke? He's a cop." Jess gave Benji a "get serious" stare. Benji reconsidered his point. "You're right. The guy's a douchebag. Wouldn't put it past him." Then Benji thought a little more. "But why would Burke do that?"

"Money. Power. He's being blackmailed. All of the above." Jess shrugged, which caused him to groan. He was still damn sore and a bundle of nerves. "It's bizarre that Burke has been in my face at least three times since I've hit town."

"Is that why you haven't called him?"

"If he was one of the guys who dragged me out there, he knows damn well what happened to me."

"You're still not answering the big question."

"Which is?"

"How the hell did you escape out of that hole?"

Jess took a deep breath. Then, he launched in.

Jess tried to evade the fangs his father was attempting to bury in his neck. He couldn't believe the strength Walter possessed. Even weakened from spending most of a night buried in a coffin beneath the desert floor, he still had forty years on his old man. But Walter quickly overpowered Jess and the guttural cries emitting from his throat were ungodly.

He shoved his hand into Walter's face to try and blind him. It was slapped away and Jess was shoved flat onto his back. Walter descended upon him once again and Jess felt a sharp scrape across his jugular vein. He felt blood spurt from his flesh and Jess let out what he was certain would be his final scream.

Suddenly a burning smell assaulted Jess's nostrils. A shrill keening filled the desert air. Jess was shocked the cry wasn't his; it came from the writhing creature that had once been his father.

The Walter-thing rolled on the ground in pure agony as smoke peeled off its back. Jess realized the smell was burning flesh and he lay on the ground gasping for air as Walter threw a coat over his scorched skin. His father's hand was covered in blood and Jess realized it was a sharp fingernail that had slashed his throat.

The monster rose to its feet, the coat wrapped around him like a shroud. Walter ran for a car parked fifty yards from the open grave. The first streams of dawn's early light tracked his father like a sniper's beam. Wherever the rays hit him, smoke began to billow. As Walter dove into the car, he let out a bloodcurdling sound so high-pitched and otherworldly, it made Jess's head want to explode.

Jess tried to stand up but was still too weak from his ordeal down below. He stumbled as the car revved to life and squealed off, kicking up a sandstorm of dust that rose into the purple morning sky like a waterspout.

By the time the sand settled, dawn was breaking and the car had vanished from sight.

Jess sat in the desert for a long time, trying to pick up the pieces of his fractured mind and meld them into something he could believe was real.

❄   ❄   ❄

Jess gripped the coffee cup tightly. The sensation of warmth on his shaking fingers did little to calm him down.

"Let me get this straight," Benji said. "Your father—who I saw dragged out of here in a coroner's wagon—is now a vampire who pulled you out of a grave, burst into flames before he could sink his teeth into you, and then drove off leaving you stranded in the middle of the desert."

"Did I mention that he was driving a Celica? My father—in a rental car?"

Benji looked at Jess like he had squirrels popping out of his ears. "Wha—?"

"C'mon, Benji. Do you think I don't see how utterly ridiculous this sounds? That you should call one of my family's rest homes and have them come take me away?"

Benji finally picked up the comic books and a half-eaten meatball hero from the floor. "Hey, man. I had trouble buying the Celica too. No way he'd be caught dead in one." He chuckled, realizing the inadvertent double-entendre. "Then again."

"You don't think I'm making this up?"

"How long have we known each other?"

"All our lives."

"And you've always been a straight shooter. You never lied to me. I wouldn't have protected you from three-hundred pound goons trying to sack you through all of high school and let you put your hands up my ass to grab the ball if I didn't trust you, Jess."

For the first time this side of the grave, Jess's hands stopped shaking. He even eked out a slight smile. "Not sure I love the specific imagery . . . but thanks."

"I'm just saying that you had one hell of a night—make that few days. You were buried alive, for fuck sake! Who knows what kind of tricks the light played on you when you got free?"

"I saw my father, Benji. I swear to fucking God."

"Jess, you're trying to convince a guy who reads two dozen comic books a month and is a card-carrying member of the Stoker Society."

"The what?"

"Vampire club. Online thing. Named after the *Dracula* author."

Jess gave his friend a dirty look.

"Never mind." Benji tossed the comics on the desk. "You say you saw your dad. I believe you think you saw him. But there has to be a logical explanation."

"And if there isn't?"

"Then you've made my lifelong dream come true and found an actual vampire."

"So you do believe me."

"I want to. I swear, I really do."

"But . . ."

Benji dumped the sandwich in the trash. "The truth is . . . who knows what's real and what isn't?" Benji pointed at the comic books. "I know all this stuff is made up, but the kernel of the ideas must come from something real."

"I don't think we're talking about superheroes here."

"No shit? He wasn't wearing a costume?" Jess frowned before Benji let him off the hook with a grin. "How'd you get back here anyway?"

"I hiked for a good two hours before I hit some kind of road. I kept walking down the blacktop with my thumb out, hoping someone would stop and give a zombie a lift."

"Guess you walked all the way, huh?"

"A couple of day laborers actually took pity and pulled over. They agreed to bring me here but insisted I sit in the back of the truck with some chickens."

"You could use a shower, man."

"I need to find out what happened to Tracy."

"It's almost been a day since they took you away, Jess. She's either at home or not. Fifteen minutes won't matter at this point, but I don't think I could stand being in the same car with you for more than five. No offense."

Jess held up a palm to make clear none was taken. "You're tagging along?"

"Hell yes. I'm not missing out on the chance to meet a real live vampire." Benji smiled. "'Live' being a figure of speech, of course."

2

Vampire.

The fact that word even entered his brain was almost enough to send Jess running for the closest loony bin to demand being locked up in a rubber room.

What surprised him even more was that he considered himself the last person to expound tales of eternal bloodsuckers.

Walter Stark had insisted on a no-nonsense upbringing for his children that didn't allow for flights of fancy. His father had never read Jess a fairy tale, taken him to a movie, or even offered up an imaginary story. Walter believed in hard truths and life lessons; he would tell Jess the world was a rotten place—one had to fight to get a toehold and not let go when someone tried to rip it away. Those lectures never offered up a supernatural being as the threat one should be looking for over his shoulder.

But as Jess rode shotgun in the Mustang toward the Jameses' house, he thought about what Benji had said in the Sands's office. The legends of vampires and people rising from the dead went back to the dawn of man. Were these really just byproducts of wild imaginations, or were they rooted in some fact, regardless of how small? Jess could make the same argument about UFOs and their alien pilots. Were we really that exclusionist to believe we were the only sentient beings in the entire universe?

A long sabbatical in the aforementioned rubber room would not change what had transpired in Palm Springs since his arrival. Sure, most of it defied a logical explanation. But Jess knew what he'd seen with his own two eyes.

Call him a vampire. Walking dead. Nosferfuckingratu. Until someone offered up a better explanation—as far as Jess was concerned—Walter Stark had died and come back to life.

He considered how this fit into everything else that had occurred the past few days. Tom Cox's death. Edward Rice having his fingers in every slice of the Stark family pie. What about the two attempts on Jess's life? There had to be a connection to what had happened to his father. He voiced these thoughts to Benji.

"So we're going with the vampire thing, huh?" asked Benji, waiting for a traffic signal to change.

"Humor me."

"Yeah. Twist my arm."

"Really?"

"I still think you're suffering from some post-grave trauma. But if you accept vampire, lots of questions get answered. The cross on the picture and the motel wall. The dead patients at Meadowland—vampires need to feed on something, right? What better than old people? Speed along their demise—their deaths don't look so suspicious."

"Good reason Tom Cox would fear for his life and beat it out of town," Jess pointed out.

"It also explains why someone would chase him down to keep the secret from the outside world."

"Our mystery motorcyclist."

"He must be in on it." Benji drummed his fingers on the steering wheel and shook his head. "Except he was out in broad daylight. Sort of rules out vampire."

"Are you making fun of me now?"

"Just trying to help you build a case."

Jess considered that for a moment. "Might explain the over-the-top outfit."

"What do you mean?"

Jess reminded Benji how his father shielded himself from the rising sun by covering his skin with a heavy coat. "That material the cyclist wears would provide ten times the insulation of a coat. Might allow someone like my father to move around during the day."

"If the idea weren't so terrifying I'd say that's totally awesome."

"Certainly explains someone trying to get rid of me a couple of times. The more I dug and asked questions, the closer I was getting to the truth. Much easier to have me out of the way."

"They think you're still in that hole in the desert."

"My father knows better."

"Who's he going to tell?"

"Whoever 'they' are—the ones that he said were 'killing' him. I'm presuming one was Edward Rice. Though I'm not exactly sure where he fits in. The man's a physician. How does that link up with the craziness we're talking about?"

"Well, sticking with classic vampire lore, he'd be considered a 'familiar.'"

"What the hell is that?" asked Jess.

"Like the Vichy with the Nazis. You throw in with the oppressors to save your own hide, and hope to be rewarded with riches and a long life."

"That describes the man perfectly," agreed Jess.

The Jameses' driveway appeared on the right. Benji steered the Mustang up the asphalt; the only car in the driveway was Jess's SUV. Benji pulled in right behind it and shut down the engine.

"Looks like no one's *en casa*," observed Benji.

"At least the cops aren't here."

But neither was Tracy.

The housekeeper who answered the door wasn't a live-in. She took the bus in from Indio each day, got off at the stop at the bottom of the hill, dutifully trudged up the driveway, and arrived at eight on the dot to start mopping, dusting, and ironing.

This morning no one had answered her persistent bell ringing. She knew the actor was tending to business back in Los Angeles, but had expected Tracy to be at home. This wasn't strange—*Señor* James and *Señorita* Tracy were always coming and going as they pleased. So she let herself in with her house key and went about her normal routine.

"Shall I be leaving message?" she asked in broken English.

Jess saw no point in dragging this woman into the madness he felt gripping him tighter and tighter. He shook his head. "My friend was dropping me off to pick up my car. I left it here last night."

He pointed at his SUV in the driveway, and then looked at the wrought-iron table in the entryway. His keys were right where he had left them. Jess felt the hole in his stomach open up even deeper.

The maid handed him his keys, convinced he was telling the truth. Jess wished he could be as easily swayed that Tracy wasn't in serious trouble.

Like in her own grave somewhere deep in the Coachella Desert.

TRACY BEFORE

Sometimes it felt like they were the two loneliest people in the world, though Tracy knew this would sound ridiculous to anyone meeting them for the first time. Jess's father owned half of Palm Springs and her famous sire pretty much ruled Hollywood. But unless one was the scion of such privileged people, she didn't expect them to understand. So they just sucked up the Poor Little Rich Girl and Boy tags and reveled in each other.

Tracy understood Jess right away. She wasn't surprised that taking over a massive real estate business was the farthest thing from his mind. Standing in the pool with her hands wrapped around his waist, listening to him tell her about the great novel he was reading or the old movie he'd discovered, she knew Jess's aspirations spun from the realm of his imagination and not toward the bottom of a balance sheet. He was a daydreamer, borne from countless hours spent alone as a child because his parents were too busy building their fortune.

"What do you think you want to do?" she would often ask. His answers would vary. Some days he wanted to pump out the Great American Novel that explored the human condition. Other times he'd talk of going to grad school and getting a psych degree. More than once he mentioned signing up for one of those charitable organizations that rebuilt houses in devastated Third World countries.

The common theme was he liked knowing what made people tick. When she pointed this out, he told her it came from being raised by a father who didn't give a shit about anyone.

"My problem is that my dad cares about everyone else," Tracy said. Clark James was a Hollywood icon who threw everything into his career. He often told Tracy there were hundreds of people depending on him to keep churning out hit after hit. The irony was that Clark's dedication to this extended family was usually at the expense of his one legitimate heir, who he left in the hands of nannies and housekeepers. For Tracy, feeling aimless with one year left to go in college was to be expected—she would have been shocked had it been any other way.

Jess changed all that. For the first time since her mother died, Tracy found herself looking forward to getting out of bed (except, of course, when Jess was in it) and attacking the day. They were constantly taking road trips deep into the California desert and explored every inch of the Death Valley National Monument. Out in the wilderness, they felt free at last, with nothing expected and no one to answer to.

It was a different story in Palm Springs. Neither of their families seemed thrilled they were together. It made Walter Stark crazy that his son had taken a job in a local bookshop just to stay close to Tracy. Walter constantly told Jess he was wasting time with that "dilettante" and that he should get on with his life. Jess shrugged it off, but it bothered Tracy more than she would ever let on.

For Clark James, it was "No one is good enough for my little girl." The few weekends the actor spent in Palm Springs put a crimp in their sleeping arrangements as they'd taken to spending most nights in Tracy's bedroom when her father was off filming. There was no way either of them wanted to be under Walter's watchful eye. When Clark was home, Jess became very proficient at hopping the fence into the Jameses' backyard, using the hide-a-key Tracy left under the stone tortoise near the kitchen door to sneak inside, and tiptoeing up the back stairs to her bedroom. More than once, Jess climbed out a second-story window and beat a quick escape as the actor called Tracy down for breakfast after they'd both overslept.

She occasionally wondered if Jess was involved with her because it pissed off his father so much. Each time she thought about bringing it up, Tracy chickened out. If it were true, she decided she didn't want to know about it.

The closest she came to asking was one night when they were curled up at the foot of her bed, eating popcorn and watching *The Graduate*. Jess had brought the DVD from home because he couldn't believe Tracy hadn't seen it. He was constantly stunned by her lack of film knowledge and she was always reminding him that just because she grew up in the home of a famous actor, it didn't mean she saw a lot of movies.

"We only watch the ones my dad starred in," she lamented.

This got the proper response—a big "Awww" from Jess, which led to cuddling and the good stuff that came with it. Afterwards, he popped the movie in and they watched Dustin Hoffman stumble into a relationship with Mrs. Robinson, only to fall head over heels for her daughter later on. Two hours later, after Ben finally chased Elaine down and convinced her to get on the school bus, Tracy was sobbing uncontrollably.

Jess was puzzled by her reaction. She wiped away the tears and said it reminded her of them—the uphill battle they faced with their families not wanting them involved with each other.

Jess said he didn't care what anybody thought, it only mattered that he loved her. It was the first time he had ever uttered the words out loud.

Tracy told him she loved him too and began to cry again.

Again, Jess was confused. Tracy said she was now crying because she was so happy.

She didn't dare tell him the truth.

3

Jess told Benji to go back to the Sands. At first his high school buddy resisted; he wanted to make sure Jess was going to be okay. He swore to be careful and bring Benji up to speed on his search for Tracy, and then made him promise to keep the vampire theory under wraps. Benji said no problem. He might have been ninety-nine percent on board but Benji knew he would sound like an inmate who had just fled the asylum to a nonbeliever.

Jess watched Benji spin the Mustang down the driveway and head toward the setting sun. Then he hopped into the SUV, gunned the engine, and followed suit. But he only drove halfway down the block and parked on the mountain-shaded side of the street. Jess settled in to watch the coming and goings at the Jameses' house. The coming side was a dead end. Two hours passed, the skies darkened, and the only thing that appeared were a few lights in the house.

In the meantime, Jess grew increasingly worried about Tracy. The lack of a police presence convinced him no one had reported her missing. The fact the housekeeper didn't know Tracy's whereabouts and was clueless about the bizarre backyard activity the previous night, like masked men clubbing people's heads and dumping them in a car trunk, made him fear Tracy had succumbed to a similar fate. Even if his cell phone hadn't died in a waterlogged coffin somewhere in the desert, Jess didn't have Tracy's number to try and reach her. He knew she'd changed it years ago.

There were a few nights shortly after he'd left Palm Springs when he drunk-dialed her, only to get a disconnect recording with no forwarding number.

So, at eight o'clock, when the housekeeper locked the front door and caught her bus at the bottom of the hill, Jess decided enough was enough. It was time to take a look at things himself.

As he climbed a tree and dropped into the Jameses' backyard, it occurred to Jess that he had probably sent Benji on his not-so-merry way because he suspected breaking and entering was in his immediate future. It was enough to entrust his lifelong friend with his vampire saga; dragging him into actions that could land them both in jail was more than he could ask.

For a moment, Jess was surprised he had no qualms about what he was doing. But what had started out as curiosity and guilt about his father had become personal. There had been two attempts on his life and he'd witnessed something no one would believe. If Jess didn't pursue it, nobody would. Plus, someone might try to kill him again—hoping the third time would be the charm. It behooved Jess to get to the bottom of everything.

There were no telltale signs of Jess's abduction from the backyard the previous evening. He hadn't been outside with Tracy for very long, and it wasn't as if it had been a knockdown drag-out battle with his two assailants, breaking everything in sight like some B-movie dustup. Jess had been sucker-smacked with the shovel and knocked out cold. If something similar had happened to Tracy, there was nothing around the pool to indicate a struggle, kidnapping, or chase had taken place. That left the inside of the house to explore. He was happy to see some things never changed; the hide-a-key was still under the ceramic turtle, and the alarm code was identical. ("Oscar," ironically the one thing the owner coveted that he had never gotten his hands on.)

A few minutes later Jess was inside the Jameses' house.

The kitchen was immaculate. Jess couldn't tell if it was because the housekeeper had scrubbed her fingers to the bone or no one was using it. The refrigerator wasn't quite bare, but in a house this size one would expect more choices than the few items that looked as if they'd been left for the housekeeper to prepare her lunch.

As Jess moved through the rooms, he grew increasingly uncomfortable. The house seemed to be unoccupied, with no indication that anyone had spent any time here. This was particularly strange since three nights earlier there had been at least two hundred people swarming through it for his father's birthday party. He hadn't felt this emptiness then. Even the previous night, alone with Tracy, it seemed more lived in. Maybe the Jameses' house was really nothing but an empty shell that was filled only when it was necessary to make a big show. Sometimes the illusion was for a ton of people, other times it could be for just one.

He had a nagging feeling the encounter with Tracy fell into the latter category, and his suspicions weren't mollified on the second floor. The housekeeper had certainly been generous with the vacuum, Endust, and Windex. Everything had been sucked up, waxed, and polished clean. It added to the preserved-for-museum-posterity feeling that crept into Jess's bones as he continued to explore.

Finally, he came to Tracy's bedroom. His hand hesitated on the doorknob. His last truly happy time had been spent inside those four walls seven summers before. He thought about not going inside, not wanting to tarnish the memories with the baggage he'd carried around with him ever since.

But with that baggage came the dissolution of dreams he'd once shared with the girl who lived inside this room. Gone were the writerly aspirations and noble ambitions of exploring the human psyche. It was simple to blame his family and past events for most of this descent, but Jess knew he had his own culpability to deal with.

Of course, standing in the hallway outside his ex-girlfriend's bedroom after breaking into her house was one hell of a time to develop a conscience.

Jess opened the door and stepped inside.

The room was clean enough to perform a sterile operation. The bed was so neatly made it was impossible for Jess to ascertain whether it was the housekeeper's doing or it hadn't been slept in for a number of days. When he had last been in Tracy's room, it was full of the trappings of a senior girl in college—rock posters, knick-knacks from college, chick-lit books, and school texts. He remembered Tracy had also lined one wall with the greeting cards he used to leave on her windshield each time he left the house; they had been interspersed with snapshots taken on their trips to the desert together.

None of those was on display now. Jess hardly expected them to be after seven years, but he kind of wished they were.

Two walls were now bare. One had a framed Clark James movie poster, some Rom-Com Jess had made a point of not seeing when it came out. The fourth had a nondescript floral painting. If Jess hadn't spent so much time there years before, he would have sworn he'd walked into a guest room, not Tracy's.

He opened the closet door and found very few clothes. He was no expert on women's fashion but thought there was maybe enough for a week's worth of changes, and that was a conservative estimate. He flipped through dresser drawers and found about the same amount of undergarments. He thought this peculiar; Tracy had said she was living at home but there weren't enough clothes for a short vacation stay. And that was even if she spent most of the time hanging around the pool in the one swimsuit he found.

Either Tracy had been living somewhere else for a good part of the past few months or she had crammed what she could into a suitcase he couldn't find and took off for who-knew-where.

He saved the desk for last. Already deeply troubled, Jess clicked on Tracy's computer to see if he could get a clue as to her whereabouts. Her email came up and he anxiously tried to scroll through it, but quickly realized it had been wiped completely clean. He hit the History bar and was rewarded with the same result. Absolutely nothing. He was left wondering if Tracy had done this—or had someone done it for her.

He didn't know which option bothered him more.

Jess was about to leave the room when he noticed the small pile of books at the edge of the bright white desk blotter. They were of no particular interest to him: a dictionary, a book of quotes, and a thesaurus. All were worn and dog-eared from the constant use Tracy must have given them in high school and beyond.

What caught his eye was the picture sticking out between them. Most likely the housekeeper had straightened up what was on the desk and had put it there to make sure it didn't end up in the trash or on the floor.

It was the photograph Tracy had shown him of Clark James and the writer standing in front of the church down in Mexico.

The last time Jess had seen it was in Tracy's hand right before he got knocked out in her backyard.

He flipped it over and saw something had been scribbled on the back. Even after all these years, he recognized Tracy's precise handwriting.

One word.

Civatateo.

Two things bothered Jess. First, he had no idea what the hell the word meant.

And second, he was damn sure it hadn't been there the night before.

4

Jess made it to the electronics store just as the teenage clerk was turning the lower locks on the sliding door. He pounded on the panel but the kid ignored him, even though they were only separated by a six-inch pane of glass. He pulled out his wallet, flashed a credit card, and promised it would be the quickest sale he ever made—five minutes tops. The teen relented and Jess made good on his promise by taking the first phone he was shown. Rather than explain the watery grave where his phone now resided, Jess said he had lost it. The kid "tsk-tsked" and said that increased the cost two-fold and he'd need a new number.

The moment he got back in the SUV, Jess used his new purchase to dial the mortuary. An operator immediately answered—people weren't always kind enough to die during normal business hours—and asked how she could help him. When she realized Jess was inquiring about the status of his father's cremation, the operator asked him to call back the next morning.

"The funeral director gets in around seven," the operator sing-songed.

"I'm afraid it can't wait till then."

He explained that he was Walter Stark's son. His father's hospitals sent a lot of business their way, and he wondered if perhaps she could make an exception. She apologized but stuck to company policy. The next thing he knew, Jess was telling her unless someone met him at the mortuary within the hour, his family would call a different company when they needed their dead picked up and it would cost the operator her job. He had to hand it to the woman; she didn't lose one iota of cool when she asked if he could hang on.

While he waited, Jess stared out at the mini-mall. Beside the electronics place, there was an all-night convenience mart, a coin laundry, and a souvenir store with "I LUV PS" emblazoned on every single object in the window. It was a far cry from the sandy roads and local hangouts his parents traversed when they first moved to the desert decades ago.

Back on the line five minutes later, the operator said, "Mr. Talbot will meet you at the mortuary in half an hour, Mr. Stark," in the same melodious tone.

Jess thanked her profusely and hung up. As he drove off, he felt ashamed for using his family's name to get what he wanted. It made him appreciate the power his father wielded over the desert community and used to every advantage. But he knew Walter would have hated him using the Stark name that way, considering how Jess had spent most of his life trying to disavow himself of it. He was sure his father would be rolling over in his grave at the thought—if he hadn't already been wandering out of it.

That last part didn't make Jess feel any better.

Talbot's first name was Larry, which Jess found oddly macabre, seeing as how it was Lon Chaney Jr.'s name in *The Wolf Man*. Jess was pretty sure he wouldn't be the first to mention it, but seeing as how he had hauled the man out of bed, he figured it wasn't a good time to bring it up. Talbot didn't resemble the hairy beast or a matinee idol; he was what you expected from Central Casting when you wanted a funeral director. He hovered around fifty, looked good in black, had a monotone voice, and was extremely pale from spending too much time in dark rooms. After Jess identified himself as Walter Stark's son, Talbot had him wait in the Serenity Suite, just off the main entryway to the Desert Funeral Home and Mortuary. The décor was muted oranges and yellows, validating the room's moniker. There was nothing dour or funereal here—the only two things separating it from a receiving room at a country club were a casket selection book on the table and an inordinate number of strategically placed Kleenex boxes.

Talbot returned holding a cardboard box and placed it in front of Jess.

"Sorry. It was a little crazy here today. We were going to deliver this to the family earlier but we encountered some employee issues. I planned to personally take this over to your mother tomorrow morning."

"I'll make sure she gets it."

Jess began to peel open the box, which gave Talbot pause. "I assure you everything is in proper order."

"Doesn't hurt to double-check." Jess removed a simple gold urn so polished a person could see their reflection from across the room. He tipped open the lid and peered in to see a gray pile of ashes. "No way of knowing for sure, right?"

Talbot reacted like Jess had just eaten his young. "Almost thirty years in this business and another thirty before that for my father guarantees our work, sir."

Jess closed the lid and held up a hand. "I didn't mean to offend, Mr. Talbot. I was just pointing out that unless you did the process yourself . . ."

"That would have been Mr. Gideon," interrupted Talbot.

"Well, perhaps I could check with him?"

Talbot went silent. Jess could see the man was torn. Clearly troubled by the semi-accusations Jess was making, Talbot was also fully aware of how much business the Stark family had thrown his way. The funeral director choked down a cough as if that would hide what he said next.

"I'm afraid that isn't possible, Mr. Stark."

"Why is that?"

"The personnel problem I mentioned earlier? That would be Mr. Gideon, who runs the crematorium. He didn't show up to work this morning."

That sent up a warning flag for Jess. "Perhaps we can try him at home?"

"He isn't there. I've tried calling all day, but haven't been able to get in touch with him. I even sent my assistant to his place late this afternoon and she got the manager to let her into his apartment. Apparently Mr. Gideon hadn't spent the night there."

The flag was now flapping back and forth. "What do you think happened to him?"

"I'm hoping he got called out of town unexpectedly. It's not like Mr. Gideon to just leave without notifying us. I don't mind telling you it's left us in quite a spot."

"But he did the intake and cremation on my father?"

"He's the only certified person here. Who else would do it?"

Jess had an answer but didn't offer it up. He was pretty sure Larry Talbot would think he was completely insane.

"What do you mean those aren't your father's ashes?"

Benji and Jess were sitting in the office at the Sands. Candles and a flashlight illuminated the room. The power had been out for a few hours—not a rare occurrence when the Santa Ana winds kicked up. Benji told Jess it was one of the drawbacks from being on the outskirts of town; they were first to lose electricity, cable, and Internet, and the last to get it back. Benji had trained the flashlight on the urn Jess brought back from the mortuary.

Jess laid out his theory. Going with the supposition that Walter had come back from the dead, he must have risen from somewhere. Talbot told Jess he'd actually seen his father's "dead" body before he left the previous night, just before Jess was almost a breakfast snack for Walter in the desert. But when the mortician came in the following morning, "Walter's ashes" had been placed neatly in the urn. Couple that with Mr. Gideon not turning up for work—it added up to a horrific switcheroo.

"You think your father 'rose' right before this guy Gideon was going to stick him in the hot box?"

"If he's become—what I think . . ."

"A vampire."

"You say that so matter-of-factly."

"Hey, I've been waiting since I was a kid for someone to come along and make a case for one. You're doing a damn good job of it."

Jess nodded, uncomfortable. Benji lifted the lid of the urn to stare at its contents. "I suppose there's some test you could run to identify this stuff?"

"I've no idea. Even if you could, think of trying to explain it."

"Good point." Benji closed the lid. "Still, seems a lot for one man to do—even an un-human one. I'll buy his first instinct would be to kill Gideon out of bloodlust, but the whole cremation thing? How would your father know what to do?"

"He must have had some help."

Benji realized Jess had already considered this—and he reached the same conclusion. "Dr. Rice?"

"Makes sense. Rice told me he'd been in contact with the mortuary. According to Tom Cox's records there were a couple of dozen deaths at Meadowland in the past year or so. I'd be interested in how many were cremated versus buried."

"Or which ones Rice had his fingers in."

"Exactly," said Jess.

Benji inched the urn away as if at any moment it might jump up and bite his hand. "I presume going to the cops is out?"

"Unless I want to get locked up in a psych ward and start regular rounds of electroshock therapy." Jess shook his head. "I'd like to know what happened to Tracy."

"You could've told me you were going to check her place out."

"No reason to risk you doing something illegal."

"Appreciate that. But I'm in pretty deep already."

Jess picked up the picture he had taken off Tracy's desk and flipped it over. He mouthed the written word. "Ci-va-ta-teo. Any idea?"

"My Spanish is rusty. What do you think?"

"That as soon as the power comes back on, I'm hitting the Internet."

"Wikipedia is awesome, man."

"At least I'm not as worried she's buried in a hole somewhere. If she was grabbed when I was, there's no way this picture would have ended up back in her room."

"You think she just split?"

"There were hardly any clothes in her room. No luggage either. It seems like she packed up and headed off somewhere."

"Back to LA?"

"I don't think so. I called the house in town. The housekeeper said Miss Tracy was down in the desert and that I should try and reach her there." Jess placed the picture on the table and continued staring at the scribbled word. "I'm thinking she saw what happened to me, got scared to death, and ran off."

"Why didn't she tell anyone what happened to you? Or at least call the cops before she left?"

"I've been thinking about that."

The wind kicked up hard enough for the building to actually shake.

"And what did you come up with?"

"I don't think she knew who to trust."

❋   ❋   ❋

Benji accompanied Jess across the dirt parking lot; they had to shield their eyes from the billowing sand. Luckily the moon was almost full, so the wind-induced blackout hadn't thrown the Sands into complete darkness.

"You don't have to walk me back to my room."

"I don't mind. Sort of get creeped out sitting in my office in the dark." Benji dug something out of his pocket. "Besides, never know who you might run into out here."

Jess stopped as the moonlight glinted off the silver object in Benji's hand. "That's not what I think it is."

Benji offered the tiny crucifix to Jess. "What's the harm?"

"I thought you were a lapsed Catholic."

"I am. Had this for years. Ordered it from a monster magazine back in college. You know us geeks—we never throw anything out."

"You expect that to protect me from my father?"

"If he is what you think he is. Like we talked about, who knows where this shit started. Crucifixes. Garlic. Avoiding sunlight. No reflections in the mirror. Having to be invited before stepping inside a room? It didn't start with *Dracula.* There was Vlad the Impaler centuries before, which is also steeped in lore and superstition."

"Superstition. Precisely." Jess started heading toward his room again.

"You're the one who he tried to take a bite out of. Not me."

This slowed Jess's step enough for Benji to catch up.

"I'm just saying it couldn't hurt," said Benji, with the sincerity that could only come from an old friend.

"Maybe you oughta keep it for yourself."

"I've got another. It was a two-for-one sale."

Jess laughed and took the crucifix. "I'm not wearing it around my neck."

"There's no hard and fast rule you need to do that," Benji said. "But I wouldn't keep it out of reach."

Jess stuck it in his pocket as they walked past a grizzled trucker, who was using a tiny flashlight to walk a mangy dog while searching for the ice machine.

"Complimentary flashlight comes in handy, doesn't it?" Benji called out.

"Be better if you had a fucking working generator," replied the trucker.

Benji gave the man his best eat-shit-the-owner-is-always-right smile. "Make sure you pick up your dog's crap, otherwise I'll double charge you."

The trucker grumbled as he shuffled off into the dark.

"It's a wonder your business isn't booming," said Jess.

The loud bang woke him up. Jess looked to see what time it was but the power was still out, so the clock radio wasn't working. He fumbled for his cell phone and found it on the nightstand. When he clicked the LED switch, he saw it was just past three in the morning.

That was when he heard his name being called.

At first he thought it was the wind playing tricks on his ears. But then the gust died down and he heard the voice again.

"Jess."

He started to get out of bed as Walter loomed up over him.

159

His father swiped at him with sharp-nailed fingers, narrowly missing Jess, who backed himself up against the headboard. The Walter-thing advanced on him, opened his mouth and the pointed teeth emerged.

Jess screamed.

And then bolted back up in bed.

All alone.

Jess had barely caught his breath from the nightmare when he heard his father calling him again.

"Jess."

This time the voice was accompanied by a scratching at the door. Jess didn't need to pinch himself to check if he was still dreaming—he'd already had the living shit scared out of him and had never been more awake in his life.

The power was definitely still out. Jess bypassed his watch this time and grabbed the crucifix. He climbed out of bed and advanced toward the door with the metal cross held in front of him.

"Go away."

He slowed down as he neared the door, the scratching louder.

"Jess. Let me in."

There was something so alluring and plaintive about his father's voice, which made Jess want to throw open the door. Even though part of his brain knew that certain death waited outside, his father's plea was so intoxicating Jess had to stomp down the instinct with every ounce of willpower he had.

He shook as he yelled, "Go away, Dad!"

The desert air was suddenly filled with the sounds of wild things in the night. It was as if a wolf had gotten loose in a zoo and all the animals were up on their haunches, defending their territory. Jess could hear the trucker's mangy dog barking and growling like it had been rabid for a month.

Tears started streaming down Jess's face as he dropped to the floor and pled through the door. "Please, Dad. Just go back." He let the crucifix drop into his lap. "Go back to wherever you came from."

The animal's screeches and cries died down enough for Jess to hear Walter on the other side of the door.

"You should leave, son. While you still can."

Walter's voice faded away. The dog began barking violently again. Then Jess heard a loud whimpering that was immediately drowned out by the squeals of the desert dwellers. He remained huddled against the door, exhausted and drained to the bone.

A few hours later, when dawn mercifully broke, Jess was still there. Even in the safety of daylight, he couldn't find a way to go back to sleep.

He wasn't sure he ever would again.

When Jess finally emerged, he came across the trucker, who asked if Jess had seen his dog. The man was holding the dog's collar in his hand.

It was broken in half.

Jess shook his head. He didn't have the heart to tell the man he should consider himself lucky.

But, a few minutes later, he laid it all out for Benji in the office. The early morning visitation; the likely fate of the trucker's pooch; the works. It was enough for Benji to lose his appetite. He put a raspberry Pop Tart back in the box.

"Either this is really happening or you're going a helluva long way to make your point," said Benji.

"I don't think that will be necessary anymore."

With the power restored, Jess was on the office computer. He had immediately logged onto Wikipedia and typed "Civatateo" into the site's browser. Jess waved his friend over to the desk and again showed him the church photograph on which Tracy had scrawled the word.

"You found out what it means?" asked Benji.

Jess nodded at the computer screen. Benji leaned over his shoulder to see the one word he had highlighted.

VAMPIRE.

5

He found Harry in the backyard hitting golf balls into a large net. Jess, as he had done on the makeshift basketball court, stood and watched his brother, marveling at the concentration and tenacity with which he methodically struck the balls. He wondered if Harry had always been this way. Was his competitive, no-nonsense determination something passed down from their father? Or was it a byproduct of growing up under Walter's heavy thumb while their mother was relegated to the backseat? The age-old question—nurture versus nature. Then again, Jess had been gone a very long time and Harry hadn't been playing team sports when he left. Maybe his kid brother was just trying to lose himself in something to avoid thinking about the past few days.

Jess wished to God he could do the same.

Harry turned around to pick up a different club and saw him. "You look like shit."

"You don't look so hot yourself." It was the truth. Harry appeared to have aged in the past two days. He really was a teenager—troubled, angst-ridden, and not squeaky clean.

"Haven't been sleeping much." Harry punched a wedge shot into the net.

"I don't think any of us are." Jess had come here specifically to ask him about Walter. He had spent the entire drive over wondering how to broach his father's return without appearing to be a madman. He knew muttering "vampire," or the newfound Spanish word he was having trouble pronouncing would only result in a call for white-coated men with butterfly nets. But Harry had inadvertently left the door open wide enough—not for the entire truth, but at least for Jess to give fair warning.

"Anything particular keeping you up?"

"My mind's still playing tricks. I keep hearing things."

Jess lowered his voice, wanting to be sympathetic, not accusatory. "Dad?"

"How did you know?"

Jess treaded carefully. "He's on your mind. It's understandable."

"I guess I'm just having a hard time accepting he's gone. The funny thing is, it's not like we got along when he was alive. I barely existed 'round here. It's like they shipped me off to school and that was it. When I came back for vacations, Dad would stare at me with this expression like, 'I thought we got rid of you.'"

"Now you *are* imagining things. Dad loved you. He just wasn't the most demonstrative guy."

Harry laughed. "You making excuses for our father. That's a good one."

"Maybe it took the guy dying to show him a little respect." Jess picked up one of the golf clubs. He twirled it in his hand before casually broaching the subject again. "So, what exactly are you hearing?"

"Dad's voice. I know that sounds nuts. It's probably just the wind and my brain working on overdrive."

"Might not be as crazy as you think."

"What do you mean?"

Jess knew there was no way to come right out and say it, but he was going to do whatever was necessary to protect his little brother. "I've been hearing things too."

"Really? Like what?"

"Voices. Calling my name." Jess hesitated. Then he came to a decision. "Trying to sound like Dad."

Harry looked confused. "Trying?"

"I think there might be someone out there who wants us to think Dad is still alive."

"Why the fuck would they do that?"

"Who knows? Dad pissed off a whole lot of people. Could be some nut trying to punish his family by terrorizing them."

"Have you told the police?"

"Not yet," Jess responded truthfully. "It just happened this morning. I thought I was having a nightmare. Then I remembered what you told me at the golf course, how you thought you heard him calling you. It got me thinking someone might be out there screwing with us."

Harry shoved his club back in the bag. "People can be pretty sick."

"Which is why you have to promise, no matter what you hear or think you see, you're not to let anyone inside the house. Especially at night."

"What? Why night?"

Jess realized he had gone too far and started to backtrack a bit. "If someone's trying to make us think he's Dad, he's not going to show up in broad daylight. We'd know he's a phony the moment we saw him. But if it's dark . . . it's easier to fool people. You hear something . . . you think you see someone in the shadows . . . that's all it takes. You open the door a crack, and before you know it they're inside and it's too late to protect yourself."

It wasn't lost on Jess that he was subscribing to Benji's theory that a vampire needed to be invited in before wreaking havoc.

Meanwhile, Harry hung on his brother's every word. He looked genuinely frightened at the thought of an intruder, but still had no idea that Jess was talking about it being an undead one. Jess placed a hand on his younger brother's shoulder.

"Just promise you'll be extra careful until we figure what's going on here."

"I promise."

"Good." Jess felt bad about scaring Harry. But if anything happened to him, Jess would never forgive himself if he could have averted it.

"You oughta talk to Mom, though," said Harry.

"How come?"

"I think she saw something too. But she won't talk to me about it."

❊   ❊   ❊

But when he went upstairs to check on his mother, Jess found her asleep with a breakfast tray lying on the bed beside her, the food practically untouched. One bite had been taken out of the rye toast and Kate had had maybe two sips of tea.

Rye toast with marmalade and English Breakfast tea. His mother had eaten the same thing every morning for as long as Jess could remember. For years Lena had brought it up on a tray and Kate ate by herself. She didn't turn on the television or read the newspaper. She sat in silence.

Downstairs, Sarah and Jess would have their breakfast at the table next to the kitchen's bay window. The nanny usually joined them; Lena would fill in on the woman's day off. It was a rare morning when Walter would sit at the same table. He was usually gone by the crack of dawn and only made an appearance on one of their birthdays or a national holiday. Even then, he would read the paper and say nothing more than "pass the salt" or "you need to ask to be excused." As soon as Harry was old enough to sit in a high chair, he ended up in the parentless breakfast nook as well, with the nanny and his older siblings left to watch and feed him.

Meanwhile, Kate sat in bed upstairs all alone. As he got older, Jess started to think of it as "Mom's Time."

She never talked about it, but Jess got the impression his mother needed this time by herself to face the day. He never doubted that she loved her children. It wasn't like Kate was born with a silver spoon in her mouth and had servants waiting on her hand and foot. Far from it; she came from a solid middle-class Orange County family and met Walter in college. But his father was larger than life, a man who ruled any room he entered. As a result, Kate devoted most of her time to taking care of his needs, which must have taken a heavy toll on her. Jess figured "Mom's Time" was what allowed and reenergized her to do this each and every day.

Occasionally, if Jess wanted to talk to his mother about something, he knew he could sit with her while she had breakfast. It was the one time they could be by themselves. He didn't abuse it—and now realized the most honest discussions he'd ever had with Kate were over rye toast with marmalade and a cup of English Breakfast tea.

Kate was a loving mother. Jess never questioned that. But her life with

Walter kept her more than occupied. She never woke Jess up in the morning or put him to bed. She never helped with homework or read a bedtime story out loud. The only exception was when he was six years old and had to spend three nights in the hospital to have his tonsils removed. Kate sat by his bed and dutifully read him the first half of *Mary Poppins*, which he eagerly listened to while devouring scoops of ice cream. But when they got home, it was the nanny who finished reading the second half of the book to Jess. At the age of six, he thought it odd his mother didn't want to find out how *Mary Poppins* ended. Today, standing by the bed watching her toss in fitful sleep, Jess wondered if Kate read to him in the hospital because for once in her life she was out of the house and free.

When breakfast was done, she'd ring a bell that echoed throughout the gigantic house. Lena would come upstairs and take the breakfast tray away but Kate would have already disappeared from bed. Minutes later she would emerge from the dressing room in perfect Palm Springs societal wear, ready to take on her role as Walter Stark's Primary Devotee.

She would appear downstairs like clockwork at nine, ten on weekends. The only exception had been the months right after Harry was born. Kate had gone through tremendous health problems giving birth to her final child and spent half a year recuperating in bed. For a while, the family thought they might lose her, but she eventually regained her strength. When she started appearing downstairs at nine o'clock, the fourteen-year-old Jess knew all was right with the world again.

Jess glanced at his watch and saw it was almost noon. Thoughts of that dark time crossed his mind again. He tiptoed around the edge of the bed and stood over Kate, checking to see if she was still breathing. A whimper escaped her lips; a bad dream. Jess leaned over and kissed his mother ever so gently on the forehead, then took a couple of steps back and waited for the whimpering to stop. The deep labored breathing of sleep eventually took over and he went back downstairs.

As he came down the steps, Jess used his new cell phone to get in touch with Cisco back in Los Angeles. Soon after taking over the dispatching seat, Jess realized that some clients didn't pay their bills. Some honestly forgot, while more than a few had no intention of putting a check in the mail and instead vanished off the map.

That was where Cisco came in.

Jess was turned onto him by an insurance company client who swore the man could find a needle in a hayfield. Cisco possessed mad computer skills that usually ran down the losers in less than a day. That made him a natural go-to for Jess who wondered when, if, and where Tracy James might have used her credit card in the past forty-eight hours. Cisco promised to get back to Jess as soon as he could and said "Adios," and Jess walked into the kitchen.

Lena immediately offered up breakfast. Jess said he would be fine with some cereal and poured a healthy dose of Rice Krispies into a bowl while she went to fetch some milk from the fridge. Then he pulled out the crinkled photograph of the church in Santa Alvarado. He flipped over the picture and once again studied the scribbled word. Its Spanish translation troubled him more than ever, and he figured asking Lena about it couldn't hurt.

"I don't suppose you've ever heard of something called the Civatateo?"

There was a large splat behind him. Jess whirled to see Lena had dropped the milk carton on the floor. Liquid was everywhere; he got down on his knees to help her clean up.

"I'm sorry," Lena said. Jess noticed she was overtly upset, barely able to get the two words out.

"It's just a carton of milk. Are you all right?"

She couldn't catch her breath. Jess tried to get her to calm down. When Lena was finally able to breathe, he helped her up on her feet. "What's wrong?"

"Why would you be interested in that?" Lena asked nervously.

"Do you know what it means?"

Lena nodded, vigorously. "The question is—do you?"

Jess wondered exactly how to handle this. He wasn't ready to unspool his suspicions under the Starks' roof for fear of how they would be met. He picked up the photograph, placed it back in his jacket pocket, and proceeded with care.

"I looked it up. It's some kind of vampire, originated in Mexico."

"Where did you hear about this?" The nervousness had not gone out of Lena's voice. If anything, it had increased.

"I saw it written somewhere. Why?"

"It's something you should stay away from," warned Lena.

"You believe in vampires?" Jess asked.

"When I was growing up in Mexico, my family would tell me stories about the Civatateo."

"What kind of stories?"

"Ones whispered by my grandparents, aunts, and uncles. About little children disappearing in the middle of the night."

Jess could see a deep-set fear emerge from the woman, the sort whose roots were in tales first heard at an impressionable age. What began as stories often festered inside and never lost their grip on one's heart, no matter how old they were.

"My aunt said it took her fiancé."

"He was taken by a vampire?"

"He went into the jungle and never returned."

"Might have been a case of cold feet," said Jess.

"Maybe. But I believe there is much that can't be explained. Just as I know there are things that shouldn't be discussed." She lowered her voice as if her dreaded Civatateo might be listening. "Why are you asking about this?"

Jess realized to get Lena to open up, he was going to have to give up a little bit himself, even if it meant twisting the truth around. "I think some people believe there might be one in Palm Springs."

Lena made the sign of the cross. "Is that what happened to your father? Was he killed by the Civatateo?"

Jess thought that through. Accepting that Walter had come back from the dead, he probably didn't rise by himself and turn into a vampire. Following this insane logic, one might conclude it took one to become one. But Jess wasn't prepared to tell Lena her late boss was making a nasty habit of hovering outside the doors of his friends, foes, and family.

"There are a lot of sick people in the world, Lena. Unfortunately, I've seen more than my fair share in Los Angeles. There are those who drink too much, pass out at night, and wake up naked the next morning with blood all over their hands. They are convinced they turned into a werewolf the night before just because the last thing they remembered was itching a lot. In truth, they had a bad reaction to really strong alcohol and went on a murderous rampage they don't remember. So I guess it's not farfetched for someone to think they've become a Mexican vampire and killed my father in a blind rage."

"Do the police believe this?"

"The cops don't even think my father was murdered. They are content saying he died of a heart attack."

"It was like that back in Mexico."

"How do you mean?"

"Someone would disappear and everyone was told they just ran off. A body would be found ripped to pieces and people were supposed to believe they were attacked by a wild animal."

"Was anyone ever arrested or caught?"

Lena shook her head. "This was a long time ago—before I was born."

"What supposedly happened to this thing?"

"It went back."

"Back where?"

"To the earth and water from where it came."

The certainty with which Lena said this roused Jess's curiosity even more. "I'm not sure I understand."

"The Civatateo came from a woman who died in childbirth. When she was still barely alive, she tried to hold off death long enough to give birth to a healthy baby boy. She desperately continued to struggle during delivery, but her grip killed the child. Then she died and they were buried together in a river beneath the ground. The next night, the child, filled with the strength from its mother's struggle that had killed them both, rose from beneath the earth. It went to the crossroads and attacked the weak and innocent. Most were thrown in the underground river where their blood mixed with the water and became a feeding ground for the Civatateo."

"You said 'most.' What about the rest?"

"They were turned."

"Turned?" The word sounded creepy even coming out of Jess's mouth.

"Into one of its own."

"How many Civatateo were there?"

"Very few. The vampire child grew into a man and was very careful about whom he turned. The Civatateo would feed on someone for months until they were ready. The victims would find it harder to be in the daylight, because it was the one thing that could kill the Civatateo."

Jess remembered his father's horror when he tried to push him into the sun. Plus, he would never forget Walter running in the desert, trying to escape the breaking dawn. "Sunlight?"

Lena nodded. "Eventually, the victims could exist only at night. That was when the Civatateo had to make a choice. Completely turn its victims so they could become one of its own, or destroy them."

"There is no other way to kill the Civatateo?" Jess was surprised and not thrilled with how easily the Spanish word now slipped off his tongue.

"None that I was ever told."

"So why didn't it just stay forever? Why go back into the earth like you said?"

"It didn't want to. Supposedly it was lured there and trapped in a place surrounded by light that never went out."

"How is that even possible?"

"I don't know," said Lena.

"Where is this place?"

She shook her head, indicating she didn't know that either. "By the time I heard the stories, that answer lay with the dead. This was good because there was less chance it would be disturbed. Less chance of the Civatateo coming back."

"Maybe someone found it."

"That is hard to believe. Most have never heard of the Civatateo. It was a local legend."

Jess realized even though he had known Lena most of his life, he had no idea exactly where she came from in Mexico. She might have told him once, but he was probably in first grade.

"What was the name of your town?"

170

"Santa Alvarado."

Shock spread on Jess's face. His hand darted to his jacket pocket.

He began to pull out the well-worn picture of the very same Mexican town.

Then he heard his mother screaming upstairs.

6

Kate's screams echoed through the house as Jess bolted up the stairs. He had just reached the landing when he heard a second person yelling. Only this voice was intelligible—with repeated protestations of "Mom . . . It's all right . . . I'm sorry." When he burst into his mother's room, Jess found that Kate was out of bed. She was near the balcony window in a long white nightgown, her entire body shaking. Sarah had her arms wrapped around their mother, trying to calm her down.

"I'm sorry, Mom." She gently stroked Kate's back, thrust into the peculiar position of a child comforting their parent. "I didn't mean to scare you."

"What happened?" asked Jess. Lena came up behind him in the doorway.

Kate screamed before Sarah could answer.

"Walter!"

This prompted another series of "it's okay" from her daughter and a sinking feeling in Jess's stomach.

"She had a nightmare," Sarah said. "She thought she saw Dad outside on the balcony last night."

"That's ridiculous," Jess said quickly, suspecting this was more than likely the truth. But he also knew there was a proper time and place for expounding vampire theories, and this didn't seem to be it, not with his mother hanging on the edge of hysteria. Jess could feel Lena's eyes boring

172

into the back of his head. He turned around and gave a "not now" stare. Lena took the cue and backed off a step.

"That's what I told her," said Sarah. She turned toward her mother. "Mom, we're all upset about Dad. I know you're not sleeping well. Nobody is. You shared a bed with him for over thirty years. I'm not surprised you'd wake up in the middle of the night thinking he was here."

Sarah might have been a royal bitch dealing with Jess but she had a way of handling their mother that he could never match. Maybe it was the fact that she was the only girl, or the special love-hate bond that especially exists between mothers and daughters. No matter what came out of Sarah's mouth, Kate usually took it at face value and didn't read anything more into it. This bothered Jess to no end growing up, because there was usually a duplicitous side to whatever Sarah would say to her mother, some self-serving need to which Kate would be blind. But this was one of those rare times when Sarah's only agenda was to make her mother feel better, and Jess was grateful for that.

"Maybe you're right," muttered Kate. She looked at her son and Lena. Her face flushed with embarrassment at standing in the middle of the bedroom in her nightgown. She let Sarah ease her back toward the bed. "I couldn't fall asleep. I've had so much on my mind, so much to take care of."

"Of course," Sarah soothed as she peeled back the sheets and helped her mother get tucked back in.

Kate pointed at a vial on the nightstand. "I took a couple of the pills that Edward gave me. It took them forever to work. I was just drifting off when I heard this scratching sound." She pointed toward the balcony. "It was coming from the window. I looked over and that's when I saw him."

"You thought you saw Dad," Jess said.

Kate nodded.

"It was just the pills, Mom," said Sarah. "Maybe you should only be taking one or we should get Edward to lower the dose."

"Perhaps," Kate replied. She gazed back to the window. "I guess I finally passed out. Then the dreams started."

"What kind of dreams?" asked Sarah. Jess didn't need to be a mind reader to predict his mother's answer. He knew what lurked in the darkness and would have whispered his mother's name.

"I dreamt Walter was alive, that he was stuck outside and had no way of getting in. He kept calling my name but I wouldn't answer." She broke off a moment, stifling a sob. "But it didn't sound like him."

"Dreams always mess things up. You know that," Sarah said. "God knows you've been under a ton of stress. Now try and get some rest."

"I suppose I should." Kate leaned back on the pillow and let out a heavy, sad sigh. "It just seemed so real."

That's because it was, thought Jess.

Jess asked Sarah if they could talk for a few minutes. She said she'd meet him in the living room but wanted to get Kate properly situated first. On the way down the steps, Jess could see that Lena was busting at the seams.

"I know you've got tons of questions, Lena, but I really can't answer them right now."

"I just want to ask one."

Jess felt he owed her that, especially after everything she'd downloaded in the kitchen. "What's that?"

"*Señor* Walter? Is he Civatateo?"

Considering Lena's stories about the Mexican vampire and what she had just heard firsthand upstairs in his mother's bedroom, Jess realized it would be hard to offer a flat-out denial.

"What if I said I don't know?"

Lena's response was to cross herself again.

"You know how ridiculous this sounds when you say it out loud, don't you?" asked Jess.

"But you wouldn't have asked me about it unless you thought it was happening, no?"

Lena had him there.

"Is it true they cannot enter someone's home unless they are invited in?"

"That's what we were always told," said Lena.

"You can do me a big favor. Do whatever you can to make sure the family stays in at night. Tell them they can't open the door and let in anyone they aren't expecting."

Lena nodded and Jess suppressed a smile. He'd love to meet the person who wouldn't be surprised when their dead father came-a-knocking.

❊   ❊   ❊

Sarah was pouring herself a drink when Jess entered the living room. She saw his disapproving look and held up one hand as she took a big sip from a cocktail glass with the other.

"You get the shit scared out of you by Mom screaming her head off and tell me you wouldn't want to calm your nerves."

Jess refrained from mentioning it wasn't even noon. He already knew he was going to punch a few of Sarah's buttons—no sense upsetting her until absolutely necessary. "What happened exactly?"

"You know how the balcony wraps around the south side of the house, goes past my room, then Mom and Dad's?"

"I did grow up here, remember?"

Sarah chose to gloss over that barb. "I was having a cup of coffee out there. I'd heard from Lena that Mom had a rough night. I was worried about her, so rather than pound on her door or squeak my way in to check, I wandered down the balcony and peeked in the window."

"And she saw you."

Sarah took another healthy gulp. "She must have thought it was somebody else, because she started screaming bloody murder."

"Sounds like she thought you were Dad."

"Which makes no sense whatsoever," Sarah said.

"Maybe your boyfriend needs to dial back the medication a bit."

Sarah slammed the glass down on the table. "Wow. That was what, two minutes? I would've thought you'd make a little more small talk before slamming Edward."

Consider the buttons pushed. "I'm just voicing concern for Mom."

"Yeah, right! After seven years of radio silence, you're speaking for the family? Just because you're now the oldest living male doesn't give you that right!"

"I never said it did, Sarah."

"What do you have against Edward anyway? You never met him before two days ago."

175

"Completely true," said Jess. "But you have to admit it's bizarre coming back and finding him so deeply involved with the family."

"I love him, Jess. I'd tell you to get used to it, but I don't expect you to actually stick around."

"I might surprise you."

"Nothing surprises me about you anymore."

"Is this feeling reciprocal between you and the good doctor?"

Sarah let out a hearty laugh. "Oh my God. You're going to hate this. You're starting to talk just like Dad. 'Is it reciprocal?' You make it sound like some kind of business contract."

"It wasn't meant like that."

"I don't give a shit. But for your information, the feeling is more than 'reciprocal.' Edward has asked me to marry him."

Suddenly, Jess felt like *he* could use a drink.

"When did this happen?"

"Last night."

Jess could have uttered a protest. He could have lambasted Edward Rice as an opportunist who was after the Stark fortune and saw Sarah as an available and vulnerable meal ticket. But Jess knew that would fall on deaf ears.

Instead, he offered up his congratulations, which he could see floored his sister. Jess wasn't going to give her the satisfaction of telling him to go to hell or that they didn't need his blessing to spend the rest of their lives together.

Besides, he was too busy thinking about the fact that the doctor proposed to his sister the day *after* Jess was buried alive.

In a grave that he was certain Edward Rice had helped dig and thrown Jess in.

Convenient.

7

As Jess drove up the curved driveway to Meadowland, he saw the same gardener fussing with perennials in the courtyard. Once again, the man straightened up and waved at Jess, then bent back down and continued to move plants around. Jess was reminded of the automatons he had seen as a child at Disneyland: Abe Lincoln rising from his chair to deliver the Gettysburg address on the hour or the Pirates repeatedly setting fire to the Caribbean. He wondered if the gardener was similarly programmed—always there day after day, in that exact spot, waving at visitors while he rearranged the same batch of plants. Jess had the odd feeling this warm greeting was meant to ensure welcoming comfort; new arrivals would love it and people wouldn't feel horrible when they left their loved ones behind to slowly wither and die.

He parked the SUV in the visitors' lot and walked toward the main building. The muted yellow pueblo structure proved the perfect backdrop for colorful desert flora and eternal blue skies, but Jess could only focus on the blandness of the walls themselves. Did the patients really appreciate the manicured grounds or did they feel doomed to a tasteful desert prison where they'd eventually just blend in and fade away?

The staff parking spaces were closest to the entrance and Jess was happy to see Edward Rice was actually working today instead of sneaking in thirty-six holes, or worse yet, lurking around the Stark family. He was headed for the double-glass doors when a female voice called out to him.

"Mr. Stark?"

A hefty nurse in tropical pink scrubs stood in the teensy-weensy designated smoking area forty yards off the entrance. Jess would have placed her on either side of fifty but could have been off ten years either way. She had the well-worn look of someone who had spent too many years changing bedpans, shoving wheelchairs, and walking beneath fluorescent lights.

"Yes?"

"I just wanted to express my condolences about your father."

"Thank you very much. Nurse . . .?"

She stubbed out the cigarette in an ashtray and wiped her hand against the scrubs. Then she extended it toward Jess. "Blake. Velma Blake."

"Nice to meet you," Jess said.

"I took care of your dad while he was here."

"Really?" Suddenly Jess was interested and not just answering by rote.

"I was so hopeful he was going to take a turn for the better when he was discharged. But sometimes they just want to go home and be with their family. If you get my meaning."

Jess nodded. "Absolutely."

"I heard the dreadful news about how he died. That must have been so awful for you."

"It was."

He was increasingly impressed by how forthcoming Velma was. "Can I buy you a cup of coffee?" Jess asked.

The lunch rush was over in the cafeteria; a few staff members were huddled in the back playing cards. Jess bought two cups of coffee and settled down at a table with Velma. He made sure they had isolated themselves out of anyone's earshot while keeping an eye on the cafeteria entrance. No sense in letting one particular doctor sneak up on them.

"Thank you," said Velma. She took the coffee and poured an inordinate amount of sugar into it.

As Jess doctored his own cup, he thought about how to get as much information as possible. He figured he would start with an element of truth and see what flowed from there.

"I'm really happy to have run into you. By the time my mother called me back to Palm Springs, my father was really sick. He died the next day and was pretty uncommunicative beforehand."

"That's such a shame."

"I didn't know he'd spent any time convalescing here. I thought he was at home during his entire illness."

Velma wiped some sugar granules off her lip and shook her head. "He was here almost two months. He really went up and down. Every time we thought he was improving, he'd go into a tailspin and we'd ship him into the ICU until he was out of the woods."

Jess knew one of the great things about Meadowland was its on-property surgery center and small hospital unit between which many long-term residents regretfully spent the last parts of their lives shuttling back and forth.

"Dr. Rice told me they really never got to the bottom of his disease," said Jess. And why would he? It was a safe bet turning into a Civatateo wasn't in any medical text the Meadowland staff would have read. Or in the case of Edward Rice, ever admit to. "Severe anemia, right?"

"That was the diagnosis. We never found the root cause."

"Did you notice my father having a particular aversion to extreme sun or even ordinary daytime?"

Velma put down her coffee cup and stared at Jess in amazement. "I can't believe that you just brought that up."

"Why's that?"

"I was the nurse assigned to your father during the day. I'd come on duty in the early morning and the night shift nurse would tell me how well Mr. Stark had done the night before—how they had long conversations about the history of Palm Springs, how he was just full of vim and vigor. I started to believe she was making it all up because your dad was practically catatonic during the day. He refused to go outside; he said the daylight was actually *hurting* him. It wasn't until the other nurse's car broke down one day and I worked a few hours overtime that I noticed the change come over him."

"What kind of change?"

But he knew what she was going to say. He'd seen the dramatic difference the day his weak father fought being pushed toward the sun off the lanai, and how much like his old self Walter was that same night at his birthday bash. The byproduct of this "disease" was their ultimate confrontation in the desert dawn where Walter fled from the emerging sunlight as it burned through his heavy coat. He couldn't tell Velma any of that, but he was certainly interested in her perspective.

"He really rallied when night came around. On that one evening, I talked more to your father than the entire two months I took care of him during the day." She finished off the coffee. "The strange thing?"

Oh, if you only knew the real strange thing, thought Jess.

"Yes?"

"That night. He acted like it was the first time he ever met me. I'd been working with him for over a month at that point. It was as if none of that ever registered on him."

Her eyes lowered. Jess could tell this woman had been deeply disappointed. Obviously, Velma Blake took her work very seriously and her patients to heart. She was the kind of nurse one would want taking care of someone near and dear. To keep the conversation going, Jess offered up an amateur diagnosis that he didn't believe for one instant.

"Maybe he had some kind of inverse sleeping disorder?"

"I actually said the same thing to Dr. Rice. He dismissed it out of hand, which I was surprised about, considering the others."

And suddenly, there was the door Jess had been looking for. He slid it open slightly with a simple question. "What others?"

Velma's professional demeanor immediately took over. "I'm really not at liberty to say."

"I'm not asking you to name names. And if you're worried I'm going to file some class action suit against Meadowland, forget it. My family owned the place for years. Why sue myself?" Seeing the doubt in her eyes, he knew he had to push it over the top. "Besides, as co-owners we could always get access to medical records, so this is really just to satisfy my curiosity more than anything."

Whether or not he could get this access, Jess didn't know. But it seemed to appease Velma, who was anxious to unburden herself.

"We treated five or six other cases over the past few years that suffered from the same disease."

"The disease you could never nail down."

She nodded. "Identical symptoms—severe anemia, extreme lethargy during the daytime, regaining of strength at night. They reminded me of a night-blooming desert flower. You know, the kind whose petals open after sundown and spread their fragrance through the air? But if you walk by the same flower at high noon, you can't distinguish its smell or appearance from a normal cactus."

"What happened to those patients?"

"They were up and down for months, just like your father. We'd run a battery of tests but couldn't come up with anything conclusive. Eventually, their hearts just gave out."

Jess was dying to ask if any of them were seen walking around town after that. But he knew the chitchat would end right there and Velma would commit him upstairs. So, he tried a different track.

"Were any similar cases reported outside of Meadowland?"

Velma shook her head. "That was the scary thing. We checked all the hospitals in the area. It got the medical staff wondering if the disease was circulating through the facility like some bacteria strain or those super bugs you read about hitting big-city hospitals. We actually spent the money to close down the hospital wing and residential sections after that to run a diagnostic sweep, but nothing came of it."

"And all of them died?"

"Most did, yes."

"Someone survived?"

"The initial one. Our very own Patient Zero."

"Who was it?"

Velma hesitated. Jess realized he'd pushed too far again. "I really don't think I can tell you that."

"Confidentiality?"

"That and the fact he carefully guards his privacy. If you really want to know more, I suggest asking Dr. Rice. He brought him here and I believe they're still in touch."

Jess rooted around in his brain; something way in the back was trying to dig its way out. Finally, it broke through.

He was really sick. We did a good job keeping it out of the tabloids.

His silence gave Velma enough time for discomfort to settle in. She dabbed her mouth with a napkin and made a big production of looking at her watch. "I really should be getting back. They're going to be wondering where I disappeared to."

Jess stood up and offered his hand. "Thanks again for your condolences. I appreciate the time you gave me."

"I'm sorry for blabbering on so. I feel like I've said too much."

No, Jess thought. *You said just the right amount.*

8

Jess was kept waiting by his future brother-in-law for over half an hour. He was certain Rice had talked to Sarah by this time, so he knew he didn't have the element of surprise on his hands. But he also didn't expect the physician to give up anything when confronted, so Jess needed a different plan of attack.

Rice's outer office was devoid of any personal touch. That included the no-nonsense secretary who had as much personality as the potted plant in the corner. The magazines on the coffee table followed suit; such thrilling titles like *Critical Care Medicine* and *Public Health Journal* threatened to put the reader to sleep before they got to the table of contents. Jess had gotten up, crossed the carpet to the window, and stared out at the Meadowland courtyard nearly a dozen times when Edward Rice finally emerged from his office.

"Sorry to keep you waiting, Jessie."

Yeah, right. "That's okay. Your assistant and I here were busy making small talk." This didn't even elicit a reaction from the dead-serious secretary who hadn't uttered a word except for, "The doctor will be with you when he can."

"Let's take a walk, shall we?"

Minutes later they were back in the courtyard and Jess got another friendly wave from the gardener.

"I like to get out and walk the grounds at least twice a day," said Rice. "Not only is it good exercise, it gives me a chance to see what's going on and make myself accessible to the staff and employees."

"I really don't give a shit what you do with your time, Ed."

Jess had to hand it to Rice. He didn't miss a step reacting to his blunt retort. "Look, Jessie. I know the two of us got off on the wrong foot. It might be a good idea if we started over . . ."

"Considering we're going to be brothers-in-law?" Jess pushed on, not giving Rice time to react. "I know my sister. No way she didn't tell you she sprung the news on me."

"I guess it would be silly to think you came all the way over here to congratulate me."

"Pretty perceptive."

"What do you want, Jessie?"

"Lots of stuff. First, I wanted to see the expression on your face when you saw I was up and around after leaving me for dead."

"What the hell are you talking about?"

"You having to call off your engagement because you're going to be doing a long stint in a jail cell."

"I know these past few days have been traumatic. Maybe it wasn't the right time for Sarah to share the news. In fact, I probably should have waited longer to ask her. But I swear that I love your sister and will do right by her."

"Promise me anything you want, Ed. It's not going to change the way I feel."

Rice put on his best bedside manner. "I wouldn't trust anything you're feeling right now. Your family suffered a terrible tragedy. I know you and your father had issues, but he was still your father. It's only natural to have an extreme reaction to the loss of a parent. It isn't even uncommon to have fits of delusion under such stress."

"I'm not delusional, Doc. I just have a lot of questions and I believe you're the person who needs to answer them."

Rice finally stopped walking. "Jessie. You're all over the place . . ."

The physician tried to place a calming hand on his shoulder but Jess shoved it away. Jess immediately rattled off a laundry list, never giving Rice a chance to slip in a word.

"I want to know who helped you kill my father. I'd also like to know where he went after he came back to life. I'm really interested in who was with you when you clobbered me over the head with a shovel and then dumped me in a desert grave. And while we're at it, maybe you can tell me what you did with Tracy James and why I can't find her anywhere. Did you put her in a hole too?"

"Jess, you're not making any sense. Are you even listening to yourself?"

"Does that mean you're not going to answer my questions?"

"First off, I'll ignore the obviously crazy accusations—chalk them up to some kind of psychosis brought on by repressed grief."

"Mumbo-jumbo, Doc. So you're just going to deny everything."

"There's nothing to deny." Rice pointed at a building across the courtyard. "There are at least two people on my staff you could walk in right now and talk to. I think they'd do you a world of good."

"I don't need help, Ed. Just a few answers. But given the severity of the questions, I understand your reluctance."

Jess started for the parking lot. The physician chased after him. Six steps and they were side by side again.

"At least let me give you something to help calm you down."

"Like the stuff you gave my mother? No thanks. She's walking around like a zombie thanks to you."

For the first time, Rice lost a little of his cool. "It might do you some good to feel a little less."

"Is that what you and your buddy thought when you walked away from my grave?"

Rice's lips narrowed as he tamped down his rising fury. "I'll say it once more. Get some help, Jessie. Before it's too late."

"I appreciate the threat. I really do."

"I presume you haven't shared any of this with your sister as I would've heard about it."

Jess reached the SUV and unlocked the door. "Like she'd ever believe a disparaging word about her dear Edward." He fired up the engine. "Don't worry. You have her right where you want—under your thumb."

Jess slammed the car door before Rice could utter a protest. He squealed out of the parking lot, leaving the troubled physician in a cloud of exhaust.

❀   ❀   ❀

Jess had picked out the spot on his way over to Meadowland. It was about one hundred yards down the road in front of a house with a SOLD sign on the front lawn. He had even peeked inside the windows to ascertain the previous occupants had moved out, so it was easy enough for him to park in the driveway facing the street.

He had brought along a Subway sandwich, chips, and a drink, figuring when he was done with lunch he could piss in the cup if relief was necessary, just like James Garner did on those *Rockford Files* reruns. He had purchased a few sports magazines along with a crossword puzzle book, to while away the time. Jess figured he might have a long wait.

He replayed his conversation with Rice in his head. He was glad that the physician had suggested walking outside. If they had been in Rice's office, Jess would have been worried the secretary might overhear the conversation. He knew when it came time to go after the physician it might get quite animated and it wouldn't help if anyone else heard Jess's wild accusations.

The moment Sarah told him about the proposal, Jess knew Rice was stepping up whatever plan he had into overdrive. He also realized the doctor had plenty of time to prepare himself for Jess's desert grave escape— going on the assumption Rice had put him in it. If Rice were involved with whatever Walter had become, he probably knew about Jess's survival from the Civatateo himself. A call from Sarah would have only confirmed it.

Jess knew he had to prompt some reaction on Rice's part. His purposeful over-the-top tirade was meant to provoke one. If Rice were truly innocent, he would immediately reach out to his mother and sister and insist that Jess was in need of truly serious help. More specifically he would urge them to institutionalize Jess. There would be nothing duplicitous, just a genuine concern for his brother-in-law-to-be.

But there was another option—kind of a Combo Plate—and the reason Jess was parked across from Meadowland. The first part still held true; he fully expected Rice to work the Starks about getting Jess medical treatment. But if Rice was guilty, Jess figured the physician might get in contact with some of his cohorts—the other assailant, possibly the mystery motorcyclist, maybe even the thing that was now his father.

Jess didn't have long to wait. A squad car pulled up to Meadowland within an hour. An exasperated Thaddeus Burke lumbered out and tromped up the path to the building. Fifteen minutes later he came out the entrance alongside Edward Rice.

The sheriff looked more beaten down than when he had arrived. Rice had dropped the friendly neighborhood doctor façade. He was pissed off. Burke was acting subservient to Rice and it was wearing on him. Clearly, the law wasn't giving the orders in this relationship. Eventually, Burke drove away and Rice marched back inside.

Jess considered the meaning of Burke's appearance. There were a lot of cops in Palm Springs. It confirmed his suspicion that Burke constantly turning up like the proverbial bad penny wasn't a coincidence.

The sheriff was in the middle of all the strangeness revolving around Edward Rice and Walter Stark's family. Jess wasn't sure how to deal with this information, but thought it best to avoid Burke for the time being. But he knew the next time he crossed paths with the sheriff, he would have to tread extra carefully.

Then the long wait began. By the time Edward Rice came outside again, Jess had finished the magazine and half a dozen puzzles. Night had fallen and he hadn't seen any familiar faces since Burke's departure.

Once Rice pulled out of his parking space, Jess started up the SUV.

He had scoped out the physician's house on the way to Meadowland. It was on the north end of Palm Springs, so he knew if Rice were calling it a night, he would turn left out of the driveway.

When the physician made a right and floored the gas like a man really anxious to get somewhere, Jess was more than intrigued.

His plan felt validated.

He followed from a safe distance.

9

Ten minutes later, Rice pulled into the parkway leading to the Palm Springs Country Club. Once Jess realized where the doctor was headed, he slowed down, allowing Rice to move into the parking lot. Jess waited another minute, then pulled up to the gate. He was delayed by the guard, a pokey methodical old-timer, because he didn't have a sticker identifying him as a member. He drummed his fingers on the steering wheel, keeping one eye peeled on the upper parking lot where Rice exited his car and headed toward the country club entrance. Finally, after convincing the guard he was the son of one of its founding (but not-as-dead-as-everyone-thought) members, Jess was waved through by the man with a grin as if he had been coming there for years.

By the time Jess entered the parking lot, Rice had disappeared inside the clubhouse. He parked far enough away so he wasn't right on top of Rice's car, checked his look in the mirror to make sure he was presentable enough for the PSCC's stuffed shirts, and then hoofed it to the front door. This time, Jess beat the staff to the punch and asked for a jacket. Once he slipped into a 42 regular, he walked over to the dining room.

Dinner was being served but it wasn't bustling; most of the membership was usually asleep by the time the restaurant opened. Jess saw that there were maybe six tables being used. Rice wasn't at any of them, which was a good thing, as it would be hard for Jess to hide in the sparsely occupied room. He was about to leave the dining room when he heard Rice's booming voice.

This outburst caused a septuagenarian couple to look up and see what was disturbing their vichyssoise. Jess followed their gazes outside the window, where the doctor was on the balcony having an animated conversation with Clark James.

He found it mighty interesting that Rice made a beeline for the actor at the first opportunity following their confrontation at Meadowland. Jess moved into the adjacent tavern room where he could sit at the bar and nurse a drink while keeping an eye on the physician and thespian. He ordered a Corona from the bartender and charged it to his father's membership number. Then he staked out an angle where it would be impossible for the two men to see him because of the light reflections in the glass. Not that they were remotely interested in looking his way. They were too busy arguing.

Jess strained to hear, but Rice and James were now keeping their voices down. The triple pane glass didn't help matters. He sipped the beer and thought about Clark James. So much for the housekeeper's intel that the actor was at his Los Angeles home. Jess was certain the Patient Zero that Velma Blake mentioned was James. Tracy had told him how sick her father had been when his movie shut down and he decided to retire.

Jess considered how the Clark James pieces fell into the jigsaw puzzle surrounding his own father. Some fit; most gave him a headache. He was still trying to sort them out when a hand touched his shoulder.

"Mr. Stark?"

Jess looked over to see Jaime Solis, the owner of the country club, standing beside him.

"Mr. Solis." For a moment, Jess thought he was going to be kicked out for Bogarting his father's membership number. But the impeccably dressed Latino offered up a welcoming smile.

"Jaime. Please. To what do we owe this pleasure?"

"End of a long day. Thought I'd stop by, try and relax a little."

"I am sure this has been a most difficult week for you." Solis motioned to the bartender. "Please don't charge Mr. Stark."

"That isn't necessary," said Jess. "I just threw it on my dad's account."

"All the more reason I refuse to take no for an answer. Have something to eat while you're at it. We forget nourishment at times of great stress."

Jess knew there was no talking the club owner out of the offer. Jaime Solis was a man used to getting his way. He politely accepted the drink and tried to let his eyes casually slip past Solis to peer out the window. Rice and James were getting more into it; their movements were increasingly flecked with anger. Solis seemed oblivious to the goings-on outside and kept his attention on Jess.

"We will miss seeing your father around here. He was very helpful to me in revitalizing the club. It pained me deeply to see him struggle with his illness. He so enjoyed watching your brother on the course."

This surprised Jess considering he couldn't remember his father attending one of his own high school football games, not even the state championship. "I know Harry loves playing here. He works hard at it."

"He's going to be quite an excellent player. I wouldn't be surprised if he ended up being club champion one day."

"If anyone could do it, it'd be Harry."

"Perhaps we'll be seeing more of you now? On the links perhaps?"

"I was never really much of a golfer. Plus I'm not sure how long I'm going to be in town. My work is in Los Angeles."

"Well, I hope you make use of the club while you are still with us."

Suddenly, Rice yelled from outside. "You're out of your fucking mind!" This caught Solis's attention for the first time and he looked over at the doctor and actor out on the balcony.

Rice was up in James's face. He had lowered his voice after the burst of profanity but was clearly agitated.

"You'll excuse me?" asked Solis.

"Certainly."

"I hope to see you again soon. Please consider having something to eat." Solis addressed the bartender. "Harold, make sure Mr. Stark gets whatever he wants."

Harold nodded and Solis took off for the double doors leading out to the balcony. Jess watched the club owner stride up to Rice and James. The commotion died down immediately as Solis focused on the physician. Rice started complaining but Solis took him firmly by the arm and escorted him out of sight. James watched them go, his face still filled with rage. Jess kept his eye on the actor and noticed him take a couple of deep breaths to regain his composure. James straightened his jacket, even though it wasn't mussed, as if he needed to be presentable for a possible photo opportunity, and then came through the double doors into the tavern room.

James sidled up to the bar and sat on one of the stools. Jess decided to state the obvious. "You look like you need a drink, Mr. James."

"What I need is my head examined for sponsoring that prick into the club in the first place." The bartender wandered over but James waved him away. "Maybe later, Harold."

"I'm wondering why they let him into the medical profession, period," offered Jess.

"Believe it or not, he's actually a good doctor. But he's become increasingly insufferable."

"So why put up with him?"

"He saved my life. Have to give him credit for that."

"Back in Mexico, right? Tracy was telling me about it the other night. During that disaster movie."

"Post-apocalyptic," corrected James. "The movie was the disaster."

"I never really heard about it."

"That's because the film was never finished and we were able to keep most of it out the rags once a few weeks had passed and they found another scandal to chase after."

"What happened exactly?"

"I tried to save some money and it came back to bite me in the ass. It was a nightmare from the start. We were down in the middle of nowhere trying to shoot with a crew that spoke no English and only wanted to know when their siestas were starting. We weren't prepared, we got behind right away, and once those location guys died, that was the beginning of the end."

"Who died? Tracy didn't say."

"Three men, one woman. One of our locations fell out and they went searching for a replacement. They'd been warned by the locals not to wander off unescorted—but try and tell a film crew what not to do and they'll just say fuck off. When they didn't show up the next morning, we went looking and found them in out in the Mexican jungle in bloody pieces."

"How could something like that happen?" Jess had a pretty good idea, horrific as it was. But he was interested in what James believed.

"They no doubt stumbled on a drug deal. Even though they knew the dangers, I still blame myself for what happened. It was my fault we were down there in the first place."

"Santa Alvarado."

For the first time, the actor eyed him suspiciously. "Thought you didn't know anything about all this."

"Tracy mentioned the town. I'd heard of it because that's where Lena, our housekeeper, is from."

"How do you think we ended up down there?"

Jess was confused. "Lena?"

"Well, not her exactly. When I was looking where to shoot *The Seventh Day*, I was at your folks' house having coffee in the kitchen. I saw a photograph Lena had from where she grew up. The village looked beautiful and mystical, exactly what I wanted to capture on film. She told me where it was; we scouted it and fell in love with the location. Unfortunately, as it turned out."

At least that was one mystery explained, thought Jess. He wondered if Lena was putting some of this back history together, and in a bizarre way, felt somewhat responsible for what was unfolding in the California desert years later.

"We shut down for a couple of days and to cap things off, I got sick as a dog. That's when we decided to pull the plug, period."

"How did Edward Rice fit in?"

"He was the movie doctor. I thought he was just one of those Dr. Feel-goods that usually end up on shoots. But he really stepped up. Got me on tons of fluids and pumped my stomach enough to have me survive the flight back to Palm Springs. He got your father to put me under wraps in Meadowland and keep the press away. Walter gave Rice a job on the staff for his efforts and I think you know how that turned out."

"I'm afraid so."

"The man is quite the accomplished opportunist."

"He somehow managed to snag my sister in the process. I just found out they're engaged."

"I'd get a good lawyer to watch your father's estate."

"I'll keep that in mind." Jess nodded toward the balcony. "If you don't mind me asking, what were the two of you arguing about?"

"It was a private matter, actually."

Jess realized he had pushed too hard. "Sorry. None of my business, really."

"No worries." James waved it off. "Just watch out for Rice, son."

"Thanks, sir. I will."

James addressed Harold the bartender. "Think I'll take a rain check tonight. Maybe tomorrow."

The actor offered his hand to Jess. As they shook, Jess asked the one question he had been saving up. "How's Tracy doing?"

"She's fine. Still trying to find her way."

"Seen her recently?"

James didn't miss a beat. "This afternoon, actually. We had a pleasant lunch up at the house."

Jess knew that was a lie. From the contents in James's refrigerator, it didn't look like anyone had cooked a meal there in days.

"Tell her I said hello," said Jess.

"I don't think so," replied James.

A sudden coldness swept over the actor's face. It made Jess question everything the man had said since he had entered the tavern room.

"You broke her heart once, Jess. I won't let that happen again."

Clark James left the room before Jess could offer a comeback.

TRACY BEFORE

"I don't think your father likes me very much," said Jess.

"Don't be ridiculous. And pass me one of those pickles."

They were having a picnic at the top of the Aerial Tramway. Most tourists knew it as a place to build a snowman in the winter after taking a fifteen-minute funicular ride up from the desert floor. But the locals loved coming to the summit because it offered a drop-dead skyline view of the Coachella Valley and was a great way to beat the summer heat. Tracy and Jess had picnicked there at least once a week since they ran into each other on Palm Canyon Drive two months earlier.

Jess tossed her one of the kosher pickles and helped himself to a second sandwich. "I'm serious," he said. "He didn't say more than five sentences to me at dinner the other night."

"You know actors. They're helpless without having someone write their lines."

"I think he's worried I'm going to convince you to drop out. "

"Miss my senior year at Dartmouth?"

"Uh-huh. He seemed pretty upset you hadn't picked your classes yet."

Tracy bit the pickle in half and made a loud scrunchy sound. "That's because I never decide till I get there. Even then, I still change my mind half the time." She finished off the pickle and talked with her mouth half full. "I think you're overreacting."

"I don't think so." He leaned over and kissed her. They rolled around for a bit on the blanket, then came up for air and more lunch.

"And just what are your intentions?" she casually asked while spreading mustard on a piece of rye.

"Regarding you and Dartmouth?"

"No. About shipping off to Iraq." She squirted mustard at him; he dodged it and they both laughed.

"I think you should go back."

The smile dropped off Tracy's face. "Really?"

"I think it's important you get your degree."

"And what are you going to do?"

Jess shrugged. "I'm definitely not going to stay in Palm Springs."

Tracy turned her back and stared down at the valley. She pretended to study the traffic patterns, but the truth was she didn't want Jess seeing the tears welling in her eyes. "You'd just leave, huh?"

"No point in sticking around."

Tracy could feel Jess staring from behind, but she refused to let him watch her fall apart.

"You okay?"

She didn't answer. Her lip was trembling.

"Trace?"

"Yeah. I'm okay."

Jess moved a little bit closer and put his arms around her. He nuzzled her ear. "I'm sorry. Were you expecting me to ask you to stay? To drop out of school?"

Tracy shook her head. "No." She raised a hand and wiped a falling tear. Then, she admitted the truth.

"I was sorta hoping you'd want to come back east with me."

Jess used his strong arms to turn her around and look directly into his smiling face.

"That's what I hoped you say."

Tracy laughed. And began to kiss him all over.

She thought it was the happiest day of her life.

10

"I'd really like to see that movie," Benji grunted between bites.

"Fat chance of that happening," said Jess. They were back in the office of the Sands Motel. Jess had grabbed burgers from an In-N-Out off the highway. He picked at his Double-Double, which was already cold from the ten-mile drive to the outskirts of the Springs. This hadn't stopped Benji from devouring two like they were marshmallows, and he was already working on his third.

"Yeah. But the footage would be a collector's item."

"I didn't get the impression from James they shot much."

"Wonder if they got the dead guys on film." Benji caught Jess's look and tried to back off the ghoul factor. "Not in the movie. You know, using a location camera or something."

"James never mentioned it, but who knows?"

"I'm just wondering if those location guys looked like your dad when you found him outside your motel room."

"The same thought occurred to me."

"What do you think James has to do with all this?"

"I've been trying to figure that out. Edward Rice was super pissed at him but James never lost his cool. Makes me think Clark is calling the shots, not Rice. Plus, whatever deal he's got going with the doctor, it's obvious James resents it. He told me as much."

Jess continued to poke at the soggy French fries. "I'm more interested in how sick James got down in Mexico five years ago."

"And the patients the nurse told you about," Benji said between chomps.

"Only Clark made a full recovery while everyone else at Meadowland died."

"You're forgetting your father."

"I wish."

"Unlike the others, your dad came back."

"*That's* the part I'd like to forget."

Benji plopped the remnants of burger number three into his mouth. That was enough to make Jess lose his appetite. He pushed his food away and Benji immediately eyed it.

"You done with that?"

"Have at it," said Jess. "Just don't wake me up in the middle of the night to get your stomach pumped in the ER."

"You'll be lucky if that's the only thing that wakes you up." Benji scooped up Jess's half-eaten burger.

For some ludicrous reason, Tom Petty's "Don't Come Around Here No More" popped into Jess's head. He reached into his pocket, pulled out the cereal box crucifix, and twirled it. "I get the feeling my dad's not dropping by any time soon."

"Told you that would come in handy," said Benji.

"I don't believe I'm even carrying it around." Jess dropped the crucifix on the desk. He began rubbing his temple, hoping he would wake up back in his El Monte dispatch office and this time not return his mother's call.

The phone by Benji actually rang, snapping Jess out of it. Benji answered it with one of his quips that only he thought was funny. "Sands. Your home away from home when you don't want to be home."

Benji listened for a few seconds. "Gimme a minute." He covered the phone with his hand and looked at Jess. "Wanna talk to Edward Rice?"

"Seriously?"

Benji extended the phone. "I've never met the guy. But that's who he says he is."

Jess took the receiver. "Hello?"

Sure enough, there was Edward Rice on the other end of the line. "I tried your cell phone but it's going straight to voicemail."

This made perfect sense since it was six feet under in a watery grave. "I lost it. But you should already know that."

Rice didn't get defensive this time. "I understand."

This caught Jess unprepared. It wasn't an admission of anything but it certainly wasn't a denial. "How did you know where to find me?"

"Sarah told me you were staying out there."

Jess tightened his grip on the phone. "What do you want, Rice?"

"To continue our discussion from this afternoon."

"You heard everything I had to say. I've got nothing to add."

"You haven't been told the truth about what happened to your father." The physician paused, knowing he had Jess dangling on the hook. "Or where he is now."

And suddenly he was reeling Jess in. "And you're going to tell me?"

"Isn't that what you were trying to pull out of me at Meadowland?"

Jess saw no need to answer that. "Where are you right now?"

"Home. I'm sure you know where that is."

"I do."

"I would have been shocked if you didn't."

"Why the sudden change of heart?" asked Jess.

"Let's just say I'm getting tired of being other people's lackey."

"Who are we talking about? Clark James?"

"You know where I am."

Rice hung up. Jess handed the phone back to Benji, who had caught Jess's side of the conversation while only overhearing dribs and drabs from Rice. Jess filled in the missing pieces.

"You want me to drive?" asked Benji.

"Not this time. Rice sounds pretty skittish. I don't get the impression he'd be comfortable talking in front of someone else."

"What if it's a setup?"

"You watch too many bad movies."

"People make a lot of fun of me because I read tons of vampire crap and look where we are now."

"You're still staying here." Jess stood up. "That doesn't mean if you don't hear from me by morning, you shouldn't send the cavalry."

"Gotcha," said Benji.

Jess headed for the office door. No sooner had he grabbed the doorknob when he turned back around and moved toward the desk.

He grabbed the crucifix and put it inside his jeans pocket.

Rice lived near the border of Rancho Mirage, the upscale community just northeast of Palm Springs. Up the street from Tamarisk Country Club and the compounds that Sinatra and Groucho Marx had built the neighborhood was Desert Toney—old money from the Rat Packers and their ilk merged with new hedge fund payoffs that needed to be dumped somewhere two generations later.

It was close to midnight by the time Jess pulled the SUV up to the curb of Rice's house, the only two-story structure on a neatly manicured block. Most of the other homes tried to stay true to the vintage fifties style from whence they came. Leave it to Rice to add a second story so he could look down on his neighbors and flaunt his newly acquired success.

Rice's sports car was parked in the driveway. A green lawn that must have been watered fifteen times a week led up to the front door. Jess bet Rice didn't even know the conscientious gardener's name. Exotic cacti probably plucked directly from his mother's garden lined both sides of the path. Jess kept glancing over his shoulder for things hiding in the dark.

He reached the door and began to knock. But realizing the lateness of the hour and the fact that he was expected, Jess tried the door handle. It clicked and he was able to swing it open.

Halfway. Something prevented it from going any further.

"Hello?" he called out softly, feeling a chill in the warm desert air.

There wasn't an answer so he pushed harder. The door refused to budge. He was barely able to squeeze through the opening and almost tripped as his foot bumped into something.

Edward Rice's head.

It was still attached to his body—but only because the neck hadn't been totally ripped apart. The lone lamp in the living room threw enough light for Jess to get a horrific look. The physician had been torn to shreds as if set upon by a pack of rabid dogs.

Jess was sure there weren't any murderous canines running amok in the streets of Rancho Mirage. He couldn't say the same about a bloodthirsty vampire fresh out of the grave.

Another light flicked on.

Jess jumped. And then was filled with woe as he heard someone coming down the stairs.

"Edward . . .?"

Jess wanted to snap out all the lights and leave.

But his sister was already screaming.

11

Sarah's screams threatened to wake the entire neighborhood. Jess's first instinct was to reach out and calm her, like when they were children and he was the protective big brother. But she backed away before he could step forward, frantically pointing a finger at him, convinced he was the monster who had committed this atrocity.

If only she knew the truth, thought Jess.

"Stay away from me!"

"Sarah, I just found him here."

Her screams gave way to tearful blubbering. She collapsed on the stair landing. She was wearing Rice's robe, a dark terrycloth number three sizes too big. As she buried her face in her hands and sobbed uncontrollably, the robe parted just enough for Jess to see she wasn't wearing anything beneath it.

Sarah must have been sleeping when Rice had gotten up to unburden his conscience and called Jess. The doctor probably settled down to wait but a vampire came a-calling before Jess could get there. Sarah must have woken up to see her fiancé was no longer in bed, thrown on his robe, and started down the stairs.

Jess glanced at Rice's mangled body. The blood was pooling beneath him. He must have been caught off guard and unable to yell for help. If he had, there was no way Sarah would have slept through it. She would have been downstairs by the time Jess arrived.

The sobs had quieted somewhat, so Jess tried to approach his sister again. Even though her hands still covered her eyes, she could sense his movement. "Don't fucking come near me, Jess."

"Sarah. I didn't do this." He took a deep breath and found himself unimaginably pleading with his sister. "I couldn't do this."

"Then what the fuck are you doing here?!"

"Rice called me less than an hour ago. He told me to come over. He wanted to talk."

"In the middle of the night? That's utter bullshit!" She took one more look at her dead fiancé and began sobbing again. She forced herself to look away and began to head out of the room.

"Where are you going, Sarah?"

"To call the police."

Jess ran after her and caught up as they entered the kitchen. It was bachelor friendly with a center island and ample wet bar and stools to match. The masculine décor convinced him that Sarah hadn't spent much time here yet; otherwise her fingerprints would have been all over the room.

"Can you just hold off a second?" Jess asked as he grabbed her shoulder.

Sarah immediately started pounding on Jess—slashing at his face with her fingernails and pummeling his chest with her tiny fists for all she was worth. He instinctively protected himself from the sharp nails but otherwise just took the assault. He figured at some level he deserved it. Finally, she shoved him away.

"Stay the hell away from me!"

Jess realized his mistake. Whatever he knew to be the truth wasn't on Sarah's radar. She had seen him standing over her bloodied lover, a man Jess hated, and now he put his hands on her. He would have screamed bloody murder too if the roles had been reversed. He slowly backed away.

"Okay, okay. I know you think I killed him. But I swear he was dead when I got here."

"You . . . you're expecting me to believe Edward called you . . . called you on the phone . . . and in the time it took you to get over here . . . someone came in and did that? Ripped him to pieces and just vanished?!"

"As crazy as that sounds, yes, Sarah, that's what must have happened."

She continued crying and reached for the phone.

"No way, Jess. No fucking way." She shook her head vehemently. "Maybe Edward called you. Maybe he didn't. I won't even say you came over here to kill him. But I know you didn't like him. You didn't like me being with him. I don't even care who started it—I understand things can get out of control—but this? You did *this* to him?" She started yelling again. "You fucking did this to him?!"

She gulped for air and once she caught her breath, started to dial. Jess couldn't help himself as he lunged and tried to grab it away.

"No! Don't fucking touch me!"

Jess eased away again. "C'mon, Sarah. You know me."

"No, Jess. I don't. I don't know who you are anymore." Tears streamed down her face.

"The police will throw me in jail. That you do know."

"If you did this, you belong there."

Jess raised his voice for the first time. "But I didn't!"

Sarah jumped at the outburst, which made Jess feel like crap for needlessly making things worse for his sister. He spoke softer. "Did you see what Edward looked like? Look at me—I'd be drenched in his blood."

Sarah pointed accusingly at Jess's right hand. "What about that?"

Jess stared at the blood on his fingers. "I leaned down to check on him. If I'd done what you think, you'd see a whole lot more. What about a murder weapon? Did you see one? Do you see me holding one?"

"You must have gotten rid of it."

"No! I didn't get rid of a weapon! The thing that killed him—"

Jess broke off. Sarah looked wild-eyed at her brother.

"What thing?"

Once again, Jess had to make a decision. What did he tell her? He wasn't dealing with someone like Benji, a man who wanted to believe the unfathomable. This was his sister, who only saw the brother she was convinced killed the love of her life.

"You wouldn't believe me if I told you."

"I thought as much," she said quietly.

Sarah dialed 911.

"Please don't do this, Sarah."

She ignored him and waited for the emergency operator to pick up.

One last attempt. "Edward wasn't the man you thought he was."

"I'm done listening to you."

"Believe me, I'm so sorry this happened. He didn't deserve it. I will do whatever I can to make it right."

"I don't give a shit what you do, Jessie." The tears had stopped. Her voice had gone ice cold.

Jess turned away and walked out of the kitchen. As he passed Rice's tattered corpse and exited the house, he heard Sarah tell the emergency operator that she wanted to report a murder.

Jess had promised to "make it right" and meant it. Of course, he didn't have a clue how to do that. But he knew it would be impossible from a jail cell. If Thaddeus Burke had the chance, he wouldn't hesitate to lock Jess away and forget where he put the key.

Jess got in the SUV's driver's seat. He shut the door and rooted around in his pants pocket for the car keys. He dug them out and started the ignition.

His father sprang up from the backseat.

Jess began to scream but Walter's cold hand grabbed him by the throat.

"I warned you to leave this alone." The Walter-thing's voice was a crisp hiss laced with static.

A panicked Jess struggled in his father's arms. He shoved an elbow into the vampire's neck and wrenched away. Jess pulled out the crucifix and jammed it in front of Walter's pale angry face.

The Civatateo swiped it away like it was a paper clip.

Jess moaned.

"Catholic superstition," Walter snarled.

He leaned forward and Jess could see him clearly in the reflected moonlight. His white shirt was covered in blood, which no doubt had previously been in Edward Rice's veins. There were plenty of splotches around the Civatateo's mouth as well.

A horrifying smile emerged on his father's face. He wiped some of the stray blood off his lip with a finger, and matter-of-factly placed it in his mouth. The slight slurping sound was the most unnerving thing of all. Jess desperately tried to hold onto his sanity. It wasn't easy. Neither was trying to comprehend how he could be in the clutches of a monster and still be alive.

At least for now.

"Why did you kill Edward Rice?"

"He had to die."

"Because he was going to tell me the truth?" asked Jess.

"Because he deserved it."

The vampire's voice was wrapped in gravel from an ancient burial ground. Jess felt like he was watching a robotic version of his father. Whatever remained of Walter Stark was in there somewhere, but buried way down deep.

"You were many things before—but never a killer."

"I'm not what I was."

Understatement of the year. "What do you want?"

"To be left alone."

"And if I can't do that? Leave it alone?" asked Jess.

Cold fury appeared in his father's eyes. His mouth darted open, revealing the razor-sharp fangs.

Jess lurched back against the car window, smashing his head. The pain was secondary to absolute fear.

Walter hovered over his son. "I would reconsider. While I can still fight off the urge."

Sirens sounded in the distance, giving Jess hope to survive one more night. He looked out the side window.

"Maybe this is a good time to all sit down and sort this thing out."

But when Jess turned around, the back passenger door was hanging open and the Civatateo was gone.

At least he didn't ask to be dropped somewhere, thought Jess.

Realizing he was on the edge of madness and hysteria, Jess leaned over and slammed the back door shut. He sped off in the opposite direction of the approaching sirens. As he made a right on the next street, he could see the squad cars pulling to a stop in front of Edward Rice's house.

Jess started to get the shakes.

He still had them when he got back to the Sands Motel after driving with all the interior car lights on.

He must have looked over his shoulder at the backseat three dozen times.

12

"This thing is totally worthless, by the way."

Jess tossed the cereal box crucifix across the motel room. Benji caught it with a nice backhanded grab.

He shook it in the air as if it were a faulty thermometer needing a good kick-start. Jess filled him on the confrontation with his father. For Benji it might as well have been the Gospel According to Bram Stoker.

"God, I wish I'd been there."

"No. No you don't." Jess couldn't have been more serious. He began tossing his scattered clothes into a duffle bag. "I think he's under the control of someone."

"The one who turned him."

"Evidently. Edward Rice must have known who that person was. I think that's what he wanted to talk to me about."

"Unfortunately, your father got there first."

"He said Rice 'deserved it.' I couldn't tell if he actually believed that or was carrying out some sort of order. But he had no intention of telling me who gave it."

Jess zipped up the duffle bag and gave the room a once-over to see if he'd missed anything.

"So, now what do we do?" asked Benji.

"*We* do nothing. I've dragged you into this enough."

"Drag away. That's what friends are for."

"You want to help? Divert the cops. It's only a matter of time before Sarah sends them here. If they ask where I went—"

"Name the place—that's where I'll send them."

Jess thought about it for a moment. "Try Los Angeles. I wouldn't mind sending Burke on a wild goose chase."

"In that case, maybe I'll send him to Canada and let him freeze his ass off."

Both men laughed. "As much as I'd love that, we've got to give them something believable," Jess said. "The best way to help is stick around town and let me know what you hear."

"Whatever you need, man." Benji wrapped him up in a giant bear hug. "Any time you're in the neighborhood hunting monsters, feel free to drop by."

"I'd rather just sit around and get drunk," Jess said.

"We can do that too." The two friends broke apart. "Where you going to crash?"

"I'm not sure. Besides, it's better you don't know. That way they won't use a rubber hose on you when the LA detour hits a dead end."

"I guess telling you to lie low until this blows over would be pointless?"

"You ever see me try to duck a blitz?"

"I saw you end up flat on your ass a whole bunch because you were too damn stubborn."

"It's coming to a head, Benji. Things were kept quiet for years, but once Tom Cox stole those files at Meadowland and showed them to my father, it started the ball rolling. They got rid of Cox and turned my father into whatever-the-hell he's become. Then Rice must have gotten out of line and threatened to spill everything to me. That made him a liability. They're getting careless and it's become harder to cover things up."

"One question."

Jess had to smile. "Only one? I can't believe what just came out of my mouth."

"Who are the 'they' you keep talking about?"

"Presumably the Civatateo."

"And how do you figure out where to find them?"

"My next stop."

The Oasis appeared no different at three in the morning than the last time Jess had been there, and it probably looked the same when it opened at eight in the morning after the mandatory five-hour shutdown. There would be three or four people hugging the bar, one endless game of pool in back, and a few patrons hunkered down in booths trying to hide from the outside world.

Jess felt bad about hauling Lena Flores out of bed in the middle of the night, but if he waited until morning, the Stark house would have been crawling with Burke and his men. Luckily she had kept the same private line in her room all these years and Jess was surprised to find the house-keeper still awake at two in the morning. She told him she had been hav-ing trouble sleeping ever since the specter of the Civatateo reemerged and was happy to talk to a "live" human being instead of imagining undead ones descending upon her.

She wasn't alone. Her daughter, Maria, was sitting across from her in the booth. Jess wasn't exactly caught off guard; Lena had suggested the late-night meeting place and her daughter worked there. What he didn't expect were the first words out of Maria's mouth.

"So the Civatateo are back?"

She kept her voice quiet as she uttered the "C" word. This didn't thrill Jess and as he dropped into the booth beside Maria, he made that clear in a look to Lena. She helplessly shrugged her shoulders. Maria caught onto the silent exchange immediately.

"Don't blame my mom. I've been hearing about them since I was a little girl."

"Bedtime stories," explained Lena.

"A bit on the macabre side," Jess pointed out.

"Not if you're warned they would come get you if you didn't behave," Maria said.

"How much have you told her?"

"Pretty much everything." Lena didn't apologize. She said it was her duty as a mother to protect her daughter. Maria lived by herself and worked at night. Since she refused to move back into the Stark house, something Jess could understand, and was "pigheaded like a mule," Lena wanted Maria forewarned.

"I think the two of you are safe. You don't pose a threat," Jess said. "Unless you start talking about it."

"No one would believe us," said Maria.

"You two believe me," Jess pointed out.

"That's because I grew up with this," Lena said. "Maria isn't so sure."

"Really." Jess stared at Lena's daughter.

"I've heard all the stories. I can't deny something came from down there. But it's most likely a freak of nature or science gone seriously wrong. Not these superstitious tales."

"That's because you've never seen one," Lena admonished.

"Neither have you!"

"Well, I have," said Jess. "My father is one."

That put a stopper in the debate between mother and daughter.

"It's time to put an end to this. In order to do that, I need to know anything else you can tell me about the Civatateo."

"I only know what I've heard," said Lena.

"Let's start with my father. Why is he the only one walking around? What about the Meadowland patients?"

"The Civatateo only turn a few. Otherwise there would be too many and impossible to stay hidden," Lena explained. "Once the victims are no longer useful as food, they are allowed to die."

"So we shouldn't expect to see Edward Rice up and at 'em anytime soon?"

"It would be hard to explain since he was left for the police to find," said Maria.

"So was my father."

"But he is in the shadows. So far, you're the only one who has seen him," countered Lena.

"I'm pretty sure he has been reaching out to my brother and mother."

"But he never entered the house."

"Because he had to be invited in?"

Lena shook her head. "The Civatateo go wherever they want. He only thinks this because that's what he was told."

"By whoever turned him," realized Jess. Lena didn't correct him. He thought back to the eerie conversation in the SUV outside Rice's house. "My father does seem to be under someone's thumb. Why can't he just resist?"

"It is difficult. Their maker's blood runs through them. It's like going against one's mother or father."

Well, that was certainly something Jess could relate to.

"Where would they be during the day?"

"Somewhere the sun doesn't shine."

"Is that the only way to kill them?"

"As far as I know," answered Lena.

"What about all the other stuff? Stakes? Crucifixes and silver bullets?"

Maria laughed and jumped in. "Silver bullets are for werewolves. The rest are superstitions handed down through storybooks. They call the Civatateo a vampire because it rises from the dead and walks at night. I know my mother told you the story about the pregnant woman who died near the crossroads. More than likely it's Mother Nature getting her signals crossed. We thrive during the day and our body craves sleep at night. But some things work conversely—blood bubbling from the moon's tidal pull or plants that only bloom after the sun sets. The fact that sunlight has such an adverse effect on these creatures might just be the opposite of the night environment which makes them flourish. Think of it as science run amok."

Jess marveled at Maria's calm and rational scientific explanation for the horrors he had witnessed. He turned toward her mother. "Don't ever say they're not teaching her anything at that college."

"She's smart, my Maria," boasted Lena.

"Don't you hate when your parents talk about you like you're not even in the room?" asked Maria.

"Better than not at all," mused Jess.

Lena took his hand. "I know you think that, Jessie. But they thought of you all the time. Your mother was never the same after you left."

"That wasn't because of me. But that's another story."

He released Lena's hand and straightened up. "So, we just have to find where my dad and his new 'father' hang out during the day, drag them into the bright sunshine, and watch them fry to a crisp."

Maria's smile was drop-dead beautiful. "Is that all?"

❋   ❋   ❋

As they walked out to the parking lot, Jess made Lena promise not to tell anyone at the Stark house she had seen him. He wasn't concerned for himself; he just didn't want Lena named as an accomplice aiding and abetting a felon. That resulted in a crying jag from the elder Flores woman that was only appeased when Jess threw his arms around her, told her he loved her, and would be in touch as soon as possible. Lena dried her eyes and, after being reassured by her daughter that she was okay, drove off, leaving Jess and Maria alone in the Oasis parking lot.

Jess walked Maria toward her car. "Where are you going now?" she asked.

"Some place Burke wouldn't think to look for me. Now I just have to find wherever that is."

"I've got a couch. I can't promise it doesn't have a dozen lumps but last time I checked it was available."

"I appreciate the offer. But I don't want you involved any more than you already are. Your mom is upset enough."

"Don't be stupid, Jess. You said it yourself. The cops are going to knock on every motel door from Palm Springs to Indio. They won't look for you in the closet-sized apartment that your housekeeper's daughter rents."

"I'm sure it's a lot nicer than you're making it out to be."

"You haven't seen the couch."

Jess protested a few more times. Then, not so much. He was dead tired with no place to go and Maria made sense. He followed her a half-mile to her apartment and parked in the covered garage to keep the SUV off the street.

The place was small but tasteful in every way possible. Jess would have admired it more but was practically asleep the moment he landed on the perfectly fluffy couch.

When his cell phone woke him at seven thirty the next morning, he was under a blanket, and Maria must have wedged a pillow under his head. Jess stared at the number, cleared his brain, and then recognized it. He sat up and hit the talk button on the phone.

"Cisco. What did you find out?"

His contact had worked his magic and gotten his hands on Tracy James's credit cards. It showed only one item purchased in the past forty-eight hours.

A one-way ticket for an airplane flight, two nights ago.

The night before Clark James said he had lunch with his daughter.

The ticket was for Puerto Vallarta in Mexico.

TRACY BEFORE

Planning the surprise party proved to be more difficult than Tracy could have ever imagined. The first problem was she had been spending practically every waking moment (and a whole lot of sleeping ones) with Jess since they got together in the near calamity on Palm Canyon Drive. They had gotten used to knowing exactly what the other was doing when they were apart, making it difficult for Tracy to make the necessary calls to pull the thing off. More than once she resorted to sitting in the bathroom, whispering to a caterer or tracking down a high school friend's address.

The second issue was where to throw the party. She had hoped it would be at one of their two houses, both of which were built for entertaining large groups, but neither Clark James nor Jess's parents offered up their places. She felt that both families were conspiring to keep the two of them apart—or at least weren't supportive of the relationship. Clark James wrote it off as just a passing dalliance until Tracy returned to Dartmouth for her senior year. She hadn't had the nerve to tell him that Jess was going to accompany her. Kate Stark was lovely, but completely dominated by a husband who was a self-absorbed asshole. Tracy knew Walter was constantly trashing her as Hollywood garbage and Jess had already had a few run-ins with his father about seeing her. Tracy was counting the days till summer ended and they could escape the Springs and, specifically, Walter's toxicity.

She finally settled on a nice Mexican restaurant in downtown Palm Springs. Multicolored decorations and table settings, a mariachi band, a giant ice sculpture in the shape of a margarita glass pouring an endless stream of tequila, and a donkey piñata made for a festive setting to celebrate Jess's twenty-second birthday. He was completely floored (or at least acted like it) when she escorted him through the door for a supposed quiet celebratory dinner for two and saw fifty partiers screaming "Surprise!" at the top of their lungs.

Tracy was gratified that Jess was so happy to see the high school classmates she had located. His good friend Benji Lutz had been unbelievably helpful providing names and numbers, and she gave him a big hug of thanks after sharing a twirl on the dance floor. Jess spent a good amount of time with the football coaches and his former Desert Chapel team-mates, reliving past glories that led to a healthy assault on the piñata by the former Triple A high school champs.

Clark James had agreed to bless them with his presence and spent most of the party holding court in a corner talking about the movies he had made. Sarah tethered herself to the ice sculpture and was completely sloshed by the time the cake arrived. She sang louder than anyone else and was dreadfully off-key, but Tracy was thankful she didn't make more of a scene. Eight-year-old Harry took turns dancing with Lena and her exqui-site teenage daughter, Maria. Kate Stark sat at a table with a couple of her friends that Tracy had invited to make sure Jess's mother had someone she could talk to during the evening. Tracy kept checking on her, but Kate insisted it was a lovely party; she was having a very nice time and more than once apologized profusely for Walter's tardiness.

As the evening progressed, it became clear Jess's father wasn't just late. He was a purposeful no-show. Tracy got angrier the later it got. Her heart broke every time she saw Jess's glance toward the door waiting to see if his father would miraculously appear, or when he would look over at his mother's table to check if Walter had snuck in when he wasn't looking. Jess was such a fantastic guy and it irritated Tracy to no end that his father couldn't see or refused to acknowledge it. The fact Jess still sought his fa-ther's approval made her even crazier.

As they lay in bed that night recounting the events of the party, she fi-nally asked if he felt badly his father hadn't shown up.

"Fuck him," Jess replied. But he smiled as he said it, kissed her deeply, and thanked her for arranging one of the best nights of his life. He drifted off to sleep quickly afterwards.

Tracy remained wide awake. As the wee hours slipped away, she grew increasingly pissed at Walter Stark.

She decided it was time to confront the prick and put this to rest once and for all.

13

When Maria first suggested she accompany him to Mexico, Jess wouldn't hear of it. He had no idea what was down there, but was certain it was dangerous; the last thing he needed was Lena Flores's eternal wrath foisted on him should anything happen to her precious daughter. That argument was immediately dismissed by Maria. She was over twenty-one and able to make her own decisions.

"You're forgetting that I have to allow you to come with me," countered Jess.

"And how do you plan on getting there? The police are looking everywhere for your SUV. Especially at the border if they're convinced you're on the run."

It was all over the morning news: radio and television, print to follow. Edward Rice, prominent Palm Springs physician and entrepreneur, discovered by his fiancée, Sarah Stark, found brutally murdered in his home. The police had released a statement that they were looking for Sarah's brother, Jessie Michael Stark, for questioning related to the crime.

"You're already harboring a fugitive."

"So, I'm already screwed. In for an ounce, in for a pound. Besides, I know you're not running—you're going there to get answers."

That was true, thought Jess. Everything that had unfolded in Palm Springs over the past few days seemed to have roots in Mexico. Fifty miles east of Puerto Vallarta, deep in the jungle, lay the tiny town of Santa Alvarado. It was where Lena had been raised in the shadow of the Civatateo. It was where disaster had befallen Clark James's movie and most likely unleashed an ancient evil.

Now, five years later, that malevolence had found its way to the California desert.

The fact that Tracy James had not reported Jess missing after the attack beside the pool had bothered him since he had escaped his desert burial ground. Her father lying about lunch the previous day was troubling, and Tracy rushing off without telling anyone even more so. Now that Jess knew she had fled directly for Civatateo Ground Zero, he was certain it wasn't a coincidence. What Tracy might find there, the answers Maria mentioned, filled him with absolute dread.

"It could be extremely dangerous, Maria."

"I know what I'm getting into. Remember, I've known about this a lot longer than you."

"Still . . ."

She let out a string of Spanish sentences that caught Jess off guard.

"What the hell was that?"

"Exactly."

"Excuse me, but I don't speak Spanish." No sooner were the words out of his mouth than he understood—that was the point. "Oh."

"It's bad enough being a gringo who's poking around trying to find a beautiful girl in a village where no one speaks English. Even if they understand you, they won't let on. They'll just hassle you. If you don't handle things right, the Civatateo will be the least of your problems."

Reluctantly, Jess recognized a valid argument when it was presented. He began to relent. "Why are you doing this, Maria?"

She casually flicked back a few strands of hair, revealing the entirety of her exquisite golden face. "Your family has been good to my mother, Jessie. She would have . . ."

Maria broke off; her deep dark eyes filled with heartfelt emotion as she corrected herself. "*We* would have been deported years ago if it weren't for them. We wouldn't have had a life. I never would have gone to high school, let alone college, if your family hadn't stood by us."

She took his hand. "I know you battled with your father when he was alive. But now he's struggling with something unimaginable and it's threatening to tear your family—*my* family—apart. The least I can do is offer to help. So please, please let me take you to Mexico."

Jess let his hand linger in her soft palm. It was hard to fathom this was the same girl who used to hide behind her mother's starched uniformed skirts. Jess couldn't believe Maria had escaped his notice all those years. But here she was all grown up, and he found it next to impossible to deny this alluring woman anything.

"You'll have to tell your mother."

Maria let go of his hand and practically yelped. "Are you crazy? She'd kill you! No, Jess. We're not telling a soul."

Jess saw something in Maria he hadn't seen up to this point. Get-the-fuck-out-of-my-way determination.

"We're going to Mexico," she said. "And we're going to send whatever that thing is back to the hell it came from."

And that, Jess thought, *was that.*

❋　❋　❋

Maria lowered the garage door and used a key to lock the SUV inside it. Jess was behind the wheel of Maria's car, a baseball cap low on his forehead. Maria had called in sick to the Oasis and had the next few days off, so no one would notice her dropping out of sight for a while. The first stop was a drugstore where she went inside to pick up a few provisions along with a pair of sunglasses for Jess.

They took off for the interstate and drove in silence for about an hour until they reached I-15. Maria was surprised when Jess started to head north instead of south, but he told her to trust him. He took the first turn-off and pulled onto the frontage road. He parked and asked Maria to give him a few minutes.

He got out of the car and walked over to a barbed wire fence that bordered a cornfield. Jess pulled out his cell phone and dialed a number. It rang only once before Harry answered on the other end.

"Where the fuck are you, Jess?" his brother whispered frantically.

Jess could hear commotion in the background. Sounded like the Starks had breakfast guests in police uniforms. "I think you know I can't answer that."

"Hold on a second."

Jess heard Harry make some kind of excuse and open a door as his younger brother obviously stepped outside the house. "The place is crawling with cops."

"Big surprise." Jess glanced at the car where Maria was watching him. He held up a couple of fingers to signify he wouldn't be long, and then turned his attention back to Harry. "I just wanted to call and tell you I didn't kill Edward Rice."

"I know that."

"Really."

"The guy was a total prick. Probably deserved it. But you don't have it in you."

Jess was comforted by Harry's belief in him. He might not have been so automatically trusting if the shoe had been on the other foot. "I'm sure the cops feel differently."

"They're ready to hang you. So is Sarah, but she'll get over it—soon as the next loser guy comes along."

Jess realized again he had been gone from home forever. Housekeeper's daughters had blossomed into ethereal beauties and baby brothers had grown wise beyond their years.

"You're going to hear a lot of stuff about me the next few days. You've probably gotten quite an earful already. Most of it isn't true. Anything I've done since being back has been for you, Mom, and, believe it or not, Sarah. Maybe one day she'll see that."

"I wouldn't hold my breath." Harry chuckled and Jess cracked a smile. But an awkward silence followed and Jess could sense his brother getting more serious, which pained him to no end.

"Am I going to see you again, Jess?"

"Of course you will, Harry."

"You have to promise me."

"I do."

He heard a sigh of relief, and then someone yelling in the background. "They're looking for me. I gotta go."

"You can't let them know I called."

"I won't."

Jess was about to hang up when suddenly words flew out of his mouth he didn't expect. "Love you, kiddo."

"Me too." Then Harry was gone.

Jess clicked off the phone and stared at it for a moment. Then he hurled it into the cornfield and walked back to the car. Maria was shaking her head as he strapped his seat belt.

"What did you do that for?"

"Cops decide to trace the phone, they'll find it off the I-15 headed north. Might make them think we're headed to Vegas."

"Not bad."

"We can pick up a disposable before we hit the border." He swung the car around and headed for the southbound ramp.

"So, who were you talking to?" she asked after they had driven a few miles down I-15.

"Does it really matter?"

"Yes. Everything matters. We do this, Jess, no secrets."

There was no wiggle room in her tone. So, he told her every single bit, including the tender sign-off with Harry.

She smiled. "Maybe you'll work out this family thing after all."

Jess didn't respond. But maybe, just maybe, Maria had gotten to the heart of the whole goddamned thing.

The ride south was pretty much a control for what played on the iPod. Jess was happy to see she had plenty of Springsteen. But after a half dozen tunes, Maria pointed out that there were other artists in the world besides the Boss. Jess feigned mock horror and demanded she back her outrageous claim. He put on the cruise control to settle non-obtrusively into the traffic flow and leaned back to see if Maria could prove her point.

He was impressed by her eclectic taste of pop, hip-hop, and alternative music. But what particularly moved him were the emerging Latino artists she exposed him to—soothing yet vibrant melodies, vocals, and arrangements that felt contemporary but from a culture much older and more storied than a two-centuries-old America.

For a while, Jess forgot about the past few days. Thoughts of fang-bearing fathers, crooked cops, and dishonest dead doctors gave way to the pleasure of being on a road trip with a beautiful girl. Maria told him a little about her studies at San Luis Obispo and he amused her with anecdotes about running a service business in the City of Angels. Mostly they just enjoyed each other's company. Jess couldn't help glancing at her in the passenger seat. She appeared perfect without a trace of makeup and wore a blouse and skirt that was considerably distractive. He wished for a simpler time and place with Maria traveling by his side.

It was only when they would pass a highway patrol car or Maria would pop into a convenience store to grab drinks while he hid in the seat that Jess was reminded of the deep shit he was in and how many people were looking for him.

When they were about twenty miles from the border, Maria suggested they pull off the road and make the switch. Jess wasn't positive the search for him had extended to the border, but they couldn't take any chances. He found it ironic he was actually sneaking *into* Mexico when hundreds of thousands had risked their lives trying to do the exact opposite over the past few decades.

At least this time, when he got into the trunk of a car, it was of his own volition.

14

Once again, the wait inside the car trunk had seemed interminable. As maddening as the drive through the midnight desert had been, at least they'd been in constant motion. Fifteen minutes after he crawled inside Maria's trunk, the car slowed down—and went through fits and starts for over an hour. Jess knew they must have reached the line to cross the border. Even though Maria had kept a steady prattle going from the driver's seat with updates, the lurches and revving made him feel like he was in eternity's squeeze box.

The last ten minutes became a countdown—"seven cars . . . six more . . . five . . ."—and he held his breath when at last Maria called out, "one more." Jess didn't let it out when she floored the accelerator and sped off; he waited at least a half minute for a siren barrage that would come when the border guards realized their mistake. Finally, Maria yelled they were clear and Jess gulped in air like he had been underwater for a month.

She kept the car rolling for a good fifteen miles before pulling off the road. They had planned to drive at least half an hour before letting Jess out, both aware the Border Patrol probably had strategically placed agents waiting to pounce on overconfident traffickers. But Jess couldn't stand it any longer and was willing to take his chances.

He got in the passenger seat and let Maria keep driving. Jess hadn't been south of the border in over a decade and Maria was familiar with the landscape; she had been coming to Ensenada with high school friends from the time they were old enough to belly up to the Hussong's bar. As they rejoined the main road, Jess noticed how different things already looked even though they were only a few miles south of the USA. Abject poverty was prominent. Beggars were on practically every street corner. But the brighter-than-bright colors on the shops and buildings—majestic purples, vivid salmon oranges, blood-red scarlets, and cotton candy pinks—provided quite the contrast. The combination of darkness and hope was Mexico's lure. Jess could understand the romanticism of going there to lose one's self.

They headed for the small airport in Ensenada and stashed Maria's car in an out-of-the-way parking garage. She did the talking as they approached three different charter services to engage a flight to Puerto Vallarta. They had previously agreed not to run up charges on Jess's credit cards lest they be traced. No one knew Maria was with him and he promised the Starks would make good on paying her back any monies spent.

They settled on a four-seater and the flight almost made Jess yearn for the friendly confines of the car trunk. Maria sat up front with a pilot old enough to have fought alongside Montezuma, and Jess was sure they hit every damned burst of turbulence and wind shear between Ensenada and Puerto Vallarta.

Darkness was falling by the time they hit the ground and Jess resisted the urge to get down on his knees and kiss it. As they took a cab into the downtown area, Maria asked if Cisco had run down a hotel that Tracy James had checked into.

Jess shook his head. "The last charge was the plane flight. I don't think she was coming down here to lounge around the pool. She probably headed straight for Santa Alvarado."

Maria stared out the taxi window at the ocean's horizon. Wispy pink and purple tendrils were all that remained of the setting sun as the stars started to emerge.

"The road, if you can call it that, is horrible. You can barely navigate it during the day. I'm not even sure we would make it in the middle of the night."

Jess wasn't all that anxious to spend a bunch of time in Santa Alvarado after sundown. He liked the idea of getting there in the bright Mexican daylight and suggested they find a hotel, get a good night's sleep, and start out early the next morning. Maria's quick agreement led Jess to think she wasn't all that keen on an overnight stay in her mother's hometown either.

But sleep was a long time coming for Jess. As he lay in one of the double beds in a Puerto Vallarta tourist trap (he had suggested separate rooms, but Maria said it was silly to spend the extra money), Jess marveled at how quickly she had fallen asleep. Normally, the big distraction would have been Maria lying six feet away—a blind eunuch would have been tempted by the way the simple T-shirt she wore to sleep clung to her every pore.

But that wasn't what kept Jess tossing and turning.

Even though Santa Alvarado was over fifty miles away, Jess couldn't stop thinking about what had emerged from the darkness there. He couldn't shake the nagging feeling it knew they were coming. He half-expected the Civatateo to burst uninvited into the hotel room and make sure neither Maria nor Jess were ever heard from again.

Nightmarish thoughts stayed with him for a long time. It wasn't until the first cracks of dawn slipped through the flimsy curtains that he could let himself drift off to sleep and remain there.

They had breakfast in the hotel's café overlooking the Pacific. Jess barely picked at his pancakes, making semicircles in the syrup that threatened to solidify into a foreign substance. Maria looked out over the railing at early morning beach joggers and the bright turquoise water.

"How many times this morning have you thought about just renting a cabana and never leaving?"

"At least a hundred," Jess answered.

He was happy to see she had the same trepidation about the journey ahead. But it didn't stop them from checking out a half hour later.

While Maria went off to rent a car, Jess found a local place to access the Internet. For a few pesos he was able to go online and find pictures of Tracy James, which were simple enough to locate—she was the daughter of a film star and had accompanied Clark to numerous Hollywood premieres and parties. Jess noticed there had been fewer and fewer over the past few years, which was easy to understand as James had retired and Tinseltown was all about "out of sight, out of mind." He found photographs of Tracy and her father arriving at the Palm Springs Film Festival six months earlier. Clark was all smiles, looking like a billion bucks and ready for a comeback. His daughter's expressions alternated between a put-upon smile and "I-have-nothing-better-to-do-on-Saturday-night?" as she clung to her father's arm. Jess blew up two shots so Tracy was prominently featured, printed up a few copies, and stuffed them in his jacket pocket beside the photo of Clark James at the church in Santa Alvarado.

He met Maria at a designated corner. She swung by in an army-green colored jeep. Jess climbed inside and she navigated the twisted maze of downtown Puerto Vallarta. Twenty minutes later they put modern civilization in the rearview mirror and headed into the Mexican jungle.

Once the trees started to overhang the road, the asphalt quickly turned to dirt. Jess had picked up a map at the Internet café and was wrestling with folds and tiny towns whose names he couldn't pronounce.

"Don't bother with that," Maria finally told him. "You won't find where we're going on a map."

"Town's that small, huh?"

"It's not big. But the truth is most people won't admit it even exists."

"That sounds absolutely crazy . . ."

"But you know better," she said.

"Unfortunately, I do."

Maria swerved suddenly. A wild hog had appeared in the middle of the road. Both of them yelled. They really were out in the middle of fucking nowhere.

Still, Jess was continually impressed by Maria's calmness and determination. He was long past kicking himself for letting her accompany him. As every hour went by he couldn't imagine being in Mexico without her.

"When was the last time you were in Santa Alvarado?"

"We came back a few times when I was a little girl. Believe it or not, Mom has an aunt who still lives there. But after the movie disaster, we stopped coming."

"You certainly know your way around."

"Some things you never forget."

Maria suggested using her great-aunt's house as a base. Jess expressed concern that if the woman let Lena know where they were, there could soon be more visitors in Santa Alvarado. Maria told him not to worry— her great-aunt didn't have a phone, along with most of the town. Jess, not for the first time, wondered exactly what were they getting themselves into.

The trees and flora became so dense that for half the journey, the jeep was plunged into virtual darkness.

"Why do you think Tracy came back here?" asked Maria as she slowed to ease the increasingly bumpy ride.

"I'm not sure. I know she spent time down here when Clark was making *The Seventh Day*. But it must have something to do with all the hell breaking loose up north." Jess shrugged, considering it all. "Maybe someone she met? Something she saw?"

"Guess that's what we have to find out, huh?"

Somehow the road got even tighter—there was barely enough room for the jeep to stay atop the dirt. Jess considered them lucky they didn't run into a vehicle coming from the opposite direction; someone would have ended up in a ditch or river trying to let the other person pass. He couldn't imagine a film crew hauling gear into such a remote place and figured a bunch of it was brought in by helicopter. Probably the same airlift service that transported the near-death Clark James back to civilization when the movie shut down for good.

Every once in a while they would glimpse something indicating that a real live human being had passed down the road. A tossed beer bottle. A sign with a Spanish word on it. ("Bridge," Maria translated for him, but Jess never did see anything resembling one.) A couple of stripped cars. The first house, or to be more specific, shack, appeared two hours after they had last seen the Pacific Ocean. Santa Alvarado may have been only fifty miles due east of Puerto Vallarta, but getting there felt like plowing through a field with a machete for a solid year.

Jess expected Santa Alvarado to be like one of those towns in the States one finds two miles past the Resume Speed sign, like the shanty villages depicted in an old D. W. Griffith movie. But when the road widened ever so slightly and the jungle began to recede, he understood why Clark James moved heaven and earth to bring a film crew to the depths of Mexico.

Santa Alvarado was indeed small. If there had been more than one hundred structures, Jess would have been shocked. But each was an architectural wonder, built by laborers who approached their work with the passion and talent of true artisans. Red adobe roofs were in abundance and splashes of vibrant color made Jess catch his breath like Dorothy when she walked out of her house after the tornado plopped it down into a place that definitely wasn't Kansas.

"It's unbelievable," Jess said, taking it all in.

"Sort of stuck in time is what I always say."

Maria slowed down as they entered the main part of the town. Most houses had simple vegetable gardens in front; some even had corrals out back. There were two buildings that could be described as places of business—a market of some sort and what must have been a café as there were two tables set up out front.

"Welcome to downtown Santa Alvarado. My great-aunt lives just around the corner . . ."

Maria broke off as they both noticed a dozen people congregated on a tiny street. "That's odd," she said, throwing the jeep into park.

"What?"

"If you see three people together in Santa Alvarado, it's a town meeting. Something's going on. Maybe I ought to go check it out?" she suggested.

"Good a place to start as any." Jess said he would wait by the jeep and Maria headed toward the small crowd. He opened the back door and picked up a paper bag with snacks from the convenience store they had stopped at before leaving Puerto Vallarta. He grabbed a pack of M&M's and threw the shopping bag back on the seat. As he watched Maria approach the crowd and start a conversation, Jess felt a tug at his leg. A child no older than six with big yearning eyes was looking up at him and the bag of M&M's. Jess didn't hesitate a beat. He offered the candy to the child, who smiled and took it from his hand. He turned his attention back to Maria, who was speaking very animatedly with the townsfolk. Knowing he wouldn't understand one word even if he could hear it, Jess looked in the backseat to see what other snack he could scrounge up.

The shopping bag was gone. Jess's eyes darted in the opposite direction to see the kid race around a corner, giggling with the bag tucked under his arm.

"Wonderful," he muttered.

Jess turned as Maria was making her way back toward him. She wasn't happy. Concerned didn't even cover it. If Jess had to label her expression, he would have said freaked.

"What happened?"

"A local farmer just outside of town heard a big commotion in the middle of the night. All the animals were screeching and out of their pens, running around like crazy. Then, he heard a high-pitched squealing that turned out to be a pig lying outside the barn with its throat slashed."

"Sounds like a coyote or something got loose," said Jess. He only half-believed it.

"That's what the farmer thought. But when he was bending over the pig, he was suddenly attacked."

"Presumably not by a coyote."

Maria shook her head. "He said it was definitely human. But it was so dark he couldn't see."

"Then what?"

"He screamed and it took off into the night."

"I guess that's good," said Jess.

Maria hesitated before adding the last part.

"But not before it bit him."

15

They located the injured man at a roadside market where his wife had brought him to pick up bandages for his wounds. The farmer was in his mid-fifties and spoke no English, but the language barrier couldn't hide that he was completely flipped out. Luckily the bite had barely scratched the surface; his wife was applying some sort of plant salve to the wound. Maria said it was a local remedy for animal attacks and though Jess doubted the man's assailant was of the four-legged variety, the balm seemed to ease the farmer's pain. Jess knew they had to wait for the long-lasting effects, and more specifically what the man would feel like when the sun went down.

At first, the farmer was reluctant to talk, but he was a (for the moment) warm-blooded male who couldn't help but succumb to Maria's charm. Within moments she had him eating out of the palm of her hand. Unfortunately, he couldn't shed much light on the attack, as it had occurred so quickly. The farmer's screams and the animal's screeches had awoken his wife, and her emergence from the house made the attacker beat a hasty retreat. A short conversation with the wife added nothing. She had rushed to the barn and her fallen husband, concerned only with his plight. Jess and Maria thanked them both, wished the farmer a speedy recovery (*Good luck with that,* thought Jess), and headed back toward the jeep.

"What are you thinking?" asked Maria.

"That Tracy might not be the only one down here from Palm Springs."

"The Civatateo followed her?"

"She came here looking for something. Maybe it didn't want her to find it."

Maria pulled up in front of her great-aunt's house. A pair of yucca trees in pebbled planters framed the structure; it was the only home that didn't have a garden out front. But there was a large one in back and that was where they found Sophia Cordero, Maria's great-aunt, weeding a flowerbed.

Eighty if she was a day, Sophia attacked the green interlopers with the tenacity of a woman half her age. The garden was incredible, a botanical paradise borne from someone blessed with a green thumb. Jess could tell this was Sophia's labor of love, her life's work. The centerpiece was an exquisite white trellis with intertwining pink and white roses that climbed up and over the top. Wind chimes hung off branches dotted with dozens of ancient ribbons that had faded to off-white from the vibrant colors they had been years before.

The moment Sophia saw Maria, she dropped her garden shears and rushed into her great-niece's arms. There was plenty of joyful crying and laughter as Jess waited to be introduced. He was surprised when Sophia approached, immediately hugged him tightly, and a melodious "Welcome, Jessie" escaped her lips in perfect English.

He was worried she had been forewarned of their arrival by someone to the north and the consequences that would bring. But Sophia quickly appeased those fears, saying Lena had written numerous letters over the decades with plenty of pictures chronicling her life in the Coachella Desert. Sophia recognized Jess the moment he stepped foot in the enchanted garden.

She also told them she knew exactly why they had come.

"The Civatateo. It is back, yes?"

Jess and Maria exchanged a quick look. Maria's almost imperceptible nod confirmed what Jess sensed immediately about Sophia—there was no fooling this woman.

"Yes," said Jess. "We think so."

Sophia surprised him further by taking it completely in stride, as if they had been chatting about a slight turn in the weather. "Then we should talk. But not on an empty stomach. You must be starving. I'm sure you haven't eaten since leaving Puerto Vallarta, unless you caught or shot something."

Jess laughed. Maria took hold of his arm and urged him toward the house. "You're in for a treat."

Maria wasn't kidding. The small kitchen didn't have an appliance built since Kennedy took office, but the ceramic wood-burning oven and vintage stove were so steeped in aromas, herbs, oils, and spices from decades of delicacies, anything prepared on them had a head start any three-star chef would salivate over. Sophia made paella from rice she had smoked the night before and Jess and Maria were given specific tasks to help. Caught up in the meal preparation and Sophia's boundless enthusiasm, Jess was grateful to concentrate on something else and he relaxed for the first time since they had crossed the border.

While waiting for water to boil and rice to cook, Sophia brought out photos from Lena and Maria's annual visits many years before. Jess made fun of Maria's attention-getting poses captured on Kodak snapshots— tongue sticking out, silly dances, way too much makeup for a six-year-old—but there was no denying Maria had always been a beautiful girl. With great pride and love, a younger Lena and Sophia watched her parade around the small house that hadn't changed one iota. Next came pictures sent by Lena of a young Jess in similarly embarrassing situations. Maria got a particularly big kick out of him in a ridiculous cowboy outfit. He was touched and a bit envious of this chronicled Palm Springs life Lena had carved out for herself, showing off the family Lena was much more a part of than Jess.

They sat outside at a hand-carved wooden table drinking sun tea and eating paella that Jess would have been content to drown in. As the meal wound down, he could feel a gloom sink in as the conversation took its inevitable turn.

"How did you know what we came back here for?" he asked.

"I heard what happened to Juan Carlos last night." She turned toward Maria. "Now you come for the first time since the madness five years ago.

There could be no other reason. I always knew the Civatateo would return."

"And yet you stay," said Jess.

"I can't leave."

"Why not?"

For the first time since they had arrived, the brightness in Sophia's eyes dimmed. A mistiness filmed over them. "Because of Luis."

Maria nodded. "Luis Mendoza."

"The love of my life," explained Sophia.

Maria had obviously heard the story many times, but urged Sophia to tell it to Jess. Even before she started, he could tell it simultaneously brought joy and sadness to the old woman—joy because she loved remembering anything about this man and sadness because there must have been a tragic ending.

"You could say we knew each other since the day we were both born."

Indeed, their mothers had given birth within hours of each other, two villages apart. Though they hadn't actually met on that blessed day, the midwife who delivered them both told Sophia's mother about the beautiful baby boy she had just brought into the world. When their mutual birthday rolled around the following year, the midwife arranged a party and the two infants crawled around together in the very same yard they now sat in. On the next birthday, the celebration was at Luis's home and Sophia's parents rode alongside as she sat on a brand-new pony to attend the party in the next village. They continued to alternate homes each year until they reached their teens. By then, Luis and Sophia were seeing a whole lot more of each other than once a year; they were inseparable, wearing out the path between their two villages, just waiting for the day they came of age and their parents would bless their inevitable marriage.

On their sixteenth birthday, both villages turned out to celebrate the nuptials of their favorite son and daughter—the love story having become a local fable—and the preparations went on for a joyous week.

Sophia pointed at the white wooden trellis. "Luis and I built that from the ground up. We carved the wind chimes and hung them from the top. Everything was perfectly planned." She hesitated, her eyes drifting up and down the trellis. "Except my wedding bouquet. Pink and white wild roses. Somehow it had been misplaced in all the preparations."

Sophia took a deep breath and Maria said she didn't need to continue. But the old woman wasn't one to not finish what she started. "So, me, being the hysterical bride, burst into tears. The whole thing was ruined, I said. But Luis, my dear, dear Luis, promised to make things right."

Luis told her he knew a place where a patch of wild roses grew and it was easy enough to fetch them. Sophia, realizing she had gotten overly emotional from pre-wedding jitters, told him he needn't bother—the offer was sweet enough and she would make do. But Luis wanted her to be happy and took off before she could utter another word.

"Luis promised to be back long before the wedding was to start. He left shortly before sundown."

The best man and father of the groom went looking once Luis had been gone two hours. Soon after, the entire wedding party took up the search. At nine o'clock, when the ceremony was supposed to commence, all the guests had joined in. By midnight, people began to give up and offered condolences to an inconsolable Sophia, who clung weeping to the white trellis.

The term "cold feet" wasn't part of the vernacular in those days. But Sophia never thought Luis had abandoned her. As if she needed proof, the next morning when the sun came up, a handful of freshly picked pink and white roses was found on the outskirts of the jungle. That they were tinged with blood didn't dissuade Sophia from clutching them to her breast with hope Luis would return after having lost his way.

He never did.

At least not the Luis Mendoza she knew and loved.

A year later, on the birthday she and her betrothed had always shared, Sophia was lying in bed unable to sleep. It was completely understandable. They had never spent that day apart. The wind chimes echoed in the night breeze. Sophia thought she was dreaming while still awake. She heard a voice, distant, buried in the breeze. She couldn't make out anything at first, but then realized it was calling her name. She knew it must be Luis— but by the time she opened the door, it had faded, and the only sound was the twinkling wind chimes on the trellis.

She had walked over to the swaying chimes. She had planted the pink and white roses they had found on her wedding night. In twelve months' time they had withered, rebloomed, and grown halfway up the notches, intertwined like two lovers holding onto each other for dear life. Maybe it was a trick played by the moonlight, but Sophia swore they were flecked with drops of blood.

When the sun rose hours later, the petals started to fall and the blood had disappeared.

The same thing happened on every subsequent birthday. She would hear Luis calling, but he would never arrive. Come morning, the ground would be strewn with bloodless petals and the yearlong wait would begin anew.

"How can I leave? How can I not be here when Luis finally finds his way back to me?"

If Jess hadn't experienced the past few days, he would have chalked this up to the ruminations of a mad woman. But he had learned, way too quickly, not to dismiss anything he couldn't rationally explain.

"You think the Civatateo took him that night?"

"I am sure of it," Sophia replied with quiet certainty. "Just as you are sure it has returned once more."

"I think it took my father. And now it may be back here chasing someone else."

Jess pulled out the photographs. He handed Sophia one of the blowups he had made of Tracy. "Have you seen her?"

Sophia looked long and hard at the picture. "Not recently. But I remember her."

"You do?" Maria asked, surprised.

"She was here when they were making the movie. Her father is the film star."

Jess flipped past the Tracy pictures and pulled out the wrinkled photograph of Clark James standing in front of the church.

"That's right," said Jess. He pointed at the actor. "Clark James. He retired after that."

"I'm afraid I don't keep track of those things," she said. He started to take the church photo away, but Sophia clung onto it.

"But you might want to talk to him," Sophia said.

"Clark James?" asked Jess. "I did, but he's back in Palm Springs. At least he was the other night."

"I was talking about *him*."

She pointed at the man Clark James had his arms around, the curly haired, Hawaiian shirt-wearing screenwriter of *The Seventh Day*.

"Perhaps this girl came here to talk to him," explained Sophia.

"The guy who wrote the movie?" asked Jess.

"He's been here all this time. Living in the strangest house you have ever seen."

16

Sophia had told them where to find the writer's house. The dirt road wound through gargantuan trees and clumps of vines, and was sparsely traveled. Jess couldn't spot a single tire tread in either direction. As they plunged deeper into the jungle, Jess thought Maria's great-aunt had led them on a wild goose chase. But then, the dense foliage cleared and the house was upon them.

Strange was hardly an exaggeration.

It sat perched atop a tiny hill like something from an Antoni Gaudí nightmare. It wasn't so much its twisting and bending shapes that the Catalan architect was known for. What was truly bizarre were the colored tiles that literally covered every square inch of the structure in a peacock-like mosaic. The setting sun glinted off the ceramic glass, casting a rainbow sheen over its surroundings. It was so completely out of place, it might as well have been an alien spacecraft.

Maria parked the jeep at the base of the hill. There wasn't a driveway, only crudely fashioned steps that forced a visitor, and presumably the occupant, to get two hundred feet of exercise every time they came or went. They got out of the jeep and Jess led the way up the stairs.

No sooner had they reached the top step, maybe fifty feet from the front door, when they were blasted by an eruption of light that could illuminate a small stadium. It poured from the ceramic tiles, en masse.

"What the fuck!" Jess yelled.

Maria gasped and covered her eyes.

There was a mechanical squawk, followed by a command. "Go away!"

Jess shielded his eyes while trying to face wherever the speaker was located. The blinding lights had him completely befuddled. "Can you turn off the goddamned lights?!"

"You must leave. Now!"

But Jess hadn't come this far to take no for an answer. He stepped forward, even though he couldn't see the front door through the swath of rainbow brightness.

"We just want a few minutes of your time! You're Tag? The writer of *The Seventh Day*?"

Nothing came from the speaker, but there wasn't another demand for them to retreat, so Jess kept talking.

"We've come from Palm Springs looking for Tracy James."

This was met by silence until the disembodied voice finally punctuated through the speaker. "Tracy James? The actor's daughter?"

"Yes! Have you seen her?" asked Jess.

"No. Why would you think she is here?"

Jess didn't know how much to say. He waffled. "We're not sure."

But Maria put it right out there. "She may be running from the Civatateo."

There was a loud clunk and the lights dimmed by at least half. They heard the clanks of locks being undone, and the front door was thrown open.

The screenwriter stood before them. He wore another tropical shirt; a thin cylindrical metal tube hung off a chain around his neck. His hair was still curly and he wore the same glasses that were in the five-year-old picture Jess had in his pocket.

But his hair was as white as snow and he looked twenty years older than he did in the photograph.

"We should definitely talk," said the screenwriter.

His name was Tag Marlowe. (The nickname was never explained.) He had once been a structural engineer who had given up a steady career to become a struggling writer. He had knocked around Hollywood for almost a decade when Clark James finally optioned his sci-fi book, *The Seventh Day*, and commissioned him to write the screenplay.

They were seated in the living space Marlowe had created. Walls had been taken down (or never built) to form one gigantic room—it was a humongous studio apartment with books, computers, mismatched furniture, and one-way tinted glass windows. Marlowe could look out the latter whereas anyone approaching the house saw only the multicolored ceramic tiles. The interior was completely unique, but Jess couldn't tell if it was being used to launch a satellite or host the world's rowdiest frat party.

Marlowe described his work as an apocalyptic Western, *The Road Warrior* meets *The Stand* meets *Pale Rider* meets *The Grapes of Wrath*. Jess found it ludicrous how Hollywood people described projects as bizarre combo plates—like *Schindler's List* meets *A Bug's Life*, though he might fork over fifteen bucks to catch that flick. Tag's story took place seven years after an alien race wiped out Earth and chronicled the last few days of a hero's Odyssian journey home after the war ended.

Enter Clark James, who fell in love with Tag's book, had him adapt it, and decided to finance the film by shooting in the heart of Mexico. They had chosen Santa Alvarado because the actor had seen the pictures of Lena Flores's hometown and was convinced it was the *only* place to film his epic. Originally, they were only going to shoot in Santa Alvarado and the surrounding jungle. Things went swimmingly for the first half of filming. Clark James played the lead with an Eastwood *Man With No Name* panache, and the director was knocking off scenes ahead of schedule.

"We were going to shoot the climactic scene in a church where we revealed that Clark's character was actually a preacher," Tag said.

Jess showed the well-worn picture to Marlowe, who confirmed it was the very same one he was talking about.

"But the minute we set up scaffolding to mount cameras, the building practically collapsed." Tag pointed at the picture. "This was taken right as we were rigging. Half an hour later you would've seen dust spilling from the walls."

Jess remembered the misguided search party. "That's when you went looking for another site."

Tag nodded. "One of the locals knew of an old set of ruins about an hour to the east. He described them to Clark, who said to check them out, see if they were worth rewriting the script. Another man overheard this and warned us not to go there. Of course, try telling Clark James not to do something."

"His ego couldn't handle it."

"Exactly. Of course, he demanded we go right away. Didn't even want to wait till the next day."

Tag glanced out the tinted window—night had fallen but one couldn't tell from the glare reflecting off the tiled lights. "That proved to be a huge mistake."

"Who went?" asked Maria.

"It was James, the cinematographer, assistant director, and location manager."

Jess found it interesting the actor had lied and told him he hadn't been on the scout.

"What about you?"

Tag fingered the dangling metal tube on his neck chain. "James had me stay behind to rewrite the script. Penelope went instead."

"Penelope?" Jess repeated, picking up on the apparent reluctance with which the screenwriter mentioned her name.

"A girl from the village the location guy had hired as his assistant. She did odd errands. Took a lot of pictures." Marlowe let out an audible sigh. "Then, my heart."

He picked a framed photo off a makeshift desk and handed it to them. A striking Mexican girl in her late twenties stared up from behind the glass.

The engineer-turned-doomed-screenwriter stared forlornly at her picture. Recalling Sophia's wedding story and his own experiences in the Sands Motel five hundred miles away, Jess played a hunch.

"Let me guess. She died shortly after that and you sometimes hear her calling your name in the middle of the night."

Marlowe looked at Jess, flabbergasted. "How could you possibly know that?"

"I'm getting a handle on how this Civatateo goes about things."

❊　❊　❊

By the time night fell, the location scout hadn't returned.

No one had any idea what had happened until Clark James stumbled into the village the next morning. The actor was bloodied and more than half delirious.

James kept saying they were all dead and he collapsed in the arms of Edward Rice, the film crew's doctor. This time, when a search party went out, Tag Marlowe made damn sure he was on it.

"I kept asking James about Penelope, if she was one of the dead he kept rambling on about. He never said yes, but he didn't say no either, so I insisted on going along."

The ruins were an hour east, but only as the crow flies. By truck and machete (a couple of times they literally had to get out and hack their way through overgrown vines strung across the road), it took the better part of a day, and getting lost along the way didn't help matters.

They finally emerged in an open field where they found half-fallen rock structures that must have been built by Mayan cousins or distant relatives of whoever put up Stonehenge. Whether the ruins had been temples, ancient abodes, or statues was impossible to tell. Besides which, Tag and the search party were totally distracted by two other things.

First, there was an inordinate amount of cracked glass spread throughout the field—it was as if a hundred mirrors had exploded. Rays of sunlight flew off fractured shards. If caught directly in the face, it was momentarily blinding.

But what commanded their attention were the three slaughtered bodies in the center of the field. Ripped to pieces, and sounding very similar to someone's handiwork in Edward Rice's living room, it took them a while to ascertain these were the A.D., D.P., and location manager.

"What about Penelope?" asked a horrified Maria.

"She definitely wasn't there. So I was filled with hope when I went back to the village later that day."

But once they returned, that dream slipped away. The movie was immediately shut down and Clark James was airlifted by helicopter back to the States with Edward Rice at his side. The three bodies were seized by local authorities, written off as victims of a wild animal attack, and burned on a funeral pyre before anyone could protest (which sounded awfully familiar to Jess). The rest of the film crew packed their bags and headed for Puerto Vallarta to party away their per diem before heading back to California looking for the next gig. Tag refused to accompany them; he stuck around and patiently waited for some word about his beloved Penelope.

As days drifted by, along with almost all hope, Tag overheard stories whispered amongst the locals. The word "Civatateo" cropped up more than once, usually accompanied by someone making the sign of the cross and muttering a prayer. He quickly realized it was some sort of vampire lore but immediately wrote it off as Old World nonsense.

Until two nights later—when he heard Penelope calling him.

He had been staying on a small farm near the jungle border. Tag was sleeping in the cottage and shortly after three in the morning was woken up by what he thought was a gust of wind. As he sat up in bed, he realized something was scratching outside the door and his name was being called.

The voice was a whisper, but he would have recognized Penelope anywhere. Tag quickly hopped out of bed, threw on a robe, and opened the door.

But nobody was there.

The moon and stars provided little light and the night shadows cast by the overhanging jungle trees didn't help. As he stepped outside, Tag couldn't see much of anything, so he detached the cylindrical tube off his neck chain and squeezed it.

A bright light blasted out of one end like a laser beam. It wasn't a constant stream. He had to pump the tube to keep it working.

Again, there was nothing.

He turned to head back to the cottage. Penelope's voice called again, this time from behind him. Tag whirled around, but he was still alone.

"Tag . . ."

It came from the jungle. Tag squeezed the thin flashlight. It picked up something moving between the trees.

He darted forward, whispering. "Penny . . ."

As he got closer to the trees, he heard approaching footsteps.

Her voice was louder this time.

"Tag!"

Suddenly, he was in the middle of the jungle and it was pitch black. He started to aim the cylindrical flashlight, but a rush of footsteps caused him to drop it on the ground.

That saved his life.

He dropped to his knees and frantically searched for the metal tube. He had just wrapped his fingers around it when the night air was split by a ferocious roar. Tag squeezed the metal tube and the light beam splayed.

First, there were just trees.

And then—growls.

He swung the flashlight left and illuminated something that looked like a man. Stunned, Tag could only focus on the sharp teeth jutting from its gaping mouth. It caused him to momentarily lose track of the creature as the light winked out. He felt something swipe at his neck but was able to squeeze the flashlight again and train it on his attacker.

The thing—and it was more *thing* than man—recoiled in pain as the light beam blasted a *hole* in its chest. The creature howled but leapt forward as Tag squeezed once more and the ray of light opened up another hole in the thing's torso.

Tag, still on the ground, scampered backwards, but the creature was already moving away, deeper into the jungle, its unholy screeches filling the night.

And then it was gone.

"I think my hair started turning white before the break of dawn," Tag said.

Jess absently rubbed a hand over his own scalp. A few more confrontations with his father and he could start a select Hair Club with the screenwriter.

But Maria was concentrating on the cylinder Marlowe wore around his neck. "What exactly is inside that tube?"

Tag detached it from the chain as he explained. "There's a lot of downtime in Hollywood waiting for that big break, so I never quite gave up my first career. Being a proponent of using nature to advance science, I started working on alternative light sources."

He squeezed the cylinder. The light that poured out was unbelievably powerful and direct. It was similar to the blinding lights from the colored tiles that had assaulted their eyes when they approached the house.

Tag let the light die. "The truth was I kept thinking they were going to shut off my power if I didn't sell something, so I figured I might as well get as much free juice as possible."

"Solar power," Jess realized.

"Turned out I had the one thing that could harm these suckers hanging around my neck."

Tag dangled the cylindrical flashlight in front of them.

"Daylight."

17

"But why did you stay here?" asked Maria. "After what happened, why wouldn't you just leave?"

"I think I can answer that." Jess gave the screenwriter a sympathetic look. "Penelope, right?"

Marlowe offered a sad smile. "Look at me. What do you see?"

He didn't really expect a response, so he pressed on. "A nerd who makes things glow in the dark. When I'm not doing that, I write fiction for geeks like myself. I won't give you a sob story or wear a 'Never Been Kissed' sign, but neither would be farfetched. It took me traveling to another country to find a true soul mate—an exotic beauty who loved my stupid stories and laughed at my dumb jokes. To have that taken away, well, it was downright cruel."

Tag stared out the one-way glass. The lightness in his eyes, which came from remembering Penelope, faded away. "To have told her to go on the scout that day, when it should have been me . . . has almost been unbearable."

Jess could feel Maria's heart breaking and hatred for the Civatateo harden. "You had no way of knowing what was going to happen," she said.

"I've told myself that, but it falls on my own deaf ears. Instead, I've embraced the burden. I know Penelope is probably dead and this creature is most likely playing games with me. But if there's a chance, any chance, she might still come back to me—I will not abandon her."

"The last thing you need is false hope," said Jess. "But the Civatateo turned my father and I've absolutely seen him since he 'returned.' I won't say he's flesh and blood; he's actually something quite different, but he is definitely back."

"Then my efforts will not have been in vain."

"Your efforts being what exactly?" asked Jess.

"I figured it was only a matter of time until the Civatateo returned. I wanted to make sure that I was ready. I made it my business to find out everything I could about it."

Tag's recital of local lore matched most of what Lena told Jess back in the California desert. The writer emphasized the desire of the mother who died in childbirth not to be separated from her baby. According to legend, this accounted for the Civatateo reaching from beyond the grave for their beloved to join them. It explained Luis Mendoza haunting Sophia. Presumably the same could be said for Penelope calling for Tag to join her in the jungle.

It made Jess wonder about his father. So unfeeling and aloof in life, Walter would never be categorized as a family man. Yet, in his new incarnation, he had sought not only Jess, but Kate and Harry as well. Had being "turned" changed his father? Softened him up to try and atone for the multitude of sins he had spent a lifetime committing?

More than anything, Tag believed the Civatateo was a creature that wanted to be fed. It only *turned* a few—if it *made* too many, it would have competition to survive. The "turned" could prove useful by drawing their loved ones close so the Civatateo would have new blood to sustain itself.

Tag repeatedly heard there was only one way to get rid of the Civatateo—exposure to sunlight. The episode in the jungle confirmed this.

He held up the thin metal cylinder. "When this flashlight wounded that creature, it got me thinking. I remembered the glass shards in the field where we found the slaughtered crew. I could tell when whole, the glass pieces had been embedded in the ground in concentric circles. They had been positioned to pick up sunlight, even on the cloudiest of days."

"Who put them there?" asked Maria.

"No one knows. The legend of the Civatateo goes back generations. It might have been an offshoot of the Mayans or Aztecs as both were cultures way ahead of their time. We now trace many roots of scientific discoveries back to ancient civilizations. Why not the harnessing of solar energy? I imagine whoever the creature first preyed upon devised a way to keep it trapped by surrounding it in constant sunshine, above and below ground. Being cut off by the jungle and local superstition kept that field undisturbed for years."

"Until an egocentric actor and his take-no-prisoners film crew wiped it out in one fell swoop," said Jess.

"Exactly."

The puzzle pieces were finally falling into place for Jess. "That explains the house, the tiles, the blasts of light. You're doing what they did in the field—you're building a trap."

Tag nodded. "That creature took Penelope away from me. It deserves to go back to where it came from. And given your arrival in Santa Alvarado, I'd say an opportunity might present itself very soon."

"Why?" Maria asked.

"Don't you find it odd Tracy James suddenly returned to the place where all this first began?"

"I knew it couldn't be a coincidence, her rushing down here right after I showed her the picture. I just couldn't put it all together," said Jess.

"You're forgetting. Her father was the only one to survive the massacre. But *Clark James was there.* And afterwards he got extremely sick."

"Like my father. Who died." Jess saw the horror of what Tag was suggesting. "And then came back."

"You only have Edward Rice's version of Clark James's recovery. I would wager James would tell you the whole thing was a blur."

Jess thought back to his conversation with the actor at the country club and that summed it up pretty well.

Tag began to pace. "Now Rice has been murdered—maybe to cover up the truth. Until you got here, I had no idea the Civatateo had even taken root in Palm Springs. Which begs the obvious question, how did it get there?"

247

Tag stopped in his tracks, as if pausing for dramatic effect. "I only see one feasible answer."

"You're telling me Clark James died and came back too?" asked Jess.

"Can you prove that he didn't?"

They carefully went over everything. The movie shutdown; James's press blockade during his illness and recovery; the quiet way he announced his retirement afterwards. There was his father's comment at the party about Clark having a Dorian Gray painting locked in an attic. The actor being *turned* fell right in line with him not aging. Jess realized he had not seen Clark James during the day since his return to Palm Springs. He suspected a Google search of James's social life would find it limited to evening functions. The actor had even refused a drink that night at the country club bar, and it made him wonder if Clark James had a different liquid refreshment in mind for later on.

Jess also rethought the two assailants at the Jameses' house. He had always assumed one was Rice. The other easily could have been Clark James. His strong build fit. It could be the reason Clark berated Edward Rice on the balcony, blaming him for Jess's escape from the desert grave.

Jess shared these musings with Maria and Tag. Saying them aloud made them even more horrible—and real.

"It still doesn't explain why Tracy would come running down here," said Maria.

"Maybe it wasn't her idea," suggested Jess.

"You think it was Clark's?" asked Tag.

"He might be along for the ride. Especially if he's what you think. The farmer who was attacked last night? What's to say that Clark didn't get a little hungry?"

Tag and Maria exchanged looks and a mutual chill. On one hand it sounded insane, but on the other, the dots connected perfectly.

"If they are both here, there's only one logical place to go," Tag said.

"Where is that?" asked Maria.

"Back where it started."

"The field," realized Jess. "Can you take us there?"

Marlowe almost choked. "No Fucking Way. Even if I was crazy enough to say yes, in the middle of the night? Did I say No Fucking Way? If you insist, I'll draw you a map."

The sketch he made was crude, but the landmarks were very specific. Tag gave them a laundry list of reasons not to go, but Jess said short of inviting Clark James up to Tag's house for a midnight tanning session, he saw no other choice. Jess promised that they would leave early in the morning and return to Maria's great-aunt's house long before sunset.

He thanked the screenwriter and promised a full report. Maria hugged Tag and tried one more time to convince him to join them. He was able to resist her ample charms; clearly one brief encounter with the Civatateo in the jungle was enough for this lifetime.

As Maria and Jess reached the door, the writer called out. They turned around and snagged the two thin cylinders he tossed at them.

"Just in case."

Jess couldn't help but notice there wasn't even a crack of a smile on the prematurely white-haired man's face.

18

The proprietor was just closing up when they parked the jeep in front of the café. Maria sweet-talked the owner into letting them get something to eat. It was only eight o'clock and she asked why he was shutting down so early. The owner explained that the attack on the farmer the previous night had killed the evening's business and people were staying close to home instead.

Maria extolled the proprietor's culinary talents, which prompted the man to practically skip into the kitchen and cook up a storm. She told Jess the old adage "the best way to a man's heart is through his stomach" was a half-truth. Lena had taught her: praise the preparer, the subsequent supper so much sweeter.

Twenty minutes later, he presented a feast of spiced chorizo with exotic peppers, succulent mangoes, two kinds of flavored beans, and rice that melted the moment it touched the tongue. Maria invited the owner to pull up a chair and join them, and Jess enjoyed watching them alternate between his broken English and a flurry of Spanish. She told the proprietor how she had visited once a year as a little girl and he actually remembered Lena bringing Maria into the café on a couple of occasions.

Jess realized Maria was paving the way to ask a few questions and he admired her smoothness and gumption; she had a natural talent for getting people to open up. He dug out the photo of Clark James and Tag Marlowe standing in front of the church and let her lead the way.

Their exchange was mostly in Spanish and Maria translated. The proprietor referred to Tag as the "crazy man in the glass house." Maria said they had just come from there and threw in a few kind words on Tag's behalf, figuring it might save the writer a few rotten looks next time he ventured into the village. She told the owner they were more interested in the man standing beside Tag.

"The actor," the proprietor said in something resembling the English language.

Maria asked if he had seen him recently. Only in old movies on the television, the man told her. He remembered the disaster years before when the film had been shot and shut down, but he hadn't seen Clark James in person since the entire village watched the chopper airlift him into the cloudless sky.

Jess offered up the picture of Tracy. The man's face clouded over immediately.

"She was here. Last night."

It was early evening and she had come in to ask directions. When the proprietor realized what she was looking for, he tried to talk her out of it.

"She wanted to know how to get to the field," surmised Jess.

Maria confirmed this and was met by a barrage of Spanish, filled with plenty of invectives, warnings, and a healthy dose of freak-out. It ended with the proprietor getting to his feet and clearing the table even though they weren't quite finished.

"Well, that put a damper on the meal," said Jess. "What did he say?"

"She wanted to see the field of glass where the men died. Angel, the owner, told her it was an evil place and no one should go there. He refused to tell her anything else."

"How did she react?"

"Really scared—looking over her shoulder every now and then."

"Doing her father's bidding?"

"Could be," said Maria.

"What happened in the end?"

251

"She left. I asked if he'd convinced her not to go, but Angel couldn't tell. He did say none of the locals would be anxious to help."

"Still, she got at least a day's head start."

"Well, we're not headed there in the middle of the night."

"That's for damn sure," Jess said as he pulled out his wallet. He handed a clump of bills to Maria. "See if you can get him to let me use his phone? And tell him the food was as good as anything I ever ate."

Maria smiled. "That ought to help."

A few minutes later, Jess forked over a palmful of pesos to Angel, who clearly wasn't happy about it but couldn't deny Maria's plea, though Jess did have to dig into his wallet twice. Maria wanted to grab a few things from the little market if it was still open and told Jess she would meet him by the jeep. Jess picked up the phone and noticed Angel standing there watching. He politely motioned to the proprietor for a little privacy. Angel begrudgingly took two tiny steps backward, but kept his eyes peeled on Jess. Figuring he would just keep his voice low and Angel wouldn't understand much, Jess turned his back and dialed. It rang at least four times before Benji picked up on the other end.

"What happened? You actually get a customer?" cracked Jess.

Benji let out an audible sigh of relief. "Jesus, man. I've been wondering what the hell happened to you."

"I'm still standing."

"Thank fucking God. For a moment I thought . . ." He stopped mid-sentence as another notion occurred. "Wait a second. This isn't that phone call they let you make from jail, is it? 'Cause I love you, man, but I ain't no lawyer."

"I'm not in jail and I don't need a lawyer. Yet."

"I'd rethink that last part, dude. You were right. Burke hauled his lard-ass through here two hours after you split. Threatened me with obstruction of justice and the rest of that TV crap for not telling him where you went. I told him to look around—does this look like the kind of establishment that requires a forwarding address? That put the bugger in his place."

Jess stifled a laugh. Thank goodness for lifelong friends who wouldn't let anything faze them.

"Do I ask where the hell you are?" wondered Benji.

"Ask away. But you won't get an answer."

"Well, it was worth a shot." Then Benji remembered something. "I did hear they thought you'd taken off for Vegas. But I'm not hearing slot machines, so that's gotta be a dead end."

Jess smiled; the phone toss in the cornfield had bought a little time for sure.

"So, what's happening there?"

"Besides you being wanted for questioning and your family freaking out—it's chill, man."

"Do me a favor?"

"If I can do it, consider it done-done."

"Find out if Clark James is still in town."

"That's it?"

"For right now."

"Need to know where he specifically is?"

"Only if he's not in Palm Springs."

"Got it. How do I reach you? And no, I'm not asking for your cell. Just in case I'm not here when you call back."

"You're always there."

"Well, that's true," Benji sadly said and sighed.

"But if by some miracle you're not, leave something on the motel voicemail—one of your corny greetings like a 'here-here' if James is in town."

"I can do that. But for the record, 'here-here' is corny. My outgoings are priceless."

"I'm not going to debate that."

"What if he's split for somewhere specific? What do I say then?"

"You're clever. You'll figure it out."

Benji was mulling over a retort when Maria started screaming outside.

"What the fuck was that?" yelled Benji.

"Gotta go." Jess hung up and reached the café door five strides ahead of Angel.

When Jess got outside he couldn't see a damn thing. The café lights were dim at best. Maria's screams came from by the jeep, which Jess could barely make out in the shadows. It wasn't until three quick bursts of lights swiped the night, the last one accompanied by a ghoulish scream, that Jess got his bearings.

As he reached the jeep, something swiped past him and moved so quickly he only saw a fleeting shape. Whatever had screeched was breathing hard and took off deep into the night. Taking up the chase wasn't an option. Jess made a beeline for Maria, who was moaning on the ground.

She was squeezing the cylindrical flashlight in an unsteady on-off pattern, jabbing at it like a drunken telegraph operator struggling with Morse code. He knelt down beside her.

"It was closed . . ." she moaned.

"What?"

He eased the flashlight out of her hand and used it to illuminate the surroundings. Maria had blood on her face and was pointing across the street.

"The market. Closed." She gulped for air. "I headed for the jeep." Another big breath. "It came out of nowhere."

"It? Who?"

Her whisper was laced with terror. "Civatateo."

"Clark James?"

"I couldn't see. It happened so fast."

She began sobbing uncontrollably.

"Shhhh," soothed Jess. He cradled her in his arms as blood dripped on his hand. "You're hurt, Maria."

"I'm okay . . ."

But not really.

She passed out.

Jess sat on the chair beating himself up. His gut had told him it wasn't a good idea letting Maria accompany him to Mexico. If it hadn't been for Tag Marlowe's invention, she would have been dead—or possibly, in a couple of days, returning from it. It would have served him right if she had turned and made Jess her first victim for putting her in harm's way. This thought made him want to protect Maria more than ever; he could only hope she escaped this attack unscathed.

He glanced around Sophia's tiny living room. It was so spic and span, it was probably allergic to dust. A cozy fire burned in a stone hearth. The house was filled with ceramic bowls, books older than Jess's great-grandparents, and rugs so colorful they put a rainbow to shame. There was a small altar in one corner—the most prominent feature being a hand-carved painting of Christ framed by two candles. Jess couldn't remember the last time he had been in a church, but strongly considered moving across the room to say a prayer for the girl.

Sophia entered from a back bedroom. She flashed a smile that merci-fully let him off the hook. "She's going to be fine, Jess."

"Thank God."

"It scratched the side of her head. Ears bleed a lot. She was scared more than anything. Now she is just tired."

"We should let her rest, then."

"She wants to see you."

"Maybe in the morning . . ."

"She's insisting."

Sophia practically pushed him in the direction of the bedroom with a smile.

"Go, go, go. I won't hear the end of it if you don't go in there."

Jess didn't need convincing—of course he wanted to see her. "Just for a few minutes."

Sophia led him to the back. Before Jess knew it, he was standing by the bed; Sophia had eased the door shut, leaving the two of them alone.

The only light source was a single candle on the nightstand. Maria grinned when she saw him, and then winced. "Hurts when I smile."

"Then I won't tell you a joke."

She was half under the covers, wearing a flimsy nightshirt that Sophia must have unpacked. The blood on her face had been wiped clean; a tiny bandage was affixed to an earlobe. If Jess hadn't seen her on the ground outside the café, he would have thought she had just awoken from a pleas-ant dream.

In the candlelight, she was a vision fit for Goya. Maria patted the edge of the bed, urging him to sit.

Jess felt his heart skip a beat the situation shouldn't have warranted. He knew Maria ought to be resting, but it didn't prevent him from gently easing himself down beside her. "So you're feeling better?"

"Frankly, I don't remember much of anything. It was kind of a blur."

"Well, you used Marlowe's flashlight like it was a light saber."

"I carried a lot of pepper spray as a teenager. Mom insisted."

They both laughed. After a few seconds, Jess began apologizing. "Maria. I'm so . . ."

"Don't." She placed a finger on his lips.

He wasn't upset when she let it linger there longer than necessary before lowering it.

"What?"

"Don't say you're sorry. You didn't ask me to come here. I insisted."

"I could have kept saying no."

"Now that you've spent a few days with me, how do you think that would have worked out for you?"

"Hmmm. Not so well?"

"So, as the song goes, 'No Apologies.' What we need to do is head for that field first thing in the morning."

"Out of the question."

"We have to go, Jess."

"Not *we*, Maria. Me. You're staying here."

"No way," she said. "I didn't come all this way to stop here."

"Sorry."

"There you go apologizing again."

Jess started to raise his voice, his guilt spilling out. "You were lucky tonight. I can't take the chance . . ."

"Sshh! Sophia will hear you."

"Maria, I'm not discussing . . ."

She lunged forward and reached inside his pocket. She came up with a piece of paper. Jess groaned when he saw it was the map Marlowe had drawn.

"You can't be serious."

"Deadly." She smiled. "You want it? Come and get it."

She slipped the piece of paper inside her nightshirt.

Jess laughed. "C'mon, Maria. You're kidding."

Her expression showed she wasn't.

"Maria, I'm not going to do that." But saying it didn't mean it wasn't appealing—or all he could suddenly think about.

Maria raised herself up and moved closer to him. She was breathing heavier.

"That's okay. You don't have to."

Suddenly she was in his arms and her lips parted. Jess was caught by surprise—but not unwilling.

Suddenly, Jess was breathing heavily too.

She kissed him for a while.

Finally Jess broke them apart, knowing how crazy this was.

"Maria . . ."

She refused to let go. "I'm not going to apologize either. I've wanted this as long as I can remember. More than anything."

They stared at each other for what seemed like forever.

Then, this time, Jess kissed her.

Because, as it turned out, he wanted her more than anything too.

❋　　❋　　❋

Afterwards, they lay in the glow of the tapering candle, alternately kissing and laughing. It was still dark outside and Jess had no idea what time it was. He didn't care. For the moment everything seemed perfect and the trip that waited after dawn was something he didn't want to think about.

But he knew Maria was coming with him. And he vowed he would die before letting anything happen to her.

"What are you thinking about?" Maria asked.

Jess decided it was a good time for a little white lie. "What your great-aunt is going to say."

"Sophia?" Maria laughed. "She practically pushed you into bed with me."

"What about Lena?"

"My mom adores you. Sometimes, growing up, I thought she loved you more than me."

"Not for one second." The way Jess said it reaffirmed the preciousness of the girl wrapped in his arms.

For a while, they lay in silence. Jess was just about to drift off when the candle snuffed out.

"You never talk about her."

It was as if Maria had waited for total darkness to bring it up.

"Who?"

"Tracy."

"What is there to say?"

"You came all the way to Mexico to find her. You even ran away from the cops to do it."

"I'm here because of my father."

"I'm sure that's true. But Tracy's the one you're looking for. She must mean something to you."

Jess thought before answering. He wasn't weighing what to say—he was trying to get a handle on how he really felt.

"She did once. Not much anymore."

Maria laughed softly. "I'm not so sure I believe that."

Jess straightened up and kissed her cheek. "I wouldn't be here with you if that wasn't the truth."

Maria softly returned the kiss. And then asked the question Jess had been dreading.

"What happened between the two of you?"

"It's not important, Maria."

"Now you're lying, Jess. Whatever you do with me, if anything is to go beyond this moment together, please don't lie to me."

Jess didn't want to. He just had never voiced any of it out loud.

"What makes you so sure I'm not telling the truth?"

"Because you left home for seven years and never came back. And no one knows why you left."

"Some do."

"Then tell me."

"I've never told anyone, Maria."

"We're a thousand miles away from whatever happened. It can stay here—right here in this room. Never to be mentioned again if you don't want. But you should tell me. Please. I want to know."

"You might think different after hearing it."

"I know I won't."

She kissed him gently and forever.

"I know you," she said.

So he told her.

All of it.

TRACY BEFORE

She had made sure that he was going to be alone when she got to the house. Kate had mentioned at Jess's party she was going to New York on a shopping trip the next morning and taking Harry along for the ride. Tracy had seen Sarah stumble off with her Eurotrash boyfriend as the night wound down and knew she'd be at his place sleeping off all the alcohol. It was Lena's day off, which Walter Stark confirmed when Tracy called him on his cell and told him they needed to talk. He didn't stop her from coming over; he knew this was a long time coming and would be in his office. Then, he hung up, brusque and rude.

He hadn't always been that way. Walter Stark could be charming, funny, and actually make you feel like you were the only person in the world when he was talking to you.

Which was why he had been able to seduce her.

It had started up the previous winter at her father's Christmas gala, Clark James's annual charity for underprivileged kids in Palm Springs. The actor opened up his home to hundreds of perfect strangers and it fell to Tracy to serve as pseudo hostess. She had been home from Dartmouth for Christmas break and was sitting in a corner, out of her mind with a smile plastered on her face while greeting friends of her father she didn't give two shits about. When Walter Stark came over and started chatting, it was a blessed relief; at least he'd been interested in what was going on with her instead of trying to mooch off her famous father.

They drifted outside to the pool and had a couple of Cosmos. The drinks eased the shock she should have felt when Walter started flirting, but the truth was Tracy had been involved with a string of older men right out of high school. Boys her age didn't interest her; a shrink would chalk it up to an only child playing substitute wife for a larger-than-life father. So, an hour later, when they ended up in the pool house tearing each other's clothes off and having sex on the floor where she used to play Monopoly with her own dad, Tracy wasn't surprised. Looking back on how it began, she couldn't swear she hadn't initiated the whole thing.

They saw each other half a dozen times over Christmas break. Walter had her come by the house whenever his family was off spreading holiday cheer. Once she dropped by his office for a noon rendezvous. The other times he got her a suite at the Grand Champions in Indian Wells, where they enjoyed room service and each other, and where Tracy fell heavily for Walter Stark.

He was a fascinating man. He had come from nothing and built an empire in the Desert. But it wasn't Walter's money that attracted Tracy— her father's fortune was nothing to sneeze at. If she had to put a finger on something, it was the power he exuded. Seldom had she encountered anyone so self-sure and so completely in control of his environment Walter possessed the magnetism one read about in presidents like Clinton and Kennedy—strong men with very visible wives and children who also had secret lives playing out on the other side of the looking glass.

It didn't matter to Tracy that no one knew about them. She didn't need that. When Walter was with her, they were alone without anyone distracting them, wanting something, expecting them to do anything for anybody. They were just together. She loved hearing him talk about expanding his empire and was continually surprised by the amount of philanthropy he did. Walter Stark could be awfully generous when he wanted.

That didn't seem to spread to his family, the one subject he rarely broached with Tracy. Walter held them to a higher standard and was disappointed Jess hadn't embraced Walter's work and joined him at his side. He would make the occasional jab calling his eldest son a "free spirit"; he thought Jess's flights of fancy nothing but a waste of time. Now, in retrospect, Tracy saw the irony of falling in love with Jess for being precisely what his father hated—beating to a different drum.

The affair continued during spring break, when Tracy canceled her annual trip to Florida with her party-all-the-time sorority sisters and instead winged west to the desert. Clark James was surprised to see his daughter; she told him she wanted to get a jump on looking for a summer job. But the only place she hopped was into the poolside cabana at the Grand Champions where she spent most days and plenty of nights romping with her much older crush. Walter even flew back east a couple of times the next month and had Tracy meet him in New York City. They kept a low profile there too, but she didn't need to be taken out to dinner or Broadway shows. She was content learning the ways of the grownup world from a man who had made such a big splash in it.

As summer approached, the calls began to dwindle. She figured it was due to Walter's multitude of business interests. So she threw herself into studying for finals while thinking of the three months they would spend together trying to stay cool in the broiling desert sun.

But Tracy didn't hear from him the first week after she got home. She knew Walter was aware she was back in town; she certainly had told him enough times school ended right after Memorial Day. Tracy had even sent him funny emails with a countdown of sorts. But she hadn't gotten a reply.

Deep inside something nagged at her, but she excused it as him being unavailable because his family was underfoot, something Walter alluded to when he finally called and invited her up to the house one night.

She should have trusted her gut instinct.

When she arrived at the mansion, she was beside herself with anxiety and anticipation. She rang the bell at the gate and Walter's voice promptly came over the speaker. "I'm out by the pool." She quickly navigated the driveway, parked, and headed for the side gate, which he had left open.

Tracy walked up the side path and entered the backyard. The only light came from the fluorescents in the pool, where Walter was dog-paddling in the deep end. Tracy smiled, seeing he wasn't wearing a bathing suit, and for one moment everything was back to normal.

Then the other girl came out of the main house.

She was carrying a bottle of champagne and three glasses on a tray. She was naked, curvy as could be, maybe all of twenty-one—and Tracy had never seen her before in her life.

"You must be Tracy," the girl said in a way too cutesy voice.

Tracy didn't answer. She wondered what would happen if she killed the girl right then and there. Walter had swum over to the side of the pool where the girl was pouring him a glass of Dom. He gave her more than a peck on the cheek, never taking his eyes off Tracy.

"What are you waiting for? Take off those clothes and join us."

Tracy stood motionless. Tears began streaming down her face.

He responded with the cruelest smile she had ever seen. "What did you expect? That I was going to leave my family and run away with you?"

No, thought Tracy. She didn't expect that. She longed to tell him she just wanted to be with him whenever she could and didn't want to share him with anyone else.

Instead, she ran off.

As she drove up toward the Stark mansion, Tracy kept thinking about that night her life had changed so dramatically.

She had rushed out the side gate and hopped in her car, her eyes blurry from cascading tears. She barely made it down the steep curvy driveway, almost crashing a couple of times because she was hysterical and couldn't see. When she finally made it to the main road, she parked the car and started walking aimlessly down the street, sobbing openly, stumbling along trying to catch her breath and keep from vomiting.

Two minutes later, Jess came barreling down Palm Canyon Drive and almost ran her over.

As she parked in front of the Stark house, Tracy thought it was funny how life formed peculiar circles. Here she was arriving at Walter's front door to see him once again, but this time armed with firsthand knowledge of what a total prick the man could be. Fueled by her own self-loathing for being sucked into his web back then, it was now ignited by anger from Walter constantly disrespecting Jess and ignoring Tracy since they had hooked up. She strode into the house and headed directly to Walter's office, determined to let him have it.

He was behind the big oak desk signing checks and didn't even look up when she entered. "What is it?" he asked, never missing a scribbling beat.

"That, for starters. Me walking in a room and you acting like I don't even exist."

Walter didn't answer right away. He kept her waiting and signed two more checks. He finally looked up with eyes so cold the temperature in the room dropped ten degrees. "As far as I'm concerned, you don't."

She had been prepared for him to be a raging asshole, but Tracy was unnerved by how directly he went about it. She was so disgusted she had actually fallen for this man; she could barely muster up an ounce of self-esteem.

"Walter, I really don't give one fuck what you think of me. But it's unconscionable the way you treat and disrespect Jessie. Not bothering to show up for his birthday party—out of spite towards me? That just really sucks."

"Who do you think you are waltzing into my house, into my office, and telling me how to handle my son?"

"The woman who loves him. And is going to marry him, whether you like it or not."

Walter actually smiled. And that was the scariest part of all. As he got to his feet and stepped toward her, Tracy realized she had made a dreadful mistake in going there.

"Over my dead body." The hellacious smile never left his face. "What makes you think that I'd let Jess marry a piece of trash like you? A woman that screwed a married man? A woman who fucked her boyfriend's very own father?"

Tracy found herself backed up against the desk with nowhere to go. "I had no idea I would ever get together with Jess. Why can't you just forget what happened between you and me and let us be happy?"

He pressed up against her. "Because I would sooner tell him the truth than let him spend his life with a philandering liar."

"I've never lied to him."

"Have you told him about us?"

"Of course not."

Walter grabbed one of her hands and placed it on his crotch. Tracy was disgusted to see that the man was already growing hard. "Yeah. I can see how telling your fiancé that you sucked his father's cock in his office while the family was having a barbecue out back would be difficult."

Tracy ripped her hand away and Walter started laughing.

"What the hell?"

Tracy turned to find Jess standing in the office doorway.

She had no clue how long he had been standing there. The expression on his face said way too long.

"Jessie . . ."

Tracy's heart broke into a million pieces as Jess turned his eyes away from her.

She didn't know what else to say.

But Walter certainly did. He grinned piggishly at his son.

"Guess you didn't know you were getting your pop's sloppy seconds when you fucked her every night, huh?"

Jess didn't respond. He looked one last time at Tracy. There was a desperate plea in his eyes.

Before she could tell him how much she loved him, he was out the door.

Jess left Palm Springs by nightfall—and didn't return for seven years.

19

Shortly after Jess finished his story, it began to rain. For a while they just listened to the staccato of drops on the adobe roof. Jess wouldn't have been surprised if Maria could hear the heavy beating of his heart.

Or the whoosh of air from a burden being eased, one that he had carried alone for so many years.

"I can't imagine what that must have been like for you," Maria finally said.

"Imagine a movie loop constantly playing in your head. It's like that song which starts 'Welcome back my friends, to the show that never ends.'"

He let out an audible sigh. "The ironic thing was I went to the house that day to lay into my father about pulling a no-show at the party. I was sick and tired of him treating Tracy like dirt." Jess let the rain pitter-patter on the roof, remembering. "I guess the joke was on me."

"That sounds awful." She gently caressed his shoulder. "You really never talked to her until you came back to Palm Springs?"

He shook his head. "She tried to get in touch for a bit. A bunch of emails I deleted, calls I didn't take. I finally changed my cell phone and email address. I think she stopped trying after that."

She was quiet for a moment, and then spoke softly. "I presume I wouldn't have cared about hearing an explanation either."

"I didn't need one. Obviously, I've had a long time to think about it. I can't fault her for getting involved with my father except for having questionable taste. We hadn't gotten together yet. And I'm sure it was over once we started seeing each other." He stroked Maria's hair as he thought back. "I finally realized what hurt most was her not telling me about it. It made me wonder what else she had kept from me. Or would never know if we tried to carve out a future together."

"What if she had told you? Would you still have wanted to be with her?"

Jess answered quicker than he would have thought. "Probably not."

"Then you understand why she couldn't."

"Are you defending her?"

"No," Maria said and kissed his cheek. "I just feel sorry for her. I think she really loved you. I bet she still does."

"I doubt that."

"Somewhere deep down, I think there must be a part of you that still loves her. You wouldn't have come this far if you didn't."

"I told you, I'm here because of my father."

"And don't you find that strange? After everything he did?" She let out a little laugh. "And they think the mother-daughter bond is challenging."

"What are you saying?"

"That there's unfinished business between you and him."

"I don't think so. Bad enough he haunted me while he was alive. I'd like it not to continue for the rest of eternity."

"Did you ever think that Walter being *turned* might have actually changed him?"

"I'd say it just brought out his true nature."

"He left that warning on your windshield. He could have killed you at least twice but didn't. Maybe he just wants your forgiveness."

"I'm not sure I'm capable of that."

"Well, I think you're wrong. Otherwise you'd be back in Los Angeles by now." She kissed him again. "And that would make me very sad."

"Aren't you uncomfortable hearing all this? My dad? What happened with Tracy?"

"No one talked before and look where that got you." She pulled him close. "If this is going to be something more than a one-night stand, and I hope it is . . ."

"It is," Jess said, knowing it to be the absolute truth.

"Then, like I said before, no lies. No secrets."

His eyes had adjusted to the darkness and he traced his finger down the slope of her neck. He felt like kneeling in front of Sophia's tiny altar to give blessed thanks for this wonder in his arms.

"Warts and all, huh?"

"Warts and all."

Maria had been right about Sophia not batting an eyelash. The old woman smiled continually as she served them a mouthwatering breakfast of eggs, chorizo, peppers, salsa, and sweet yams; at one point she even whistled a wistful tune. There had been no commenting on the sleeping arrangements. Instead Sophia kept making natural references to "you two," as in "you two clean your plate" or "make sure you two get back before sunset," as if Maria and Jess had been together for years instead of hours.

Her only show of concern came when they were getting into the jeep. Sophia threw her arms around her great-niece and Jess, making them promise they would see her that evening.

"We'll be careful, Aunt Sophia," said Maria. "We're just going to go find Jess's friend Tracy, and then we'll be back."

Jess marveled at Maria's acceptance and grace. After hearing his tale in the darkness, he thought it unbelievable she would proceed on this journey without an iota of reluctance. But then he saw whom she had gotten it from.

"I'll set an extra place for dinner," said Sophia.

As they drove away from the house, Jess hoped not to disappoint her.

This time, Jess was behind the wheel. Maria had Marlowe's map in hand and guided him out of Santa Alvarado and into the jungle. At first it was a dirt road surrounded by huge trees that all looked the same. At times it got so dark Jess had to put on the headlights to see where they were going. He was worried they wouldn't be able to differentiate the landmarks Tag had drawn on the map, but he was able to breathe a little easier when Maria spotted the first one out the driver's side window.

"Twisted trees shaped like a heart."

Sure enough, two gigantic trees had wrapped themselves around each other like Daphne and her laurel leaves.

"Wonder if Tracy has one."

"One what?" asked Jess.

"A map. Angel certainly didn't tell her where to go."

"You're forgetting Clark was on that scout. He could tell her where the field was."

"Maybe he's with her."

"Doubtful," replied Jess. "If Clark James has been turned, he belongs to the night. Hard to believe he'd risk being trapped by daylight in the middle of nowhere."

"But he has to be down here, right? The attack on the farmer, the attack on me."

"I'd say that's a safe bet. Benji couldn't find him."

Before they had set out, Jess had given more pesos to Angel for another phone call. Benji didn't pick up, but the recording for the Sands Motel had the phrase "Gone Baby Gone" wriggled into it.

"He's probably lying low somewhere in the village during the day while Tracy went to the field."

"What is she looking for?" asked Maria.

"No idea. Hopefully we'll find out once we get there."

The deeper into the jungle they traveled, the more apparent it became someone had paved the way. They could see fresh tire tracks in the dirt road ahead. Occasionally the road narrowed from overhanging leaves and brush, but had been half-cut away by something propelling through it— most likely whatever vehicle Tracy had been driving.

The most disturbing fact was that the tire tracks headed only one way. Jess started doing the math. Tracy had asked Angel about the field the night before last. It was hard to believe she had gotten an earlier start than they had that morning and most of the tracks were pooled with water from a passing shower. This meant they had been there since before it began raining. Jess told Maria his calculations and she came to the same conclusion.

"She spent the night out there?"

"Either that or found a different way back no one knows about."

But given the lack of upkeep on the "main" road, neither believed the Santa Alvarado Highway Committee had constructed a second one.

They passed the last of Tag's landmarks—a purple and orange flowering tree that stretched to the heavens. Minutes later they emerged into one of the oddest places that Jess and Maria had ever seen.

The field looked like a giant crater had fallen off the moon and landed in the middle of the Mexican jungle. Jagged rocks sprung from the ground, pointing in every direction. The field was almost a perfect circle, surrounded by the canopy of jungle palms and bamboo. Jess figured it had been created like that by a superstitious group of locals years before to entrap the creature that had terrorized their village.

But the most eye-catching sight was the multicolored rays of light that burst into the sky. This came from hundreds of pieces of glass spread throughout the field, reflecting off the sun and harnessing its power in a primitive system that pre-dated solar power by decades.

The prism of light drew their attention, but it was quickly diverted by the mud-covered pickup truck parked haphazardly fifty yards away. The truck door hung open and Jess could see water dripping off the side panels. It filled him with dismay, confirming the timeline they had figured out. Maria had noticed it as well.

"Why would she still be here?"

"Maybe she's not alone." Jess dug the thin flashlight out of his pocket. Maria was already holding hers tight in her right hand.

"You don't have to do this," Jess told her.

"That thing tried to take a chunk out of my head. God knows what it might have done to her." She waved the flashlight. "I owe it one."

Jess forced a smile. Brave, brazen, and beautiful—boy, had he hit the bull's-eye. The key now was to survive long enough to enjoy each other.

They got out of the jeep and cautiously made their way into the craggy field. Jess shielded his eyes from the refracted multicolored light. When it hit his pupils dead on, it was like staring into the center of a kaleidoscope.

Jess called Tracy's name, but his voice bounced off the rocks and echoed into the rainbow-tinted sky.

It wasn't until they reached the middle of the field of glass that Jess first heard a low moan.

It came from belowground.

"Tracy! It's Jess. Can you hear me?"

The moan grew louder. Maria pointed toward the dead center of the field where two rocks, larger than any others, jutted up in the air. They looked purposefully placed. A few broken shards of glass were affixed to the rocks. Jess wondered if there had been more at some point in the past. As they got closer, Jess could see something inscribed in the stone. The words looked like they were in Spanish.

Maria told him it was an old dialect, one with which she was unfamiliar.

"I can make a guess," said Jess. "I imagine it's some kind of warning."

Maria didn't disagree. Jess called out Tracy's name again, and when the moan came this time, their eyes drifted to a crevice between the two stones.

The opening was rectangular in shape. There were bits of broken colored glass at both edges where the crevice met the large rocks.

"It almost looks like there was a window here," said Maria.

"There probably was, until the film crew came and smashed it."

Jess looked up at the sky and noticed how the sunlight darted toward the two huge rocks. Some of the rays boomeranged into the crevice. He didn't possess the structural design talent of a former engineer like Tag Marlowe, but he thought a whole lot more light would have poured into the crevice if a multicolored glass window had been set in place.

His train of thought was thrown by another moan from down below.

"I'm going to go check it out. You stay here," he told Maria.

"Like hell."

Jess was at least able to convince Maria to let him go first. Cragged stones formed narrow steps, so they were actually able to walk down into the crevice. The trickling sunlight provided enough illumination to make their way to the rock floor, twenty feet below the surface.

Suddenly, they found themselves in a cavern. Jess took a couple of steps and heard something crunch. He looked down at his feet.

He had stepped on the remains of a human skeleton.

It looked like there was more than one nearby.

Maria yelped.

"You okay?" Jess whispered.

"Not really."

Jess nodded, in total agreement. Then he called out. "Tracy?"

This time the moan was less than ten feet away.

Jess pulled out the flashlight and started to squeeze it, but something surged out of the darkness and swiped it from his hands.

"Don't!"

The cylinder skittered into the blackness as Tracy half-emerged from the shadows.

She was pale and her eyes were feverish. Maria fumbled for her flashlight—and Tracy lunged at her.

"Noooo!"

Tracy grabbed it out of Maria's hands and retreated into the dark. They heard her whimper, which was accompanied by a soft sizzling sound.

Jess stepped forward.

"It's okay, Tracy. We're here to help protect you from it."

"You can't!"

He grabbed hold of her fleeting arm. Tracy resisted but Jess pulled her toward him into the light.

And then let go—right after he saw her arm start to burn where the sunlight hit it.

Exactly like his father's skin had burnt when he'd tried to escape the rising dawn in the desert.

Tracy's scream was unnerving.

"Don't you see?? I am *it*!"

Maria stepped back in horror. "Last night. It was you who attacked me?"

Tracy was back in the safety of darkness. Her voice was laced with tears. "Yes. I'm sorry . . ."

She quieted down, the sobs giving way to deep, labored breaths.

"But I was hungry."

PART THREE
DAWN'S EARLY LIGHT

INTRODUCTION TO THE JOURNAL OF EDWARD D. RICE

I am a cautious man by nature.

I have never had great ambitions such as bettering mankind or saving the world. I just want to be comfortable, provide for a family if I am lucky enough to ever have one, and hope people will remember me in a way that isn't abhorrent.

I went into medicine because I embraced the precise. I believed there was a scientific explanation for everything. It was that semblance of world order that brought peace and solace to my life.

Some might consider me a control freak. I find that judgment somewhat harsh. I'm just not fond of surprises.

What began in the jungles of Mexico and spread its way to the Coachella desert turned my life upside down. It made me question everything I ever knew and long for the rational world to be restored. But I don't see that happening any time soon.

I am writing this all down to examine if I could have done things differently and somehow prevented this. I am pretty sure it would have happened regardless of my involvement. I just paved the way for everything to occur a little quicker.

I also wanted to leave behind a record should something catastrophic happen to me. Perhaps it will help someone else accomplish what I was unable to.

Stop them.

I admit that I really never attempted to do that. But I think I had a very good reason.

To put it simply—I was losing my mind.

EXCERPT FROM THE JOURNAL OF
EDWARD D. RICE

May 26

I knew something was drastically wrong when the scout party didn't return by sundown.

Up until that point, the film shoot had been uneventful and way ahead of schedule. I had never been the physician on a movie set, and never imagined I would end up in the godforsaken Mexican jungle. A huge HMO had taken over the hospital where I had just finished my residency and the staff position I thought was mine vanished with the new restructuring. So I was in need of a job and went to interview with Clark James—but I had my principles.

I made it clear I had no desire to become a Hollywood Dr. Feelgood, a quack who was part of some matinee idol's entourage, their sole purpose supplying pain pills to mask their injuries, narcotics to help them sleep, and uppers to keep them going. If James wanted that, he better get himself a different doctor. I was assured that wasn't the case, and needing to keep myself fed, I signed on to the film.

Clark, the cinematographer, the location manager, and assistant director had left for the ruins early that morning after it became too dangerous to shoot in the church. The director shot coverage without Clark because the actor insisted on being part of all creative decisions on the film. I couldn't blame the man. He had invested a ton of his own money. When it got dark, the director started going crazy, insisting we send other crew members after the scout party. How was he going to shoot the following day without an actor and a cameraman? But he was talked out of it by a couple of locals who said they would never find the ruins in the dark.

Now, looking back, I realize they were deathly afraid of going there.

The following morning, the crazed director was assembling a search when a bloodied Clark James stumbled out of the jungle. He had crashed his jeep into a tree, but I could immediately tell that his injuries were not sustained in the wreck. Maybe a few cuts and scrapes, but he had a lot more problems.

276

He collapsed in my arms. His eyes were cloudy, his body retching with nausea. I could tell he was running a malaria-type fever from one touch of his forehead. He had somehow navigated the jeep back to the base camp, but whatever malady he suffered from weakened him so much he crashed into the trees.

The director, an effete specimen given to fits of rage that were only condoned because he had won an Oscar, tried to control the situation. I could see he was only interested in his shooting schedule and told him to stay the hell away from the actor.

"If you don't let me do what I was hired for, pretty soon you're not going to have a star on your hands. He'll be a dead man," I told him.

How prophetic.

It was Clark James himself who put the idea of shooting to rest.

"Dead. They're dead. All of them."

He muttered it repeatedly, then passed out.

Thank God for the screenwriter. He convinced the director they needed to look for the missing crew members. This finally knocked some sense into the director, who threw his manic energy into ordering half a dozen people to head for the ruins.

Hours later, I heard they had arrived back with three dead bodies in tow. (I learned about the missing girl from the screenwriter right before we airlifted out of Santa Alvarado. He was drunk and despondent by then, and my heart went out to him.) There was nothing I could do for the victims, which was a blessing because I had my hands full with Clark James.

Here I was, trying to keep one of the biggest stars in the world alive, in a place time had forgotten. Clark was in and out of delirium and constantly throwing up. He had developed a particular aversion to being in the heat and sunlight. It was only his bloodcurdling screams demanding shade that made me move him into a tent where he calmed down enough so I could try and attend to his injuries.

I convinced one of the local women to help me undress him and try to clean up his wounds. We had no sooner exposed a couple of deep gashes in his leg and neck when the woman crossed herself and ran out of the tent.

I first thought the wounds were from a knife. They were striated, as if the assailant had used a ragged edged blade. But there was something peculiar about them. Just as I traced a delicate finger across the one by his neck, James bolted up and stared at me with genuine horror in his feverish eyes.

"Teeth! Those teeth!"

I cradled his head, steadying him before he fell off the table. Clark was so terrified he actually started to whimper. That was when I realized what was so odd about the wounds. They weren't from a knife at all.

They were bite marks.

"Something bit you."

Clark nodded, frantically.

"What?"

For a moment, Clark struggled to reply. But his eyes clouded over and his voice was just a sad whisper. "I . . . I don't remember."

The more I pushed the issue, the more vague he got. Clark finally passed out, unable to tell me anything more about what had attacked him.

But I found out soon enough.

1

Tracy remained in the darkness as the three of them stood in eerie silence. Oddly enough, Maria was the first to break it.

"Why did you come all the way to Mexico?"

Tracy didn't answer. Jess, whirring through the ramifications of having just learned of Tracy's turning, offered up a theory.

"You're looking for something to reverse this."

"Yes."

"And what did you find?"

"Not a cure." Her voice was laced with disappointment and fury from being told a lie. "But it has helped fight off the hunger."

She pointed toward the deep recesses of the cavern.

"You don't expect us to follow you back there," said Maria.

"I promise I won't hurt you. Even when the craving was at its worst, I couldn't bring myself to really attack anyone."

"The farmer. Was that you?" Jess asked.

He could make out Tracy nodding in the shadows. "I couldn't go through with it. There's this yearning deep inside for blood, but when it came to actually cutting through flesh to get it—it just made me nauseous." She lowered her voice. "Some people aren't *made* for this, I guess."

The irony of the phrasing wasn't lost on Jess. Even turned, Tracy had retained more than a shred of her humanity. The girl he had once fallen head over heels for was still there, and it broke his heart.

"I keep thinking I should just walk into the sunlight and get it over with."

Jess flinched. He was still struggling with the idea that part of Tracy was gone forever. But for her to just go and end it entirely?

"Tracy . . ."

"Don't worry, Jessie. I'm too much of a chickenshit." She looked over her shoulder. "At least this offers an option I can *live* with." She turned back toward them and offered up a sad smile. "Bad pun intended."

"Just what is back there?" Jess asked.

"Depends on how you look at it. Hell. Or salvation."

Jess and Maria remained in the streaming sunlight as a trust debate continued for a while longer. Maria, still feeling the swipe across her throat from the previous evening, was understandably cautious about accompanying whatever-Tracy-had-become deeper into the cavern. Jess said it would have been easy for her to attack them after knocking the flashlights from their hands, giving further credence to Tracy's claim she couldn't take a human life. Maria was already coming around to Jess's side when the two cylinders landed at their feet. Tracy had picked up the flashlights and tossed them back from the darkness.

She stood near the edge of the cascading daylight. "What's in those things?"

Jess explained Tag Marlowe's invention.

Tracy instinctively backed further into the shadows. "Maybe you can keep them pointed away from me?"

Jess and Maria agreed—for the time being.

"So are we good?" Tracy asked.

"I'd hardly say 'good,' but I want to see what's back there," Jess responded.

"Then follow me."

Maria was still unsure. "How do you know where you're going? Do you . . . have some kind of night vision?"

Tracy let out a little laugh. "Don't I wish?" She produced an ordinary flashlight from her back pocket. "I brought my own. Far as I can tell, AA batteries won't make me burst into flames."

That bit of levity propelled the three of them deeper into the cavern. Tracy used her flashlight to illuminate the cave walls while Jess and Maria were extra careful to keep Tracy out of their solar beams.

The walls had plenty of cragged nooks. Stalactite formations hung from the ceilings and they needed to duck more than twice. As they traveled farther, Jess became aware of a rushing sound.

"What is that?" he asked as they rounded a narrow bend and it grew louder.

"You'll see soon enough."

Maria hung close by Jess and eventually took hold of his arm. He was happy for the human contact and gave her hand a tight squeeze. Up ahead, something glowed in the deeper recess of the cave.

"I don't presume that's sunlight," Jess said.

"I brought a lantern."

Jess wondered if Tracy had been a Girl Scout and adhered to the "Be Prepared" motto. Then he remembered that was the Boy Scout credo, and he was anything but ready for what lay around the corner.

"What's that smell?" asked Maria.

All of a sudden, Jess smelled it too. It was sickeningly sweet and had a metallic feel.

Tracy stopped outside the entrance to a deeper cave. "Not pleasant, right?"

"Disagreeable, I would say," said Jess.

"That's how I know things have changed." A dangerous edge had slipped into her voice. "I find myself craving it."

She walked into the glow of the cavern ahead. As they followed, Jess kept hold of Maria's arm. The rushing sound was loud, the smell even more acrid.

A lantern on the ground washed light over a hollowed-out cavern. The walls sparkled, partly from the minerals buried within, the rest from the condensation coming off the body of water below.

But it wasn't quite H_2O. It had a more gelatinous consistency; thicker.

It was also tinged with red.

Jess suddenly understood the smell and Tracy's attraction to it. "Blood."

"Not completely. It's definitely water-based. But I don't think a scientist has been down here to take a sample."

Maria turned her face away; the smell was so overpowering.

Tracy knelt down and dipped a finger in the bloody river, which she brought up to her parted lips. The ensuing slurping sound sent a shiver up and down their spines, causing Maria to stifle a gag reflex and Jess to momentarily squeeze his eyes shut.

When he opened them, Tracy had just finished licking her finger clean like the last vestiges of a favorite dish. "It curbs the hunger."

"How often do you need to . . .?"

Jess couldn't find the right word to complete the question. He realized he didn't want to.

"Every day or two, I think. I'm just getting used to this."

Pained by what she had become, Jess turned away. He took in the strange surroundings. "I presume you learned about this place from your father."

"He described how to get here. But he wasn't the one who told me about it."

Jess turned to face her again. "Who did?"

Tracy looked up at them from the river. A helpless look fell over her. "I don't know."

After witnessing the ghoulish spectacle of Tracy feeding from the river, Maria, clearly unable to take any more, exited the cavern room. Jess began to follow but then spotted something near the entrance. He bent down and gingerly examined a pile of bones.

"I think they were sacrifices," Tracy said. A few crumbled in his hands; others didn't seem so old.

Tracy came up behind him. By the time Jess looked up, she had wiped her mouth clean. All traces of the ghastly aperitif were gone.

"Sacrifices?" Something in the remains glinted: metal. Jess started to finger through the remains.

"To replenish the spring," she said, pointing at the river of blood. "Whatever it's made of seems to regenerate, but it helps getting a new infusion every so often."

Jess picked out a few metal objects, stuck them in his pocket, and straightened up. "And you know this how?"

"I can't explain it. I just knew after I was turned."

"Like what? A shared consciousness? Is that what you're saying?"

"More like a whisper that kept wiggling inside my ear, running through my head. I can't tell you where it came from, but by the time I was fully aware, I just knew all this stuff."

"By fully aware, you mean after you were . . ." Jess broke off, unable to finish the sentence, as if by refusing to do so, he could possibly undo it.

"Attacked. Bitten. Turned. Whatever you feel comfortable saying."

"I don't feel comfortable saying any of it. When did this happen?"

"The night they came for you at my house. I screamed but they knocked me to the ground and dragged you away. I got up to run inside and call the police but never made it that far. He was waiting for me."

"Your father?"

"Not mine, Jessie. Yours."

Tracy's eyes brimmed with tears once again.

"It was Walter who turned me."

2

Jess knew that one day he would end up talking about his father with Tracy, but in his wildest imagination, he never thought it would be in a situation like this.

They had moved out of the cavern room. The metallic odor of the spring had finally become too much for Jess. Tracy held the lantern to lead the way. Maria was nowhere in sight.

Jess realized Maria thought he should be alone with Tracy. After unburdening his darkest secret the night before, he could tell Maria knew there was unfinished business between them. Lena's daughter's sensitivity and maturity continued to amaze him.

"My father attacked you," Jess said after they found a spot far enough from the cavern room.

"I actually don't remember."

"You said he was standing there."

Tracy nodded. "But everything immediately went black. I might have passed out; I can't say for sure. I thought your father was dead. The shock of seeing him was the last thing I remember."

"Then what?"

"It's hard to explain. I drifted in and out. I kept hearing this voice, whispering . . ."

"Was it Walter?"

"No. I had never heard it before. The words were jumbled—I didn't understand them. It was like when you're swimming underwater and someone tries to talk to you. Garbled like that."

Jess nodded, encouraging Tracy to continue.

"When I woke up it was nearly dawn and I was on the living room couch."

That explained her bed not having been slept in, thought Jess.

"My father was sitting beside me. He was crying. I hadn't seen him do that since I was a little girl—when my mother died."

Tracy paused. She looked around the cave, trying to comprehend how she had ended up in such a strange place so far away from home.

"And then I knew, I could just feel it. I had died too. And my father was grieving once again."

Jess tried to line it up with all the fantastical things he had experienced the past week. He had learned enough not to reject anything out of hand, but still had questions.

"You knew what had happened to you?"

Tracy nodded. "I realize now it must have been the whispers. I didn't understand what they were at the time, but I knew so much more when I woke up. It was like when you have a strange dream where nothing makes sense while it's happening, but in the morning you remember the nightmare. Only in this case, it was my new reality."

"You understood that you had been turned."

"Pretty much. What I didn't get at first, my father explained to me. That was actually the hardest thing, wrapping my brain around my father being the same as me."

"You had no idea before?"

"That my father had died and come back to life?" Tracy managed a slight laugh. "Are you kidding? If it had occurred to me and I said it out loud, someone would have committed me. Hell, I would've done it myself."

Jess knew the exact feeling.

"All I knew was that he had gotten really sick in Mexico and made a remarkable recovery. I totally got him retiring and going into seclusion afterwards."

"What about the fact that he didn't go out during the day? Or eat?"

"He was an eccentric movie star. Also, remember I went to grad school for a few years. He urged me to. Of course, now I understand why. And it wasn't like we spent a ton of time together. It was mostly parties and premieres in the evenings. I occasionally saw him during the day, but it was always somewhere inside. I once asked about his weird hours and he said he loved sleeping in to make up for decades of crack-of-dawn movie calls. He did say he was happy to get a second chance at enjoying life. A couple of days ago I realized the irony of *that* statement."

Sitting in the darkness with the woman he had once loved so deeply, Jess could appreciate it too.

"So it was totally surreal waking up to my find my father sobbing beside me."

"He'd lost his daughter, at least the one he knew."

"Maybe. But I think he felt responsible for what had happened to me."

"How so?"

"Because my dad told me he had turned Walter."

"Why would he do that?"

"Walter found out about the deaths at Meadowland . . ."

" . . . from Tom Cox."

"Right. Walter started asking questions and Dad ran the risk of being exposed, not to mention having his blood supply run out."

"Why not just kill him? He certainly possessed the 'skill' to do it."

"Dad said that wasn't enough—he wanted Walter to suffer, just like he did."

"How come?" asked Jess.

Tracy hesitated. Long enough for Jess to ask the question again.

"Tracy. Why would he want that?"

She lowered her head and answered. Softly, and painfully.

"Because of what happened between Walter and me."

Jess's heart sank.

"My father said he wanted Walter to—how did he put it? 'Feel a ravenous thirst for blood he couldn't quench and fear the approaching dawn.' He thought it only a matter of time until Walter 'threw himself upon the mercy of sunlight and experienced the excruciating death he deserved.'"

"But it didn't work out like that."

Tracy shook her head. "Walter came for me instead."

"When my father was alive he perfected the art of finding someone's Achilles' heel and exploiting it. I suppose it's no different in death."

"I don't know what was worse. Waking up on that couch and understanding what had happened to me, or finding my father on his knees telling me how sorry he was."

"What did you tell him?"

"That I knew he would never do anything to purposefully hurt me."

"That was pretty understanding."

"More than you were."

Jess flinched. He probably deserved that.

"You never gave me a chance to beg you to forgive me," said Tracy.

And suddenly, after all these years, in the most peculiar place, they were finally talking about it.

She mentioned the numerous attempts to reach him by email and the unreturned cell phone calls. She told him how she locked herself in her room and didn't come out for a week after he disconnected his number. When she could no longer hear Jess's voice on his outgoing message, she felt a lifeline had been severed.

As for what happened with Walter after Jess found them together that day, he didn't want to hear about it. Seven years later the wounds were still deep enough that scratching would only make them bleed anew. But Tracy didn't back off—she knew this was probably her last chance to make her mea culpa.

"I actually kicked him in the balls and left him groveling on the floor."

Jess raised an eyebrow, eliciting a smile from Tracy.

"You never knew that, did you?"

Jess told her no.

Tracy proceeded with the rest, the stuff he never knew.

She talked about the night they first met and why she was crying her eyes out on Palm Canyon Drive when he almost ran her down. He felt horrible hearing how she went to see Walter after the surprise party; declaring her love for Jess and standing up to the man he had spent most of his own life trying to get out from under.

Jess realized she was still suffering because of what had transpired between her and the Stark men—and might very well continue to do so now into eternity.

"Why didn't you tell me once we got involved?" he asked.

"Because I was afraid that you'd look at me like you did when you saw us in the office that day, and walk out of my life like you did."

When Jess spoke next, his voice was soft and laced with a trace of shame. "You're probably right. Not that I'm proud to admit it."

Tracy took some solace in that admission. "You never thought about me?"

"Of course I did. For a while, I thought of nothing else."

"But you couldn't bring yourself to get in touch."

Then Jess told her what he never imagined sharing.

"I did come to see you once."

"You did? But I thought you never came back to Palm Springs before this."

"At Dartmouth. A few months after you went back."

"I had no idea."

"I realize that." Jess struggled with the admission. It was difficult to reveal this vulnerable moment. "It was during that weeklong party in January where everyone gets really drunk and does crazy things in the snow . . ."

"Winter Carnival."

"Yeah, that's it. I headed up then. I sat parked in a car I'd rented, freezing my ass off because the heater wasn't working, watching your sorority house."

"Wow. My very own stalker."

"Do you want to hear this or not?" Jess immediately regretted snapping and tried to take the edge off by shrugging it away with a smile.

But Tracy looked like she'd been stung. "Of course I do."

"I guess I wanted to see if you were suffering as much as I was."

"More. If that was possible."

"Well, it didn't look like it."

Tracy recoiled, like she had been slapped. "What are you talking about?"

"I was working up the nerve to go bang on the door when this older guy, I don't know, he looked like a teacher, came by and you got into his car and took off."

"Oh my God. Was he in his fifties, receding hairline?"

"Yeah. Sounds right."

"That was Professor Tiltson, from the science department. He'd convinced me to help him work on one of those giant ice sculptures for the Carnival. He'd noticed me moping in class and suggested I get off my butt and do something. That's all it was." She laughed. "Me and Tiltson, that's a good one. Believe me, Jessie, your father cured me of older men."

Then her eyes misted. "The only thing he didn't cure me of was you."

Jess had no response. It just plain hurt.

"So you left without ever seeing me?"

"I was so fucked up by that point, I needed to get away," said Jess. "I ended up hiking my way through Europe for a while, eventually made my way back to Los Angeles. You know the rest."

Tracy eked out the saddest of smiles. "Talk about star-crossed lovers."

"Yeah."

"Now look at us."

Tracy reached out and took Jess's hand. He started to shy away, not out of fear or from Tracy's intent, but because it was so cold.

Tracy was well aware. "It's the first thing I had to get used to. Your body temperature drops really low."

Jess didn't let go, but her icy grip brought everything into focus. She couldn't have been more right. Fate had dealt them the cruelest of hands and there was nothing to do about it.

"I know we'll never be together now, Jessie. I get that. But know that I love you and always will. Most of all, I'm sorry. So terribly sorry about everything that happened back then."

"Me too," Jess said.

And he meant it.

Footsteps approached and Jess dropped Tracy's chilled hand just as Maria rounded the corner. Jess wasn't sure if she saw anything but knew he would rectify the situation later. He had learned the hard way about not coming clean.

Maria didn't let on either way and used the solar flashlight sparingly, making sure to keep its beam off Tracy.

"It's getting dark," Maria said.

The statement filled the cavern with dread. Jess realized decisions needed to be made.

Right away.

3

The arguments started almost immediately. The first was whether Tracy should remain in the cavern or come with Jess and Maria. Tracy wanted to stay; she was still terrified about the threat of sunlight and the blood spring at least curbed her hunger. Jess had no intention of leaving without her because despite her best intentions, Tracy was too much of a threat on her own. He said she knew where the cavern was and could always return if necessary, but they would make sure to provide her a food supply. To prove the point, Jess emptied a couple of gasoline cans from the rental cars, returned to the blood spring, and filled both cans to the brim. Tracy, realizing neither Jess or Maria would let her stay behind and could force their mandate with the solar flashes, reluctantly agreed, but not before taking a healthy last gulp of sustenance from the blood water.

The second battle was basically over before it began—one car or two. Since Jess wasn't letting her out of his sight, Tracy driving by herself was a nonstarter. He finally agreed they should all pile into the pickup truck; that way there was no debating who would sit in front or guard the vampire in back. They would all sit together and there was more protection from the sunlight with the pickup's closed roof than the jeep's exposed overhead window.

Jess urged Tracy out of the cavern, saying the quicker they left, the more time they could travel under the cover of darkness. Tracy was reluctant to leave the safety of the spring. She had been lured there by the whispers which promised salvation lay in the cavern depths. Jess argued it didn't provide the cure she had been hoping for and promised to take her somewhere safe. Afterwards, he and Maria would hunt down Walter and her father to get the answers she so desperately desired.

Minutes later, with Tracy looking nervously at the field of glass glistening in the moonlight, the two jutting rocks beckoning her to return to the cocoon of the spring, the three of them squeezed into the front of the truck and headed back into the jungle, intent on getting Tracy to safety before the emerging dawn.

The ride back to Santa Alvarado was treacherous. Nothing much was said inside the pickup. Jess was behind the wheel, with Tracy squeezed between him and Maria. Occasionally, one of the women would point out an obstacle in the dirt road and a couple of times Jess needed to pull over so that Maria could use the solar flash to illuminate the landmarks on Tag's makeshift map. Luckily, a full moon was in the sky and between the lunar light and pickup's headlights, they slowly but surely made the trek back to the village.

Jess thought back on his heart-to-heart with Tracy. It had been a long time coming and though there was a sad but wistful air of What-Might-Have-Been to it, he figured it could have been a whole lot worse. Tracy, the ultimate scorned woman, could have literally ripped his head off and feasted on his remains. But here she sat, still hoping for some miracle to reverse her horrible fate.

Jess wondered about his own culpability in what had befallen Tracy. Numerous scenarios and plenty of "what if's" peppered his brain. Suppose he had never walked in his father's office seven years ago—would he have ever found out about them? Would he and Tracy be approaching a decade of wedded bliss together? But going down that road wouldn't have stopped

Walter from digging up the conspiracy at Meadowland and being turned by Clark James. What was to say Walter wouldn't still seek vengeance against the actor by going after Tracy anyway?

Jess tried to concentrate on the matter at hand. Tracy physically separated him from Maria. Perhaps it was only right that Jess do whatever he could to find some peace for the woman he had once loved in order to clear a path so he might try and find happiness anew. He began asking Tracy questions that might steer him in the right direction.

"Do you have any idea where my father is?"

Tracy shook her head. "The last time I saw him was when you were taken from my house."

"What about Clark? Would he know?"

"If I had to guess, I'd say no. He was so upset about Walter turning me, I'm sure he would have gone directly after him if he knew where to look."

The mention of Walter turning brought a question to the surface that had been nagging Jess. "What about the Civatateo? That was what attacked your father five years ago, right?"

"That's what he said."

"Whatever happened to it?" Jess couldn't affix a gender to the creature that had emerged from the cavern. Not to mention that he didn't want to humanize it that way.

"Dad told me not to worry about it anymore."

"It's dead," Jess realized.

"That's what he said. I tried pressing him, but he refused to say anything more."

Tracy looked out the pickup's rear window, as if she could still see the field of glass. When she turned back, her expression was as forlorn as Jess ever remembered.

"I thought it was the Civatateo whispering and it was still down here, where it all started. I hoped it was luring me back to give answers so I could move on with whatever this new *life* is." She lowered her eyes, not wanting them to see the pain there. "But you saw the place—nothing had been down there for a long time."

Surprisingly it was Maria, not Jess, who took Tracy's hand this time. If fazed by the icy flesh that now carried the bloodline of the Civatateo, Maria didn't show it. "Don't give up hope, Tracy. Not yet."

Maria glanced over at Jess. He nodded in agreement.

"What she said."

Jess offered up a smile of thanks to Maria; he was amazed and thankful for her graciousness.

They drove in silence until they reached the outskirts of Santa Alvarado. Jess steered the pickup away from the center of the village. Tracy was immediately alarmed.

"Where are you going?"

Jess asked her to be patient.

Ten minutes later they could see the glass house on the hill, lit up in all its solar glory.

Even though Jess parked the pickup at least five hundred yards from the breadth of the solar panels, Tracy began screaming.

"What are you doing? Why are we here? What is this place??"

She tried to scramble over Jess to get out of the car. He gripped her tight and urged her to be calm in his most assured tone. "I'll get them turned off."

He looked to Maria with an unspoken question in his eyes. Was she all right being left alone with Tracy? A slight nod and seeing the solar flashlight was in her lap, inches from her right hand, gave him the answer he needed.

"Take her back to Sophia's if I'm not back soon," Jess told Maria. He turned his attention back to Tracy. "Tag's a good man. You'll see."

Tracy was still shaking, but knowing she had to trust Jess, she forced a compliant nod.

Five minutes later Jess was pounding on Tag Marlowe's door, his eyes practically blinded by the light, begging to be let inside. Eventually, a sleepy-eyed Marlowe appeared in the doorway.

"It's three o'clock in the morning," Tag scolded.

"I wouldn't be here if it wasn't an emergency."

The screenwriter gathered his wits—enough to comprehend someone was missing. "Where is your friend?"

"Down in the car waiting."

"How come?"

"That's what I need to talk to you about," said Jess.

"You're out of your fucking mind."

Jess had expected this reaction from Tag and launched into why it was the only choice. He rushed through the explanation, worried Tracy wouldn't last long in the pickup without totally freaking out, but he made sure to fill in all the necessary information for Tag. Jess had to hand it to the writer; he didn't kick Jess out on his ass but was still showing more than a little reluctance.

"There has to be another option," Marlowe said.

"I wish I could come up with one."

Jess had no choice but to play his trump card. He reached into his jeans pocket and pulled out one of the items he had picked up off the ground in the cavern beside the blood spring. It was a simple chain with a small gold "P" hanging from it. Jess handed the chain to Tag and told him where he had found it.

"This belonged to Penelope," Tag murmured. "I gave it to her right before she disappeared."

"I thought as much."

The ensuing quiet might as well have been a funeral dirge. Both men knew Penelope was never coming back.

"Whatever you've been hearing in the middle of the night is something screwing with your head, man," said Jess.

Tag closed his fist around the chain. His grief was already starting to give way to anger and revenge.

Jess pointed out the multicolored window. "I owe that girl down there my best shot. I figure you might want to give yours the same. Let's get rid of this fucking thing once and for all."

Tag put the chain in his pocket.

Then, he shut down the lights.

When Tracy James and Tag Marlowe first met five years before, she had been fresh out of college and bored out of her mind for the entire week she spent on the location shoot. Tag had barely said hello because he was frantically rewriting *The Seventh Day*, serving every whim and fancy of Clark and the mercurial director.

Once reunited, they held a morbid fascination with each other. Tag could see a woman who was decent, sad, and lost, but now borne of the same creature that had killed his beloved Penelope. Tracy only had to glance around the room to appreciate the screenwriter's brilliant mind, the very same brain that had constructed a house that was deadly only to Tracy and her unholy kin.

Both kept their guards up, Tag explaining in very specific terms what he had constructed and why. Tracy responded with minimal words and nods. But Jess could see her paying rapt attention to Tag, something he had counted on, and it allowed Jess to excuse himself for a moment and return to the pickup truck.

Once there, he uncovered the tarp of the truck bed and picked up the two gasoline cans full of blood. As he lugged them up the hill to the house, he thought them heavier than he remembered. Maybe it was just exhaustion from a long day and harrowing night, but Jess suspected the real burden came from what he was about to do.

The moment Jess reentered the glass house, the solar lights flared back on. Artificial sunlight flooded every inch of the property for at least a good hundred yards. Tracy stifled a scream but Tag told her to relax. He toggled it on and off with the remote in his hand.

"Did you tell her about the override?" asked Jess.

"I was just getting to that."

A look passed between the two men. Maria caught it first. "What override?"

Jess placed the two gasoline cans on the floor next to the door as Tag pushed a code on the remote. The lights came on once again. Tracy backed away from the door.

"It jams the signal so the lights can only be turned off by this remote," Tag told them.

Jess immediately pulled Maria toward the door.

"C'mon . . ."

Maria realized what was happening and shook him off. "Jessie, you can't! She'll be trapped."

"It's our only choice."

Before Maria could respond, she was dragged out the door by Marlowe. Tracy started screaming.

"Jessie!"

He lingered in the doorway, making sure he was bathed in enough solar rays to stay out of Tracy's reach.

"I'm sorry, Trace. I really am."

"Don't leave me here!"

This time there was a guttural sound buried in the scream. It was the first time since they found her groveling in the cave that the beast within struggled to gain control. But the same feral survival instinct kept her away from the light.

Jess slammed the door shut. He stood outside it bathed in faux sunlight, yelling at the top of his lungs.

"There's enough in the gas cans to last at least a week, maybe two if used sparingly. I will be back before that!"

A howl came through the door. It almost shook the house off its foundations.

"Noooooo!"

"Tracy, we need to end this! Once and for all. This is the only way I know how!"

Jess's words were spoken as much for Maria and Tag, who were huddled together a few yards behind him.

"I will not leave you here! I will be back! I promise, Tracy!"

Jess's eyes welled up. Maria stepped forward and put her arm around him. She nodded, a tacit understanding and agreement, and began leading him away from the house. They hurried down the stairs to the pickup truck with Tag hot on their heels.

Tracy's cries echoed into the night.

"Jessie! Jessie!"

He knew he would still hear her later—that night, to the border, and beyond. Jess suspected her screams would ring in his ear long after he had returned to the desert.

EXCERPTS FROM THE JOURNAL OF
EDWARD D. RICE

May 28

    Getting a helicopter to airlift Clark out of Santa Alvarado turned out to be no small task, starting with finding a phone in the tiny village. Eventually we located one in a café operated by a man named Angel, who for a price would let you call the States. After lots of pleading, a few rounds of mistranslations, and the healthy weight of Clark James's checkbook, a Medevac chopper was finally chartered and due to arrive within the next twenty-four hours.

    While we waited, more details emerged about the search party's discoveries. I was told about the field covered with shards of glass and even got a look at the dead bodies hauled back in one of the jeeps. They looked like they had been sliced by a machete and then feasted upon by wild animals. The locals wrote it off as drug war casualties but I noticed inconsistencies that bothered me, especially when I thought about James's bite marks. But my protests were met with great resistance by the locals who wouldn't let us reclaim the bodies. They loaded the corpses onto a funeral pyre and burned them that same night. I sat in the tent, drinking more than I should, and watched the flames rise while keeping an eye on Clark, who was stable enough that the vomiting had stopped and moans quieted down. I noticed that the night air agreed with him as opposed to the sunshine he constantly complained about—but I didn't understand the significance of this yet.

    By the time I did it was much too late.

May 29

Clark's anguished cries roused me from a deep sleep and I saw him huddled in a corner of the tent, crawling away from the rays of morning sunlight that came through the opening in the canvas.

Fighting off pulsing hangover pain, I scrambled off my cot and closed the tent flap. As I got Clark settled back down, something nagged at me, but I tossed the concern aside because the actor was sweating profusely and breathing heavily. Yet his eyes were wide open and focused for the first time since he told me the rest of the scout party had died.

"Palm Springs," he grunted.

"What about Palm Springs?"

"You have to take me to Palm Springs."

I told him we were lucky to get the chopper on such short notice, but it was only contracted to return to Puerto Vallarta. Clark insisted he return to Palm Springs and would compensate the pilot handsomely for his trouble. I argued we needed to get him to a hospital right away, but Clark became so agitated, I agreed to ask the pilot if he could reroute. It turned out offering money, especially the amount James suggested, spoke much louder than common sense, so in a matter of hours we were on our way to Palm Springs.

It wasn't until we were moving Clark from the tent that I realized what had been tugging at my brain ever since I awoke with a pounding head.

As I let the Medevac pilot and his gurney inside, I found myself staring at the tent flap . . .

I distinctly recalled fastening it before falling asleep the previous night, but remembered the sunlight streaming through the opening that had awakened Clark and caused him to cry out.

What was it doing open?

That triggered a hazy but strange memory of a dream I had that night. At least I thought it was a dream. Now, staring at the flap, I began to wonder.

The dream-memory floated back into my brain. I remembered stirring briefly because someone was murmuring nearby. I had turned to look at the sleeping Clark where I saw a figure hovering over him, whispering in his ear. But the fog from the consumed alcohol, my dreamy-drifty state of mind, and the vague shadows convinced me I was more asleep than awake. I gave in to the pull of deep sleep and didn't wake till morning.

Now I wondered if someone had actually walked in and knelt down by Clark James in the middle of the night. It seemed preposterous, so I didn't wrestle with it for long. I wrote it off to stress and alcohol-induced delusions and forgot about it.

Until a couple of weeks later when I saw the very same figure in Clark James's room at Meadowland.

4

They dropped Tag off at a small house in the village. It belonged to a friend who didn't ask many questions, was used to the eccentricities of the screenwriter-inventor, and not thrown by him showing up at five in the morning. Before they parted ways, Tag told Jess he would drop by the glass house each day to make sure Tracy was still locked inside. He swore not to enter lest Tracy go into attack mode, and reassured Jess there was no way for her to outmaneuver the override. Jess threw his arms around the man and thanked him profusely.

"Just get back here as soon as you can," said Tag.

"One way or another," Jess promised.

Jess rejoined Maria in the pickup. Both were exhausted and rode in silence the short distance back to her great-aunt's house. Sophia threw open the front door before they exited the truck; she had been sick with worry and wearing out the living room rug. The heavy smell of incense greeted them upon entering the house, and Jess wasn't surprised the old woman had lit more than one candle for them during her daylong vigil.

Jess had planned to just pick up their things and immediately start back to Puerto Vallarta to catch a plane north. But Sophia wouldn't hear of it, insisting they get some rest. He knew it was pointless to argue and went back with Maria to the small bedroom.

Maria was out before her head hit the pillow, but Jess lay awake in the darkness. Not wanting to disturb her with his tossing and turning, he slipped out of bed. He headed out back and sank into a chair on the edge of Sophia's garden.

As Jess stared into the darkness, mulling over what to do once back in Palm Springs, he couldn't stop thinking about Tracy's plaintive screams. They echoed in his head like an eerie mantra and hadn't eased up when the sun began to rise an hour later.

It was only when the rays of light gleamed off the pink and white roses climbing the wedding trellis that he grasped a glimmer of hope. Their ability to rebloom year after year gave Jess solace. Maybe death didn't have to conquer all.

Tracy's cries slipped away with the emergence of the sun and the gentle hand that touched his shoulder.

"Come inside. You need to sleep."

If he didn't know better, he would have said an angel had descended from the heavens above. Maria was wearing only the T-shirt and her hair glistened in the early dawn.

Jess let her lead him back inside, where they lay down on the tiny bed. They wrapped their arms around each other as sleep was thrown to the wayside. Their lovemaking was desperate and they clung to one another long after they were both satiated. When they fell asleep, neither would let go, as if that living bond would protect them from the undead they knew awaited their return to the California desert.

Later that morning, Angel, the café owner, got a bunch more pesos off Jess when he used the phone to call Benji. After listening to his old friend belt out a few "Hallelujahs" that Jess was still amongst the living, he got an update on the Palm Springs situation. Jess was still wanted as a "person of interest" in the murder of Edward Rice. Thaddeus Burke had dropped by the motel a few times and on his last visit, Benji let the sheriff go through the room Jess had occupied.

"He was threatening to get a search warrant and I figured it wasn't like you'd left a road map where you guys were headed." Benji sounded apologetic and Jess assured him he had done nothing wrong.

Jess told Benji they were headed back to the Coachella Valley. On one hand, Benji was happy they were returning, but he was simultaneously worried the only thing Jess would see was the inside of a jail cell.

"That's one of the reasons I'm calling. I could use some help."

"Just tell me what you want me to do."

Jess did.

He heard his high school buddy's sharp intake of breath on the other end of the line. "That's kind of crazy, man."

"So is looking for the undead."

"Touché." Benji laughed, but Jess could hear the nervousness in it. Still, the motel owner was game and said he would arrange things. Jess started to tell him he didn't have to do it, but Benji stopped him midsentence.

"C'mon, man. You want me to start singing 'That's What Friends Are For'?"

"No thanks. I've had my fair share of horrifying things recently."

Jess hung up and looked across the café. Angel was eyeing him, but he had no idea if the man had overheard him or understood a single word. Jess doubted the latter, figuring the café owner would have run for the hills. Jess nodded thanks, gave Angel a few more pesos for his troubles (which was all the man was probably looking for), then headed down the road to say goodbye to Sophia.

Something else he hadn't been looking forward to.

She had packed a picnic lunch for them. Once again Jess saw where the Flores women had inherited their caretaking nature—the elderly woman was only happy when tending to others' needs. It made the loss of her dear Luis so much more tragic. Sophia had lived an entire life unable to bestow her gifts and love on the person who mattered most.

They said farewell in the garden out back as Sophia couldn't bear to watch them depart. Jess knew she was afraid they might never return and did what he could to assuage those fears. He said they would return. He had already made a promise and would die before not fulfilling it.

"Take good care of each other," Sophia said.

"We will, Tía," Maria told her. The women hugged as Maria whispered some form of endearment in Spanish into her great-aunt's ear. Sophia immediately started to sob; Jess couldn't tell if they were tears of sadness or joy.

Then it was Jess's turn. He looked at Maria, who was wiping tears from her own eyes. She nodded at him, as if giving permission. He sighed, then reached into his pocket and pulled out a silver locket. It was in the shape of a heart and more than slightly tarnished—after all, it had been lying on the floor of an underground cavern for over half a century.

"I believe this was meant for you," Jess said.

Sophia took the locket from his hand and her fingers shook as she opened it. Inside was a black-and-white picture of a young teenage couple, circa early 1940s. When Jess had first seen it he easily recognized the young Sophia Flores gazing happily into an ancient camera lens. He knew the handsome bronzed teen had to be her soon-to-be-wedded Luis. Sophia's tears flowed again as she read the engraved Spanish inscription on the locket's inner face. Maria had translated it for Jess when he first showed it to her: "A life together—forever"

"August 30, 1946. Was that your wedding date?" asked Jess.

Sophia nodded, fingering the locket. "I had no idea this even existed." She tapped the photo. "But I do remember taking it. There was a photographer who would come to the village maybe once or twice a year. He would charge to take a picture, much more than any of us could afford. Luis wanted one but I tried to talk him out of it. We needed every penny for the wedding. But he insisted and wouldn't tell me why." She snapped the locket shut and kissed it gently with her lips. "Now at last I know."

Sophia threw her arms around Jess and held him tight. "*Gracias*, Jessie. It's the perfect wedding gift." She said it with so much love and affection that Jess felt he had been blessed.

She crossed to the trellis and hung the locket on one of the pink and white rose stems. Then Sophia turned to face them. "In case he wants to come and visit, he'll know where it is."

Both Jess and Maria's hearts broke. Finally, after more hugs, tears, and drying of eyes, Maria took Jess's hand and led him out of the garden so they could begin the long trek home.

It wasn't until they were on the plane halfway back to Ensenada that Maria mentioned Tracy.

"Did we do the right thing leaving her there?"

"I wish I knew. I just don't think we could run the risk. Look what she almost did to you."

"But you heard what she said. She couldn't bring herself to hurt me."

"We've no idea how any of this really works. She might eventually lose control and then what?"

Maria considered this, and then shook her head. "I think you are who you are. She seems like a good person. It's easy to understand why you fell in love with her."

"And that doesn't bother you? Everything we're doing to try and help her?"

"It has nothing to do with us, Jessie. I know you wouldn't have started up with me if there was still something between the two of you. I wouldn't have let you."

"You know there's no chance of that anymore."

"But I didn't when we headed down here. Neither of us knew what she had become." She took his hand and kissed it gently.

"How'd I get so lucky?" Jess asked after returning the kiss.

"I think you were long overdue."

They retrieved Maria's car from the parking garage at the Ensenada airport and headed up the highway to the border. Jess got in the trunk once again—even though he doubted the authorities would be looking for him *reentering* the country. His anxiety proved unnecessary as they sailed right through the checkpoint. They made great time heading up Interstate 15 and reached the outskirts of Palm Springs in less than a couple of hours.

By the time they hit Palm Canyon Drive, the sun was just descending. Which didn't make Jess feel a whole lot better.

5

Benji was waiting for them when they arrived at Maria's apartment. They had vetoed the Sands. Jess wasn't quite ready should Thaddeus Burke pop by for the umpteenth time. He wanted to get all his ducks in a row first. Benji had picked up sandwiches and they sat around Maria's table in her tiny kitchen as they filled him in on their trip into the Mexican jungle.

"Sounds like you had no other choice," Benji said when Jess got to the part about imprisoning Tracy in the glass house on the hill.

"I keep telling myself that," Jess responded. "Doesn't make me feel a whole lot better. Everything status quo with her father?"

"It's a go. Though I still don't love the idea." Benji reached into his pocket and pulled out an envelope. "As requested—one ticket."

Jess stuffed it away. Maria said she wanted to come along—and not for the first time; the same discussion had occupied most of the drive back from the border. He repeated the same reasons for Maria staying behind. He had dragged her into enough already and it was fifty-fifty Clark James would even talk to him. Those odds would diminish rapidly if he weren't alone. Realizing she would never win this battle, Maria finally relented.

Jess took a quick shower, changed into his version of something presentable, and then went over the last part of the plan with Benji.

"How long till I make the call?" his former teammate asked.

"Once I get there."

"Can I go on record again and say I am not in favor of this?" Benji asked.

"I second that," Maria added.

"Duly noted."

He kissed Maria goodbye, bear-hugged Benji, and two minutes later retrieved the SUV from her garage and headed toward downtown Palm Springs.

The last few guests were making their way into the Palm Springs Cinema when Jess drove past, looking for a parking space. He thought it a good omen when he nabbed a spot only a block from the movie palace. As he approached the theater, Jess pulled out his cell and quickly punched in the number to the Sands. Benji, recognizing Jess's cell, abandoned the usual come-on cutesy quip.

"You there?"

"Just about to walk in. Call him."

Benji couldn't help asking one more time. "You sure about this?"

"No," Jess said. "But call Burke anyway."

"You got it," Benji said. "Good luck."

Jess disconnected, knowing he would need a whole lot of it.

The sign on the marquee read "An Evening With Palm Springs' Clark James." As long as he was breathing, Jess was sure the actor wouldn't miss out on a self-congratulatory affair. When Jess was down in Mexico and began to realize Clark's culpability in the tragedies that had occurred in the desert, he realized it would be best to confront him in a very public place.

Jess waited to enter the lobby until a few minutes after the lights flashed, signifying the program was about to begin. When the house lights dimmed, Jess walked in the theater and managed to find a seat in the back just as Clark James took the stage to thunderous applause.

As the actor began speaking, Jess watched him with a different perspective. He had known Clark James for the better part of his life. He had been that "movie star" friend of his parents and then, for a brief summer, the father of the girl he loved. Now, as the handsome leading man enthralled his audience with tales of Hollywood and his off-screen antics, Jess realized he was performing the role of a lifetime: pretending to be himself.

If Jess hadn't known better, he would say the actor on stage was the same egotistical ham he had been since his first big hit thirty years earlier. If anything, Clark was more animated and bombastic than before the creature in Santa Alvarado turned him, and that concerned Jess. His own father had exhibited unnatural strength, even for a healthy man his age, when he had rescued Jess from the desert grave. He realized the change both men had undergone not only brought them back to life but also revitalized them beyond belief. It made going up against the spawn of the Civatateo all the more intimidating.

Meanwhile, Clark had the audience eating out of his hand, which Jess found ironic; he knew the actor would rather be sucking the blood out of theirs. James answered questions with more humorous anecdotes. As he wound down his opening remarks and set the stage for the screening of *Pathfinders*, perhaps his most famous film, a Western that had garnered Clark the first of three Oscar nominations, Jess headed to the aisle on one side of the theater. Cloaked in darkness, he was able to move towards the stage where Clark finished and took three more bows than necessary to the ensuing applause. The lights winked out, the film projector flickered, and the movie started.

Jess caught a break.

He was pretty certain Clark James would head for a spot in the audience to watch the film with the crowd. Jess had been prepared to confront him in the darkness as he went to find his seat, but was saved the trouble when James stepped to the side of the stage. Jess realized Clark was either going to watch from the wings or make a quick exit, so he picked up the pace before the latter could occur, and suddenly the two of them were alone backstage.

Jess pulled out the solar flash from his pocket and called softly to the actor. "Mr. James."

The moment he turned around, Jess flicked on the flash and traced it quickly across Clark's neck and shoulder. There was an audible singe accompanied by a muted cry from James.

Jess felt vindicated, but also at the point of no return.

"Your daughter sends her regrets. She wanted to be here tonight but is having a hard time getting out of Mexico."

He had to give James credit. Once confronted, the man didn't pussy-foot around the situation. Jess thought he caught a glimpse of sharper-than-normal incisors at the corners of his taut mouth.

"I knew we should have killed you in my backyard instead of burying you in the desert," said the thing that was once the famous actor Clark James.

6

Jess had been to the Palm Springs Cinema at least a hundred times. He had spent many a Saturday afternoon at bargain matinees escaping the heat and real life in the mansion on the hill. But he'd never watched a scene on the Cinema's screen that rivaled the surreal one he was currently starring in—standing backstage against the flicker of celluloid with a movie idol who had retired because he had become a vampire.

"Who thought of the grave in the desert?" asked Jess. "Edward Rice?"

The actor nodded. "Too many bodies were piling up. First Tom Cox, then your father. It was easy enough to write them off. The first was a tragic road accident. And Walter had been sick for months—people would think he succumbed to his disease. But you were a different matter."

"Because I was poking around. I show up dead and somebody else starts asking questions. But if I vanished . . ."

" . . . no one would think twice," finished James. "You already walked away once for seven years."

"So nobody would question a permanent disappearance," Jess said.

"That was the plan, until your father got involved with his rescue operation."

"How did he know where I was?"

"I've no idea. I didn't even know he'd saved you until Rice told me. I have to presume he followed us."

"Right after turning your daughter."

The expression on Clark's face changed to something bordering on murderous. Jess inched backwards and bumped into the stage wall. "Your father will pay dearly for that."

Jess thought back to the conversation with Tracy in the cavern and her telling him about Clark's blood grudge against Walter. "When did you find out about him and Tracy?"

"Shortly after you left."

"How?"

"My daughter told me. She was clearly unhappy and I knew you had broken her heart. I was getting angrier and making rumblings about hiring a private eye to find you. Tracy was afraid I would do you bodily harm. I won't say it didn't enter my mind."

"No one ever came looking as far as I could tell."

"That's because Tracy begged me not to. She still loved you, despite everything. The sad thing is I think she still does."

Jess didn't respond. He didn't know how.

"Hearing all this from her was . . . difficult." His lips tightened. "Especially the part about sleeping with my best friend."

"Yet you and my father saw each other socially for years afterwards."

"Men like me and Walter do a lot of things for appearance's sake." He pointed out toward the stage. "Like what you just saw. The public sees one person. Very few know what I really am."

"That's because you've destroyed anyone who does."

"I didn't ask for this, Jessie. Remember that." Clark James loomed in close and Jess found himself scrunched tighter against the wall. "The thing that did this to me killed three men and a woman. I thought I was lucky to escape. It wasn't until I got to your father's hospital that I realized I would've been better off butchered in the Mexican jungle. Instead I am doomed to this wretched eternal thirst."

"Which you kill others to quench."

"Men and women who are going to die anyway. They are already wasting away at Meadowland. I actually give them peace as they drift into the great beyond. They are oblivious to pain by the time I am done."

Jess thought this sounded like Clark James trying to justify his actions the past few years. He knew it didn't hold water for all his victims.

"My father said you were killing him."

"Walter Stark ruined my daughter's life!"

A few disturbed movie patrons "ssssshed" from inside the theater. James backed off a step.

"Why did you wait all this time?" asked Jess. "You knew about him and Tracy five years ago."

"Because even a man like your father should be spared this fate. It wasn't until he started meeting with Tom Cox that I had to take matters into my own hands." Sorrow took over his face. "And because of that I was punished even further."

"When he turned Tracy."

"I will drag him into the sunlight myself for that."

"Where is he?"

"I've no idea."

"How can that be?" asked Jess.

"Simple. I don't know where he is. Do you think we belong to a fraternity and hang out together in some sort of vampire clubhouse?"

"I thought you would know because you turned him."

"It doesn't work that way. He's trying to adapt, I'm sure. So far, he's made a lousy go of it. Attacking Tracy was unforgivable. Killing Rice, well, not the greatest loss in the world."

"Especially if I end up going to jail for it."

"A fringe benefit." The vampire smirked. "What did you exactly plan to accomplish here?"

"Get myself off that hook and prove what you are," answered Jess. He withdrew the solar flash and the actor promptly snatched it from his hand.

"What in hell is this thing?" he asked.

Jess was more than a little unnerved by the vampire's swift reflexes. "Remember Tag Marlowe?"

"Of course."

"He made it. Call it Instant Daylight."

He tried to grab it back but Clark James quickly pocketed it. Jess was beginning to think things couldn't get much worse when a voice called from behind him.

"I thought that was you!"

Both men turned to see Sarah Stark standing there. Jaime Solis, the owner of the Palm Springs Country Club, was at her side.

Jess was wrong.

It could actually get a whole lot worse.

The quartet quickly moved to the lobby upon Solis's suggestion so that their raised voices wouldn't bother the movie patrons.

"Nice to see you're out and about so shortly after the death of your dearly beloved," Jess told his sister the moment they came into the light.

She moved close and whispered in his ear. "Fuck you, Jessie." Then, she stepped away and spoke in a normal tone. "Jaime was kind enough to suggest it might take my mind off everything."

"Nice of you," Jess said to Solis.

"It is my pleasure," Solis politely responded.

"The cops have been looking for you, Jessie. Where the hell have you been?"

"Out of town."

"They think you fled because you killed Edward."

"If that was true, why would I come back?"

"Hell if know!" seethed Sarah. Solis tried to step between the sparring siblings but Jess fended him off.

"I suggest staying out of this."

Solis pointed at the lobby. "Maybe this isn't the proper time or place."

But Jess wasn't hearing any of it. "I didn't kill Edward Rice."

"I saw you standing over his fucking body, Jessie! What am I supposed to think? That someone got there right before you?"

"Yes, that's exactly what you're supposed to think!" Jess yelled.

Solis stepped forward, and this time was able to separate them. "Perhaps we should calm down. I'm sure your brother has a reasonable explanation for what he was doing there . . ."

"I told her that night. Rice called me."

"I didn't hear him," insisted Sarah.

"Maybe you were already asleep. You were when his killer showed up," suggested Jess.

"You should know," accused Sarah.

"It wasn't me!"

"Then who the hell was it?" Sarah screamed back.

"You wouldn't believe me if I told you."

"Of course not! Because I'm looking at him." Sarah's hysteria slipped away and sadness took over. "I've known you all my life, Jessie. It's been a long time since we got along. We've had lots of differences but I never thought you were capable of this."

"I'm not, Sarah. I swear."

Sister and brother stood there, somber and worn out. Solis was the first one to notice someone else had entered the lobby.

"Jess Stark. You're under arrest."

Jess turned around and saw two things that caused his heart to leap into his throat.

The first was the business end of Thaddeus Burke's pistol pointed directly at his chest.

The second was that Clark James was nowhere to be seen.

Which was worse was a toss-up.

For Jess, they both just plain sucked.

EXCERPTS FROM THE JOURNAL OF EDWARD D. RICE

June 7

    Clark James summoned me to Palm Springs Medical early that evening. I hadn't seen him in a few days, and after spending that first week fending off the press at his request, I was happy to be back in my apartment trying to reassemble my life after the ill-fated trip to Mexico. I was filling out applications for any possible staff opportunity when I got the call.

    "I want you to get me out of here," Clark rumbled when I arrived at his room.

    "Shouldn't this be something you discuss with your doctors instead of me?"

    "They don't think I'm ready."

    "Perhaps they know best." I had checked his chart upon entering. He still wasn't eating much; what went down usually came right back up. He had received a few blood transfusions that seemed to help. But he was still fading during the daytime, which befuddled the team of physicians that descended on him like fresh meat.

    "You saved my life down there. I'm going to trust you with it," he told me.

    "I looked at your chart, Clark. You're hardly in any shape to go home."

    "I know that. I just don't want to be here."

    That was when he first mentioned Meadowland and Walter Stark.

June 9

It took a couple of days of Clark throwing his weight around and Walter Stark's patronage to move the actor from Palm Springs Medical to the convalescent facility. The PSM staff made Clark sign tons of releases, and he wasn't the only one. I also had to put my name and reputation down in ink on numerous dotted lines.

I didn't have much choice. My medical career was in shambles. I quickly discovered most doors were closed before I even got to them. It seemed my adventures in Mexico and subsequent involvement with Clark James upon his tumultuous return to the Desert had tarnished me as a viable candidate. In many circles, I was blamed for Clark's worsening condition; somehow I should have done more when treating him in the jungle. Other employers found great fault with the way I had dealt with the press regarding the actor, citing me as being unprofessional and overstepping the bounds of the patient-physician relationship. I was shocked, thinking I had just been protecting Clark from the rabid media horde. I was extremely disheartened to hear terms like "starfucker" and "glory-seeker" bandied about in tabloids and whispered in hospital hallways where I was trying to gain employment.

So when Clark James said he could secure me a position on staff at a reputable institution like Meadowland in exchange for getting him transferred there—I saw it as an opportunity I couldn't pass up. When I asked how he could guarantee me a job, he told me he'd known Walter Stark for a couple of decades and the man owed him big time.

That was how I agreed to take full responsibility for Clark James and signed the six-inch stack of appropriate documents facilitating his move to Meadowland.

I've come to regret that decision more than I can ever tell.

I began feeling that way almost immediately.

All it took was Clark James dying two days later.

7

"Why did you leave the country?"

Sitting in the sheriff's office, Jess considered the best way to answer the question. The only good thing about his situation was Burke hadn't thrown a murder charge at him yet. So far it was just conspiracy to withhold information pertaining to a crime. Unfortunately for Jess, he knew the real cause of Edward Rice's death was not easily explained—unless Burke was in on the whole thing. And Jess had a hard time believing this bureaucrat was, as Benji had put it, a "familiar" to Clark and his brethren. If anything, he suspected there was some kind of fiscal arrangement, possibly blackmail, getting Burke to look the other way at Cox's and Walter's deaths.

Jess went with a "What? Me Worry?" attitude. "I took a little vacation."

"Hours after standing over Edward Rice's body."

Sadly, Burke was born without a sense of humor, so Jess moved on to option two: telling the parts of the truth that would keep him out of a straitjacket.

"Don't know how many times you want to hear me say it, but Rice called me over to see him and was dead by the time I got there . . ."

" . . . which we only have your word for."

"Check his phone records. You'll see he called me at the Sands Motel."

"I'm not disputing that. We got hold of the phone company. What bothers me is why you would sneak out of town in the trunk of Maria Flores's car and cross the border into Mexico."

This caught Jess off guard. He could see the sheriff got more than a little pleasure from it.

"Not as stupid as you think, huh, Stark?"

Three or four smart-ass answers popped into Jess's head, but he decided it wasn't the time to let them escape his lips. Instead, he thought it best to let the cop show off a bit so Jess could see exactly how much deep shit he was in.

"How did you find out about that?"

Burke proved Jess's supposition right by immediately starting to brag. "We found the cell phone you tossed and quickly ran the Vegas lead into the ground. It got me thinking." The sheriff actually tapped his forehead with an index finger. "Maybe he went the other way. We ran down a list of all your known associates, family, that good-for-nothing friend of yours Lutz, to see if we could pull a match for flights and border crossings, and just this morning got a hit on Flores at the border. I thought it was the maid so I was kind of shocked when I saw the car was registered to the daughter. Got yourself a new girlfriend, do ya?"

Jess tried not to grit his teeth as he told Burke, "Maria has nothing to with this."

"That's where you're wrong. How 'bout aiding and abetting a suspect in a murder case for starters?"

"Anything you want to charge her with, go ahead and put on me."

"Sensitive? I get it. She's a damn good lookin' piece of ass."

Jess started to get out of his seat, ready to throttle Burke's neck. Then, realizing the man was probably itching for him to make exactly such a move, Jess settled back down. The sheriff chuckled, which infuriated Jess more than ever, but this time he didn't rise to the bait.

"Easy, son," said Burke, with the smoothness of a man who took great pleasure in getting under people's skin. "I just need you to talk. But don't think I won't make good on that threat to haul your girl in and lock her the hell up."

Jess considered his surroundings. At least he was sitting in the sheriff's office and not an interview room. That led him to believe Burke was going to have a hard time making things stick. The sheriff would have Jess shackled to a metal table if he had a rock-solid case. He thought the man might be playing him—placing Jess in a more relaxed atmosphere where he would be more liable to slip without realizing it. Jess presumed someone was right outside Burke's door ready to pounce and read him his rights the moment he screwed up.

"What exactly do you want to know, Sheriff?"

Burke leaned back, smug and satisfied. "I assume asking you why you killed Edward Rice is a nonstarter?"

"You assume right."

Burke pulled a pad off his desk and uncapped a pen. "How about skipping town? Want to explain why you went, and more importantly, why you came back?"

"I thought it was the best way to find evidence to expose the real killer."

"Evidence? Down in Mexico?"

"That's right."

"Where?"

"Outside a small village called Santa Alvarado. Ever heard of it?"

"Can't say that I have." Burke's blank look convinced Jess the man was telling the truth. Which was going to make explaining things a whole lot harder. "Did you find something there?"

"Actually, yeah."

"Feel like sharing?"

This was the tricky part. Open the undead door and a guy like Burke, unless he was in on it, was likely to slam it in your face. Jess thought maybe there was a different track to come in on.

"Why do you think I had Benji Lutz call and tell you to come down to the theater tonight?"

"I figure you were sick of running and decided to confess. But that's clearly not the case. Care to enlighten me?"

"I was going to present you with proof."

"Proof?"

Jess took a deep breath. Then, figuring what the hell, just came out with it. "That Clark James was involved in the deaths of Tom Cox, Edward Rice, and my father."

Burke laughed. "That's quite a mouthful, son. And an even bigger accusation."

"It's one I can prove."

"With something you found in some shit-hole South of the Border."

"Exactly."

"All right, then. Where is it?"

This wasn't the first time Jess kicked himself for letting Clark James grab the solar flash out of his hand and then disappearing. He chose his words carefully.

"James took it with him."

"Of course he did."

"I'm telling you, Sheriff . . ."

A sharp rap on the door interrupted Jess's protest.

"Not now!" Burke called out.

The rapper ignored this, hit the door harder, and pushed it open. It was one of the deputies who had accompanied Jess in the squad car from the theater. He wasn't much more than a kid, old acne scars threatening to come back and eyes flickering with nervousness at busting in on his boss. Burke didn't help matters by jumping down the young man's throat.

"What the hell do you want?!"

The deputy coughed, struggling to find his voice. When he finally did, Jess was probably the most surprised person in the room.

"Stark's lawyer is here."

Burke frowned. He looked at Jess. "Don't remember you asking for one."

Before Jess could tell the sheriff he had made no such request, the door swung open wider and a man in a three-piece suit that was as crisp and spiffy as when he put it on fifteen hours earlier popped in the door. Jess immediately recognized him, though it had been close to a decade since he last saw him.

"J. S. Summers," said the attorney who had been Walter Stark's deal-closer and go-to legal counsel for almost thirty years. He had close cropped hair, was perennially tan, and glanced at a watch worth six months of Thaddeus Burke's salary. "You've got fifteen minutes to release my client."

"On what grounds?" Burke asked.

Summers proceeded to unleash a stream of civil rights violations and illegal statutes that Jess lost track of by the third one. All he knew was that with each passing minute, Burke shrunk deeper into his chair and the deputy got more of a kick out of his boss getting the shaft. Jess was ceremoniously shown the exit with the proverbial warning not to leave town.

He thanked Summers profusely for showing up, but the attorney said it wasn't his idea. He told Jess his benefactor was waiting outside in the parking lot.

Jess walked out of the sheriff's office to find Kate Stark sitting behind the wheel of her Mercedes. She rolled down the passenger window and motioned him toward the car.

"It's late, darling. Let's go home."

Jess didn't need to be asked twice.

As he got inside the Mercedes, Jess thought the old saying was true. Sometimes, the only thing a boy really needed was his mother.

EXCERPT FROM THE JOURNAL OF
EDWARD D. RICE

June 11

Clark James seemed to thrive from the moment he arrived at Meadowland.

Walter Stark was there to greet us when the ambulance arrived that first evening. Stark embraced the actor, but I could tell it was a put-on façade. I don't think I would have noticed it had Clark not told me that Walter Stark "owed him." It made me realize this was a business arrangement and nothing more. But Clark seemed happy to be in a gated facility. It kept the press away and he didn't have a dozen poking doctors trying to figure out what was ailing him.

"You're my doc," he told me in front of Walter Stark. Right after we got James situated, I signed an employment contract with Meadowland. I thanked Stark for the opportunity, but he was indifferent, confirming I was just a by-product of a deal between the two men. He wanted nothing to do with me.

I think that was where my resentment began toward Walter Stark. I don't like to think my future involvement with his family came from a Machiavellian place, but I believe at some subconscious level I wanted to prove to the old man I wasn't just a piece of dirt under his thousand-dollar loafers.

The paperwork complete, I became Clark James's primary physician. He immediately began to show marked improvement. Clark went a day without a blood transfusion and said his appetite was returning, though I don't recall him actually eating anything. He had a couple of visitors—his daughter, Tracy, who had been a constant companion since his return from Mexico, and Walter Stark. I was constantly monitoring him, but Clark said I didn't need to keep checking on him so often.

"You're on staff now, Edward. You're paid weekly, not by the office visit."

I took his blood pressure and was satisfied to see it running only a tad low. "Just showing my appreciation to my benefactor."

Two hours later I found him collapsed on the floor. I checked his pulse and vital signs. He wasn't breathing—and wouldn't be doing that again anytime soon.

He had detached himself from the heart monitor and shut it off before getting up, which was why I hadn't been alerted. I rooted around for the call button just as someone entered the room behind me.

The first thing I noticed was the motorcycle suit that encased the man from neck to toe. I told the new arrival he had to leave. "You can't be here right now."

But the man closed the door and took two steps into the room. His voice was simultaneously mellifluous and terrifying.

"I think I can be of help, Doctor."

I was immediately paralyzed because I remembered where I had heard that voice before. It was from my half-dream in the tent, what I thought had been an apparition hovering over Clark James. Now I realized it had actually been real, not a phantom from a nightmare.

Its mouth opened. The teeth were pointed.

That was the first time I met the Civatateo.

8

The last time Jess remembered his mother driving him somewhere, he had been in seventh grade and the principal had called her to pick him up. He'd gotten into an altercation with his archenemy, Stewart Trank, over what most adolescent boys do battle over—a girl.

It had been Valentine's Day and Jess had a crush on an eighth-grader, Wendy Clemmons. Shy, Jess found it difficult to speak to her, but worked up enough courage to slip an anonymous card in her locker. The four-line poem was the eighteenth version he had composed before committing to it in pen below the standard greeting.

He watched from down the hall, half-hidden by the water fountain, as she opened the locker on her lunch break. She squealed with delight upon finding the red envelope and her eyes lit up as she read the poem more than once. This reaction emboldened Jess to step forward and claim his rightful place as the card-giver, but Stewart Trank, who made it his life's work to fuck with Jess Stark's head, beat him to the punch. He had seen Jess place the card in the locker and walked up to Wendy to claim the card as his own. Stewart asked if she liked the poem and Wendy said she loved it. Even worse, she agreed to go to the Valentine's Dance with Stewart, which was the sole reason Jess had composed the card in the first place. Something to help him work up the nerve to invite Wendy himself.

Jess wanted to tackle Stewart right there, but wasn't going to make a scene in front of the girl he secretly admired. He waited until Wendy returned to class to confront him, but barely got a word out of his mouth before he heard, "Snooze you lose." Which was punctuated by shoving Jess into the bank of lockers. Still, Jess resisted the urge to fight back.

But then Stewart Trank, that stealer of hearts and greeting cards, delivered the coup-de-grace. "I'll let you know if she puts out."

Jess went ape-shit. "She's not that kind of girl!" he yelled, causing all the kids to turn and stare.

He launched himself at Stewart Trank.

By the time the teachers pulled Jess off his sworn rival, Stewart had lost two teeth and a lot of blood on the floor. What felt good at the time was fleeting. On Sunday morning, Jess heard Wendy had spent the entire dance fawning all over Stewart's wounds. Jess wanted to kill himself, which was exactly how he felt when his mother dropped by the principal's office to pick him up and start his two-week suspension from school.

It took the entire drive home to pull the story out of him; Jess was embarrassed and not used to telling his mother anything about his private-thirteen-year-old-so-miserable life. When they parked in front of the Stark mansion, Kate shut off the engine and stared at her oldest son for what seemed like forever.

Jess dreaded the scolding and punishment he was certain that was coming, so he was completely knocked off guard when his mother finally spoke.

"That was pretty gallant."

"What? What was?" asked Jess, truly in a quandary.

"Standing up for a young woman like that. Especially one who doesn't even know you exist."

"That's only because she's in the grade ahead of me."

His mother had smiled, incredibly touched. "I wish someone had done that once for me."

Thinking back on it years later, that was the first inkling Jess got into the complicated relationship between his parents.

Now, riding alongside his mother who had rescued him from the sheriff's station, Jess looked at her in disbelief and simultaneous awe. He wondered how she had stood by Walter all those years—and how would she react if she learned he really wasn't dead and buried?

"How did you know where I was?"

"Your sister came home and couldn't wait to tell me what happened at the theater."

"She probably has me ready to be strapped into a chair and injected."

"Sarah has always been . . . how should I put it . . . overly dramatic. Don't get me wrong, I think she loved Edward, or had convinced herself she did. Whether it was reciprocated on his part or he was just trying to marry into this family, we'll never know."

She kept her eye on the road to navigate a turn, but could sense Jess's dubious raise of an eyebrow. "And yes, I was guilty of letting Edward become entrenched in our lives too quickly. Regardless, your sister lost the man she thought she was going to spend the rest of her life with. You have to give her a little room to work her way through that loss."

"By going out on the town with Jaime Solis?"

"We all handle grief differently, darling."

Jess thought back to how his mother had taken to her bed when Walter died. She looked remarkably better. Perhaps she needed something to rally for, like her eldest child getting dragged into custody.

"I take her rants and raves with a shaker of salt." She turned to look at Jess. "But I know you couldn't have killed Edward."

"What else are you going to say? You're my mother."

"It's more than that, Jess. I gave birth to all of you, but three children couldn't be more different. And even though I was remiss in not spending enough time raising you, I know you all better than anyone. Harry is impetuous, says what he believes, and doesn't have a mean bone in his body."

"That's for sure."

"Sarah is your classic middle child who feels like she has to fight for attention. You would think being the only girl would have been enough, but she's always resented that you were the first and your brother the baby. Couple that with a domineering father, it's no wonder she's drawn to men that she feels the need to please. I just keep hoping it's a stage she'll eventually grow out of."

"We can wish."

"And then there's my sensitive, introspective first born. I know we have never been close. I also know I had to back your father in situations you not only disagreed with but might have felt were a betrayal."

And there it was. Suddenly, Jess realized that his mother had known the darkest secret of all.

"Tracy?"

Kate nodded.

"How did you find out?"

"I told your father I'd leave him if he didn't tell me what he did to make you disappear."

Jess was still reeling from this revelation. "How did you know it was Dad?"

"Because who else but your father could make you run away without even saying goodbye?"

Kate exhaled loudly while waiting for a signal to change. "That's how I know you didn't murder Edward Rice. If you were ever going to kill someone, it would have been your father seven years ago."

Jess thought about it as they pulled up the driveway to the mansion. It was the sort of illogic that chillingly made sense. "But you stayed with him . . . all these years."

"What good would walking out have done? It would have just let him off the hook, allowed him to continue a life of debauchery with no consequences." She looked up at the mansion. "He deserved the coldness that fell upon this house."

When she turned back, her eyes had gone icy. "That way he got up every day and went to bed each night having to live with the fact that he cost me my son."

Jess realized something else about his estranged family. He had always thought Walter held all the power. But it was Kate Stark who wielded a sword and should never be crossed. As horrible as he felt for everything his mother had endured, there was a tiny part of Jess becoming increasingly fearful of her.

"At least you finally came home," Kate said.

"I'm sorry it took Dad dying to do it."

"Me too." Her sad smile tugged at his heart.

Once again Jess wondered if things would have turned out differently if he had never returned his mother's phone call that day.

"Did he ever ask you to forgive him?" wondered Jess.

"Constantly."

"What did you say?"

"Nothing. I just stayed. I guess that was answer enough. Eventually he stopped asking."

She looked up at the house one last time.

"The person he should have been asking forgiveness from all this time was you."

EXCERPT FROM THE JOURNALS OF EDWARD D. RICE

June 11 (continued)

It didn't take me very long to realize I had been set up—by a two-hundred-year-old Mexican vampire and a film star.

It was pretty clear the thing in front of me (even though it looked like a man, I still, to this day, regard it as a "thing") was not a normal human being. I'm not sure it ever was, even though it has spent time masquerading as one. But I could suddenly attribute a lot of the strange occurrences since the deaths in the jungle to the "thing" hovering over Clark James's dead body—the sliced-up film crew, James's bizarre malady and aversion to sunlight, the bites on his body, and inability to remember what had happened to him.

The Civatateo, which he quickly identified himself as, laid out the sticky situation in which I found myself.

"I see three options. One, let me help Mr. James while there is still time. If it is not done soon after he has stopped breathing, it will be too late."

I started to ask what "it" was, but the Civatateo kept talking.

"Second, I could leave him here and let you suffer professional ruin that would come from the way you mishandled Clark James's case beginning to end. I would think you would never work in the medical profession again and could face criminal charges, most likely resulting in a long prison sentence."

I managed to find my voice at that point. "What if I choose neither?"

The thing moved so quickly, I didn't even see its arm thrust out. I was suddenly hurled across the room. I crashed into the wall and crumpled to the ground.

"You will suffer the same fate as the men in the jungle." The Civatateo bared its teeth once more. "I should mention it is beyond painful."

The fact that I didn't offer up a protest gave the Civatateo the desired answer. It advanced on the dead Clark and bent over him.

The horror that followed I will take to my grave.

To a man of science, there was no earthly explanation, but I knew I had entered a world that no medical book or school could ever teach you about.

The Civatateo rolled up the sleeve of its bizarre motorcycle outfit and lowered its pointed teeth into its own forearm. Dark blood flowed like ebony from the puncture mark. The Civatateo leaned over and cradled Clark James's head in his lap. It opened the dead man's mouth and let the blood trickle down his throat.

I was frozen in horror at this sight. I kept waiting for the moment when I would wake up and find myself having fallen asleep filling out job applications in my tiny apartment. I opened my mouth to protest at the vile act but was stopped by something more unbelievable.

Clark James began coughing and choking in the thing's arms.

I leapt to my feet and started to approach the two of them, but the Civatateo snapped up its head up and glared. Never in my life had I felt closer to my own death. I knew if I took one more step, the Civatateo would rip me to shreds like a lioness protecting its newborn cub. I had no choice but to back off and watch.

The ebony blood continued flowing into Clark James's mouth. He stopped choking and began to suckle, as if receiving mother's milk from a surrogate savior.

Eventually the Civatateo removed his arm from James's lips, but not without a struggle as the actor had regained a considerable amount of strength and wanted more sustenance. But the thing quieted him down, stroking his forehead like an Impressionist Madonna pampering her supine child.

Clark's breathing became steady and normal for the first time since he emerged from the jungle. He lay in the thing's arms, his eyes closed, softly murmuring.

To my amazement and horror, Clark James seemed healed.

And most frightening of all, content.

"What have you done?" I managed to ask.

"He has been turned."

"Into what?"

The Civatateo told me.

I knew my life was never going to be the same.

9

The first thing Lena wanted to do was feed him. Forget the fact it was one in the morning. Lena would sooner run naked down Palm Canyon Drive than allow a Stark to walk out of her kitchen if she suspected an empty stomach in her midst. Jess realized he was actually hungry and scarfed down the omelet Lena whipped up in one quarter of the time it took her to make it.

Kate sat with them at the kitchen table and nursed a cup of tea. This was also a foreign concept for Jess; growing up the children never sat with the adults.

Sarah traipsed through the kitchen at one point, gave her mother a disparaging look, made a crack about locking doors lest they should be murdered in their beds, and went back upstairs. *At least she didn't scream or attack me this time*, thought Jess. She might have been coming around, but was more likely deferring to their mother's wishes under her own roof.

Kate insisted Jess spend the night in his old room. His earlier plea to be dropped off at the theater to pick up the SUV had fallen on deaf ears. Kate simply stated she would take him first thing in the morning—that was that. She got up, leaned over, and kissed him good night. He thanked her again for rescuing him from the evil clutches of the sheriff and then Kate went upstairs to bed.

That left Jess sitting with Lena, the mother of the beautiful girl he had fallen so hard for in Mexico. He wondered if she knew what had happened between them, and if not, whether he should be volunteering any information. As usual with Lena, she was way ahead of him and immediately made the situation a whole lot easier.

She reached across the table and took his hand. "My Maria is very happy."

He didn't quite do a coffee spit take, but he did have to fumble for a few words. "Th-that's good."

"She's also worried about you."

"No reason to be. Mom and her lawyer got the sheriff to back off. It's going to be okay."

Lena shook her head. "I'm not talking about that. I know you didn't kill Dr. Edward. None of us think that." She glanced up toward the ceiling like she had X-ray vision. "Even your sister. You know what she's like."

He used his mother's words. "Overly dramatic."

"*Sí*." She still was holding his hand. "I'm talking about what happened down in Santa Alvarado."

Jess couldn't tell how much Lena knew. "What did she tell you?"

"Nothing. That's the problem. Maria never keeps anything from me."

Jess gently withdrew his hand.

"She told you about us, didn't she?"

"Only because she didn't want me to get mad at you for taking her down there."

"Believe me, Lena, it wasn't my idea. She insisted on going."

"I know. *That* she told me. It's what she's not saying that has me worried."

Jess made a decision. Even though he had first learned about the Civatateo from this woman who had helped raise him, he thought it best not to burden Lena with the particulars.

"We're okay, Lena. Both of us."

"You say that now."

"I would never let anything happen to Maria. Please trust me."

"I know that. I'm not concerned about the two of you." She smiled. "In fact, it's what I always secretly wished for."

But her face quickly darkened as she looked out the window. "It's what's out there that worries me. I'm pretty sure that also troubles both you and my Maria."

Jess was struggling for a response when his mother called from upstairs. It wasn't quite a scream but enough to make them rush out of the kitchen.

They found Kate at the top of the stairs. The color had drained from her face; she had aged at least ten years in the same number of minutes. Jess reached her first.

"What's wrong?"

She pointed to an open door across the hall.

Jess froze. It was Harry's room.

"I went in to check on him," Kate said. "He wasn't there."

Jess moved past her and entered the room. Moonlight illuminated a typical teenage boy's domain—sports posters, rock gods, books, and clothes strewn everywhere—along with an empty bed.

"It's one thirty in the morning. Where could he be?" Kate asked, hysteria creeping into her voice.

Jess didn't have an answer. If he did, it wouldn't have been good.

He was too busy staring at the open window leading out to the balcony.

They searched the house—upstairs, downstairs, inside, out. There was no sign of Harry or any indication he had gone out the doors. Jess knew they needn't look further than the balcony window where Harry told Jess he had heard Walter calling him. But he also realized he couldn't come right out and say Harry was wandering through the desert with his father who had returned from the dead.

So, the exterior lights were thrown on and everybody, including Sarah who showed genuine concern for her brother's disappearance, covered every inch of the grounds. But the teen was nowhere to be found. Kate phoned the parents of a couple of Harry's friends, hoping against hope that he was knee-deep in some mischief she would normally ground him for but in this case would celebrate. All she got were angry sleepy responses, so they decided it was time to call the police.

Jess was less than thrilled to spend time with the authorities again, especially so soon after his narrow scrape with Burke. At least he was spared the sheriff on this occasion—a couple of local uniforms responded to the call. They questioned each member of the family, and then Lena, who was the most visibly upset by Harry's absence because it fell on her watch. She told them he went to bed around midnight, unable to wait up for his mother's return to the house with Jess. The cops took a few snapshots featuring Harry, alerted the department he was missing, and told Kate to stick close to the phone in case her youngest called. Before leaving, they tried to reassure her that they saw this all the time. Harry would phone and want her to pick him up somewhere or waltz through the door at any moment. It was probably just a teenager being a teenager.

Jess tried to echo the sentiment for his mother, but was having a hard time being convincing. He knew Harry hadn't left of his own volition. And it was tearing Jess up inside. He'd been afraid of something like this happening since the moment he saw his father was out of the grave.

As dawn approached, everyone was still awake. Lena had called Maria about Harry and she came rushing over. Benji had checked in to see what happened at the theater and Jess had brought him up to speed. He was perturbed to hear it had all gone to shit with Clark fleeing, Jess dragged in for questioning, and Harry suddenly missing. Benji insisted on coming by and Jess was happy for the company and support.

Maria and Jess sat on the living room couch in silence. Benji paced back and forth, his eyes straying to the window as if willing Harry to appear in the frame. Lena, Kate, and Sarah could be heard in the kitchen mostly murmuring, but Jess could pick out the occasional sob. Finally, Benji couldn't take it anymore.

"Shouldn't we be putting out an APB on your father?" he asked.

Jess motioned for him to lower his voice. "An APB on a walking dead man?"

"Okay, I admit it's nutso but we should be doing something—at least be out there looking for him," Benji said, frustrated.

"We don't even know where to start," Maria said.

335

Jess nodded in solemn agreement. His cell phone rang. He looked at the number, didn't recognize it, but answered anyway.

"Hello."

The voice caused his heart to skip a whole bunch of beats.

"It's Clark James. Are the police still there?"

"They left about an hour ago," Jess said. Maria and Benji stared at him, all synapses on alert at the strained tone in Jess's response.

"Then, let's discuss what to do with your brother," James said.

10

"You better not harm him or . . ."

Clark James's chuckle interrupted Jess's threat.

"Or what? You'll kill me? Sort of missed your chance." Another laugh trickled through the phone line and tore at Jess's chest.

"What do you want?"

"Much better," said the undead actor. The connection was a little muddled, almost underwater. But Jess could hear the menace in Clark James's voice just fine. "We can make this a simple negotiation. Do exactly what I tell you and the boy comes back unharmed."

"I'm listening."

Benji and Maria hung on every word of Jess's side of the conversation. "Do I call the police?" Benji mouthed. Jess shook his head no.

"By the time I emerge tonight you need to have confessed to Edward Rice's murder. I hear you're locked up in custody, and then your brother can be home for a late dinner."

"And if I don't?"

"You've seen what I did to your father. Perhaps he would like to be reunited with his youngest son."

The thought made Jess nauseated. "Please don't hurt him."

"That's up to you, Jessie," said James. "Though it would be quid pro quo for what Walter did to my daughter."

"That won't be necessary. I will do what you ask."

"I knew you'd understand."

The connection futzed again as Jess heard a mechanical sputtering. Clark must have shifted his position because the sound faded away and he was much clearer when he resumed speaking. "It goes without saying all this talk of creatures returning from the dead needs to stop. Your two friends in particular, the girl and seedy motel owner."

Jess whipped his head around, wondering if Clark James could possibly be lurking nearby. The actor immediately answered the unasked question.

"I saw them arrive at the house shortly before dawn. Their silence is part of the bargain. Remember, I hear any more tales of vampires and bodies disappearing, it is easy for Harry to wander off in the middle of the night again, only this time he won't come back."

"Say I do what you want. What's to stop Harry from saying anything?"

"He won't remember any of this."

"How is that possible?"

"My daughter told you what happened when she was turned."

Jess recalled Tracy's story about her mind being clouded in the presence of the Civatateo. It made Jess fully realize the power of what he was up against.

"She told me."

"Then you know I'm not someone to fuck with, Jessie," Clark threatened. "Sundown tonight. You know where I want you to be."

The line disconnected.

Benji and Maria immediately besieged Jess with questions. He quickly repeated Clark James's demands. The two of them looked crestfallen.

"That's so messed up, man," said Benji. "You're really going to turn yourself in for a crime you didn't commit?"

"Unless we find him before dark."

Benji grinned. That was more like it.

338

Jess laid out what he was thinking.

Clark had mentioned the word "emerge." Jess figured the actor must be lying somewhere low to stay out of the sun.

"Maybe an attic or basement at the house?" wondered Maria.

"I'd check there for starters."

"What about that housekeeper there?" asked a worried Benji. "She could be some kind of sentry keeping guard while he sleeps during the day."

"Eva?" Maria made a half-scoffing sound.

"You know her?" asked Jess.

"She and my mother have been friends for years," Maria explained. "I would never mistake Eva Lopez for the undead's gatekeeper."

"I wouldn't have picked out Clark James as a vampire either," said Jess. "We need to proceed with caution there."

He addressed this to Benji, and Maria took exception to it. Jess started to reiterate his unwillingness to involve Maria further, but it was barely out of his mouth when she began protesting.

"Clark James already knows we're involved. Why should you be the only one taking the risk?"

"Because I'm the one whose ass is on the line for murder."

"Eva might not talk to you, but I bet she would if I was around," Maria said.

"Maria . . ."

She put a finger to his lips. "I waited years for you, Jess. I'm not letting you go without a fight." Then she kissed him on the very same lips. When they broke apart, Jess gave Benji a helpless shrug as if to ask: You got a better idea?

"What she said." Then Benji managed a smile. "Without all the lovey-dovey stuff."

✳   ✳   ✳

Twenty minutes later, they piled into Benji's Mustang and headed down the Stark driveway. Benji drove them to the Palm Springs Cinema where Jess was relieved to see the SUV still on the street with a ticket on the windshield. Maria and Jess switched to the bigger vehicle, followed

Benji to a long-term parking lot where they dumped the Mustang for the day, then proceeded to the James estate.

Jess felt bad about the lies he had spread before leaving the house. He'd told his mother, sister, and Lena that he had heard from Harry, who had been lured by school buddies to a late-night party and stayed out much longer than intended. Jess was letting Harry sleep it off, but would get him home before sundown. Kate and Sarah were so relieved they bought it at first blush. Jess wasn't so sure about Lena, but Maria got her mother to back off with a strident nod and "trust me" look. Jess knew the truth would be impossible to explain and, even if they miraculously believed it, a full-scale panic would ensue. *No sense in that,* thought Jess, who was worried enough for all of them.

When they reached the front gate of the Jameses' house, Jess let Maria ring the bell and do the talking. Maria was right. Her fluent Spanish not only had the gates open in a flash but a welcoming Eva was already waiting for them by the time they hit the top of the driveway. Maria told the housekeeper they had come to pick up a few things for Tracy, who was joining them on a weekend trip to Mexico.

Eva buying it so readily told Jess a couple of things. Maria was as personable and loveable as a girl could be, but if Clark James was holed up somewhere inside, Eva would have never let them through the gate, let alone the front door. Even if he were occupying a basement labyrinth Eva had no clue existed, the woman would have been under strict orders regarding drop-by visitors. All of this, coupled with Jess's once-over of the house when he came looking for Tracy a few days ago, led him to believe they were barking up the wrong tree.

Eva accompanied Maria upstairs to gather clothes for Tracy, the two of them prattling away in Spanish at fifty miles per minute. It allowed Benji and Jess to look for a secret hideaway. But there wasn't a hidden passage, or even a basement, on the premises. Maria eventually found the guys in the backyard, staring at the country club below.

She had a small suitcase in tow. Then, as prearranged, Maria asked Eva if she could trouble her for something to drink before they headed out. The housekeeper, happy to be doing something, went inside to fetch beverages.

"Anything?" Maria asked.

Benji shook his head. Jess had moved over to one of the flowerbeds. There was a sprinkler box hidden by a tree. He slid open the panel and flicked the dial to the "manual" setting.

"What are you doing?" asked Maria.

"Give me a couple of seconds."

He quickly ran through the stations. Water sprayed in an arcing soft drizzle over various landscaped areas. Jess shut them down just as fast and closed the panel.

"That would've been too easy."

"What are you talking about?" asked Benji.

"I heard this rushing sound when I was on the phone with Clark James. I thought it was bad cell reception, then realized it was sputtering water. The first thing that popped into my head was the sprinkler system here at the house. But this is like a soft rain. What I heard was more industrial. Like . . ."

Jess stopped midspeech.

He hurried across the backyard just as Eva came out of the house with a drink tray. The housekeeper tried to hand one to Jess but he strode past her to the edge of the property. Benji took his glass and one for Jess.

"Sorry. He gets distracted when he's thirsty," Benji said.

Maria took the third glass and muttered something to Eva in Spanish. The woman smiled, offered up a "*No problema*" and returned to the house.

"What's going on?" Maria asked, watching Jess stare into the distance.

"I don't have a fucking clue," answered Benji.

Jess was studying the immaculate green fairways and bright white sand traps of the country club five hundred feet below. His gaze settled on the red bridge leading from the driving range to the practice area.

Jess had been standing on it a few days before with Harry. He remembered his brother hovering way too close to the edge, staring into the gorge below. Harry had practically been in a trance when he told Jess he thought he heard his father calling him.

"Jess? What's going on?" asked Benji. He had come up right behind him with Maria.

Jess snapped out of it and looked back at the adjacent driving range.

Big industrial sprinklers kicked into gear—watering one section of grass after shutting down the previous one.

Jess tore his eyes away and turned to face Maria and Benji.

"I think I know where they are."

EXCERPT FROM THE JOURNAL OF
EDWARD D. RICE

June 14

The press conference was held at night.

Everything in Clark James's life would happen after sunset from that point forward. It was one of the many things the Civatateo had told me after he had "turned" the actor.

I didn't have to fill in much. Things fell quickly into place. I realized it had been trapped by the refracted sunlight in the field of glass for a couple of centuries before the film scout came along and broke open the window to see what was below. The Civatateo, free at last, had immediately attacked the intruders and been strengthened by the infusion of fresh blood. It only wounded Clark James—and I learned this was purposeful. The Civatateo had a use for the actor and, ultimately, me.

Perhaps the ability for the dead to rise and prowl at night could trace its roots in science. Certain organisms thrive under the lunar pull or regenerate on a regular basis (orchids, roses, seasonal trees). There was even Henrietta Lacks, the African-American woman whose cancer cells became immortal and are still used for medical research, six decades after her death. Maybe the Civatateo was a similar genetic mutation that could be explained in a laboratory, but that would never happen because it would kill the researcher before allowing it.

After accepting this creature could return from the dead (which I had to considering it happened right in front of me), there was another thing I couldn't explain—the willpower the Civatateo held over those it "turned."

It must have started when it first bit Clark James back in Mexico. The actor couldn't remember what happened. I realize now the Civatateo was able to cloud its victim's mind when it wanted; it actually told me so at Meadowland as it cradled the newly turned Clark in its arms.

"He shall learn as it becomes necessary. As shall you."

The Civatateo must have whispered its desires in the fevered Clark's ears that night in the tent, which explained why the actor awoke the next morning begging me to take him to Palm Springs. It was all part of the creature's plan, just as it had mapped out Clark's death, subsequent return, and the part I was going to play.

I wish I could have stopped it right there. But I was in complete shock at what I had witnessed and knew no one would believe the truth. I was also absolutely terrified the creature would lash out at my slightest resistance and turn me into something destined for a slaughterhouse, like the bodies I'd seen in Mexico.

And of course, there was the temptation of what it was offering.

As the doctor who had successfully headed up Clark James's recuperation from his death cot in the Mexican jungle, my career would suddenly be on the upswing. Before the appointment at Meadowland, that career was nonexistent; here was an opportunity to actually better myself.

That was how I ended up leading the press conference in the Meadowland lobby where Clark James said he was on the road to recovery and stunned the film world with his sudden retirement.

What else was Clark going to do? He looked stronger than ever, but unless his films only took place in the dead of night, it was going to be difficult for the "turned" actor to find a suitable project. He told the media after the disastrous crew deaths in Mexico, and Clark getting a second chance at life, it was time to step down with his legacy intact and spend time with his daughter before she headed off to college.

I spoke a little about his recovery, making things sound medical enough to satisfy the paparazzi and explain the life change Clark James was about to undergo. I knew he wasn't going to be seen during the daytime anymore, not unless he wanted to immolate right in front of people, because that was the last piece of wisdom the Civatateo shared.

Eternal life was the gift, but sunlight the curse.

"Before he was turned and suffering from the after-effects of the bite, he became susceptible to the sun. A weakened state," explained the Civatateo in the Meadowland room that night. "He might be stronger during the day now, but that doesn't offer protection from the solar rays."

The Civatateo indicated the bizarre motorcycle outfit that covered most of his body. "Even though this allows me to be in daylight for a short time, I run the risk of being exposed, so it is only under dire circumstances that I tempt fate."

The creature said Clark would lead a similar life as long as he remained *careful. And if I accepted the role of helping him, I would be substantially rewarded.*

As I ended the press conference, telling the media Clark needed his rest, I *knew I had been sucked in completely. In the literature of vampires, I guess I was what one would call "a familiar"—the mortal who aided and abetted his unholy master, allowing it to rest undisturbed during the threat of day and run rampant at night.*

Things remained calm for the next few weeks. I worried someone would *unearth the truth of Clark's recovery or there would be vicious unexplained attacks in the streets of Palm Springs. Yet my concerns seemed to have been for naught. The retired actor settled into a life of quiet parties in the evening and lying low during the day. I began relishing my increasing responsibility at Meadowland and ability to do some good as a doctor. Most importantly, the Civatateo had disappeared. For a moment I thought my life might return to normal.*

Then, the patients started to get sick.

11

Jess ditched them halfway to the sheriff's station.

The plan was to pick up Benji's car from the long-term parking lot and head over to the station, where they would convince Burke to make the trek with them to Palm Springs Country Club. Jess casually suggested Maria ride with Benji while he checked in with his mother. A few minutes later he lagged behind at a light, and once the Mustang turned a corner, he spun a U-turn.

He wasn't happy about leaving Maria and Benji behind, but felt he had no choice. No amount of persuading would convince them he had to head to the country club alone. Armed with only the one remaining solar flash, which he had taken from Maria earlier that morning, he couldn't afford the two of them confronting Clark defenselessly.

Jess figured he had maybe an hour head start before Maria and Benji reached Burke's office and realized they had been tricked. By the time the cavalry arrived at the country club, Jess would either have seized his window of opportunity and rescued Harry or been hauled off to jail if he was wrong about Clark's hideaway.

Jess didn't even entertain the third possibility—that he would come out of the gorge on a coroner's gurney or worse yet, "turned" like Clark James or his father.

This time, the guard at PSCC recognized Jess and his SUV. He waved him through and Jess quickly parked in the guest lot. He asked one of the employees where he could find the golf course superintendent. Jess was steered toward a small office near the pro shop where he had a five-minute conversation with Mort Lonnigan, the eternally tanned septuagenarian who had groomed the green fairways since the course was built decades before.

Lonnigan was surprised by Jess's interest in the gorge. "Haven't had to tend to it in at least a few years," he said. "Once the bridge was put in, there was no need. Pretty much rocks and cacti below. There's nothing for us to take care of nature won't do. The golf architect liked how the course organically surrounded it. Worked out fine for me because I have my hands full just trying to keep the fairways green."

"You're doing an excellent job of it," said Jess, figuring it couldn't hurt to bolster the man's ego. "When was the bridge put up?"

"Let's see," Lonnigan said, thinking back. "Maybe four or five years ago."

That certainly fit, thought Jess.

"Did Clark James have anything to do with it?"

"Actually, he paid for it." For the first time, Lonnigan gave Jess a suspicious look. "How did you know?"

"Lucky guess." Jess thanked him for his time and took off before Lonnigan could ask questions Jess didn't feel like answering. Armed with new facts that fueled his supposition and filled him with dread, Jess headed down the path toward the driving range and the blood-red bridge that loomed beyond.

The drop to the desert floor was probably a good hundred feet. Once again, Jess recalled the day he found Harry standing precariously close to the edge. If his brother had taken one false step, no way he would have survived the fall. More than likely, he would have landed on the cragged rocks jutting out of the sand and cacti.

Jess couldn't help but notice the landscape below was very similar to the field of glass in the Mexican jungle. He wasn't all that surprised—the Civatateo was a creature of habit, so why not take shelter in a place that seemed like home?

At first, a descent into the gorge appeared impossible, especially if navigated by Clark James before the break of dawn, or for that matter, ascended shortly after the gleam of twilight. But Jess spotted a thin break between some rocks at the north end of the bridge. Moving closer, he saw a narrow path on the other side of the boulders, which he thought might have evolved from five years of steady traipsing by the Civatateo.

Jess waited for a couple of golf carts to pass over the bridge before he stepped between the rocks and trekked down the path. Just enough sunlight peeked through the rock clumps to light the way and the temperature dipped considerably as long as Jess was covered in shadow. Occasionally he spotted a footprint in the dirt—sometimes more than one set, the second considerably smaller. Convinced the latter belonged to Harry, he could only imagine his baby brother being forced down the path by the turned actor. This thought propelled his descent even quicker, not wanting Harry to spend one more second than necessary with Clark James.

When he reached the desert floor, Jess was bathed in light as the rocks parted to let rays of sunshine pour through. Patches of red-tinted shadow from the bridge sporadically dotted the sand like scarlet clouds painted on a white canvas. Jess scoured the outcroppings of rock for an opening and finally found one at the northwest end of the gorge. He saw the two sets of footprints in the sand by the entrance and knew his hunch in Clark James's backyard had been right.

With one last glance at the sun up high that could be his salvation or that he would never see again, he stepped through the opening in the rocks.

❈　❈　❈

The minute he walked into the darkness, Jess smelled the familiar odor of musty iron. Once again he heard the faint sound of rushing water. He used the solar flash to navigate a tiny path and headed in the direction of the noise.

He had traveled about fifty feet when he heard the moans.

Jess kept a tighter rein on the flash's spread of light as he moved forward. He was about to call out for Harry when he spotted the body on the ground.

The moan became a muffled scream when the solar flash darted across its prone legs.

Jess realized that it wasn't Harry.

It was his father.

Walter, barely conscious on the cavern floor, rolled away from the solar beam that burned his outstretched leg.

Jess dropped to the ground and trained the solar light on the wall so the area was lit, but Walter could still remain in the shadows. He gingerly approached his fallen father, but made sure not to get too close.

"Dad?"

Walter was barely able to turn his head. Blood dripped from his neck, and even in the semi-darkness, Jess could see his skin was abnormally pale with practically an alabaster sheen to it. Obviously wounded, Walter looked even worse than the night he had died in his son's arms.

He muttered something Jess couldn't understand.

"What was that? Who did this?" Jess asked.

Walter started to crawl away on his belly farther from the light. Each movement produced another groan, but he kept at it. Jess pointed the light in the direction his father was moving.

The flash illuminated a trickling stream of blood at the base of the cavern wall.

In that moment, Jess understood, more than ever, the true horror of the fate that had befallen Walter, Tracy, and even Clark James.

The never-ending thirst.

Even on the brink of death, and in excruciating pain, the sole thing that mattered to Walter was sustenance—which could only come from blood.

It also explained the location Jess had tracked down. The golf course above had plenty of water from its man-made lakes. It would have been easy enough for Clark, with his riches and resources, to divert enough to this hidden cavern and prime it with blood to provide a food source for himself, just like the original Civatateo did in the Mexican jungle.

Suddenly, Jess felt something he never thought he would—sympathy for his father.

He moved over and grabbed hold of his father's shoulders and gently pulled him closer to the stream. But the moment Walter started to lick up the blood, Jess backed away, alternately repulsed and tortured by his father's plight. Jess forced himself to concentrate on the matter at hand.

"Dad. Where's Harry? Is he down here?"

At first he didn't think Walter heard him. But finally, his father turned to look back at his son. His mouth was filled with blood, and he was still weak. Walter motioned with his head toward the deeper part of the cavern.

Jess grabbed the solar flash and started moving. His father made the same guttural noise as before. Jess was able to make out the garbled words this time.

"Clark," muttered Walter with gasps of breath. "Kill him."

Jess didn't respond. But he knew that he would do just that if left with no other choice. Walter lowered his mouth back into the stream. The horrendous suckling sound began anew and Jess turned away.

He descended into the darkness.

He used the flash sparingly, just enough to avoid bumping into anything. Again, he found scattered bones and understood they must have been either vagrants or unaccounted-for senior citizens that Clark James used to replenish the underground stream of blood.

Up ahead, there was a faint gloaming; Jess clicked off the flash. He knew he must have been entering the cavern's innermost chamber, most likely where Clark James and now Walter Stark evidently retreated each morning. Keeping a death grip on the flashlight, he rounded a piece of jagged stone and found himself staring at a lantern-lit blood-red pond, maybe half the size of the one in Mexico.

But his attention was drawn to the figure leaning up against the wall ten feet from the lamp.

His eyes were open, but Harry's body was motionless.

Jess raced over and lowered himself so he was eye-level with his brother. Relief immediately washed over Jess upon hearing a soft but steady intake and exhale of breath, but the boy appeared catatonic. Jess leaned closer to try and shake him awake.

"You should have stuck with the arrangement."

Jess turned around to find the risen-from-the-dead actor looming above.

Clark James's bloody lips curled in a smile, revealing sharp teeth.

12

Jess flicked on the solar flash and aimed it at Clark James.

The beam swiped across his face like a laser, lacerating his right cheek and jawbone. Blood spurted forth and the Clark-thing howled, bringing his hand up to his face that was already smoldering. Jess darted the flash across the actor's chest and his clothes began to burn. James screamed, frantically patting and clawing at his body to tamp down the flames. Jess pointed the beam at Clark's head but the monster darted out of the way, its feral roar echoing through the cavern.

For a moment, he lost Clark James in the darkness. Jess, his hand shaking, aimed the flash in every direction and caught Clark just as he lunged from the right side. The beam landed on the vampire's right arm and sent it bursting into flames. This time, Jess screamed, bombarding the recoiling creature with blasts from the solar flash as if firing at mechanical ducks in a shooting gallery. He missed more often than not, but enough hit home to set the better part of James's torso on fire.

The flames made it easier for Jess to focus on a target. A little surer of himself, he went for the stumbling Clark's head and waved the beam across his ear. Clark screamed in agony, turned away, and began to run. Jess was caught by surprise and by the time he gave chase, the burning man launched himself through the air and into the blood-red pond.

Jess trained the solar flash on the pond, searching for the thing that had once been Clark James. The only sign was billowing black smoke where he had disappeared below the surface. Jess's heart pounded in his chest, his heavy gasping breaths echoed throughout the chamber. He stood at the scarlet water's edge, waiting for the vampire to reemerge, but the surface only grew calmer and the smoke began to dissipate.

Finally, able to catch his breath, Jess raced back to Harry, who was still leaning against the wall in a catatonic state. He tried to rouse his brother with a bit of shaking and prodding.

"C'mon, Harry. Snap out of it."

There was no response. Not wanting to spend one more moment than necessary in the cavern, Jess hoisted Harry up and over his shoulder. The boy was total dead weight and Jess didn't even want to consider how he had gotten that way. They just needed to get the hell out of there.

It wasn't easy going. Harry wasn't the eight-year-old kid he had left behind years before. He wasn't overweight by any means, but the fireman's carry utilized the better part of both his arms and hands, so Jess had trouble navigating the path because he wasn't dexterous enough with the solar flash. And it was just damn dark. Jess would have difficulty finding his way back with the use of both hands and a trail of breadcrumbs marking the way.

Harry didn't moan, speak, or even mumble as Jess hurried along. At one point, the boy's face brushed up against a low-hanging rock Jess couldn't see. His brother didn't even cry out. At least he could feel Harry's breath on his back and was just thankful to bring him out alive.

For the moment, that was the only goal—getting Harry home in one piece. Jess would deal with everything else later.

The journey back through the cavern seemed infinitely longer than the descent. For a moment, Jess thought he had lost his way, but then recognized the skeletal remains he'd seen on the way down, which confirmed he was on the right track.

Finally, in the distance, Jess could see a sprinkle of light and knew it was the cavern entrance. Using that as a focal point, he picked up the pace and raced toward it.

He was maybe fifty feet away and thinking they were home free when he tripped.

Jess crashed to the ground. Harry tumbled out of his arms and actually cried out when he hit the floor. The solar flash skittered out of Jess's hand.

There was a groan just off to his right as Jess realized he had stumbled over Walter.

In his determination to rescue Harry, Jess had forgotten about his father. He couldn't fathom what to do about Walter. First he had to get Harry out of the cavern and into the sunlight where he would be safe. One side of Jess's head was throbbing; he had taken a good hit when he fell, and was having a hard time getting oriented.

His initial instinct was to search for the solar flash, but it had rolled into the darkness and Jess feared it might take forever to find it. There was just enough light from the entrance to see where Harry lay crumpled on the ground and Jess crawled over toward him.

Haul his butt out of here and deal later. The mantra ran through Jess's head as he put his arms around his baby brother. Jess was on his knees trying to lift Harry when a monstrous roar filled the cavern.

A shape rose from the darkness and hurled itself at him.

His legs were knocked out from under him and suddenly Jess was back on the cavern floor. His arms were pinned to the floor, his chest practically crushed by the weight suddenly upon it, and he felt something sticky and wet dripping on his face.

It was blood coming off a crimson-covered Clark James. The Civatateo was sitting on top of Jess.

Half his face was charred, punctuated by open sores and pustules. Blood continued to fall onto Jess as he struggled in vain to get out of Clark's clutches. The sounds emitting from the vampire's scarlet mouth were not so much words as guttural ferocious growls.

Then, another cry filled the cavern. Both Jess and the thing straddling him turned to see it was Harry unleashing a spine-tingling scream. Jess was entirely helpless to come to his terrified brother's aid, especially when his head was snapped back by the Clark-thing.

Its mouth opened and craned toward Jess's neck.

The sharp teeth protruded.

Jess yelled.

There was a roar—but it didn't come from Clark.

Walter Stark leapt out of the darkness onto the monstrous actor. "Leave my son alone!"

Whether it was renewed strength from the blood stream where Jess's father had been drinking or Clark's weakened state courtesy of the solar flash hits, Walter was able to propel the stunned James off Jess and toward the cavern entrance.

Clark tried to push Walter away, but the ferociousness behind his attack allowed the older man to overpower the actor. Jess watched as his father shoved James farther down the path. The two vampires grappled, their feral cries bouncing off the hollow cavern's walls.

Jess crawled back to Harry. The teen had fallen back into his catatonic state and this time Jess didn't bother trying to shake him to his senses.

Jess hefted Harry back onto his shoulder and turned toward the entrance just in time to see Walter yank James hard enough to send both spawn of the Civatateo sprawling out of the cavern.

Into the sunlight.

Unearthly screams rocked the cave as Jess hurried forward with Harry slumped over his shoulder. When he emerged from the cavern onto the desert floor, he froze in his tracks.

He wouldn't forget the sight in front of him for as long as he lived.

Clark James and Walter Stark rolled around on the ground, their bodies bursting into flames from the rays of sunshine slipping into the gorge.

Walter managed to get atop Clark and put his hands around the actor's bloody, charred throat. James roared in anger, his mouth snapping at the older man's fingers. Jess could hear the hideous sound of oversized incisors clacking together.

Finally James, still the stronger of the two, was able to wrench Walter's hands off his neck and hurl him aside. Once free, Clark instinctively headed for the safety of the shadows. Walter tried to crawl after him but was overcome by the heat of the flames shooting off his body.

Transfixed, Jess finally managed to move. He put Harry in the safest place he could find—the bright sunshine—then made a beeline for his father, who he shoved with all his might under the shadow of a huge rock. Walter crumpled in a heap, groaning as his body kept smoldering.

Jess noticed Clark James crawling back toward the cavern entrance. Flames continued to lick his body. The blood from the pond was scorched black. His breath was more like snorts, punctuated by growls. Once in the shadows, James pulled himself to his feet. He stomped out the remaining flames with his bloody palms.

In the moment Jess weighed what to do—get Harry back up top to safety or deal with Clark before he disappeared inside—the actor made the decision an easy one.

Clark's murderous gaze landed on Harry, who was maybe twenty yards away, albeit in the bright sunshine. The vampire didn't even wrestle with a choice; he started in Harry's direction. Jess was on Clark before he took one step out of the shadows. He ignored the burning sensation on his hands as he grabbed Clark by his flaming clothes and dragged him away from Harry and into a huge pool of sunshine.

Clark screamed in agony and tumbled to the ground. His body erupted into flames again as he groveled in the sand to try and return to the shadows. Jess stomped down on Clark James's flame-ridden chest and kept him underfoot.

"Enough," Jess said through gritted teeth.

He kept his foot in place until the flames took the fight out of James. Then, with flickers of fire crawling up his pants leg and Clark's screams ringing in his ears, Jess threw himself onto the sand and rolled around until his jeans began smoldering.

By the time Jess got back on his feet, Clark James's body was folding in on itself like the charred remnants of flaming parchment. Seconds later, all that remained of the actor who had graced America's movie screens for decades was a pile of black ashes.

Jess checked his own body to make sure he was in one piece and not on fire. He glanced at Harry and saw his baby brother still lying in the sand, stone-faced but breathing.

Finally, he turned to face his father.

Walter was also crawling on his knees, but not toward the entrance.

He was trying to reach the sunshine.

Jess raced across the desert floor. "Dad! What are you doing?"

Walter, growing weaker by the second, barely managed an answer.

"It's time."

Walter inched forward. Jess tried to block him from the light, but his father waved him away.

"Let me go, son."

Jess understood what Walter wanted. But he wasn't sure he could actually handle it.

After all, how many sons had to watch their fathers die twice?

13

The sun was inching closer to where Jess lay with his father.

"There's got to be some other way," pleaded Jess.

Walter shook his head. "There isn't. Clark made that very clear when he turned me." He started coughing. "Eternal damnation or the sun. Those were his words." The coughing fit continued as blood trickled from his mouth. "He always had to be so fucking dramatic."

Walter's eyes strayed toward Harry, who was lying on the ground passed out. Jess was relieved his brother didn't have to witness this.

"At least the two of you are safe for now," Walter said. He looked back up at his oldest son. "It wasn't my idea to take him."

"I know."

"When he returned with Harry last night, I tried to persuade Clark to let him go. He wouldn't hear of it."

Thus, finding his father beaten to a pulp on the cavern floor, thought Jess.

The sun crept closer. There was a sharp sizzling sound as the rays flicked across Walter's leg. He moaned and Jess pulled his father into the shadows.

"Don't!"

Jess let go of him.

"It's better this way."

"Dad . . ."

"I did a lot of horrible things in my life. Especially to you, son. I had this coming."

"No. No one deserves this."

Walter reached out and took his oldest son's hand.

"If you believe that—then let me go."

Jess looked into his father's bloodshot eyes and saw what he would never expect.

Contrition.

"That way I know you will forgive me," said Walter.

Jess desperately held onto his father's hand and finally did the hardest thing he had ever done.

He let go.

Walter used the little strength he had left to shove himself away from Jess and roll into the sunlight. Flames immediately encircled his writhing body. His eyes never left his eldest son.

Jess couldn't bear to watch but knew if he turned away it would be like his father had died alone.

"I'm so sorry about Tracy," he cried out. "I just couldn't stop it."

There was a huge burst of flames and Walter Stark was swallowed up whole.

Jess heard another scream. He thought it might be Harry, but his brother was still unconscious on the ground. Jess looked up and could see three silhouetted figures peering over the edge of the bridge. The light shifted enough to make out that one was Maria.

It had been her scream that he had heard.

By the time she made her way to the desert floor, with Benji and Thaddeus Burke in tow, Jess was cradling the ashen remains of his father and openly sobbing for the first time in as long as he could remember.

Dealing with the sheriff actually turned out to be quite easy.

It didn't hurt that Burke had gotten quite an eyeful from atop the red bridge, along with an earful from Benji on the way to the country club. Watching a man self-immolate in the afternoon sun was something one didn't see every day. It also helped that the last time the sheriff had seen Walter Stark he had been a corpse on a gurney outside the Sands. Suddenly Burke was willing to approach the situation with quite the open mind.

The sheriff's head hurt worse the more he heard about vampires on the loose in the Coachella Valley. It didn't take much convincing to persuade him the best course was to let Walter's and Clark's remains literally go from ashes to dust. When Benji asked if this let Jess off the hook for Rice's murder, the sheriff told him not to push his luck. But the quiver in Burke's voice and uncertain dread in his eyes indicated it was only a matter of time before the physician's death was slid under the carpet as well.

In the end, Jess saw Thaddeus Burke for the functionary he really was. His suspicions that the sheriff had been in on the whole conspiracy went out the window the moment he saw how shaken Burke was by the events in the gorge. Maybe Clark James passed money under the table, but Jess was sure Burke saw it as looking the other way on shady business deals, not covering up the dark secrets of something called the Civatateo.

All that mattered was getting Harry back safe and sound—and how Jess was going to explain to his mother that his brother was in a catatonic state.

❋   ❋   ❋

Miraculously, that resolved itself shortly before they returned home. Harry woke up as Jess turned the SUV into the driveway.

Maria was in the backseat. She had helped strap the unconscious Harry in the passenger seat and insisted on coming along. Jess realized it was best not to argue. He still had to make amends for the fast one he'd pulled earlier.

"What's going on?" Harry asked, clearly in a haze.

Jess was so surprised he nearly steered the car off the road. "How you feeling, kiddo?"

"Completely out of it," his brother answered. Harry looked at the Stark mansion on the hill. "What the hell am I doing here?"

Jess locked eyes with Maria in the rearview mirror. She shrugged; this was foreign territory for her too. Jess turned back to his brother and treaded carefully.

"You've been kind of out of it, Harry."

"Last thing I remember is going to bed and now I'm in your car? No shit, I'm out of it. What the fuck is that all about?"

Maria laughed at this sudden outburst. Jess felt an enormous amount of relief flood over him. Harry was returning to his normal self, colorful vocabulary and all. He didn't seem to recall a thing about the whole ordeal.

"I think you've been sleepwalking, buddy."

Another quick look back at Maria got him a tacit nod. She was down with this approach.

"Go figure." Harry tried to shake the cobwebs out of his head. "For how long?"

Jess pointed at the digital readout on the car dashboard. "Most of the night and a good part of the day."

Harry's eyes widened. "One thirty? Jesus Fucking Christ."

Jess let out a laugh. He knew he shouldn't be condoning Harry's propensity for cursing, but it was just so damn good his baby brother was safe.

"Where did you find me?"

Interesting question. Jess remembered the phone call the night before and Clark James telling him about the Civatateo's ability to cloud one's mind. Jess decided it was time to put it to the test.

"The country club. Got a call from someone that you were there."

"No shit?"

"No shit." It was the truth—if you bent it enough. "You don't remember?"

"I'm telling you, my head hit the pillow and that was it." Harry scrunched up his face, trying to recall anything. "Strange dreams though."

"Such as?"

"It's all messed up." He stared out the window, as if the answer was right outside. "I was in some dark place. Like a cave. But I don't know 'bout any caves around here. Do you?"

"You'd know better than me, Harry. I've been gone, remember."

"Maybe I've got to cool it with the snacks before bed." He turned around to face Maria. "Could be something in your mom's cookies."

"Who knows?" said Maria. "She'll never tell me the ingredients."

"Yeah, that's Lena."

Then, Harry did a double take that threw a scare into Jess until he realized his brother was gawking at Maria. "Wait. What are you doing here?"

"Umm . . ." Maria started to fumble for an answer. Her eyes sought out help, but Harry beat her to the punch.

"Are you two together? You know like doing . . ."

Jess cut him off with a smile. "That's enough."

Harry shot back a wicked grin. "Hey, that's super cool." He tossed a look back toward Maria. "Though I sort of hoped you were going to wait for me to grow up."

"If only you had said something," Maria said with a twinkle in her eye.

"Does Mom know?" Harry asked Jess.

"I'm not sure." This was honest on Jess's part. He had no idea. But it did bring up the next hurdle. "Speaking of Mom, we should discuss what we're going to tell her."

❋   ❋   ❋

The first order of business was getting Harry to tell a little white lie. That wasn't a big deal. After all, he was a teenager. Jess, knowing the answer was a definitive "No," asked him if he had ever sleepwalked before. When Harry gave the expected reply, Jess told him it might be good not to worry Kate that her youngest son was wandering around aimlessly in the middle of the night. She had endured enough grief in recent days. Should another sleepwalking episode occur, which Jess was confident would never happen (given that the whole thing was one big fat lie), then Harry should get checked out by a doctor. Jess suggested they stick with the story he had already put out there to his mother and sister that morning—Harry had gone out with friends the previous night and passed out before telling his mother his whereabouts.

When Harry said that was well and good for Jess, that he wasn't going to be the grounded son, Jess told him the grief angle worked both ways and he would take care of everything and work on their mother.

Kate made it much easier. She had been so worried about Harry that she immediately wrapped her arms around her youngest son and implored him to "Never scare me like that again." Harry actually had the audacity to wink at Jess and Maria, but Kate was way too busy hugging Harry for dear life to notice.

Jess suggested Harry go upstairs and take a nap. His brother almost overplayed it by giving his mother a pout and loving kiss with the promise never to do anything like that again. Once Harry left, Maria excused herself to go visit Lena, leaving Jess alone with Kate. He told his mother she should go easy on Harry.

"He's been through a lot."

"We all have," agreed Kate.

If only his mother knew the half of it.

"I think we all have our own ways of dealing with what happened to your father. It doesn't surprise me that Harry would act out like this."

"I had a long talk with him. I don't think it will happen again." Jess said it with such certainty his mother seemed to believe him.

"It would be nice if you could stick around a while and find out."

"I might just do that."

Jess's eyes drifted out the living room window. Maria was walking by the pool with Lena. He knew she was relaying her version of the morning's events to her own mother. Jess didn't know exactly what tale she was spinning, but was gratified to see a teary-eyed Lena give Maria a tight hug. Finally, they broke apart, Lena went back inside, and Maria stared out at the vast Coachella Desert.

Kate watched her son and a bemused look came over her face. "I get the feeling you're not telling me something."

Jess returned the coy smile. "Maybe."

"She's a nice girl, Jess."

"She's a *really* nice girl, Mom."

"Then it would be awful if you broke her heart."

"It's the farthest thing from my mind," said Jess, and he absolutely meant it.

"So, what about the other one?"

Wow. Just when you think mothers can't know everything, they still find their way to the heart of the matter.

"Tracy?"

"It is over with her?"

"Almost," said Jess.

One last piece of unfinished business.

"Does Maria know this?"

"She knows everything, Mom."

"That's good. You don't want to lie to her, Jess. Not about the big stuff. If there's one thing I learned after all those years with your father, it's that you're always better off telling the truth. Otherwise it all catches up."

"You're definitely right about that."

Jess thought about where he'd been just a couple of hours before. Things had certainly caught up with his father in a way no sane person could ever fathom.

"You were also right about Dad."

"How so?"

"I wish I had forgiven him a long time ago."

Tears formed in Kate's eyes. Jess gently kissed her cheek and then headed outside to Maria.

❉　❉　❉

She was still looking out at the desert when Jess walked up beside her.

"Is this our first fight?" Jess asked.

"I'm just hoping it isn't our last one."

"What was I supposed to do, Maria?"

She finally turned to face him. "How about telling me what you were planning? After everything in Mexico, did you really think I was going to try and talk you out of it?"

"No, I thought you would insist on coming. I had already put you in enough danger. I couldn't take the chance."

"Of what? Losing me?"

"Well, yeah."

"And what was I supposed to do if something happened to you?"

That tongue-tied Jess. He wasn't used to someone declaring outright feelings, especially toward him. It had been many years since that had happened—and look how that worked out for Tracy.

"I guess I didn't think of it that way."

"Well, we're going to make one hell of a couple if you keep doing that."

Jess couldn't resist smiling. "I'm just glad you still want to be a couple." When she didn't offer up an answer, the smile dropped off his face. "You still want that, don't you?"

"More than anything," Maria said.

"That goes double for me. Am I allowed to say I'm sorry now?"

Maria looked back at the house where Jess was sure two mothers were watching their every move.

"Maybe later," she said, finally allowing a grin.

But Jess took her in his arms and kissed her. When they came up for air, Maria looked ready to admonish him.

"Don't worry," Jess assured her. "I know for a fact that they're both rooting for us."

And then he kissed her again.

They spent the next hour making plans. Jess tried to get Tag on the phone down in Mexico, but it was impossible to get connected to the tiny village. He knew he was going to have to head south again in the next couple of days—just like he knew Maria was coming with him.

Jess didn't know yet what to tell Tracy. Her father was dead and the secrets of the Civatateo had gone to his second grave with him. But Jess was determined to find some kind of answer and thought Tag Marlowe might hold the key. If he was smart enough to come up with a small flashlight that could destroy the Civatateo, perhaps he could invent something that would return Tracy to the living, or at least allow her to move among them in the daylight.

Inside the house, Harry was fast asleep. Sarah was back to her old routine of not talking to Jess and getting ready for a quiet dinner with Jaime Solis. Sadly, Jess was becoming convinced his sister was one of those women who weren't happy without a man in their lives; he could only hope the country club owner was better than the previous one. Kate and Lena told him they were going to bed early and would make sure Harry's window was double-locked.

Jess dropped Maria at her apartment and said he would be back in a little while. Benji had called him and asked if Jess could drop by the motel. He wanted to bring Benji up to date anyway; his friend deserved that for all his help. He kissed Maria goodbye and told her he was looking forward to more apologizing later in the evening.

Dusk had fallen by the time Jess pulled into the Sands parking lot, and as he got out of the SUV, he glanced at the room he had occupied upon his arrival just over a week ago. He had gone to sleep that first night more pissed than ever at his father with no idea what was lying in wait for him on the dark sands. It made Jess look forward more than ever to spending the night in Maria's bed, back in her arms again.

Jess hadn't had time to fill Benji in at the gorge, what with the sheriff present and the need to get Harry back home. They grabbed a couple of beers as Jess gave a blow-by-blow description of the confrontation down in the cavern.

"That would make an awesome graphic novel," said Benji as he clinked bottles with Jess.

"I can't thank you enough for everything."

"Most excitement I've had here since the celebration after we won State. Those girls from Tech?"

"I don't even know what you're talking about," Jess said, feigning amnesia.

"Sure you don't." Benji drained the bottle, and then actually remembered something. "Oh, I almost forgot . . ."

He reached behind the counter and picked up a package. It was a thick manila envelope addressed to Jess Stark, care of the Sands Motel. Jess flipped it over. Scribbled on the back was "E. Rice, MD." The word "Urgent" was underlined three times.

"When did this come?"

"A few days ago. I really suck at running down to the post office and I hate paying bills. Plus, with everything happening, I didn't get there till this afternoon."

"What is it?" asked Jess.

"Do I look like I have X-ray vision? Which, of course, would be super cool."

"You could've peeked."

"It's your mail. Besides, I figure you'll tell me. You hungry?"

Jess realized he hadn't eaten since the night before and said he could do with a snack. Benji went into the adjacent kitchen to scrounge up something and Jess opened the envelope.

He pulled out a thick notebook.

Printed neatly on the first page were the words *"Introduction to the Journal of Edward D. Rice."*

Jess began to read.

By the time Benji brought over some food, Jess had lost his appetite.

EXCERPT FROM THE JOURNAL OF
EDWARD D. RICE

July 23

No one had died yet at Meadowland, but two elderly patients had become severely anemic and refused to take their afternoon constitutional. I talked to both of them and the moment they told me they were finding the sunlight bothersome, I was barely able to contain my anxiety and fury. I told the nurses to keep them in their rooms during the day and put a close watch on their doors. When asked why the security measures, I said I was investigating a couple of medication violations and would fill them in when the time became appropriate.

I asked if either patient had recent visitors. It turned out Clark James had dropped by two evenings before to spread good cheer amongst the residents.

Good cheer, I thought. Ironic name for it.

The nurse thought James might have popped into one or both of the ailing patients' rooms. I didn't need confirmation. I knew that he had.

I went into my office and paced on the carpet, staring out the window until I saw the sun go down and knew Clark James would have awoken from his unholy sleep.

"What is it, Rice?" he asked. The actor was irritated to be called so early in his "day," but changed his tune when I told him my theories concerning the patients.

"We should talk," he suggested.

I agreed to meet him in the bar at the Palm Springs Country Club.

I hadn't yet joined the country club set. I had one lunch there a few weeks before with Walter Stark when he wanted a status report on the medical staff. I must admit I was enamored of the genteel surroundings, gracious wait staff, and overall ambience, and had entertained thoughts of asking Clark to sponsor me at some future date.

I'm sure having a drink with a member-turned-vampire wasn't going to be listed as an extracurricular activity on my application form.

When I arrived, Clark James was entertaining the regulars and nursing a Scotch I knew he would later spit out. He waved and put on a friendly face, then motioned for me to join him in a corner of the room.

I told the bartender I would order something later and got right down to business.

"What do you think you're doing, Clark? My patients at my hospital? Are you out of your mind?" I struggled to keep my voice at a whisper even though I wanted to scream it out loud for all the sane world to hear.

"Clark needs sustenance. Why not from where it is safe?" asked a familiar voice.

I turned around and my heart sunk deep in my chest.

Clark James smiled. "Edward, have you met the new owner of the club? Jaime Solis?"

The handsome Mexican in a splendid suit offered up a well-manicured hand.

"Nice to see you again, Dr. Rice."

It was the Civatateo.

14

"Jesus Christ."

Jess stopped reading the journal and kicked himself. Of course the Civatateo was still alive. He had been stupid believing Clark James's claim it died years before.

Jaime Solis was the Civatateo.

The same Jaime Solis who happened to be having dinner that very minute with his sister Sarah.

Benji knew Jess's outburst couldn't mean anything good and pointed at the journal.

"Bad plot twist?"

"The worst." Jess quickly summarized everything he had read.

Benji, clearly shaken, tried to take the matter in stride. "Can't say much about your sister's taste in men."

Jess pulled out his cell phone and dialed the house. Lena picked up on the second ring and was happy to hear his voice. He couldn't help asking if everything was okay, but she said that it was quiet; Harry was still sleeping and his mother was upstairs watching television.

"What about Sarah?" he asked, unable to keep the anxiety out of his voice.

"She's in the backyard with Mr. Solis. He seems like a nice man."

No, Jess thought. *No, he's not.* But there wasn't any point in telling Lena the truth at this very moment. "How long has he been there?"

"Maybe a half hour." Suspicion crept into her voice. "Is something wrong?"

"No," Jess lied. "I'm probably going to stop by for a few minutes. There was something I forgot to do earlier."

Yeah, he thought. *Deal with another vampire.*

"Well, you know I'll be here," sighed Lena. "I'm always here."

"I'll see you in a bit." He started to hang up, then thought to add something. "Lena? Don't tell anyone I'm coming."

One of Lena's best qualities was knowing when not to ask questions. She told Jess she would be waiting for him and they disconnected.

"Want company?" asked Benji.

Jess had learned his lesson the hard way—enough of going maverick.

"I'll take all the help I can get."

※　　※　　※

He let Benji drive so he could sit in the passenger seat and flip through the rest of the journal. Jess came away with a quite different impression of the departed doctor.

"I don't think he started off with bad intentions," he said to Benji. "Rice was a victim of circumstance more than anything else." He cited the critical point where the Civatateo presented Rice with the option of his career going up in flames or letting the creature turn Clark James.

"Once Rice allowed that, the Civatateo had his hooks into him." The physician must have realized this when the vampire emerged in his new persona as the charming owner of the country club. And clearly Jaime Solis wasn't going anywhere. Edward Rice was along for the ride whether he wanted to be or not.

"You think Solis killed him?" asked Benji, who was having difficulty keeping the Mustang under the speed limit.

"Had to be. The fact Rice sent this to me means he must have been ready to talk." Jess tapped the notebook in his lap. "I'll bet Solis doesn't know Rice kept a journal, let alone gave it to someone else. Otherwise, his house would have been turned upside down when I got there."

"Why couldn't it have been your dad? He was there that night. You told me he surprised you in your car."

"The one thing I know about my father is he didn't take orders from anyone." Jess shook his head. "I'm starting to think he was trying to stop Solis the whole time."

Jess began itemizing like a defense lawyer making his closing argument. "He uncovered the deaths at Meadowland with Tom Cox. There was the warning on my windshield; then him following Rice and James out to the desert and rescuing me from the grave. He even tried to stop Clark from taking Harry into the cavern. None of that lines up with him killing Edward Rice."

Benji swung onto Palm Canyon Drive. "I presume this isn't a random social call we're paying on Solis? You've got a plan?"

"I'm working on it."

"Long as it doesn't involve that cavern."

"I don't think he's going back there so quick after what happened today." Jess picked up the notebook. "Actually, seeing as how Solis has been masquerading all these years as a legitimate businessman, I thought he might be open to a deal."

Jess ripped out the first couple of pages from the journal. He put them in his pocket, and then placed the notebook on the dashboard. "You have somewhere good to hide this?"

"Absolutely. I've stored stuff in places that I can't even remember."

"Perfect."

Lena had left the gate open for Jess. Benji eased the Mustang up the driveway. He parked right beside the other guest, obviously Jaime Solis.

Moonlight gleamed off the polished chrome of the motorcycle.

The distinctive scarlet helmet hung off the headrest.

Lena was at the door before Jess could ring the bell. She was surprised to see Benji, but Jess explained they needed to spend a few minutes with

Jaime Solis. Jess could see a dozen questions running through Lena's head, but was happy she chose not to ask them. She led them through the house and out into the Cactus Garden.

Solis was on a stone bench in front of the greenhouse, sitting much closer to his sister than Jess would have liked. He was suddenly plagued by visions of the country club owner leaning over and taking a healthy bite out of Sarah's neck, and he had to check himself from shoving Solis to the ground. Despite all the acrimony between Sarah and himself since returning home, Jess was still overly protective of his sister. It left him with hope that one day his family might return to a state of normality—though he knew that wasn't possible until the creature on the bench was no longer in their midst.

"What are you doing here, Jess?" Sarah asked. He knew the curious tone was only for the benefit of Solis, who acknowledged their presence with a courteous nod. Otherwise, Jess was certain Sarah would have snapped his head off.

"We were wondering if we could talk to Mr. Solis for a couple of minutes."

Sarah took immediate umbrage at the request. "We're trying to have a quiet evening here. I'm sure Jaime would be happy to see you during his normal business hours."

Just as Jess realized he was going to have to get more insistent, Solis saved him the trouble.

"Why don't you give us a few moments, Sarah? I'm sure your brother wouldn't have come here unless it was important."

Lena, who had been hovering behind Jess and Benji, motioned to the girl. "Come inside. You can help me with the coffee."

Sarah reluctantly got to her feet, but not before taking Solis's hand, which might have been the most frightening thing Jess had seen since coming home. It took every ounce of willpower for him not to throttle the Civateateo right then and there. "I'll be inside if you need me," Sarah told Solis.

She walked past Jess. "Five minutes," she said under her breath, then went inside the house with Lena.

Jess noticed that Solis's eyes had been on him from the moment they stepped into the garden. Once the women were in the house, Solis reached into his pocket.

"I believe this belongs to you."

He tossed the object at Jess, who caught it one-handed.

It was the solar flash he had dropped in the cavern that morning. It was cracked in half.

"I'm afraid it's broken," Solis said with a mocking shrug.

Then, he smiled slightly. Jess knew if he opened his mouth wider, his pointed teeth would sparkle in the moonlight.

"So, what did you want to talk about?" asked the Civatateo.

15

"I know who you are and *what* you are," Jess told the Civatateo.

"I'm not disputing that," said Solis. "It still doesn't tell me why you interrupted my evening."

"I want you to stay away from my sister."

"Sarah's an adult. She can make her own decisions about who she spends time with."

"The problem is she's a lousy judge of character."

"You misconstrue my intentions, Jessie. I'm just offering moral support to Sarah. She's taking the loss of Dr. Rice awfully hard."

Benji spoke up for the first time. "That's convenient, seeing as how you're the one who killed him."

"Then it's the least I could do, wouldn't you say?" The smile was back on the vampire's face.

Jess had to give the Civatateo credit. He didn't pull punches.

"I wonder how she would feel if I told her the truth," Jess said.

"I'd think she wouldn't believe you."

Jess dug the journal pages out of his pocket. "That might change after reading these." He thrust them at the Civatateo, who casually took them as if being handed a menu by one of his waiters.

Solis gave them a cursory glance. "I might have underestimated the doctor. I didn't think he had the nerve or fortitude for something like this." He handed the pages back to Jess, nonplussed. "Fairy tales."

"You know they aren't," said Jess.

"Anyone who reads that, and I assume there's more you've put away for safekeeping, will think Edward Rice was a nutcase who needed to be committed. Short of me signing it as a confession, I'm afraid you'll have to do better than that."

"It would get someone like Sheriff Burke asking questions," suggested Benji. "He saw what happened to Clark James and Jess's father."

"And just how is that investigation proceeding?" asked Solis. The Civatateo made an elaborate show out of an idea suddenly occurring to him. "Oh, that's right. Burke dropped it before it even started."

"Doesn't mean it can't be revisited," said Jess.

"Have you met our good sheriff? He is as lazy and inefficient as any man I have ever encountered. And I've been around quite a long time."

The emphasis on the word "long" wasn't lost on either of them.

"Instead, you ought to be thanking me, Jessie."

"And why is that?"

Solis looked up at the second floor of the house. "For making sure your brother doesn't remember what happened earlier today."

Jess didn't respond, but Solis could tell he had struck a nerve for the first time since they began talking—and the Civatateo continued to press down on it.

"You seriously don't believe Clark James had the ability to cloud young Harry's mind."

"He said as much," replied Jess.

"If I'm not mistaken, Clark also told you that I was dead. Perhaps he even led you to believe he had killed me."

By getting no response, Solis had the answer he was looking for.

"Clark James didn't do anything without my blessing. His compliance was inbred with becoming part of my bloodline. I knew if someone stumbled on his secret life as the two of you did, it wouldn't hurt for them to think he was the last of the Civatateo."

"That changed when he turned my father," said Jess.

"Walter was supposed to slip away and die. Clark didn't think that was enough because he hated him so much."

"For what he did to Tracy seven years ago."

The Civatateo nodded. "Which is why I made sure Clark James paid the price for going against my wishes to settle a personal vendetta."

Solis grinned. And suddenly the last piece of the puzzle dropped—the most horrifying one of all. Jess wanted to rip the smile off the vampire's face.

"*You* turned Tracy. Not my father."

I just couldn't stop it.

Walter's last words. The operative word being *"It"*—with a capital "I."

Jess had thought Walter meant he couldn't stop himself from attacking Tracy—when he actually had been trying to tell his son it was the Civatateo who had turned her.

Solis was quite pleased with himself. "Clark needed to fall back into line. He told you that your father did it because I wanted you to believe I no longer existed."

The vampire's sanctimonious tone made bile rise in the back of Jess's throat. "Meanwhile you destroyed Tracy's life."

"Or you might say I gave her a second one."

"Never seeing the light of day? What kind of existence is that?"

"One I've managed for a couple of centuries. You learn to survive." He took a step closer to Jess and Benji. "Because that's what I am, Jessie. A survivor. Nothing more. Nothing less. I was around years before either of you were born and I expect to be here long after you die. I spent close to a century beneath that infernal glass waiting for a chance to rejoin the world of the living. I'll be damned before going back."

"I'd say you were damned a long time ago."

This seemed to get under the vampire's skin. For a millimeter of a second, Jess saw the flash of the Civatateo's temper and teeth.

"Watch what you say, son. You saw what I did to Tracy. Imagine how easy it would be to do the same to your brother, sister, or mother."

"Leave my family out of this."

"Or perhaps I should pay a visit to that Mexican girlfriend of yours. After all, she's more my type than yours." Solis unleashed the hideous smile again. "*Sí?*"

Something finally snapped inside of Jess.

He threw himself full force at the Civatateo.

They crashed through the greenhouse window. Shards of glass flew as both hit the ground. Jess was on top of Solis and began to pound at him with bloodied fists. The Civatateo let out a roar and revealed its teeth with a snarl.

Jess was suddenly overpowered by the brute strength of the creature as Solis threw him onto his back. The Civatateo opened his mouth and started to lower himself toward Jess as Benji rushed in to try and help.

The vampire violently shoved Benji aside like he was made out of papier-mâché. Benji crashed into the wall near the greenhouse door and crumpled to the ground.

Solis turned back to Jess. Sarah could be heard screaming somewhere in the distance but the two men ignored it, continuing to grapple. Jess was quickly succumbing to the power of the Civatateo, who was pumped up from its lust for blood and edging ever closer with its pointed fangs.

For a few seconds that was all Jess could see.

Then, something came into focus above the vampire—the large industrial lights that lined the greenhouse ceiling.

"Grow Lights," as they were commonly known because of their ability to replicate sunlight and allow plants to thrive at any given time.

Especially in the middle of the night.

Jess turned his head and saw Benji struggling to his feet. The Civatateo had his hand around Jess's throat—preparing for a feast—but Jess was able to croak out a half yell across the greenhouse.

"The lights, Benji!"

For a split second, the Civatateo looked as confused as Benji.

Then, Benji got it and stumbled toward the door. Solis looked up at the greenhouse ceiling and screamed at the top of its lungs. He leapt off Jess to try and stop Benji before he could reach the switch.

Benji got there maybe two seconds before the Civatateo.

He flipped on the switch, and the greenhouse was flooded with bright light.

The sound that came out of Solis's mouth was unlike anything Benji or Jess had ever heard. It was feral, ancient, and most of all, painful.

The Civatateo was blasted by the Grow Lights and it fell in extreme pain to the floor.

Solis's scream was cut off as his body burst into spontaneous flames.

Jess leapt to his feet and joined Benji at the door.

They stood there watching the thing that had been Jaime Solis writhing on the floor.

By the time Sarah arrived, screaming at the top of her lungs, all that remained of the Civatateo were its tattered clothes and ashes.

EPILOGUE
LIGHT OF DAY

POSTSCRIPT TO THE JOURNAL OF EDWARD D. RICE

TO JESS STARK (OR SHOULD HE NOT BE ALIVE, WHOEVER RECEIVES THIS):

If you have finished reading this journal, you now understand most of this falls on the doorstep of the man calling himself Jaime Solis. He might have taken a modern Spanish name along with a good deal of money from Clark James to start a new life, but to me he will always be the monster I first saw in the tent five years ago in the tiny Mexican village of Santa Alvarado.

The Civatateo.

I was put in the untenable position of either having my career destroyed or throwing in with Solis. I chose the latter because I was weak of spirit and had a fondness for the things in life that had been previously unattainable. I presume there was the third option of trying to stand up to this two-hundred-year-old creature—but I was afraid had I done so, it would rip me to shreds.

It still might.

Clark James just told me at the country club how displeased the Civatateo is that you escaped from the grave in the desert. He blames me, since I was the one who suggested it instead of killing you right there in the backyard, as Clark wanted.

I expect to pay the price for his displeasure.

It is why I called you. I am sure time is running out to explain my complicity in all that has transpired since my return from Mexico.

It is important that you know a few things.

I truly love your sister. Sarah is a remarkable woman and believe it or not, I think she has missed you dearly.

I feel like I shall forever be damned for my part in what happened to Clark James.

If I had been stronger, I wouldn't have let the Civatateo near him and perhaps your own father would still be alive.

I am certain that Tracy James would be.

I regret all of this more than any words can ever convey.

God forgive me.

Edward D. Rice, M.D.

P.S.S.

It is time to put this in the mail.

I feel like I'm being watched.

It took a couple of days before Maria and Jess were able to leave for Mexico, mostly because of the Civatateo's demise. Getting Thaddeus Burke to dispose of Solis's remains had not been a problem. Assured by Jess this was the end to the sheriff's vampire problem, Burke was happy to keep something off the record he could never explain to his superiors.

Sarah was more difficult. Her mind almost blown by what she had witnessed in the greenhouse, it took a couple of hours to just calm her down to where she could form a coherent sentence. Jess gingerly tried to explain what Jaime Solis had been, but wasn't getting through to his sister. None of this was surprising: it had taken Jess a while to wrap his own brain around it all—and he had been privy to much more mayhem before being pulled out of the grave by his dead father.

Finally, Jess landed upon the journal. He hoped the fact it had been written by the man she had hoped to marry would carry weight with his sister. Jess sat across from Sarah for an hour while she read each page. He watched her expression go from bewilderment to horror; then begrudging acceptance; and finally at the end, when she got to Rice's pledge of love, she shed tears of sadness. Sarah fell into Jess's arms and he tried to comfort her as her body quaked with wracking sobs. He couldn't remember the last time he had held his sister. He must have been a teenager.

Eventually she regained enough composure to head upstairs to bed, but not before extracting a promise that he not leave home so quickly. This brought some inner peace at long last for Jess with his family, but he never could have imagined the price he had to pay to get it.

Jess drove the motorcycle back to the house Solis owned near the golf course, figuring it would just add to the illusion the country club owner had suddenly packed up and disappeared into thin air. He used Solis's key to let himself inside to explore the house. The décor was sparse; clearly the man did most of his entertaining at the country club. Jess figured Solis had spent most of his days holed up in the dark bedroom avoiding the sun when he didn't descend into the cavern to quench his thirst from the blood pond. In the bedroom closet he found half a dozen identical motorcycle outfits, which had provided the Civatateo a way to move around during the daylight hours.

The next morning, Jess said goodbye to his mother and promised to return within a couple of days. Kate had not asked many questions about what had transpired in the greenhouse a couple of nights before; she was too busy tending to the needs of her younger children. Jess got the impression his mother knew more than she let on, not an uncommon thing for Kate Stark. She told him she was glad he had decided to stay for a while. His family needed him. They always had. It warmed Jess's heart and he tried to hold onto that feeling as he boarded the plane with Maria for the journey he had been dreading.

Jess appreciated being able to take a commercial flight from Los Angeles to Puerto Vallarta instead of having to sneak across the border in a car trunk or worrying about being hauled into jail for fleeing the country. As the plane crossed into Mexico, Jess took Maria's hand and held it for the longest time. They hadn't talked much about what they might find on their return to Santa Alvarado, but both were filled with a sense of unease and foreboding. Jess hadn't been able to get Tag Marlowe on the phone. Maria had reminded Jess of the village's remoteness and accessibility to technology.

But neither bought that as the real explanation. They just didn't want to consider alternatives. It was bad enough they were returning to Tracy with busted promises of a cure and no clear game plan. They also had to tell her that Clark James had perished in the sun-baked desert.

They spent the night in the same hotel in Puerto Vallarta. They lay in each other's arms until the light of day crept through the window shade, filling them with hope that nothing sinister could befall them when the sun was up in the cloudless sky. They made good time traveling to Santa Alvarado and Jess pulled the jeep into the center of the village just past noon.

They immediately went to the small home of Ramon, where Tag Marlowe had gone to stay. Ramon, an artist who painted in vibrant primary colors, told them Tag had left the house two days before and hadn't returned. The painter didn't seem troubled; Tag was a free spirit and Ramon was used to his friend not adhering to any kind of set schedule.

Jess wished he shared Ramon's lack of concern.

They stopped by Sophia's. She was overjoyed to see them and insisted on making lunch. Maria and Jess didn't need much persuading as neither looked forward to their next destination. When they both kissed Sophia goodbye, the old woman held onto each of them extra tightly, worried she might never see them again. She murmured something in each of their ears in Spanish. As they got back into the jeep, Jess asked Maria what Sophia had said.

"A prayer," Maria simply replied.

Half an hour later they arrived at the glass house on the hill.

Jess began feeling sick to his stomach.

Tag's car was sitting at the bottom of the driveway. It looked like it had been there for a while. One touch of the hood confirmed that the engine was ice cold. Maria was looking up at the house, her eyes transfixed on something.

"What do you think is causing that?" she asked.

Jess looked where she was pointing. Bright colored lights criss-crossed in the sunlight above the house. He didn't have a clue but instinctively felt it couldn't be anything good.

When they climbed the steps and got to the top of the hill, Jess's suspicions were proven right.

The colored lights were sunbeams refracting off hundreds of pieces of broken glass—the byproduct of a couple of shattered windows. Worse yet, the front door was wide open.

Jess insisted on entering first. Maria was right behind him; she wasn't going to remain outside by herself.

The living space looked like a mini-tornado had blown through. Most of Tag Marlowe's possessions lay on the floor in ruins. The gasoline cans were nowhere in sight. There was blood on the floor where Jess had left them. It didn't take long to see Tracy was nowhere to be found. That didn't stop him from calling her name at least a dozen times. He didn't want to believe that she was gone.

Maria was the one who found the override remote. It was on the floor close to the door. There were dried flecks of blood on it. Jess took it from her hand, stared at it, and cursed. Maria placed a gentle hand on his shoulder.

"You told Tag what he was getting himself into."

"Then why would he come inside?"

"Maybe he just couldn't help himself."

Finally, they were left with no choice but to close the door. Jess used the override remote to click on the lights, even though he knew it was worthless.

He was sure that Tracy was never coming back here.

They talked about heading for the field of glass and cavern, but realized it would be dark before they got there. So they went back to Sophia's house, had an early supper, and went to bed not long afterwards. But Jess had a hard time falling asleep. He half-expected to see Tracy appear outside the window, but all he ever saw was the half-moon and glimmering stars. He wasn't sure if he was disappointed or relieved. As he finally fell asleep, he assumed it was a little of both.

The next morning they got an early start and drove out to the field. The jeep Jess had left behind the week before was nowhere in sight. Either Tag had managed to get out there and return it before his fateful trip back to the house of glass, or perhaps Tracy was using it under the cover of darkness. Jess knew long before they reached the blood pond that he wouldn't find Tracy. It made no sense that she would flee one prison for another. He would never forget her screaming his name when he locked her in the glass house—he couldn't imagine Tracy returning to this dreary place of her own accord. But they knew they had to search the cavern from top to bottom. They had to at least exhaust all the obvious places.

They remained in Santa Alvarado for the better part of a week. During the day there wasn't much to do except wonder where Tracy might be and what had happened to Tag Marlowe. Jess feared he was dead, victim to Tracy's unquenchable thirst. At times he thought perhaps Tracy had turned him. Jess took a small amount of solace in that; at least Tracy wouldn't be totally alone.

At night Maria and Jess would stroll through the village. The streets were pretty much deserted but Jess suspected they always had been, ever since the Civatateo appeared two centuries before. They kept looking for some hint of Tracy, but found none.

When Maria finally suggested they think about heading home, Jess was more than ready.

❋　　❋　　❋

Jess returned to Los Angeles and spent a couple of days there. Rose agreed to take the dispatch job until a suitable replacement could be found, and he gave notice on his Echo Park apartment. He didn't know how long he was going to stay in Palm Springs, but knew he was done biding time in the City of Angels.

He spent the next couple of weeks helping Kate deal with his father's estate. It was a process that would continue for a number of months; there were numerous holdings and it gave Jess plenty of time to figure out what he was going to do next. He had no clear plan. For the moment he was just happy spending time with his family, a concept that had been foreign practically all of his life.

Jess still didn't feel comfortable staying under the Stark roof—mostly because of Maria. They wanted to be together whenever possible but found the prospect of sleeping in the same house with both of their mothers too much to handle.

So each evening they returned to Maria's apartment. It was their own little cocoon and Jess went to bed each night and awoke every morning counting his blessings that this amazing woman had fallen into his life.

✻   ✻   ✻

It was about a month later when he first heard her.

Maria lay beside him sleeping. Jess was trying to make heads or tails out of some complicated business deal his father had been involved in.

Jessie . . .

At first he prayed it was the wind playing tricks on him. But then he heard it again.

Jessie . . .

He looked over at Maria, thinking it would awaken her, but she continued to sleep. Jess climbed out of bed, threw on a robe, and walked outside.

The night air was filled with the smell of blooming acacias in the front yard and nothing more. He sat on down on the front step and lingered there for a good fifteen minutes, waiting for the girl he had left behind in the jungles of Mexico to emerge from the desert—but nothing came.

He sighed and went back inside.

He stood at the foot of the bed and stared for a long time at Maria as she slept.

Then, he crawled into bed and wrapped his arms around her.

He tried to fall asleep but couldn't stop thinking of the wedding trellis in Sophia's backyard and the white and pink roses climbing up it, their petals intertwined; how they floated to the lawn together each autumn, only to be reborn anew the successive spring.

Jess thought of the sad writer who once lived in a lonely glass house atop a hill after losing his love in the jungle years before, and hoped he had finally found some peace.

Then, he thought of Tracy, wandering somewhere in the darkness.

He held Maria tighter. Then, he heard it again.

Jessie . . .

"Go away," he whispered softly.

Jess buried his head close to Maria's neck, trying to will the voice away.

Jessie . . .

ACKNOWLEDGMENTS

Guess I start with my mom. She always asked me as a kid, what I was doing wandering around the house with my nose buried in a mystery or horror novel? Well, here's the answer finally. I only wish she were still around to see this. I'm so glad that most of my family is.

Thanks to my literary agent Victoria Sanders, who made this dream come true with such great guidance and grace. Bernadette Baker-Baughman was unbelievably helpful along the way.

My TV agents, Robb Rothman and Vanessa Livingston, have been part of my life forever and have been so supportive of this journey. Thanks guys for everything.

I am so thankful for Benee Knauer's belief in what I was doing, always pushing me to do better, and being there to make sure it all made sense in the end. You're a true friend.

It's no easy task getting me to go out and talk about the novel, as I'd like to think the work speaks for itself. Erin Mitchell has done that by making the process smooth, super creative, and unbelievably fun.

Thanks go to Victoria Griffith, Daphne Durham, and Alex Carr at Amazon and 47North for asking me to go on this ride with them. Here's hoping we get to do it again and again. Also, a toast to Clarence Hughes for making the editorial process such a breeze and pleasure.

I'm grateful to my super-talented novelist friends, Charles Ardai, Michael Koryta, Karin Slaughter, and F. Paul Wilson for reading early drafts, all their advice on how to make things go "boo," and their total support. Heartfelt appreciation to Jon Feldman, Ellen Klapper, AJ Konowitch, Cindy McCreery, Daniel Pyne, and David Reinfeld, who read stuff before anyone and told me to keep going.

I'm indebted to my TV partners Lloyd Segan and Shawn Piller for not complaining all those times I was home writing instead of in the office and for being at the front of the cheering section.

And of course to Holly, who has been championing me doing this for years. I hope it was worth the wait, honey.

A NOTE TO THE READER

Sharp-eyed readers may notice that in *Descending Son*, several characters refer to a film entitled *The Seventh Day*. Fans of Scott Shepherd's work will be delighted to know that *The Seventh Day* is, in actuality, another novel by Scott Shepherd—and it is available now from 47North.

Please read ahead for two chapters from this harrowing post-apocalyptic, science fiction adventure.

THE SEVENTH DAY

BY SCOTT SHEPHERD

1

Joad couldn't believe his eyes.

The pirate ship floated across the desert floor as if gliding over an ice-covered lake.

He hadn't seen one since he went to Disneyland as a child and begged his father to take him on the ride. Of course, the ship hadn't been genuine; it was just a façade built for the attraction. But it made him recall the movies it inspired, and for just a moment, Joad wondered if the boat moving across the stark white sand was a retrofitted refugee from the days when images flickered across silver screens.

As much as Joad wished he were back in those innocent times, before everything went topsy-turvy, he had to quickly discard the notion.

This ship was gargantuan and extremely real.

The blood-crimson sails, at least a hundred feet high, could wrap around half a dozen houses. The canvas flapped in the wind like thousands of blackbirds winging en masse for the Southern Hemisphere; the sound was deafening but strangely soothing. Billions of sand pebbles bounced off the ship's varnished ebony wood and were ground to dust beneath dozens of gold-chromed wheels on the underside of the boat.

Joad dismounted from his horse and dropped behind a huge sand dune. He made a quick hand motion and grunted a command. The horse immediately lay down by his feet, and Joad was thankful he had spent so much time teaching and coercing his longtime companion to do his bidding.

Joad heard a clacking sound that increased in volume with the ship's approach.

A man's scream rose above the noise.

Joad's horse whinnied. He gently patted the animal's long jaw, encouraging him to remain still. As the horse quieted under his soothing touch, Joad eased himself up just enough to peer over the lip of the sand dune.

The pirate ships of his youth—be they from movies, comics, or picture books—all had two things in common: a flag identifying the vessel, and the figurehead affixed to the bow of the boat. Usually, the former was the family crest of a thieving scoundrel, or emblazoned with the requisite skull and crossbones. The figurehead was typically a carved mermaid or some other mystical creature from the deep dark sea.

But this gliding crimson and black behemoth had neither.

Instead of a flag, dozens of skulls were strung together on pieces of rope, unfurling from atop the highest mast. They bounced off each other, causing the cacophony of clacking.

There wasn't a statue carved into the bow. Instead, a wiry man hung upside down off a grappling hook. Naked from the waist up, his back was bathed in blood. A black-bearded, longhaired man hovered over him, whipping a cat o' nine tails. Despite the ship's velocity and bumpiness, the whip landed on the hanging man's back with a resounding crack. The hanging man moaned.

And the horse whinnied again.

Joad dropped down to calm him again. While stroking its massive chest, he could feel the animal's heart racing.

Along with his own.

"Where did you find them?"

Fixer peered up at the dark bearded man through half-opened eyes. He thought the man's name was Primo, but couldn't be sure. Everything was a mishmash from the time they'd grabbed him out of the shed. *Leave it to my luck, thought Fixer. Finally, a semi-decent roof over my head; I'm getting the first solid night's sleep I've had in months, and the door busts open to reveal four bearded brothers—each more frightening than the last.*

"I didn't," Fixer muttered.

His answer was rewarded with another lash of the whip.

Primo leaned over the ship's bow and brought his seething face inches from the hanging man. "I'll ask again. Where did you get the cells?"

Fixer hadn't seen any in over six months. His upside-down brain was pretty scrambled, but he knew that answer wouldn't hold much water with his tormentor. It didn't help that these men were convinced he had cells in his possession—even though Fixer had denied this more times than Peter had done Christ. Left with options that would only further bloody his back or find him dumped off the ship and squished like a bug, Fixer offered the only possible response.

"What if I took you to them?"

A gratified smile spread across Primo's face. Which only made him look scarier to Fixer than before. "That's more like it."

Yeah, thought Fixer. *Until you realize I'm lying through my teeth and just stalling for time.* At least the whipping would stop.

As if on cue, the cat o' nine tails rose into the air and smacked the side of Fixer's head. A cut split open on his temple; blood sprayed out and down his face.

"You better not be lying. If you are, the pain you're feeling now will be just a prelude to what's coming."

This threat should have unnerved Fixer, but he was more disturbed by the gleam in Primo's left eye.

Because the other one didn't shift in the slightest.

It was only then that Fixer realized Primo's right eye was made of fine glass, its green pupil a direct contrast to the sepia brown of the real deal. For the first time, Fixer got a good look at the skin on the right side of Primo's face. It was mottled, like the underbelly of a turtle. It didn't appear natural, so Fixer didn't think it was a birth defect. He couldn't imagine it was something a man would have by choice, but suspected he wouldn't be around long enough to learn where it came from.

The one-eyed glare demanded an answer.

"Point taken," Fixer feebly offered up.

"Where to?"

"Back where you found me. The shed."

"We searched it high and low. There was nothing," growled Primo. He gripped the whip tightly, preparing to lash out yet again.

Fixer shook his head vigorously, causing the blood to drip down his face. "It's near there."

Primo cocked the cat o' nine tails. "I warned you. . . ."

"No, no, no. Think about it. Having them handy—right where a man such as yourself might take them away from me—that would be foolish. Right?"

"Very foolish, indeed."

Fixer nodded. Blood seeped into his eyes as he stammered away. "Yes, yes. The prelude thing you said. Don't want that. Definitely don't want that."

Primo considered, and then pushed back onto the ship deck and called out to his brothers. "Turn it around! We're going back!"

The hierarchy was clear. The three men began the Herculean task of rerouting: climbing masts, shifting sails, steering the ship. Primo leaned over the rail once again.

"You better not be wasting my time."

Fixer tensed, awaiting one more strike of the whip. When nothing happened, he breathed a sigh of relief as Primo's footsteps retreated on the deck. The reprieve was fleeting, however; his head was immediately besieged with thoughts of what would happen the moment Primo and his brothers realized that Fixer was leading them on a wild goose chase. It caused him to visibly shudder.

The boat lurched and swiveled. Wind blasted sand high into the air. It stung his face, particularly the open wound on his forehead. As the boat swung around, Fixer shook his head from side to side, trying to rid his eyes of the trickling blood.

That was when he saw the man on horseback.

Just beyond a sand dune, the stranger sat high in the saddle, watching the pirate ship turn around.

Fixer thought about yelling, but realized his scream would be swallowed up by the wind. And only catch his captor's attention. Waving his arms was impossible; they were bound behind his back. He could only look imploringly at the horseman, but was certain the man was too far away to see the expression on his forlorn face.

More blood dripped into his burning eyes.

Fixer closed them tightly, then sprung them open, trying to clear the blood.

By the time he could see again, the stranger was gone.

Fixer had chosen the old bowling alley for a number of reasons.

It was on a deserted strip of two-lane highway in the middle of nowhere. Before The Seventh Day, it had served as a roadside diversion for families on long treks through endless fields of wheat and corn. Fixer remembered the first time he ever came across it on a trip to visit his grandparents with his mother. BIG AL'S BOWL-O-RAMA: the neon sign rose out of the cornfields like a dragon from the sea, wondrous and shocking. Fixer's mother had propelled the ancient station wagon right past it, and he had repeatedly pounded on the headrest until she finally gave in and agreed to head back. His mother said they could only play one game, but she quickly got into the spirit of the whole thing: the hollow clack of scattered pins when she bowled a strike, the brain freeze that came with the quick gulping of a black-and-white malt, the licking of her lips after tasting the crinkle-cut French fries served up in their cardboard boat-shaped plates. By afternoon's end they had bowled half a dozen games, eaten more junk food than even a ten-year-old could handle, and laughed continuously. Even now, decades later, as he was literally hanging on for his dear life, remembering that rarest of occasions when his mother seemed happy without a care in the world warmed Fixer's heart.

He was glad the windows had been smashed. It would give him an excuse when Primo and his brothers came up with an empty haul. Fixer would try to convince the brothers that someone had gotten to the stash beforehand. He didn't expect Primo to believe him—he just needed time to formulate a plan. To come up with something. Anything.

As long as he could escape.

Fixer had been working on his wrist bindings to no avail. He had tried to get the ropes to uncoil themselves, but they had no interest in obeying. That meant resorting to the old-fashioned way: wiggling and scraping. But all he'd gotten so far for his troubles were scratches and cuts from the twine burying deeper into his already way-too-sore flesh.

Trey, the smiliest member of the quartet, emerged from the building with a bowling ball that had so many colors it resembled a rainbow sno-cone. A big grin was plastered on his broad face. "Will you look at this? Who the hell would use something like this?"

His giant guffaw was quickly wiped away by Primo's scowl. "Why in the world would I care? That's not what we came here for."

"I know, I know. But imagine what this looked like rolling down the lane? Like one of those thingamajigs you hold up to your eye and all the colors go spinning by. . . ."

"A kaleidoscope?"

Trey nodded vigorously. "Yes, that's it! A kaleidoscope."

Primo swatted the ball out of his brother's hand. It landed with a re-sounding thunk, narrowly missing Trey's foot by an inch. "What did we come here for, Trey?"

"Cells." He pointed up at Fixer. "He said he saw cells."

"Does this look like a cell?"

"No, it doesn't."

"Then get your ass back inside and find me some."

Trey obediently scooted back inside the bowling alley. Primo crossed the parking lot, which was empty except for a couple of car frames stripped of everything worth taking, and even the parts that were useless. The pirate ship, parked in the middle of the asphalt, was as out of place as a rocket ship in a vineyard. Primo stopped at the foot of the boat and stared back up at Fixer. The wiry man bobbled on the grappling hook.

"Where exactly did you say you saw these cells?" Primo called.

"Under the counter. Where they kept the shoes."

"First place we checked. It's been cleared out."

Fixer knew he was near the point of no return. All that remained was his flimsy lie. "It's been at least a few weeks since I was here. Someone must've beat you to the punch."

"Or the cells were never here to begin with."

Fixer gave his best casual shrug. "That would mean you think I'm lying."

"Imagine that."

"Maybe you ought to let me down and help you look."

"I'm not an idiot."

"I wasn't suggesting that."

"You look fine just where you are. For now." Primo headed back inside to help his brothers with the search.

For now.

Those two words echoed in Fixer's ears.

Joad's initial instinct had been to ride off in the opposite direction, putting as much distance as possible between himself and the pirate ship. With less than a week left after a seven-year trek, it was hard to believe anything could pull him off his chosen path. But distractions had been thrown his way more times than he could count on the journey home, and they usually took him hundreds of miles out of his way.

As he followed the pirate ship across The Flats, even though it was heading south and his destination lay to the northeast, Joad suspected this was a similar situation.

He just couldn't help himself. His interest was piqued—not only by the ship, but the plight of The Hanging Man. The unfortunate guy was certainly outnumbered by the pirates (Joad knew they weren't actual "pirates" but was content to refer to them as such); it would have been easy for them to put him out of his misery. But they clearly wanted something from The Hanging Man, (as Joad was beginning to think of him). Joad was curious enough to stick around and find out exactly what.

He was fairly certain the pirates were unaware of his presence. He knew The Hanging Man had spotted him; Joad had seen the pleading look on the man's face. The last thing he needed was getting involved in another man's troubles.

And yet, here he was, still following along.

Big Al's Bowl-o-Rama. Joad suspected, from the building's dilapidated state, that Big Al had left the premises a while ago. More than likely, he wasn't anywhere really. Just ashes and dust. Like most everyone else.

Gone.

Angry screams snapped Joad out of his thoughts. The pirate leader, swarthy and black-bearded, had emerged from the bowling alley, totally infuriated. His three mates, cut from the same swarthy cloth (which led Joad to believe they were related) were right behind him. The sole fair-haired specimen displayed his displeasure by ripping the door off its hinges and hurling it at the ship. It bounced off the bow, not too far from The Hanging Man's head.

The brute strength of the man was impressive. The door must have traveled at least seventy-five yards. The only thing saving The Hanging Man from being crushed was Blondie's awful aim.

"Nothing!" screamed Black-Beard. He shook a fist at The Hanging Man, then turned to the marauding trio.

"Kill him!"

The order was so matter-of-fact, he might have been ordering a cup of coffee.

The other three men's reaction sent a chill down Joad's spine. It was as if they shared the identical menacing smile. Lions let loose in a butcher's shop couldn't have been happier.

The last thing Joad heard as he rode off were the screams of The Hanging Man.

The boat picked up speed, tossing up enough sand to create its own dust storm. Fixer was still strapped to the ship's bow like a mauled mermaid. Primo was leaning down so his face was once again next to Fixer's. He held a knife to the strung-up man's throat.

"Last chance to talk," said Primo.

"What do you want me to say?" Fixer begged.

"Just tell me where the cells are."

Tears formed in Fixer's eyes. He finally managed to blubber out two words. "I can't."

"And why is that?"

"Because I really don't have any and I have absolutely no idea where any are."

Quattro, the youngest brother, moved toward the railing. Slick and slim, he was impulsive and possessed a fiery temper.

"That's a lie."

Quattro reached into the folds of his vest and pulled out a small model car that was dwarfed by his open palm. "You had this! I saw it move!"

"It wasn't cells!" pleaded Fixer. "Open it up. Check for yourself!"

Quattro ripped off the model car's bottom and exposed its undercarriage. He shoved his fingers inside, mangling the works to shreds. He threw the car at Fixer's face and screamed.

"It's a trick! You must have used something to get it to work."

"You wouldn't believe me if I told you." This came out of Fixer in the hushed tone of a man who knew he was doomed.

Primo slashed out with the knife, cutting the main rope holding Fixer to the rail. The cord unfurled with breathtaking speed, sending Fixer shooting down the front of the ship until it snapped taut and he was hanging just feet above the swirling sand.

"Enough!" Primo yelled, waving the dagger in the air. "The truth! Tell us or I'll cut the rest!"

Fixer's body kept bumping against the front of the ship as he dangled precariously above certain death. He tried to look up at Primo but it was next to impossible. He swung back and forth, still upside down.

"Please! I'm telling you. . . ."

Fixer's plea was cut off by a resounding wallop, followed by the rope snapping in half. The force of the split catapulted Fixer through the air; he landed on the sand in a heap, just clear of the speeding ship.

Primo and Quattro exchanged bewildered looks.

"What did you do?" screamed Quattro.

Primo, the dagger still in his hand, stood motionless. "Nothing!"

They frantically looked around. Primo saw a copse of brambled trees to the west. He could barely make out a figure nestled in the upper branches.

A tall man, dressed in grizzled gray, was reloading a slingshot that only seconds before had been fired at the ship.

Quattro didn't see him. He was busy on the deck grappling for his crossbow. He picked it up and leaned over the railing—trying to get a bead on Fixer, who crawled through the sand, trying to get away from the pirate ship.

The gray-clad man shifted the aim of his slingshot toward Primo and Quattro. Primo tried to reach for his brother and push him out of the way, but Quattro shoved him aside; he had his sights set on the crawling Fixer far below.

"I got him."

Primo made one last lunge for Quattro.

But the man in the tree had already unleashed his second shot.

It made a direct hit on the crossbow, which flew out of Quattro's hands. Reaching for it, he tumbled over the railing and fell one hundred feet to the desert floor.

"Nooooo. . . !"

Primo's scream echoed through the air, bouncing off the mountains.

The moment Quattro's body hit the sand, his legs were crushed as the fifty-ton ship rolled over them from stem to stern. Scarlet blood splattered the desert and hull of the pirate ship.

Primo immediately started yelling for his brothers to bring the boat to a halt.

Which took more than a few minutes.

By the time Primo had climbed down the ladder to rush to his fallen brother, there was no trace of the man in the brambled tree. The Hanging Man was long gone too, and Primo was left cradling his youngest sibling in his arms. He rocked him back and forth and began to keen. His grief echoed through the desert canyon, peppered with the screams of undying revenge.

2

Rabbit.

Joad had developed a begrudging taste for it. Back when there were restaurants, it would have been the last thing he'd ever order off a menu. But over the years, he found it the easiest thing to shoot with a slingshot; it needed little cleansing before being roasted over an open fire, and one catch provided enough for a couple of meals.

Not that his diet totally subsisted on creatures that definitely didn't taste like chicken. Joad was happy to scour through canned goods when he was lucky enough to come across them in abandoned stores. But by the time Joad reached what was left of the cities, the establishments had been pretty much foraged by Remaining.

Night had fallen and Joad was half asleep as he cooked the rabbit. Leaning against a broken Chevy, he stifled a yawn as the crackling fire was punctuated by a soft snap. Joad's eyes immediately popped wide open. He reached behind him with the alacrity of a close-up magician and produced the slingshot. In one motion, he loaded and fired a stone into the darkness.

"Ooomph."

This was accompanied by a painful expulsion of breath. Joad started to reload the slingshot.

"No, no! Please don't do that again!"

The Hanging Man emerged from the cover of night, hands raised in surrender. He had managed to find a shirt, the material of which was blotched by the dried bloodstains from the whipping. Joad lowered the slingshot.

"What are you doing here?"

"Looking for you."

"That makes no sense. I don't even know you."

"You saved my life, didn't you?"

Joad sighed. He dropped the slingshot, and turned back to his roasting rabbit.

The Hanging Man gingerly stepped forward and extended a closed fist.

"I found this in the sand near the boat." He opened his palm to reveal a slingshot pellet.

Joad rewarded him with a slight nod. "You didn't look like you were having much fun up there."

"No. Not my idea of a good time."

Joad grunted. The Hanging Man took this as an invitation to join him and moved closer. Joad stopped him mid-stride with a glare, but The Hanging Man wasn't willing to back off just yet.

"Did you know those brothers?"

"Never saw them before in my life," replied Joad.

"You're lucky."

Once again, Joad tried to end the conversation by cooking dinner. The intruder shuffled around, nervous.

"Anyway, I just wanted to say thanks."

"By trying to steal my horse?" Joad asked without taking his eyes off the roasting rabbit.

"Oh. You noticed that."

Joad ripped the hare off the spit, put it on a metal plate, and began pulling the meat apart. The Hanging Man watched, obviously hoping to share, but quickly realized no invitation was forthcoming.

"Speaking of horses. I was just thinking. Maybe you could help me find another one?"

Joad chewed and swallowed. "Think again."

His finality of tone left The Hanging Man with no choice but to retreat into the darkness. Joad continued to work on the rabbit. A few seconds passed before he called out.

"Leave the horse *alone*."

The Hanging Man's mumbled curses could be heard as he shuffled off into the desert.

A slight but satisfied smile creased Joad's lips.

* * *

Shooting stars darted across the night sky. Framed against the Milky Way, their tails left streaks of color in the heavens. Vibrant reds, blistering oranges, and emerald greens.

It must be that stuff The Strangers left behind, thought Joad.

He rolled over on the raft, his stomach lurching from the choppy sea and days without food. The water sparkled as if dotted with silver sequins. Joad didn't think this was a natural phenomenon either. There weren't enough sea creatures or algae to illuminate an entire ocean. This also had to be a byproduct of the visit by The Strangers.

Joad tried to remember how long it had been since he'd caught a fish. His watch had stopped working the moment it got wet, so all he had to go on were rising moons and setting suns—of which he'd long ago lost count.

He shifted around on the bouncing raft, trying to find a position that was comfortable. But it was next to impossible; his body cramped up the moment he tried to move in any direction, and his nausea was worse than ever.

Joad cast an eye out at the swirling sea. Sparkling beads of water moved into a concentrated area, crissing and crossing until they took on a distinctive shape.

A woman's face.

As it formed, the beads clinged and clanged. Joad shook his head in disbelief. He knew that face better than his own.

"Rebecca. . . ."

He mouthed her name in a haunted whisper. After all this time, dreaming of her for so long, actually seeing her beautiful face took Joad's breath away.

As the sparkled drops continued to cling and clang, Joad wondered if The Strangers were trying to tell him something.

Or was he just . . .

❋　❋　❋

Dreaming?

Joad awoke on the backseat of the old Chevy. He squinted as sunlight poured through cracks in the shattered rear window. The clanging noise he'd heard in his dream continued to sound, and Joad tossed aside the saddle blanket he'd used to cover himself.

He climbed out of the car and emerged beneath the remnants of a giant Exxon sign that glistened in the stark desert light. The station was a trashed three-pumper on a long stretch of deserted highway that bisected The Flats. Joad's horse was tied to the base of the sign and snorting, also apparently annoyed by the clanging sounds.

Joad crossed over to soothe the horse with a gentle pat, then moved toward a torn-apart limo where The Hanging Man was pounding away at a piece of metal. A tinted windshield lay in pieces at his feet. He looked up and gave Joad a healthy grin.

"Morning."

"Couldn't you do that somewhere else?"

"Almost done." The Hanging Man held up a pair of sunglasses he had fashioned out of bumper chrome and chopped-up tinted-window glass. "Want me to make you a pair?"

"No, thanks."

"Wouldn't be any trouble. Give me an hour. Two, tops."

"Don't have the time," said Joad.

"What the hell are you talking about? All we've got left is time. It's not like any of us has to punch a clock or something."

Joad shook his head and moved toward his horse. The Hanging Man leapt to his feet and followed, quickly scooting around in front of Joad.

"Hey. We were never formally introduced. People call me Fixer. On account of how I like to fix things." He pointed over to his makeshift workspace, then held up the newly fashioned sunglasses.

"Yeah. I heard."

Fixer finally read the annoyed look. "Oh. Sorry. Didn't mean to wake you. At least this way we can get an early start."

Joad stopped walking. "We?"

"You wouldn't actually leave me stranded out here, would you?"

Joad stared at the empty landscape. No reason to state the obvious.

"Don't answer that. Just let me ride along till we come across some Remaining," implored Fixer.

"And I would be doing that for what reason exactly?"

"Companionship?"

Joad continued to glare at him.

"Okay. Scratch that. How 'bout I be your navigator?"

"That's not necessary. . . ."

"You been through these parts before?"

"Nope."

"Then, I could prove useful. I've been prowling 'round here for years now."

"I tend to stick to myself," said Joad.

Fixer pointed at the desert. "Plenty of trouble out there. I can help you stay clear of it."

"Like you did those brothers?"

Fixer attempted a casual shrug but didn't pull it off. "Oh. They sorta snuck up on me."

"Thanks. I'll take my chances."

Joad continued over to his horse. He rolled up the blanket and quickly stowed it in the saddlebags. He threw a leg up and over his mount, and got settled in the saddle.

Fixer trotted over. Joad marveled at the man's persistence—he was like one of those blowup clowns that kept bouncing back up no matter how many times you knocked it down.

"I'd think those brothers would be pretty pissed at you," said Fixer.

"Why is that?"

"You hurt Quattro pretty bad."

"Quattro? That's a name?"

"It means four."

"Yes. I know that."

"He's the youngest brother. Primo, Secundo, Trey, and Quattro—that's what they call themselves."

"To each his own."

Joad urged his horse forward. Fixer raced around and cut him off.

"They'll come after you."

"You don't know that."

"Neither do you." Fixer inched closer. "If they do show up, two stand a much better chance than one. And I've got a bone to pick with 'em. I don't take to hanging and whipping much."

"What did they want from you?"

"Something they thought I had."

Joad stared long enough at Fixer for The Hanged Man to realize he couldn't get away with just that. The wiry man coughed up the rest.

"Cells."

"That's what they were looking for in the bowling alley?"

"I sent 'em on a wild goose chase. Unfortunately my goose was about to be cooked, but then luckily you came along."

"Why did they think you had cells?"

Fixer stiffened slightly. Joad noticed the hesitation.

"They thought they saw something. But they were just imagining things."

"Uh-huh."

Joad studied the man. Something he wasn't saying. Over the past seven years, Joad had met more than his fair share of men like the brothers. They didn't waste time on random Remaining like Fixer—unless there was something more to such people than met the eye.

The more Joad thought about it, Fixer might prove useful. It was true that Joad had never been through The Flats before. Certainly not on horseback. He and Rebecca had buzzed along the highway back when it was called something else, on the way to the coast for a vacation. They'd spent most of their time singing along to the radio and were too caught up in trying to read a map to notice much. Having a guide might not hurt.

Besides, if Fixer was right, and the brothers pursued Joad, two men might split the quartet's focus. That would allow Joad an avenue of escape by putting this man directly in the brothers' sight.

"What do you say? Let me ride along? Till at least we find me a horse?"

Fixer gave Joad his most winning and convincing smile.

"I promise I won't slow you down."

That's for sure, thought Joad. *He'd make certain of it.*

He finally nodded and patted his horse.

"Climb on up."

ABOUT THE AUTHOR

Scott Shepherd has worked in television as a writer and producer for over twenty-five years. While studying as an undergraduate at Stanford, he developed one of the first courses on mystery and detective novels, which remains part of the curriculum. His television credits include *The Equalizer, Miami Vice, The Dead Zone, Quantum Leap,* for which he received an Emmy nomination, and "The Outer Limits," for which he received a Cable Ace Award. Scott has collaborated with numerous best-selling novelists including Karin Slaughter, Harlan Coben, and Stephen King, whose novel *The Colorado Kid* was the basis for the current SyFy hit *Haven.* In addition to his television work, Scott teaches writing at the prestigious graduate program of University of Texas, Austin. Scott lives in Los Angeles with his wife Holly.